D0765621

A DEATH IN
GENEVA

A
NOVEL

A DEATH IN
GENEVA

A. DENIS CLIFT

Naval Institute Press
Annapolis, Maryland

Naval Institute Press
291 Wood Road
Annapolis, MD 21402

© 1987 by Denis Clift
All rights reserved. No part of this book may be reproduced or utilized
in any form or by any means, electronic or mechanical, including
photocopying and recording, or by any information storage and
retrieval system, without permission in writing from the publisher.

First published by Ballantine Books in 1987.

First Naval Institute Press edition published in 2014.
ISBN: 978-1-61251-798-8
ISBN: 978-0-87021-051-8 (eBook)

Library of Congress Cataloging-in-Publication Data is available.

(∞) Print editions meet the requirements of ANSI/NISO z39.48-1992
(Permanence of Paper).
Printed in the United States of America.

22 21 20 19 18 17 16 15 14   9 8 7 6 5 4 3 2 1
First printing

For Artie and Ann

Each character in the novel *A Death in Geneva* is the invention of the author. Any resemblance to any person living or dead is both coincidental and totally unintentional.

"A most peculiar name for the yacht, you know. The
Matabele *were called the vanishing people, Zulu in origin,*
whose sole business was war."

—Captain William Roger Renfro, DSC
Royal Navy, Retired • St. Georges, Malta

• • • • • **Chapter 1** • • • • •

The rain had continued for days, often violently, with savage gusts of wind tearing through the ivy of the mansion. Now, in the momentary lull at early evening, rays of sunlight fanned through the racing banks of black clouds, illuminating the yellow of a goldfinch darting to his imperiled home.

Thirty feet beyond the nest, the silhouette of a woman crossed behind the drawn lace curtains of French doors off the second floor balcony.

"Are we late, Ellen?"

"It's going on seven-forty, Mrs. Burdette. You have an hour. The dinner is set for eight-thirty. You are not expected until eight-forty-five, very comfortable time, no need to worry."

Constance Starring Burdette strode across the thick yellow rug of the bedroom tying the sash of her satin robe. She seated herself at the glass-topped dressing table, tilted her head back as she switched on the hairdryer and swiveled around to face her companion. "Seven-forty; are we the same as London?"

"We're five hours ahead of the States, the same as London," the maid replied.

For a few moments, the drone of the machine was the only sound in the room. The newly appointed American ambassador to the European Offices of the United Nations thought through the distance which separated her from her family. Facing the mirror, she contemplated her face in silence. The guilt never goes away, does it? she thought And yet, I shouldn't . . . the self-recrimination was fleeting. "It's almost three in the afternoon, Memorial Day. The children said they were taking a gang to the Hamptons . . . what did Bruce write . . . run an audit on the Long Island beer industry." A silver-handled hairbrush coursed through shining black waves of hair, pacing her words.

"Mr. Burdette called while you were showering." Ellen set down a silver tray bearing cigarettes and a glass of sherry. "He said he was at the university grading finals . . . didn't want to trouble you, wished you luck, wanted to tell you he was looking forward to coming over next month."

"Thank you, Ellen, just what I need." She took a long sip of the sherry. The rings on her fingers traded beams with the chandelier as she set to work, applying a rich emollient on her face, working gently around the eyes, stroking firmly from the lines at the corners of the mouth up over the still smooth cheeks. With a deft application of paint and powder, the features of the face were highlighted, a touch of rouge to accentuate the broad cheekbones, mascara to enhance the eyes which were somewhat too narrow, a coral lipstick to the generous mouth. She sat back to draw deeply on a cigarette, followed by another sip of sherry.

"That will have to do. What am I wearing? Yes, good," as Ellen held up the white silk suit.

"It's elegant, Mrs. Burdette. All eyes will be on you."

Ambassador Burdette absorbed the praise without comment. Her eyes caught the leather document case, seal broken, on the bed where she had been poring through its contents just an hour before . . . The fools, she thought, the worthless fools, harassing Tommie with their idiot schemes . . . dangerous, mindless madness. Half the world's tonnage laid up, a worldwide slump idling the cargo fleets, transport rates continuing to dive, only the Towerpoint fleet making a profit . . . and Adrian and the other directors pressing him to diversify . . . the Australian mining industry! . . . God give me strength. Her brother had continued to forward his most confidential, personal reports on Towerpoint for her eyes only. He trusted her judgment more than any other than his own. . . . Australian mining! . . . so he should!

She snuffed the cigarette against the crystal of the ashtray. "Ellen, remind me to call Tommie tomorrow, very important! I'll want to have those papers. Don't forget."

The telephone rang punctuating the assignment. "It's Mr. William Pinkerslaw, Mrs. Burdette, calling from downstairs. He has your papers for this evening."

"Have the . . . the butler, I must learn his name . . . tell him I'll be down in a minute. Make sure he is offered a drink."

She dressed quickly. "I should wear the flag tonight, don't you think?" Ellen removed a richly wrought creation of sapphires, rubies, and diamonds from the bottom drawer of one of the jewel cases and opened the clasp.

"I don't look like a marine, do I? Perhaps the sapphire and diamond spray would . . ."

"The flag is stunning, Mrs. Burdette. Shall I bring your sherry downstairs?"

"No," . . . a quick check in the floor-length mirror—"no; we should go. You have my speech?"

● ● ● ● ●

"Good evening, Ambassador Burdette." The deputy chief of mission rose, closing a notebook and tucking it under his left arm. He gave a quick twist to his red-and-black-striped bow tie as he stepped forward to greet her.

"Let's sit down over here, Mr. Pinkerslaw. Do you have the president's statement at Arlington today?"

"Yes I do, Ambassador Burdette. A telegram of the advance came in two hours ago." He handed her the text. "I have taken the liberty of having the paragraph on America's friends and allies retyped in speech type, thinking you would probably wish to use it this evening." He drew his copy of the speech from his notebook. "I thought, if you agree, that it might read well up near the front, top of page two, right after your introductory remarks where . . ."

"The President was eloquent today"—she handed the message back to him—"a strong, good statement . . . Now, Mr. Pinkerslaw, what do you propose?"

"That you take this paragraph, Ambassador, and use it here."

"I see . . . yes." She placed the text on the round glass coffee table. "Do you think the speech will be well received?"

Pinkerslaw instinctively fumbled with the pipe in his sports coat pocket. Courage restored, he ran a hand along the sharp crease of his trousers. The speech was his, his personal product. He had sacrificed his weekend mixed-doubles match to the speech. He had researched his new ambassador's past, her earlier public statements, to give it just the right personal touches. The few points of fresh substance had been cabled back, cleared with Washington.

The pipe emerged. He pointed the stem at the ambassador's reading copy. "It is an extremely good speech, Ambassador; in all candor, I was truly impressed by the way you took the draft immediately after that long, overnight flight. It makes all the right points, and does so in a very refreshing, personal style. The American Club is a good test. They're looking forward to meeting you. Your speech is the perfect introduction."

"Louison, the president of the Club, will introduce me? You have the names of everyone I should recognize?"

"Louison, yes, marvelous person . . . and the others, yes, Ambassador." Pinkerslaw produced two three-by-five cards from his notebook. "There are only two, the phonetics are in parentheses." He passed the cards to her and leaned forward as she studied the names.

"Lou-duh-man? Du-ba-tee-a?"

"Perfect, Karl Luedemann and Jacques Debatier." He felt as if he had just guided a jumper over the toughest stone-wall obstacle.

"Fine, fine." The cards disappeared into the speech folder. She checked her watch, rose, and disappeared into the adjoining study to return with another folder. "How is the mission reacting to Ambassador Burdette, Mr. Pinkerslaw?"

"You will be pleased with the staff. With very few exceptions, they are a very capable group, and if I may say so, you have brought some very impressive credentials, not the least of which was your swearing-in in the Oval Office. . . . And, that wasn't lost on the UN crowd or the Swiss either. You will find that the mission has some very busy periods, and some quite slack. The new mission, of course, is a vast improvement over the quarters on Rue de Lausanne. . . ."

"So I understand. . . ." She removed the speech from its folder, folded it once, taking care not to crease it, and placed it with the cards in her evening bag. "Well, time . . ."

They followed her from the drawing room. Her eyes caught the carved walnut secretary with its brass pulls—top brass pull on the left, concealed security alarm—first briefing the day she had arrived. "Thank you, Mr. Pinkerslaw, for having come out; I do hope I haven't ruined weekend plans for you." She held out her hand. "You're off duty now. I'll be soloing this evening; my first Geneva solo. Thank you, Mr. Pinkerslaw." She smiled again and shook his hand.

His disappointment did not show. He pursed his lips and nodded his head vigorously in approval. The chauffeur slid from his seat to open the rear door of the gray limousine at the first glimpse of Ambassador Burdette descending the marble stairs, accompanied by the butler who held an umbrella to protect her from the rain that had begun to fall again as twilight deepened in the hills south of Geneva. The tires crunched against the gravel of the semicircular drive. The limousine paused at the high-walled gate, then turned on to the road.

Pinkerslaw waved his notebook. "She is the accomplished performer, isn't she? No staff, first Geneva 'solo,' good call on her part, wouldn't you say, Ellen?" He beamed a professional smile. "I'm looking forward to the Burdette era."

"Goodnight, Mr. Pinkerslaw."

● ● ● · ·

The beam from the reading light shut out everything but the text of the speech in her lap. She worked her way slowly through the pages once more, penning diagonal strokes at each spot where she would wish to pause . . . *pace the audience, have them with you,* she reminded herself . . . applause following the first paragraph, for the head table, for the President's quote . . . don't push ahead, feel the rhythm, let them feel your confidence. Her mind skipped to Bruce and Evelyn, glorious young people racing into the freezing Atlantic surf. Her husband's voice, calm, antiseptic, crowded in: "It is, of course, your decision, Connie, and I will respect you for it. We'll miss you, but we will be very, very proud of you. It is *your* decision. . . ."

She carefully refolded the speech, returned it to her purse, and turned off the lamp. "Are we nearly there?"

"We are in Geneva proper, now, Ambassador. That's the flower clock on the right. Normally, you'd see the *jet d'eau* behind it, out in the lake . . . pumps are being repaired."

She felt the stones on her fingers as she looked out through the rain-speckled window following his tour. "Is it Lake Geneva or Lake Leman? I've seen them both on the maps."

"Either will do, Ambassador. Most Americans stick with Geneva. This is the Pont du Mont-Blanc, lake on the right, the Rhône River takes over on the left. If we still had some light, you would see the white swans; the parks are nice here." The limousine left the bridge. "I believe you wanted to go by the old mission. Is that right, Ambassador?" Looking in the rearview mirror, he saw her nod as she continued to look out at the city.

"Business district?"

"A little of everything, business, several auto outlets, shops, hotels, a good number of apartments." He slowed and pulled over. "This is it on the right. The arcade was the entrance. You took the elevator up to the mission, the upper floors."

"I see. I'm glad we left. Looks like an office, not an embassy. Thank you, driver."

The limousine pulled away from the curb again. She leaned back and closed her eyes. The chauffeur frowned as a motorcycle came alongside. The faceless rider in visored helmet, leather jacket and pants glistening with the rain, held his position abreast for a moment and then fell back. Too close, wet roads, fool. A silent curse from the chauffeur.

Another set of lights was close behind him. Idiots! He slowed, anticipating the light at Avenue de France. The lights slowed. In the mirror he saw the cycle rider alongside a van. Van driver giving him hell, good! With the green light, he turned left, north up Avenue de France. The lights of a train passed silently beneath as the limousine crossed the bridge. The 8:35 to Lausanne.

The motorcycle was alongside again. The chauffeur's impulse was to roll down the window, give him a yell, a shake of the fist . . . an impulse easily dismissed, too many years with the mission for such nonsense. Too many years! The instinct and security training hit him like an icy spike in the base of his neck. He drew himself straighter, glanced at the ambassador. She was resting. . . . no need to disturb her . . . false alarm. He flipped the safety on the 9mm SiG Sauer pistol he kept in the left front door holster, placed it on the seat beside him. His hand went to the radio mike, squeezing the button as he brought it to his mouth.

"Rampart, Rampart, this is Chariot, over." He continued along the rainswept Avenue de France, cleared his throat. "Rampart, Rampart, Chariot, over!"

The rain was much heavier now. He could no longer spot the motorcycle. The van was so close its lights were blinding in the rear window, the mirrors. His thumb snapped at the buttons. Typical, new ambassador, Sunday night, no response. . . . I'll have Weems's ass, file a report in the morning, security officer! What the hell sort of security is this? He touched the pistol, then grabbed the mike again, slowing, pulling far to the right, indicating the van should pass. It stayed with him.

"Rampart, Ram . . ." At the intersection of Chasse Eugene-Rigot he spun the steering wheel and floored the heavy, gray limousine, which fishtailed coming through the hard right turn and then raced ahead through the darkness.

"What is it, driver?" Ambassador Burdette struggled to regain her balance. "What are you doing; is there a problem?"

"I hope not, Ambassador . . . have to be certain." The chauffeur's turn had taken the pursuers by surprise. He had gained one hundred fifty to two hundred feet, but there were still three lights in his mirrors. The motorcycle was back in the lead; they were closing. "Probably some drunks, Ambassador. They chase a set of diplomatic plates for the thrill, doesn't make it any more right . . ." He turned hard again, right on Avenue de la Paix, blazing past the night shapes of the Botanical Garden, right again, skidding, powering ahead onto Rue de Lausanne. The limousine was racing in a circle, aiming for the heart of Geneva where he would find police.

Ambassador Burdette's mouth was dry. Fear, fear of the limousine's hurtling speed in the winding wet darkness confused with oncoming lights. She squinted out of the rear window, her right hand instinctively reaching for the diamonds on her ring finger. "Who are they driver, not thieves for heaven's sake. Where is the police station?"

"Please move to the side *now*, Ambassador. Do not let yourself show in any window. Stay low!" The big car ran a red light, swerving left and southbound along the lake, then right on Rue Chateaubriand. "The primary radio does not seem to be working, Ambassador. Please hand your telephone receiver to me."

She did as she was asked. Fear turned to bitter frustration. This mad chase. Radios that don't work. She would get on top of things . . .

fast! The driver, good God, the driver would have to go. She had been told he was excellent. Now, she was late. She would arrive at the dinner disheveled, flustered, not in control. Her mind clutched at a decision; the speech would be canceled, no, postponed, another evening.

"This is insane," she burst out. "Everything will be ruined for the future. It will be in the press. Good God, no! Stop the car, driver. Stop immediately!"

Her command was ignored. The limousine continued its dash along Rue Chateaubriand. Ahead, through the rain, a car with its trunk lid up . . . someone was loading or unloading. She was thrown against a rear door as the limousine moaned through a skidding turn into Rue Jean Charles Amat. "Rampart, Rampart, this is Chariot, Condition Red, repeat Condition Red, this is Chariot . . ."

The motorcycle slid alongside. The bullets from the first clip of the machine pistol riveted the driver's window and door, the fat, unbroken taps of a woodpecker drilling a tree. The chauffeur kicked down on the brakes with all his strength. The street was too narrow. He snapped the limousine into reverse, swinging out to the left, but the van was on top of him.

The second wave of the attack was swift. Two HK-53 machine pistols emptied a salvo against the weakly armored glass of the chauffeur's side window. The main assault of armor-piercing bullets clicked smoothly through the curved clip of an AK-47 automatic rifle, tearing with deafening slams into the glass and body of the limousine. Blood streaming from his face lacerated with glass splinters, a black, growing wound in his neck, the chauffeur fired twice through the broken window in the direction of the nearest barrel flashes. He threw the limousine into forward, ramming and dragging the motorcycle before crashing, the machine wedged beneath, into cars parked on the side of the street. The spit of bullets continued. In the next second, two caught him in the left ear and temple.

When the first spray of glass and gunfire exploded into the front seat and the blood splattered from the chauffeur's neck, Ambassador Burdette pitched forward, desperately grabbed the telephone and dove to the rear floor. The terror, the noise almost overwhelming, she squeezed the receiver handle, "We need help. We're being shot!" Her hand froze tight on the instrument. "This is Ambassador Burdette. We're being killed!" Her voice had risen to a scream. "We're in the car; we're being shot!"

A gloved hand thrust through the window's jagged hole, flipped the release, yanking open the chauffeur's door, grabbing his body and shoving it to the wet pavement. The street for a second was quiet. An apartment window opened: A voice called out in unsure complaint. Two figures appeared, hesitated behind the glass of a hotel entrance, then vanished. In this second, Ambassador Burdette, lying face down on the lushly carpeted floor, thought that rescuers had arrived. Her mind stammered in the emptiness following the stunning, ripping shocks of gunfire, the splintering starbursts in the car glass, and the explosion of the front of the limousine collapsing under the assault. The police, she thought, I'm alive! Thank God I'm alive . . . they're here . . .

The chase, from the chauffeur's first warning, had lasted less than four minutes. An eternity. Thank God the police have stopped the shooting. Her chest burned. Her throat and mouth were numb. There was blood on her skirt, her legs, her hands. She pushed herself up, still clutching the phone.

"You are Constance Starring Burdette?" The voice was strange, high.

"Yes, yes." The ambassador forced a smile as she struggled back onto the seat, struggled to thank her rescuers. Her relieved, thankful eyes locked in horror on the insanely zig-zagged ski-masked head, the hands leveling a pistol inches from her face. There was not time to shudder, to protest, to raise her bleeding hands in defense. The machine pistol ripped a lethal path from her forehead to the jeweled flag which laid shattered, its gems still glistening in the growing bloodstain on her lifeless body.

Fifty miles west of Lisbon, the *Towerpoint Octagon* was steaming on an easy southerly course in the predawn when the radio shack came alive.

"Mr. Starring, sorry to awaken you, sir." It was the ship's captain on the telephone. "An urgent message, sir."

Starring, barefooted, in a deep blue robe trimmed in yellow, met the captain in the passageway at the entrance to the owner's suite. He rubbed his eyes, his jaw, peered at the black ink of the message printout:

/ / / / / / / F L A S H/ / / / / F L A S H/ / / /

From: OpsCenter TPI
FOR: Thomas Starring, *Towerpoint Octagon*
BEGIN TEXT

1. Tommie—regret devastating news. Connie murdered, shot dead in Geneva. Killer(s) still at large. Local police, U. S. Mission security set attack at 8:30 p.m.

2. President called personally. He is stunned, grief stricken, hopes you will bring Connie back to Washington for honors, service.

3. President has ordered military special mission aircraft to Lisbon to meet you for flight to Geneva. Special mission aircraft will await your arrival. Please confirm.

4. Join with you in mourning Connie's passing

Your brother, Adrian.
END TEXT

"Some bastards just killed my sister!" He snapped the message, his eyes flashing. "She had just arrived, new ambassador, Geneva . . . the bastards!" He thrust the message back at the ship's captain.

"Horrible, horrible, sir; my most sincere condolences. Absolutely horrible. In recent years, Europe . . ."

"Send the following reply, Captain. 'Confirm travel on president's special mission flight from Lisbon, deepest appreciation to president . . . my duty to accompany Connie'. . . . Separate message to her family: 'Robert, children . . . devastated, deepest sympathy . . . we can be forever proud of your mother . . . fell in service to country . . . love . . .' usual sign-off. Third message to Sullivan: 'Sullivan, meet me on arrival Washington.'"

"Sir, I will pass the details to Geneva. Is there anything else?"

"The stewards should not wake up Mrs. Starring." He glanced at his watch, "0445. Have my bags aboard the helicopter for 0600 departure."

The captain saluted, then departed. Starring stepped across the steel coaming onto the weather deck. The damp teak planking was cool, soothing. He stood with his arms folded, facing the wind, his eyes gauging the elevation of the brightest morning star.

· · · · ● **Chapter 2** ● · · · ·

Tommie Starring cut a dashing figure at fifty-eight, trim with a bearing that demanded attention, fine, handsome features beneath a crown of carefully sculpted white hair. Strength flowed from his voice and from his hands, which punctuated his speech with authority. His face was dominated by penetrating gray eyes. A glance could reward or punish; his mind and his soul were concentrated in those eyes.

A descendent of President James Madison, to believe the genealogists, and third-generation heir to his family's STARCO tramp steamer operations, Starring had walked his first steps on the shipping wharves of Portland, Maine. His life was shipping fueled by profit and dressed in patriotism. As a boy, his greatest joy was passage, unaccompanied, aboard a succession of his father's coal-burning freighters plying between Atlantic ports from St. John's, Newfoundland, to Havana, Cuba. He knew each ship from stem to stern in minute detail. He observed and absorbed the different patterns of loading, hauling, and discharging of cargoes. School years were endured; shipping was his passion.

Starring's first marriage was a business venture, bringing the daughter, the riches, and the opportunities of the Endeavor Line into his house, paving the way for merger of the two companies five years later, with Starring the youngest president and chief operating officer of any line in the United States. That marriage was abandoned without children, matter-of-factly, following the intense, adroit maneuvering which brought the reins of power into his hands.

Still in his late twenties, he again outmaneuvered larger competitors, "stealing" the most lucrative contracts of the trans-Atlantic trade, and feeding the profits into the first of a growing network of repair yards and support facilities, launching the dominating era of Towerpoint which continued to climb with a great rocket's speed toward a zenith never before dreamt of by the entire industry.

Starring took pleasure from the charge that he was boring, one dimensional. His avocation, if it could be described as such, was his responsibility as trustee of the National Creative Performance Arena, a role which had grown from the raw, necessary act of cash endowments to a deep interest in the theater and, in particular, in the strength and drive of its most successful actors and actresses.

Early in the successful years, he had experimented with game hunting. But the exotic, brilliantly mounted heads and full skins bagged from India to the American West were soon removed from his executive offices to be placed in permanent, forgotten storage. His instincts returned him to the only prey with any meaning—competitive builders, rival shipping.

The ledgers of the World Trade Center corporate headquarters carried Towerpoint International assets in the billions. Starring knew the columns of figures, the victories they recorded, the guidance they offered, as well as he knew his ships, his installations, his people. The dynamism of Towerpoint flowed from his energies and, in turn, Towerpoint was the only valid reason for his life.

● ● ● · ·

A pencil beam of light revealed Starring in the darkened first class compartment of the jetliner, midway across the Atlantic on the night run from Washington. He folded back the cover page of the rush congressional transcript, hand-delivered to his secretary minutes before they had departed Dulles. Hearings of the Subcommittee on National Preparedness . . . His eyes skimmed the introduction, dropped to the opening remarks.

Chairman Drake: The subcommittee will come to order. The subcommittee continues today its hearings on the posture of our national defense.

Voices of grave and legitimate concern are raised across this nation, concern over an increasingly perceived weakness of America's Armed Forces in a crucial era of challenge from abroad. It is vital that we identify and remedy such deficiencies and shortcomings as we may have, if we are to survive, if we are to maintain our vitality and strength as a people, if we are to remain the leader, the foremost free society and free people on this earth.

Regretfully, and all too often, such weaknesses are exacerbated by internecine conflicts within our own official family of government over the priorities to be accorded . . . or not accorded . . . in the stewardship of our national defense. These hearings have as their goal the stilling of such conflict and the direction of our energies, our strength and our resources so as to maintain our superiority against those nations who would overturn the United States.

We begin our consideration today, and I speak for all members of the subcommittee, in saying that we are greatly honored to have with us this morning the chairman of the board of Towerpoint International. Mr. Thomas Madison Starring, who has agreed to be with us . . . to appear before this subcommittee . . . on very short notice and under the most tragic of circumstances.

Yesterday, the Congress passed a unanimous resolution honoring the memory of your distinguished sister, Ambassador Constance Starring Burdette, and condemning her heinous murder by terrorists abroad. It was not my privilege to know your sister, sir, but she is immortalized in the ranks of America's heroines. You have our deepest sympathy, sir. We are greatly honored by your presence at this inquiry. You may proceed.

Mr. Starring: Thank you, Mr. Chairmen. I am honored to appear before this subcommittee of the Congress. I thank you and the members of the subcommittee for your tribute to my sister, Connie. I will be brief. You have other expert witnesses. I have no prepared statement. With your agreement, I will address that aspect of our national defense with which I am most directly involved . . . sea power.

Chairman Drake: Please proceed, sir.

Mr. Starring: Mr. Chairman, members of the subcommittee, as a shipbuilder, fleet operator . . . and as one engaged in expanding the frontiers of undersea technology, I am keenly attentive to America's status as a sea power. We are, sir, in a state of decline, a state of dangerous decline, and that must be a cause of deep concern for each of us.

I will not mince my words. We have declined as a maritime power. We have declined as a naval power, and there should be no mystery. The Department of the Navy no longer speaks with a clear voice. That voice has been lost for too long in the erroneously conceived Department of Defense. The Navy is underfunded. This is reflected in the fleet, in the air arm, and in vital research and development.

Fix, find, and destroy. It is an old saying, Mr. Chairman, but as relevant now as at the time of John Paul Jones and the *Bonhomme Richard*. The facts are that in recent years the few ships the Navy has ordered have been undergunned from time of contract. I say that, sir, to include all ships' weaponry undergunned and with design specifications no better than mediocre.

I submit that you should not ask today's frigate skipper to put to sea, to prepare for combat, with a single-screw ship, with a single gun mount, with a single missile launcher . . . anymore than your predecessors in the Congress would have asked our frigates of two centuries ago to set forth with a single sail.

Today's, and tomorrow's, man-of-war requires the seaman's common sense and good judgment just as much as it requires advanced technology. At Towerpoint, we have fought faulty contracts as specified by the Navy Department; we have fought proposals for inferior design. But, Mr. Chairman, we have not always won.

We are in a period of naval decadence. Alfred Thayer Mahan used this term—naval decadence—more than a century ago to describe the depths to which this nation had fallen. Mahan also taught that the Navy serves the nation, protecting not only our shores but also our seaborne commerce. In recent decades, Mr. Chairman . . .

● ● ● ● ●

Starring returned the subcommittee document its envelope. The words had been transcribed as he had spoken them. The message had to be hammered home whatever the odds against corrective action by the Congress. Ahead of the jetliner, a horizontal thread of orange in the blue-blackness signaled the coming of dawn over Europe. Starring rested. Connie, "immortalized in the ranks of America's heroines . . ." He savored the words. . . . part of history. Good work, Connie.

The return of the coffin, the ceremony at the Air Force base, the interment at Arlington, every moment precise, dignified. We're at our best with the dead, not the living, he thought. His head shook as he recalled his sister's burial, young Evie griefstricken, pressed against her brother. I should have poked him in the nose! Starring detested his brother-in-law, "a lump of academic dough." He had urged his sister repeatedly over the years to move ahead with her own interests . . . good years when she was running London . . . guts, tenacity . . . the presidential campaign . . . then, Geneva. The president had taken him aside at the cemetery, placed a hand on his shoulder, asked the secretary of state to join them. "I've got the best there is on this, Tommie. Interpol, the rest, are cooperating fully. We're dealing with the animals, but we'll crack it, crack it fast. Connie was representing me. . . ." He had looked at the casket above the grave as the caisson drew away, his voice dropping to a whisper. "Connie, Connie . . ." He clasped Starring's hand and departed.

Starring's reverie was broken by the bustle of the flight attendants. "Sullivan, the stewardess has a hot towel for you. Wake up, have some breakfast. We have some dictating to do."

Muriel Sullivan, Starring's secretary, organized herself quickly. Pen and pad emerged from a traveled leather satchel. Starring bent over his linened tray, a napkin at his throat, speaking quickly as he ate. "Have New York wire a full review of the planning for the end of June family session. Remind Hensen this is a *formal* dress rehearsal for stockholders meeting. London has done some good work, but I want a better analysis of the coming decade in the Irish Sea and the entire Spitzbergen as well as the tote sheet on North Sea construction and production . . . need an honest statement on rig construction decline . . . some highlighting on the shift in tanker charters, shows them we're anticipating, not asleep."

"Tell Baltimore the Mexican LNG report, more attention . . . projected employment figures . . . projected regional energy requirements . . . report needs more fight . . . being nibbled to death by small-timers."

He folded his napkin over the half-finished breakfast. "Make a separate note, Sullivan. Want to see Oats Tooms first thing tomorrow, go over this Mexican business . . . Towerpoint receiving bad press, talk to him in the morning." The secretary kept pace with these instructions, then flipped back to an earlier page as he resumed work on the June meeting. Starring's voice snapped through the agenda. He bore in on the improvements to be made to the defense contracts presentation.

"Tell Adrian . . . film is terrible, put the entire crowd to sleep . . . infantile narrative. Scrap it, gives the wrong impression. Each division responsible for sharp, three-dimensional models . . . includes the off-shore division, far more instructive . . ." He was interrupted by the landing announcement. "Fasten your seatbelt, Sullivan. I'll have two more paragraphs in the airport."

● ● ● ⋅ ⋅

Muriel Sullivan winced at the intensity of the clerk's cologne; he was leaning across the glass counter to demonstrate the 35mm camera. Two small boys raced through the concourse, their shoes slapping loudly in the nearly empty terminal. Oblivious to the announcement in French, German, and English of a departing flight, one snared the other by his sweater. They wrestled, pulled apart, and resumed the chase.

"You will appreciate, madame, the professional quality; the very best, madame. The lens is firmly in place with one twist . . . you hear the click . . . the very latest zoom. It will make excellent close-ups." She looked through the viewfinder, focused on the alert face of a German shepherd guard dog seated beside an airport sentry, automatic rifle, barrel down, hanging from a shoulder strap. Guards; only hours since Mrs. Burdette's death. The thought made her neck and shoulders ache.

In the distance, a lanky figure with the hunch of a backpack was crossing the terminal. She zoomed in on his curly blond hair, aviator's sunglasses, mustache . . . a good camera. She told the clerk she would take it, tucked in one end of the green silk scarf knotted loosely at her throat to soften and give life to the tailored gray suit she was wearing.

Muriel Sullivan was a petite woman, fair-skinned and red-haired, at Starring's side professionally for fifteen years, her life given over to the pulsing existence of Towerpoint International. He treated her the way a ship's captain treats a second in command. He relied on her to be aware of the smallest details *inside* the Towerpoint structure. Her dedication ran around the clock eleven months each year. September marked her annual pilgrimage to the cottage on the coast near Dun Laoghaire south of Dublin Bay. Her forbearers had come from the east center of Ireland, from Kildare, Wicklow, Dublin. The cottage stayed in the care of a cousin. Starring had first fought unsuccessfully then endured with melancholy this annual disappearance, had said it would be more profitable to put the entire operation in drydock while she was away.

Muriel was as unassuming as she was efficient. There was nothing unusual in Starring's reliance on her to purchase a camera for his second wife, Tina.

He looked to Muriel to provide a constant burnishing to this outward appearance of attentive husband. It was good for business, good for the image, a mask for hardened emptiness in his heart.

Now, with the second announcement of their onward flight, Starring gave the purchase a disinterested glance and passed it back to be packed in her satchel. They moved from the distinguished visitors' lounge to the tunnel leading from the main terminal to one of the smaller, satellite arrival and departure terminals in the center of the airfield. Starring offered his secretary his arm, which she declined, when they stepped onto the people-conveyor belt that would transport them the length of the clean, efficient tunnel. He admired such Swiss workmanship, the attention to detail. Very Strange, his mind jumped, very strange that they had still not captured the killers, not like the Swiss.

It was when they were halfway through the tunnel that Paul Andrew Head followed them onto the conveyor. He did not know them, was unaware of their presence. His right thumb and forefinger ran along his mustache, stroking the false hair, pressing it into place. He kept his left arm close to his side. The bullet had done no real damage, carved a trench, cracked a rib which they had patched before they had separated from him.

He was careful with each breath. He did not want pain; it would make him sweat. Sweat would betray him in the cool terminal. He rode in silence, his mind on his new identity . . . *Cranston, Henry Cranston*. He stepped from the belt, climbed the steps to the departure lounge . . . more dogs, police with automatics, an armored personnel carrier, small but distinct in the distance through the glass.

Easing the backpack from his right shoulder, he dug into a pocket for a cigarette. . . . No complaint. It had gone well . . . rebound from near disaster. The twin clouds of smoke from his nostrils drew an angry stare. He casually moved a few paces, turning his back, pushing the pack along the floor with his foot. . . . Tracking, kill, getaway had been clean, under control. He had taken them to the border transfer, returned the weapons, except for his pistol, to the cache, and driven back into Geneva.

The final contact by the tennis courts at the Parc des Eaux-Vives had been to the minute. The bigger the crowd, the greater the traffic, the less chance for the gestapo. Work right under their noses. The van, wiped clean, was gone. It was then he had realized he did not have his papers. They had kept all sets of papers in one pouch throughout the operation. He had forgotten, his mistake; his passport was in a farm truck heading south through Italy. Bloody bastards!

He stubbed out the cigarette, listened to the boarding announcement for the U.K.I. flight. There was a long line, full bloody flight. That was alright; he was in no rush now.

Cranston, he took no satisfaction from having killed him, an act of survival. Head had first learned survival, and terror, in the red mud of the veldt, and in the bundu nightmare of the Rhodesian bush. It had started for him with the acts of the Crocodile Commando, the murders of families in farmhouses and on empty roads. His entire nation had been at war against the terrorists then. He was still in his teens, in the Security Force Reserves guarding villages which had been secured as safe havens from ZAPU and ZANU attacks. He had lost his nerve, cracked in the grisly, deafening chaos of a night attack, hidden, fled south across his country, across the Limpopo into South Africa.

From Durban, he had continued his flight by ship to Europe, to Rotterdam. His first brush with his present was in the communes of Amsterdam where he had absorbed the intense discussions, the rising excitement in voice after voice, face after face, over the successes of the Red Brigade, the other movements. He had let it be known that he was a trained, expert killer, a member of Rhodesia's elite Selious Scouts, disillusioned by the racist actions of his country. To establish his worth, he killed. And, he had been accepted.

Head had been cautious in tracking the American from the American Express offices to his hotel. "It's 311." The desk clerk had checked as he turned to the pigeonholes for the key. "Right," the American had replied, "311, until the morning." He would do. They were similar in appearance, coloration, no more than two inches apart in height. The American's hair was shorter. He had a mustache; it would be on his passport.

Having selected his prey, Head made his way across the city to a woman barber. While she was making change in the back of her shop, he stole the blond wig from one of the four wigged heads in the window, tipped her, and was gone. The heavy, double-faced tape was harder to find, a department store back in the center of Geneva. He shaped a trimmed mustache from the cloth-backed flaxen hair and placed it in his wallet with four trimmed pieces of the adhesive.

Cranston had been punctual, a good boy, checked out at 9:00 a.m. sharp. He had met him on the street, at the rental car delivery bays. He had addressed him by name, recalling their schoolboy acquaintanceship, asked if he might catch a lift.

Cranston had been flabbergasted, gone chalk white when Head jammed the pistol into his side. He had handed over his wallet and papers. Head checked them as they left the city. . . . Excellent—passport, two credit cards, several hundred Swiss francs, travelers checks, letters of some description.

"What are these?"

"Letters," Cranston had blurted, "letters for the university, from my professor."

Halfway to the airport, Head had given him a hard jab with the pistol, "Here, left, turn!" The car had moved slowly along Chemin du Pommier, one more turn. Head looked carefully. "By those trees, stop!" The Cemetery de Petit-Saconnex was on their left.

"Your tie, shirt, jacket! Off! Now!" Cranston, breath coming in shallow gasps, did as he was told.

". . . and shoes, dammit, the shoes . . . leave your pants on." Head took the keys from the ignition. Keeping the pistol, covered by the shirt, on the American, he stepped out on the road, opening the boot of the car as he crossed to the other side. He waited as one, then another car passed.

"Out, out! Fast! Into the boot . . . the trunk, the trunk, fast!" Cranston had jabbered in protest, grabbed at him, sending a spear of pain through the wounded ribs.

Head slammed him back into the trunk lid, gave another look in each direction. "Quick, damn your bloody ass! I need the money. Get your bloody ass in the trunk if you don't want to be killed!" It was cramped, but Cranston fit. Head pushed his shoulder down, shot him twice in the head, and slammed the trunk lid closed. He returned to the front seat, closed the door, stuffed the shirt in his pack, folded the tie into a pocket of the jacket, flicked through the papers again . . . stopping at the passport.

Hair . . . parted more in the middle . . . bigger eyes, sunglasses would take care of that . . . mustache, mustache! He worked quickly.

The false hair was in place; it stayed. . . . Have to be careful not to set the bloody hair on fire.

He yanked Cranston's shirt back out of the pack, wiped down the passenger's side of the front, then stepped out again, banging against the dead man's shoes as he exited. The shoes! He looked at them; no prints . . . leave them! He moved to the other side again, wiped the outside of the door, then the trunk lid. He climbed back into the driver's seat, and the sedan continued its journey to the airport bearing two Henry Cranstons.

Three stops were required en route; the pistol disappeared in pieces. Henry Cranston was not armed. In the airport lot he finished the wiping down of the gearshift, emergency brake, steering wheel, rear view mirror, inside and outside of the driver's door. The sedan was clean. He locked it, locked the trunk, tested it with a kick. Another car pulled in beside the rental sedan. He ignored it, heading toward a sewer grate, wiping the keys as he walked. The plan changed with the approach of a refuse truck. The keys disappeared down the road with the airport's morning trash.

Head's first stop in the terminal was at Trans-Global. He purchased a ticket, one-way, for Henry Cranston to Cairo, gave the girl a good look at the passport. The American bastards played a bloody tougher game; this was the test. The passport was returned . . . okay. He paid for the ticket in francs, circled the terminal, bought a paper, moved on, tossed it into the trash, then walked to the U.K.I. counter where he again requested a ticket.

"Name, please?"

"Harold Gosden."

"Valid passport, please?" He flipped it open. Her eyes flicked only momentarily toward the document, then back to the emerging printout of her computer. "How will you be paying, please?'

"Francs, Swiss francs."

She slipped the ticket into its folder, took his money and gave him his change. "Thank you. Have a good flight."

● ● ● · ·

The Maltese islands appeared off the port wing, three yellow sand and limestone tablets in the blue of the Mediterranean; first Gozo, tiny Comino, to the southeast the main island of Malta.

"There it is, Sullivan. Your first trip, isn't it?" He didn't wait for an answer. "Starring's new school for oceanographers and retired pirates—Catholic country, Sullivan. You're going to be right at home. Here, change seats." He stepped into the isle. She shifted to the window, and he leaned over her, peering out at the coastal cliffs, looking inland across the rocky fields, gaining his bearings.

"There! Dead in the center, Malta's old walled capital—Mdina—dates back to the Roman occupation more than a thousand years ago. Catacombs there; the cathedral was destroyed by an earthquake, rebuilt in the 1700s. But that's current events; there are temples here dating back to 4000 B.C.

The plane was descending. He sat back for a moment, then leaned toward the window again. "Dry here, very dry. They have crops, but they have to scratch. See that stone archway running off to the east—the aqueduct—old waterworks running into Valletta. Can't see the harbor, off on the other side. There's an excitement about this place, Sullivan, the fortifications, the battles."

The U.K.I. flight touched down hard on the Luqa Airfield runway, rose slightly, then settled. Twelve rows behind the two Americans, Head adjusted his sunglasses and caressed his mustache. Only half awake, he ignored the first efforts at conversation by the elderly man seated beside him. He pulled the necktie in his jacket pocket partway out, stuffed it back. The passport, letters . . . Henry Cranston, student . . . airline ticket, Gosden? . . . bloody mistake at the other end . . . name's Cranston . . . get your bloody act together. He worked the wad of documents back into the pocket, organized his thoughts for the Maltese authorities.

Starring and his secretary had already been ushered through the arrival formalities and departed for the harbor in his Continental convertible by the time that Head cleared customs and immigration. No questions, everything in order. A warm breeze blew through the open windows of the bus carrying him to Valletta. He studied the dashboard, which the driver had transformed into a religious shrine. One skirmish over . . . new war just beginning . . . bloody bus. He slid further down into the seat turning sideways toward the window, his arms crossed tightly in front of him to protect the wound.

· · · · · ● **Chapter 3** ● · · · ·

Four miles north of Luqa Airfield, near St. Julian's on the northeast coast of Malta, Oswald Tooms sat on the terrace of the Malta Hilton savoring an ale. The first swallow produced a guttural growl of satisfaction. His eyes followed a speedboat skimming along the coastline just beyond the surf, pulling two water-skiers weaving back and forth across the wake, ducking under the towlines as they crossed, their solo skis trailing arching rooster tails of water.

"Speechmaking ain't easy," he remarked to no one in particular, "not when you're inside and this spectacle is out here." The canopied tables were crowded with participants enjoying a break in the afternoon's session of the Oceanic University of the World Conference.

"I should not think that speechmaking would be bearable when the words are those of a hypocrite." The young woman who had taken a chair beside his leaned forward to place a manila envelope on the terrace tiles. As she spoke, the graceful line of her breast was exposed by the half-buttoned front of her denim shirt.

"I'm not smart enough to be a hypocrite, just wise enough to say what folks don't want to hear. It makes the game more interesting, stirs up the real debate, keeps me in touch with all manner of people." He took in the long tanned legs beneath the white shorts, the shoulders, unusually broad, on her lean figure. She had a small nose and a cleanly defined jaw, almost a boyish look, strengthened by her tousled, sun-bleached brown hair and by a fine scar, etched against her tan, running from beneath the right eye down across the cheek.

"You see, Athena, or is it Diana," he read the tag LESLIE RENFRO MALTA on her shirt, continued in his deep southern voice, "if we are all agreed at the start, there's no reason to get together in the first place, is there? Cigarette?" She declined with a shake of her head. He speared one for himself with thick fingers. "A beer, gin and tonic? Lent's over."

"Coffee, thank you, with cream."

"I gather you have my name. Oswald Tooms, O.T., call me Oats—in the employ of Thomas Madison Starring, this conclave's patron saint and benefactor. I see your name tag, now. Is it Miss Renfro, or Mrs. . . . or Ms.—titles getting as bad as the academic bullshit, if you'll pardon the expression."

"Leslie Renfro, Dr. Tooms. I know quite well who you are, and you are a very shrewd speaker."

"Leslie Renfro, a pleasure. Twelfth address this year, Leslie; they're improving, vintage wine—"

"I found your speech insulting, Dr. Tooms. The people in this conference are dedicated to the future of the ocean environment." She fingered the white periwinkles around her neck. "And you deride their efforts. You condone and assist in the destruction of the oceans."

"The folks here"—he chuckled—"are a traveling company of actors permanently between engagements, a hand-to-mouth gang that survives on all manner of misguided grants and the largesse of some well-to-do folks who don't mind a steady dose of flattery. . . ."

"Are you aware, Dr. Tooms, of the number of people who have died in Italy alone in recent years from cholera?" She sat straighter. "Cholera contracted from contaminated shellfish? Are you aware—or do you find it more convenient to ignore—the quantities of mercury and radioactive waste that are dumped into the Mediterranean each year? Have you really dismissed the mercury poisonings in Japan? Do you know just how many people are contracting dysentery, hepatitis, and typhoid fever when they swim in the Mediterranean?"

"I make my living from this sea, Dr. Tooms." Her eyes were intent on his face. He lazily shifted his gaze to the skiers. "And, you and your people are destroying that living! If it lines your pockets, you condone . . . anything at all! Raw sewage? You love it. Toxic wastes, tanker oil, of course—"

"Black coffee?" A spoon rattled on the saucer as the old, olive-skinned Maltese waiter served them.

"Coffee, yes indeed—with cream, right, Princess? Keep on talk-ing." Tooms poked his bar tab toward the waiter, slid down in his chair, relaxed, his fingers clasped across his ample stomach. "I like the trim of your sails, Miss Renfro. Usually when a lady gets fired up she gets the trembles and shakes, but you're as steady as a tanker loaded to the Plimsoll, makes listening worthwhile."

Tooms gave her his broadest whiskered smile, breathed a contented sigh, and crossed his ankles. He had the physique of a fireplug, five feet six, barrel chested, and heavily muscled with a layer of fat. He wore his black hair in a brush cut which contrasted with his lordly, graying goatee. Eyeglasses on a cord lay across his shortsleeved safari shirt; tan shorts, black socks, and brown, crepe-soled canvas shoes completed his rig.

Leslie sipped from her coffee as she watched an Indian incline his turbaned head toward Tooms and deliver effusive congratulations. The admirer moved on to another table. "It is estimated, Dr. Tooms, that between ten and fifteen million tons of oil are deliberately dumped into the oceans by tankers each year, and—"

"Tankers are like dairy cows, Princess. They provide the juice to keep civilization on the move, cars rolling, houses warm, bakeries baking . . . of course, they do leave a few cow pies."

"Millions of tons of oil, Dr. Tooms, represent an equal quantity of toxic hydrocarbons, carcinogens, poisonous compounds that lin-ger and systematically contribute to the irraparable long-term dev-astation of the entire marine resource food chain. A single spill off a coastal marsh wipes out everything: the invertebrates, shellfish, fish, and plant life. It permeates the sediment and, as you well know, Dr. Tooms, it lingers and goes on killing. It breaks down very slowly, if at all, and its toxicity remains."

The shadow of a single cloud drifting beneath the sun added to the brilliance of her green eyes. Tooms traced a path through the sweat of his bottle, wiping the cool moisture on his brow. "What I like about you, Miss Renfro, is the artful way you make your point."

She swung toward Tooms, her voice cool and even. "The point is self-evident. You have given a paper ridiculing this conference, chastising universities, governments, and international organizations for their so-called misguided efforts to dominate ocean affairs, which you consider best left to private enterprise. You certainly must find it expedient to do so, given that you are in the pay of Towerpoint—"

"Aha! Now that's better; a clean and simple charge of prostitution." The waiter hovered at the table again, flicked at an invisible crumb, shuffled the ash tray. Tooms indicated another round. "I won't deny it." He sat up, checked his watch, leaned forward with his elbows on his knees, his hands clasped.

"You know, Princess, I've been around the water a goodly number of years. Way back before you mounted this crusade, I was soaking wet eighteen hours a day sliding around open decks as an able-bodied deckhand"—he banged his stomach and laughed—"on a salmon purse seiner working the North Pacific. I'd migrated there from my apprenticeship on shrimp boats in the Gulf. Up in the Pacific, we worked places like Tongass Narrows, Bristol Bay, the Skeena and Frazer systems . . . a nice part of this earth . . . forty-eight pounds of fish to the standard case of canned salmon. In a good season, the Pacific fleet would land three-and-a-half million cases of that plump salmon . . . chinooks, chums, pinks, silvers, reds."

Tooms took a long pull from his fresh bottle. "I was still growing up, impressed with what the sea could do for an empty belly. But, I was also something of an idealist, perish the thought. I came ashore, got some academic degrees, and made my way over to the FAO, that great international mecca of food and agriculture in Rome." He wagged a finger toward the north. "I got caught up in the West African fisheries game, fairly heady stuff for a young North Pacific fisherman.

"*Des peches pour l'Afrique* was my guiding standard, sewn on my nightshirt. I would come swinging through from the Head Office. We had two good professional fisheries types in the West African region, and a few stellar, nationally sponsored local research stations manned mostly by Frenchmen—good scientists, lousy politicians; not your usual Frenchman. All in all, a team with great promise.

"Now then, Miss Renfro, spicing this particular bouillabaisse was my discovery that the fisheries research and the catches were almost totally eclipsed by the politics of it all. Skilled international folks, not the scientists, the bureaucrats flown in from capitals, would convene

one of their regular conclaves. There'd be tough, nationalistic infight-
ing by the big boys working the waters—the Russian bear, France,
Portugal, Spain to name a few, and no one in sight interested in the
pious thoughts of FAO, the little boys ashore, or the coastal states
of West Africa. There was good fish to be sure—mackerel, sardine,
tuna—but not much making its way to the average residence of
Pointe-Noire, Accra, and Dakar.

"The little boys were just getting their freedom in those days. It
was slow at times. There would be opening speeches at each conclave, with the newly independents glowering at the imperialists and
the former overlords returning the compliment. But my colleagues
and I were undeterred. We continued to plug for improved regional
research and a level of catch that could renew itself and still set aside
the required amount of protein for the new African small fry.

"You're very patient, Miss Renfro, and if there is a point to this, it
is that I enjoy your newfound company and am prepared to filibuster
to keep it, and . . . when we were working with these West Africans,
we didn't say 'No' to anybody. We didn't pretend that the tropical
Atlantic was some sacred reserve to be locked away!"

"Every time you come to one of these clambakes, doesn't matter
where . . . Valletta, Kingston, London, Tokyo, Turtle Bay . . . you can
always count on some wild-eyed grantee to regurgitate his 'freshly
minted' thesis on demilitarization of the Pacific, of the Atlantic, of
the Caribbean, the Indian Ocean, or the Med. It makes no sense to
natter about demilitarization, about creating international machinery to stop this or stop that. It's simply not what the oceans are about.

"The Mediterranean is the perfect example." He waved toward the
distant speedboat. "Resorts, fishing, commercial shipping, defense of
the Free World . . . the U.S. Navy, the allies; that is what the water is
there for. The trick is not to say 'No' but to say 'How,' to shape our
use of this sea and the rest in a way that keeps them useful, doesn't
wear them out. And, Princess, history teaches mighty plainly that the
little guy on a rolling deck hauling for his life on a net—the entrepreneur—private enterprise and competition have brought more good
and rational use of the seas than any international organization ever
could. In there"—he jerked his head back in the direction of the conference hall—"I was just reminding folks not to sell private enterprise
short. If there's a real hypocrite, Miss Renfro, it's my audience."

"You're Starring's chief scientist, aren't you?" Her words came quickly. He squinted, flattered himself with the thought that he detected a hint of conciliation.

"You can call me that—I'm part, a small part, of his corporate brain. Towerpoint is a big operation. I suppose I'm the one person on the payroll who's paid to keep the profits down, help Tommie Starring fold some of his money back into the 'pure' side of the ocean business. Starring is a pioneer, writing a positive page in the history of the world. He gives considerable thought to his legacy. . . . And what about you, Miss Renfro? You're too tan to be a bureaucrat. Judging by that arm, looks like you might be a lion tamer."

She glanced down at the long, shallow cuts, half-healed on her left forearm. "The boat," she said, smiling at Tooms for the first time, "just a scratch from a frayed hawser."

"I've met a few in my time. They come looking for me—hawsers, booms, blocks—main cabin lanterns have always liked my head. What kind of boat?"

"A ketch, Dr. Tooms; I sail it out of Marsamxett. That is my living. I sail tourists on day cruises, overnight, by the week—skin diving, scuba diving, snorkeling, marine archeological expeditions."

"Outstanding; strange that I haven't come across your name. I always read the local rags, even when I don't know the native tongue. I've got a good eye for that sort of ad—"

"No advertising, Dr. Tooms, word of mouth, regulars, fairly steady in season, and not too bad out. I gather you have done some diving, the watch you are wearing?"

"A bit, a bit." He paused, drained his ale. "Diving is what brought me and my current benefactor together. I had cast my net wider than West Africa by then, done a hitch teaching coastal research, mariculture. We included some diving, really just for the sheer pleasure of it—one atmosphere, is that what you're doing?"

"Yes, primarily one atmosphere, bottled air."

"Well, back then when I was mariculturing, we were thinking a bit bigger as a nation, dreaming, designing laboratories on the continental shelf—return to Atlantis, you know. I got caught up in a fancy operation, Navy-funded, plenty of dollars, and we put together a long-endurance saturation diving program. When I wasn't underwater or compressed in a steel pipe somewhere," he said, laughing, "I was talking to folks—second only to the astronauts in those days. people loved to hear about the pressures, what they did to a person, the dangers, the prospects for sustaining researchers and work crews underwater, the prospects for those 'colonies' on the deep-sea floor."

"Tommie Starring got wind of one of my talks, probably had Sullivan pull together some of my papers, asked me to meet him. Halfway through the first cup of coffee, I was telling him that the Gulf of Guinea was lousy with Soviet bloc trawlers and factory ships, that this was the tip of the iceberg, bigger than fishing . . . and, that we were in the process of losing an important game." He looked at her. "Do you follow, Miss Renfro? You couldn't put into a single port for thousands of miles without bumping into one or more trawlers flying the hammer and sickle. Well, Starring and I swapped a few yarns, found we liked each other's politics, and I joined him. Towerpoint was expanding its wings, out front in off-shore technology . . ."

"Go on!" The harshness had returned.

Tooms seemed not to notice. "Well, started out with some diving. The science role emerged in the second year. I've been with him now for upwards of twelve, thirteen years. Ummph!" He started to heave himself to his feet. "I'd like to learn more about your charter opera-tion, Miss Renfro. I'm due inside again, a panel."

"Yes, the future of Mediterranean resources."

"That's it; glad you knew at least. I'd like you to take me diving, Miss Renfro—haven't had the pleasure of looking around off Malta, long overdue. In the meantime, given my sanctified bachelor's status, perhaps you will do me the honor of joining me for dinner this eve-ning. There used to be a nice joint up the coast from here, the Green Dolphin, very tasty Mediterranean resources. What do you say?"

She was on her feet. "No thank you."

"Tomorrow evening, Miss Renfro, Starring is having a reception in the Grand Harbor. He has the flagship here—six o'clock on the fan-tail for cocktails. I'd like you to meet him, might do you both some good. Come to think of it, half of Malta will be there . . . all the grant-ees. Best to let them work the trough over first. The second sitting will settle in at a more genteel pace at about seven o'clock. Do you accept, or is there a husband lurking in the forecastle?"

"Thank you, Dr. Tooms, I would like to attend your reception—"

"Grand, grand. You continue to surprise me. Tell me again, where will I find your ketch? You said the Marsamxett . . . ?"

"I will meet you at the customshouse wharf at six-thirty, Dr. Tooms." She turned away from him. They entered the conference hall separately. At the tables along the rear wall, she scanned the conference literature until she found the schedule for the following day, confirming:

1700—reception hosted by the Honourable Thomas M. Starring, Grand Harbour. Apply at conference administration centre for transportation.

She swept this and various other papers into her envelope, and turned toward the dais, the raised tables covered in blue felt, a spotlight playing on the Ocean University's emblem of sea creatures imposed in a swimming circle on a Maltese Cross, in turn centered on a field descending from emerald green to indigo.

Tooms, blinking in the change of light, scratched at an ear, made his way up the stage steps to his panelist's chair. He swiveled toward the pale, bald, little rabbit of a man beside him. "Lemaire, Monsieur Dr. Lemaire! Well, well, well; we're really going to give them their money's worth today. The late fifties Lemaire, in Tunis; we were both handsome then. I'd hate to think I might learn something, but I just might this afternoon." Tooms's hand darted out, squeezed the Frenchman's knee. Lemaire, with a flash of teeth, kicked his chair out of Tooms's range.

With the *thunk, thunk* of the chairman's pencil on his microphone, Tooms settled down, peered out through the lights. Leslie Renfro had departed.

·····●Chapter 4●·····

The following evening, the freighter *Thrakikon Pelagos*, a ten-thousand tonner, rounded Ricasoli Point, leaving St. Elmo Lighthouse to port and setting a northeasterly course for her return voyage to Greece. Her empty, rusting hull, coated gray with dust from the cargo of cement just delivered, rode high in the water. Her propeller broke the surface with each blade's revolution, chopping a frothy green marble wake in the blue of the Grand Harbor.

Towering astern, the fortress city of Valletta rose on the spiny peninsula of Mount Sciberras. At the seaward tip lay Fort St. Elmo, behind it, bank upon bank of white and pastel-colored houses, apartments, and shops reaching high above the harbor walls, presented a façade of urban and natural grandeur of a magnitude, sweep, and architectural impact unparalleled through the centuries.

The far side of the harbor was more intricate. At the narrow entrance, Ricasoli Fort guarded the seaward approaches. Inside the breakwaters, five creeks divided five peninsulas, each jutting into the harbor's main basin. Looming over all stood the great rock rampart of Fort St. Angelo, before independence the headquarters of the Royal Navy's Flag Officer Malta and three hundred years before that the home of Grand Master La Valette and the Knights of St. John. Tucked behind this enduring fortress, the shipyards of Malta, so vital to her livelihood, lay at the headwaters of Dockyard Creek and French Creek. The community of Senglea divided the creeks with shoulder-to-shoulder houses rimming the waterfront, many with tunneled stairways, carved in the living rock, running down to the water's edge. From Senglea, a ferry running to the customshouse linked the two sides of the harbor.

Tooms's cigarette died with a hiss in the water flowing past the customshouse. He was on the wharf leaning against a bollard, arms folded, observing the skyscraping caged elevator rising slowly from harbor level to the streets of Valletta. Starring had laid the wood to him that morning, a classic performance. "Here's what I want done; why the hell don't you have it done?" Tooms had closeted himself for the rest of the day, with charts and papers, inventory records covering every working surface of his shipboard laboratory. It was coming, he had reflected with some satisfaction, but damnation, I'm getting too old for these instant creations.

The workday also was over for the Maltese; the harbor was at peace. Only the tourist boats, Arabesque, double-prowed dghajsas, rowed by capped Maltese oarsmen standing amidships, continued to ply the waters. The light, the sun low in the west, was good for photographs at this hour, and the temperature was cooler.

Tooms watched an elderly couple, fair-skinned, Scandinavian to his eye, maybe German, embark in a dghajsa, the taximan holding the graceful craft steady. The gentleman assisted the lady to the bench in the stern, and then immediately helping her up again, they turned around holding each other by the waist and exchanged places. From beneath his green plastic visor, the man gave a nod of approval to the taximan, gesturing with a broad sweep of the harbor to confirm his order for the deluxe tour. The taximan repeated the gesture, tipped his cap to the couple, shoved off with a foot, and headed up harbor, pushing the dghajsa with short sweeps of the oars.

"Well, Dr. Tooms, you are punctual, necessary I suppose when you place yourself in someone else's hire. Punching time clocks must be the same even in the grasping clutches of Towerpoint."

"Miss Renfro, charming as ever. You do me great honor keeping this date; the current crop of Knights of St. John would have arrested me for loitering in another minute." He pushed away from the bollard extending his hand in greeting, which in a glance was seen and ignored.

"You are looking absolutely charming, Miss Renfro, the belle of the Towerpoint ball." His admiring gaze took in the pale blue shirt and matching espadrilles, the white skirt and familiar shell necklace. He scanned the waterfront, spotted a kelly green hull with gold scrollwork and waved the skipper over. Tooms was pleased to have Leslie Renfro in tow. He valued his psychological insights; they helped in his game. He had savored the impact of her harsh words, had played with the language in his mind since their first conversation on the hotel terrace. Throughout the day he had been toying with various roles for her in his new scheme. None had fully crystallized, but there had been a place for her each time, and it had worked well. This was the extra facet of Tooms's character that Tommie Starring valued. Starring expected, demanded, that he keep pulling rabbits out of hats. Tooms was looking forward to showing off the young mermaid to the boss.

Leslie stepped lightly into the dghajsa. Tooms eased himself down into the small craft with a grunt. "You have a seaman's manner, Miss Renfro, and that's said as a compliment. Have you been on the high seas today or back at the front office sorting through your investments?" He waved his cigarettes toward her knowing she would decline and took one for himself, pausing to give directions to the dghajsa skipper before flicking his lighter.

"I have had a good day, Dr. Tooms. Two couples, three children, have booked for a week's cruise. They are neophytes, here for a fortnight, and in a hurry to get under way. Actually, it is much easier with the beginners, no ingrained errors to correct. I sent them into the city with a shopping list, and my crew and I have spent the day outfitting the ketch. We sail tomorrow."

"Where to?"

"West, along the north coasts; circumnavigate Gozo and Comino; skin diving; a night at anchor in the Blue Lagoon; a side excursion to the Blue Grotto Caves; good variety. I would invite you, Dr. Tooms, but we are already at full capacity. Do you speak again at the conference? I will miss the closing session."

"God forbid, God forbid! You ought to book some of the grantees, Princess, let them work a little *mal de mer* into their next presentations. As for me, there'll be time. I'll make time—your cruising invitation's accepted."

The dghajsa's long oars, lashed with heavy line to the wooden peg oarlocks, continued their rhythmic splashing sweeps through the water. As the taxiboat pushed further into the harbor, the port bows and hull of the *Towerpoint Octagon*, flagship of Starring's Towerpoint International, loomed before them riding at her black iron mooring buoy.

"It's an ugly ship."

"The very finest in the world, Miss Renfro, a sweetheart, an able ship; the best oceangoing research platform you or I will ever see." Tooms turned to the taximan. "The accommodation ladder's rigged on the outboard starboard hull, skipper; take us once around before we board."

More than a flagship, the *Towerpoint Octagon* epitomized Tommie Starring's determination to prevail, displaying his defiance of the general decline of sea power in America. An oceangoing catamaran, she ran some three hundred feet from bow to stern. Her twin hulls were divided by a thirty-five foot well, giving her a maximum beam of more than eighty feet. The hulls were a glistening midnight blue with *TOWERPOINT OCTAGON* painted in eight-foot block letters of gold on each outboard hull. The octagonal superstructure was white, with the twin stacks taking up the blue of the hull, each with the corporation *T* in gold.

Leslie Renfro scanned the ship's profile.

"One of a kind, custom-built, alive with machinery—helo platform aft." Tooms leaned back, one elbow on the dghajsa's thwart, following the line of her observations. Her skin glowed golden in the sunset's rays, a filmy down on the arm raised to shade her eyes. "Massive overhead crane, submersible, no . . . yes, two of them, buoys on the forward decks . . . built for underseas support."

"Damned good," Tooms growled. "You have a keen eye. She's a converted submarine rescue ship, *Neptune* class."

"You mean a warship."

"She's civilian, alright, but don't let the paint fool you. She's was laid down for the Navy. Starring built her in his yards, one of a new class—one too many as it turned out. Starring kept the Navy's feet to the fire, wouldn't let the brass hats cut corners on quality. The *Neptunes* were built to handle rescue missions for the nuclear missile subs. He wanted them to be as good as the submarines. There were God-awful contract disputes, entire armies of lawyers maneuvering

on the Potomac flats, more budget cuts wringing more money out of
the Navy's hide. Then—they put a hold on the entire class, no more
construction while the folks in Washington read their bones. Starring
laid them flat, Miss Renfro, knocked the air out, left the Pentagon,
White House, Capitol Hill, and points east gasping. With the last of
the hull plates not even welded, he renegotiated, closed out the contract, took over the ship as she stood in the ways and finished the job
with Towerpoint money—quite the sensation at the time."

"I do not share your admiration, Dr. Tooms. Either the man is a mega-
lomaniac squandering millions, or he is engaged in military support."

Tooms gave a burst of laughter, "Spoken like a deckhand, Princess.
I am increasingly bewitched by your diplomatic lilt."

A Maltese customs launch was pulling away from the accommodation ladder as they rounded the starboard side. The president of
Malta, a diminutive figure in dark suit with his straw hat crushed in
one hand against the rail of the launch, gave a farewell wave in the
direction of the catamaran. With the departure of his boat, the Maltese flag was struck from the *Towerpoint Octagon*'s signal yard. Two
ship's launches and a flock of dghajsas that had been circling off the
catamaran moved in to collect the first wave of Oceanic University
conferees leaving the reception.

The sun's evening rays had turned the walled city of Valletta into soft,
glowing amber, a scene framed in the long triangle of signal flags dressing the ship, running from the jackstaff up to the mainmast platform
ninety feet above the waterline, aft down to the ensign staff at the fantail.
Tooms was struck at once by the spectacle and by the effect it seemed
to have on his companion. She was silent, facing the hulking *Towerpoint
Octagon*, deep in thought, slowly turning a fine silver ring on the little
finger of her left hand, her expression questioning.

"Okay. You board now." The dghajsa skipper maneuvered the taxiboat
to the ship. Two deckhands in crisply laundered uniform—white shirts,
blue shorts, white calf-length socks, and deck shoes—manned the landing
float at the foot of the ladder. The taximan waved off their offer of assistance, allowing his port oar to skim along the top of the float and brake
him. He held the boat fast with a sculling motion of the starboard oar.

"Thanks, Skipper, a fine cruise." Tooms's adrenaline was flowing
with excitement of the party. He pressed two more notes into the
taximan's hand. "Hope your folks let you stay out after dark, Skipper.

Keep a weather eye on that helo pad. When the last cork pops we'll be needing a return lift, like to give you the business."

The taximan laughed, rubbed his gray stubble, "*Sahha, sahha,* I will be here."

At the top of the ladder, they were met by the ship's second officer. "Mr. Starring has been asking for you, Dr. Tooms. You and your guest are expected on the helicopter deck." He saluted and turned to pick up the ship's phone.

"This way, Princess; Maritime Academy. They don't teach them how to laugh anymore. You two could have a dandy evening together."

She avoided his hand as he guided her aft. In six steps, they were in the waist of the ship. A thirty-six-foot waterjet speedboat rested in a cradle on the starboard side of the center well. Above it, the powerful, girdered structure of the well bridge crane dominated the ship. A teardrop submersible, midnight blue with golden sail and diving planes, hung suspended from the crane, its twin portholes peering down like myopic eyes. She studied the rig. The crane's controls were forward in a glass-enclosed operator's booth two levels above them.

"Like one for the ketch?" Tooms was beside her at the guardrail. "Powerful, built to move the width of the ship, starboard hull, to center well, to port hull and back, with load positioning fore and aft the length of the well.

"The way Starring operates this ship, one-third yacht, one-third research, one-third commercial operations, she doesn't carry everything she was built for. If she did, these decks would be packed—two of the deep-rescue minisubs, the personnel capsules, and the new compression chambers. We don't have the minis; we carry that teardrop, have two good work chariots below decks, one capsule and one decompression chamber. The *Octagon* has had some major work below decks, work shops, storage compartments reduced, relocated to make space for the boss and his guests. We'll get to that in good time."

From the main deck, they climbed to the 0-1 level, to the helo deck. Starring sprang from a cluster of white deck chairs, "Oats, where in God's name have you been? You missed a good reception. The conference is a success; your ears should be burning. Your speech was excellent, by all accounts."

"Thank you, sir, thank you. This is Leslie Renfro, conferee." Tooms took satisfaction from Starring's obvious approval. They joined the circle of chairs. Starring was beginning to relax. For two hours he had stood accepting condolences for his sister and praise for his gifts to Malta. The words had sat well, but the chatter had been a bore. He had accepted each utterance, clasped each hand, his eyes unblinking, locked on each speaker. With the reception over, he was reinvigorated by Tooms's arrival. "My friends, I believe you all know Dr. Oswald Tooms—Oats, and his lovely guest . . ."

"Miss Renfro, Tommie, Miss Leslie Renfro, a native, a conferee, a mermaid—"

"Yes, Leslie, my friend," Starring continued, "my wife Tina, Dr. Joseph Ghadira of the University of Malta, and Mr. Gus Anderson of Oklahoma City." The men rose.

Tina smiled at the newcomer, tapped her ivory cigarette holder into the ashtray at her side, then turned her attention to Tooms who had crossed to her chair. "What have you brought us this time, Oats?" she murmured.

He chuckled, planted a kiss on her cheek. "Strictly business, madam, strictly business. You're looking marvelous as always."

Tina Starring was a stunning woman. Her well-defined features had pouted from many a magazine cover and billboard poster. Blonde, slender, taller than her husband, with graceful, tanned arms, ankles, and neck at the extremities of her white satin cocktail suit. The flimsiest of extravagant silver-strapped high heels had been chosen for the evening. One heel burrowed into the great Persian rug spread on the flight deck. The other danced on her crossed legs, its performance highlighted by a golden ankle bracelet wrought of links as fine as horsehair.

Modeling had presented her beautiful face to the world, had led French actor Jean Montpellier to her. Their love affair had been exotic in its passion. His adoration and influence had provided the entree to the setting of her dreams, live theater.

The beauty, sexiness, and presence of Tina Montpellier leapt from the covers of magazines to the footlights and the growing love of audiences in Europe and America. The crush of so many thousands, their love, took her from Montpellier. His psyche rebelled at such sharing. He sought solace, the beginning of their separation, in four-months' on-location filming in China. The hurt of his departure was soothed by the excitement of her youthful success. Their final separation was little more than a year old when she won her greatest acclaim in a leading role at the National Creative Arena. The Directors' Night performance had stunned Tommie Starring. He had returned a second and a third night to watch Tina Montpellier perform, and to decide that she must become Tina Starring.

Stewards in white linen jackets appeared with additional chairs, and the circle, defined by the rug, was enlarged to admit two more. Starring swept in behind Leslie. "Have a seat, my friend. Relax; enjoy this finest of evenings."

Her husband's hovering over this new girl caused Tina to give Oats Tooms a long stare and a mock, reproving smile. If there was jealousy, the feeling was lost to her, buried deep beneath enduring scars of their marriage. The courtship and wedding had burst on the social pages as the most exciting matchmaking of several years. Their first months together had been a succession of joys culminating in her pregnancy.

Starring had been crushed, first by concern for her and then by self-pity, when her physicians had advised that the pregnancy was outside the womb, in the fallopian tube, and would have to be terminated. Deep within him, Starring had resented her abortion as an act of failure, an act which mocked his power. He had been white as chalk when she had been wheeled from surgery into the convalescent suite. His journey through the hospital's corridors, the strong medicinal odors, the sight of so many pale, prostrate forms on stretcher beds, had brought on the uncontrollable reaction of fear and nausea that the world of medicine had always inflicted on him. Weak as she had been, Tina had been alarmed by his appearance. Beneath his pallor, she saw the look of betrayal, which was to haunt her for months. The outward tokens of love and affection returned soon enough, a reflection of Sullivan's—not Starring's—tasteful hand. Starring had left their marriage bed at the start of her convalescence. Long after she had physically mended, he had not returned. From his rebuff of her first enticements and the predawn tempest of her injured fury and screaming recriminations that had swirled from the master bedroom through two floors of the town house, there had not again been mention by either of the physical estrangement. She had summoned their personal attorney that same day, her mind throbbing with the imperative of divorce. For weeks she had resisted his caring, velveted counsel, had fought against the future often raging aloud during a seemingly endless succession of sleepless nights. For weeks longer, she had measured that counsel, with its powerful underlying argument of ledger, of her remaining Tommie Starring's wife.

This personal disharmony at the apex of Towerpoint International had remained beyond the public's view, but it had troubled Adrian Starring deeply. As did his sister, he accepted his older brother's leadership eagerly, the springboard for his own comfortable corporate rise. Unlike Connie, he had welcomed, even thrilled to Tina's celebrity entrance into the family. Her aborted pregnancy had sorrowed him, truly a family loss. Her difficulties with Tommie, whatever their cause, presaged a bleak uncertainty he feared could only play negatively in his and the family's fortunes.

Tina had accepted the younger brother's first overture, an invitation to lunch, with indifference. Without doubt, his solicitude had been heartfelt. They lunched again, some ten days later. With her guarded responses, she had encouraged him to carry the conversations, his flow of words forming an increasingly polished mirror in which to study her future as a Starring. As Adrian had led her out of her dark forest of despair, he grew in confidence and in hope. She was reemerging, her spirit brightening, and in this he took tremendous satisfaction—a subconscious sense of contribution to Towerpoint's destiny.

As their meetings continued, there was soon too much to be said over the silver and linens of a restaurant table. He shaped his professional calendar to permit their conversations to extend from luncheons, to the cab back to her house, and through the shifting light of mid-afternoon over drawing room coffees. More than half a year had elapsed when one such afternoon he took her hands to say good-bye and brushed her cheek with his well-practiced brotherly kiss. She had kept his hand gently, told him she needed his advice, and had led him to the master bedroom where she had turned and kissed him with enveloping passion.

There could be no doubt as to Adrian's loyalty to his brother, but his eyes over the months of conversation, his physical adoration, had betrayed his weakness. She had made love to him that afternoon with such seeming desire that Adrian, in his dazed excitement, had climaxed almost immediately. She had held him in her. She had run her hands along his aroused flesh until she too trembled in orgasm, shuddering triumphant in victory over Tommie. That same evening, as Tina sat with her husband at the head table of a black tie charity gala, she would sweetly whisper her affair with Adrian into his ears, a message to be permanently submerged by both in silence, her contribution to the revision of their marriage.

"Oats!" Starring's voice rose across the circle. "During your truancy, Dr. Ghadira and his houseguest Gus have been regaling us with fascinating tales. They share the rare distinction of having had the George Cross conferred on them by His Majesty George VI at the height of the Second World War. Dr. Ghadira, you Maltese have become legendary as the heroes of sieges. Is there some unique strain of bravery the parents endow to the sons and daughters of each new generation?" Starring retook his seat as he spoke, unbuttoning his green blazer, and accepted a Scotch.

"Mr. Starring . . ."

"Tommie. Call me Tommie, my friend."

"Well, Tommie, we didn't think of it as bravery—maybe afterwards but not while we were defending our homes. I was almost seventeen when the Italians started in on us in June of 1940. The first half year was more excitement than hardship. Mussolini's bombers had an extreme distaste for anti-aircraft fire.

"The British, while their resources were very limited, had us well organized. My father was a gunnery sergeant, battery northwest of the capital. I was at the aerodrome, totally entranced by the RAF, running errands, anything to be part of the action. It wasn't too long before there was plenty of it, with the Italians giving way to the Nazi dive-bombers in early '41. I was with a runway repair crew then. The Nazis would blaze across each day cratering our strips. We would pop out, patch over the holes—"

"My God, how horribly dangerous. What about your family?" A faint line appeared on Tina's forehead as the fine brows drew together in a frown.

Ghadira's eyes sparkled with the pleasure of his tale. "I had four sisters, two brothers, five of whom are still alive. Our families were strengthened by faith, Mrs. Starring. There were times when I was sure my mother and grandmother carried the entire island on the strength of their prayers. We rode out the worst of the Nazi bombardments in caves. Malta is a rock. And so, we lived in caves, not comfortable but safe."

"Sounds like an aunt of mine," Tooms growled.

A steward appeared at Leslie Renfro's side. "I ordered you another wine, my friend," Starring broke into the conversation, "a splendid Bordeaux just laid in." In the growing darkness, he was conscious that she had been staring at him from the moment of her arrival. As he had caught her green eyes from time to time, he had been flattered, surprised to find that his mind had drifted from the lilting words of the Maltese professor. The first tinglings of sexual arousal had snapped his mind back to the conversation. He jumped to his feet to regain command. "Dr. Ghadira, what brought you and Gus together? You were a pilot, weren't you, Gus? I didn't know we had people here."

Anderson shifted in his chair. He was a big man, pale, with light-brown hair growing in profusion from the open neck of his shirt, down along the heavy forearms resting on his knees, ending, a forest's edge, on the backs of his long-fingered hands. He rolled his pilsner glass between the fingers. "Joe and I are brothers," he said, winking at the short, bald professor.

"Now, who is Joe?" Tina recrossed her lovely legs.

"Tina!" Starring's voice was firm. "Go ahead, Gus." With the coming of darkness, the stewards had lit candles in hurricane globes at each of the cocktail tables. Long-poled kerosene torches flamed just beyond the periphery of conversation, the light playing across Anderson's long facial features. Silver trays of hors d'oeuvres were borne around the circle.

"Joe? Dr. Ghadira." Anderson aimed his empty glass toward the professor. "He was my honorary plane captain. We had regular crews, RAF, but Joe was there when we scrambled and ready with the chocks when we landed. At the worst of it, in late '41, '42, he slept on a blanket between the plane's wheels, guarded her like a watch dog. I arrived in Malta in October '41, came down from the U.K. I had been a mail pilot, Oklahoma, further west, had sensed the war, but couldn't wait for Pearl Harbor. We had a mixed bag of good pilots down here, Limeys, Aussies, Kiwis, Canadians, Rhodesians. We were flying Hurricanes until the first of the Spitfires joined us in '42. The Hurricanes were good, had proven themselves against the Luftwaffe's Messerschmidt 109Es in the Battle of Britain."

"Heroic engagement, carved in stone." Starring directed his words to Leslie Renfro, who continued to watch him like a cat studying the occupant of an adjoining cage.

Anderson accepted another hors d'oeuvre, downed it in a gulp. "We'd come over this harbor flying out to tangle with the Junkers 88 bombers, their brothers the 87 dive-bombers, and the Messerschmidts. The first Hurricanes were classy birds, old-fashioned, fixed-pitch wooden propellers, fabric wings cradling eight Browning machine guns—"

"Better armed than some of today's blowtorches in the Sixth Fleet." Tooms swirled the ice in the dregs of his bourbon; at the sound, a steward bore the glass away to the serving bar.

"You may be right. They were slow, though, three-hundred max. The MEs ran circles around us except in a dive; we could catch them in a dive. The air used to be thick, forty, fifty bombers, twice as many fighters, like clockwork every day, working over Valletta, the airfields, the dockyards—"

"And the fleet when it was here."

"You're right, there, Mr. Starring. We counted as many as three-hundred bombers and fighters on more than one sortie. They had an easy run, just sixty miles from their fields in Sicily. Now, when the Spitfires came"—Anderson spread a hand across the sky—"what a marvelous fighting machine they were; fast, simple, clean cockpit, no more instruments than a Cadillac, machine-gun firing trigger built right into their joysticks. I was still flying Hurricanes. I envied those boys. Together we took our toll."

"And the island held! Magnificent achievement! When did the king actually present the George Cross?"

"Who can forget that, Tommie? April 14, 1942. He awarded the Cross to the entire population. We were all quite staggered."

"And, you have kept this friendship between you. I think that is very lovely." Tina rose, made her way gracefully to a vase of cut flowers to reseat a dangling anemone. As she bent over the vase, she turned to Leslie. "You're very quiet, darling. Are you all right? Canapes and catamarans are not everyone's cup of tea." Leslie's cool smile warned her away. She moved along to Tooms, rubbed a hand through his bristly hair. "Tell me again, Oats, where did you and Miss Renfro find each other? She is a most attractive young lady, and I am on the verge of being quite jealous."

Tooms leaned back and stretched his arms, allowing one to come to rest on Leslie's chair. "We just met yesterday, my dear Tina, over a cold beer and a hot, black—"

"Tina! Muriel was not feeling well this afternoon. She is in her cabin. Make sure the doctor is keeping an eye on her." She crossed over to her husband as he spoke, her hands with ten perfect ovals of rose-painted fingernails resting gently on his shoulders.

"Of course, Tommie. Poor Muriel, my co–wife. I don't think the canapés and catamarans agree with her. I'll have one of the stewards look in on her right now—and, really,—we all should have something to eat." She continued her careful stroll around the outside of the circle, gave her instructions, and took her chair again.

"What I find so astounding"—Starring picked up the earlier thread—"is that the last war was merely a footnote to the greater sieges centuries before."

"I must agree," Ghadira said. "The weapons may have been more modern, the statistics greater in terms of tons of explosives, but the tactics, the intensity of struggle, the barbarism, the *cause* were far more dramatic in the sixteenth century."

"The Turk, Suleiman, wasn't he? Suleiman of the Ottomans, Suleiman the Magnificent." Starring moved to the rail on the flight deck's starboard side. The *Towerpoint Octagon* had swung on her mooring with the gentle northerly breeze. The others followed, looked out toward the mouth of the harbor across the dark, rippling water reflecting the lights of the city.

"My favorite of his titles, he must have had twenty," Ghadira said, "was Possessor of Men's Necks. . . ."

"When did the siege actually begin?" Starring asked."

"In 1564." Leslie's voice brought a quick turn their heads.

"A student of the siege, too, Princess?" Tooms added to his file.

"When you live here"—her eyes stayed on the water—"it becomes part of you. It is living history despite the passage of the years, the repeated devastations."

"'Living,' that's excellent, very apt." Starring resumed, one foot on the bottom rung of the raised safety railing. "Suleiman was in his seventies, wasn't he? He had driven the Knights from Rhodes forty years before, The Emperor of Spain had given them Malta as a place of refuge."

"Charles the Fifth," Dr. Ghadira confirmed.

"It was the Knights of St. John, I learned earlier this evening, who gave the islands their cross, each of the arms a virtue, each point on each arm a beatitude. Suleiman was obsessed with ridding the world of them, launched his forces from Constantinople in two hundred galleys and sailing ships. What were the Knights' defenses?"

"De la Valette had two fortifications, Tommie, a small fort, St. Elmo, off to the left at the outer reaches of the harbor, and the main point of defense, Fort St. Angelo."

"And, the Turk's plan was to sweep quickly across St. Elmo and then move in for the kill on St. Angelo—"

"Tommie, dear guests, the buffet is set."

"Not yet, not yet." Starring brushed her away.

"Tina, you're the most delectable morsel afloat. No need to bother with more food," Tooms called. "Tell me about this well-earned vacation of yours."

"*Jaruka, thumma, jaruka, thumma jaruka.*" She kissed him, a warm, lingering kiss on the cheek.

"I know," Tooms answered, "felt the same myself countless times. What brought that to mind?"

"Arabic, Oats, my darling scholar. Don't your fish know the tongue of the desert? 'Your neighbor, then your neighbor, then your neighbo,—very philosophical, don't you think?"

"Good for apartment living."

"I am reading, reading a great deal about the Arabs, slowly transforming myself into a desert almanac. A camel, dear Oats, does four miles an hour at a walk, eight if he holds to a steady trot, and thirteen running as fast as his little feet will carry him. There is a new play—too soon, but it is there, with a benefit in less than a month. It is speckled with Arabia, and so will I be." She glided away. Tooms gave her a bon voyage wave without moving from the rail. Ghadira had carried the Grand Siege to the fall of St. Elmo.

"Correct me, my friend"—Starring grasped the professor's wrist— "the Turks were so bitter when they finally took St. Elmo that they mutilated the bodies of the few Knights they found, sliced out their hearts, hacked off their heads, nailed them to crosses, and floated them over to St. Angelo?"

Ghadira nodded, "The most brutal episode of the entire siege. De la Valette took one look, immediately executed the Turkish prisoners held within his walls, loaded their heads into cannons, and fired them back into the Turkish lines." Starring pounded his fist on the rail in excitement.

They moved back into the ring of light and chairs, pausing to be served from a table richly spread with salads, smoked trout, whitefish, salmon, lobster, hot breads, and pastries. Tina returned to her chair with a champagne in each hand. "A new diet, Gus, darling. Do have some more and do give me a cigarette." She reeled back from the flame of his lighter. "A light, darling, not a sun tan." Her voice was louder. "I have a very fair skin, and I am very envious of Miss Renfro's glorious color. Do you have regular sessions at the beach, darling?"

Leslie Renfro had mapped her strategy for the evening before setting foot on Starring's ship. She ignored the baiting, passed her plate to a steward with the meal untouched.

"Delicious, delicious." Starring had already finished and punctuated his verdict with a flourish of his napkin. The Maltese professor had resumed his history. When he finished, the islands still safe in the hands of the Knights, Starring rose.

"Brilliantly told, my friend; a splendid tale of a proud people." He proposed a toast to Ghadira and to the success of the Oceanic University of the World Conferences.

"Tommie"—Ghadira's glass was raised in response—"as our president said this evening on this very deck, none of this would have been possible without you. Your announcement this evening of the new pier and laboratory was colossal, absolutely colossal, banner headlines fully deserved tomorrow."

"Oats sketched out this project for me two years ago. He deserves the credit."

The chief scientist beckoned to one of the white jackets. "One more of Kentucky's finest; the praise has made me dry."

Starring continued. "The Towerpoint fleet plies the Mediterranean—plies every ocean, my friends. This is only the first. Malta will be the model. We'll work together, Dr. Ghadira, Towerpoint and Malta. We'll put the knowledge of your graduates to work, no lacking attention . . ." He again had looked toward Tooms's guest as he had addressed the words.

She leaned forward, hands clasped tightly across her knees. "I do not expect to alter your idea of what is right and what is wrong, not this evening. You are wrong. People will . . ." She broke off. Her words had flowed quickly, with rising emotion. Tooms heaved himself upright in his seat.

Starring had moved a step closer. "Mistaken idea? Hardly, Miss Renfro, and a perception on your part, my friend, I attach importance to correcting."

"Our mermaid is setting off on her own expedition, Tommie. She'll be back, my personal crusade, for the complete two-dollar tour of this tub."

"Excellent, Miss Renfro. Towerpoint is about to embark on one of the most dramatic research projects ever conceived. If you are a scientist it might be of interest to you—"

Tina's champagne glass fell to the rug unbroken, swinging in a half-circle around its base before rolling to a stop at Anderson's feet. He scooped under the stem and placed it on a waiting tray.

"Tina has given the signal. Ladies get their wraps; gents their canes and hats." Tooms pushed himself to his feet. The others rose, except for Starring's wife. As the candlelight played on her face and hair, she was so lovely, so composed, it was barely apparent she was asleep.

"Oats, are you seeing Miss Renfro ashore?"

"Taxi's just around the corner, Tommie."

"Ahhhhh!" The entire party exclaimed, as the sky over the city exploded with brilliant bursts of fireworks: pinks, whites, golds, and green blossoming from thundering puffs into expanding, rolling, shimmering globes.

"Night flares," Anderson laughed. "Junkers on the way. Come on, Joe, got to get out to Luqa, get the Hurricane up to meet them." Starring laughed with them.

"Church festival," Ghadira said. "A true friend of Malta must love fireworks, Malta's soul and passion."

"The sky flashed again, flowering, banging bursts of red and white which opened, separating into petals before falling and fading into the night. Ship's lights, playing on the submersible, spotlighted the *Towerpoint Octagon*'s presence in the harbor as the party made its way to the ladder on the main deck.

Tooms hesitated at the head of the ladder, shielded his eyes. "There he is, faithful skipper, Princess, lying off about twenty yards. He hailed the dghajsa, boarded with Leslie. The taxiboat sculled silently back across the harbor to the customs wharf, its way lit at intervals by the bursts of festival rockets.

·····• Chapter 5 •···· ·

At the moment Ambassador Burdette had slumped dead in the smoke, blood, and shattered glass of her limousine in Geneva, the young lieutenant navigator of the Soviet cruise ship *Omsk* was bent over a chart penciling in his ship's position north of Cape Hatteras.

He checked his sun-line computations against the loran bearings and marked a circled X. This done, he slid the parallel rule across the chart, drawing a line from the ship's location to the Chesapeake Light, then walked the rule to the nearest compass rose, took the reading, and jotted down the course heading.

His mind ticked off the coming sequence of events. The pilot would swing aboard at the Light, take them through the bridge-tunnel channel cleaving Cape Henry and Cape Charles, and up the bay. He placed the points of his dividers on the breadth of the channel, too narrow, dangerous, the great engineering Americans.

Emerging from the chart house, the navigator walked the twenty paces to his captain who was on the starboard wing of the bridge, legs set apart, binoculars to his eyes, studying a faint hull shape on the horizon. "One of their new cruisers, that pyramidal shape forward. What dreamers!" The young officer saluted, reported the *Omsk*'s position and recommended new heading. The captain acknowledged the report, stepped into the bridge house, ordered left rudder, waited until the ship steadied on her new heading, then returned to the wing.

"They are a strange nation, Mr. Navigator. That unit is standing out for their Sixth Fleet where he will join the rest of their fish in the Mediterranean barrel. Meanwhile, Mr. Navigator, do you not find it strange the *Omsk* is permitted to proceed along their coast without so much as a patrol plane? Can you imagine an American ship steaming off the Soviet Union unsurveilled? Quite remarkable, isn't it?

"Irresponsible, Captain."

"Yes. They place their faith and their defense in God. They believe that coastal defenses are a strategy of the past—no more ships, no more planes, no more troops. They build their automated light-houses, fit them with modern navigational aids free to all, and God will provide. Remarkable isn't it? He does provide—illegals, unde-sirables swarming ashore stealing, robbing the American worker of his job, parasites infesting their nation. He provides narcotics by the ton, heroin, cocaine, and the rest poisoning their sick society. Quite remarkable." He stepped back inside the bridge house, placed his bin-oculars in the rack beside his chair, left instructions with the watch, brushed his uniform, and departed on a stroll of the passenger decks.

Hundreds of miles to the north, well above the entrance to the bay, Memorial Day traffic moved smoothly over the twin spans of the Chesa-peake Bay Bridge, despite construction on the westbound span which had reduced the flow from three lanes to two. Orange fluorescent cones and an arrow of blinking yellow lights diverted the traffic from the left lane just beyond the first tower of the bridge's suspension span. At the highest point, 187 feet above the 1,500 foot main channel, three white aluminum trailers and an electrical generator unit were parked at intervals behind the cones. The generator's engine periodically coughed into life, its elec-tricity flowing to the trailers in cables laid along the bridge curbing. Five gallon cans of red lead and aluminum paint were stacked in two piles. Air compressors and coils of line added to the maintenance clutter.

Funnels of yellow plastic fitted to the open doors of each trailer on the side facing the bridge rail ran over the rail, down to the span's catwalk beneath the roadway. Additional yellow sheltering material had been rigged to provide a roof connecting the three funnels.

Four men sat beneath this roof waiting. Their leader, Hanspeter Sweetman, shifted uncomfortably on the aluminum case he was

using for a seat. Tall, in his early thirties, bald with a monk's fringe of
black hair, he looked down through the gray rails of the catwalk at
the weekend yachts cutting along the bay. Sweetman had a delicate,
almost boyish face for so big a man, a high Irish tenor voice, thin
nose, fine lips and white, freckled skin, all of which were very decep-
tive given his great strength and his profession.

A breeze ruffled his fringe of hair. Oblivious to the hum of traffic above,
he shifted his gaze to the bridge's second span, and beyond, farther to the
south, to the hazy hulls of the ocean traffic anchored in the Annapolis road-
stead, ore carriers, coal carriers, container ships, a few earlier generation
cargo ships studded with masts and king posts. They were riding out the
weekend, many prepared to remain at anchor for weeks to come, awaiting pier assignments before proceeding to the sprawling port of Baltimore.

Sweetman yawned. He continued to give his watch an occasional
glance as the digital seconds flicked past. "Coming up on 1600." He
spoke loudly enough for each man to hear. The words were directed
to the team communicator. The four wore painters coveralls, splattered
with impressionistic orange and grays. "Radio check, all stations; confirm
twelve hours." Sweetman leaned back, enjoying the bay air, eyes closed,
hands behind his head, listening to the clipped professional exchange.

"Revere One, Revere One, Church Tower, radio check."

"Church Tower, this is Revere One, out." The patrol plane communicator's voice responded almost instantly from the aircraft far to
the south over the Atlantic.

"Revere Two, Revere Two, Church Tower, radio check."

"Church Tower, Revere Two, out."

"Revere Three, Revere Three, Church Tower, radio check."

"Church Tower, Revere Three, out." Two more radio responses,
the first from a cabin cruiser anchored on fishing grounds off Thomas
Point Light eight miles to the south; the second, a few hundred yards
away, from a catwalk on the eastbound span.

"Revere Four, Revere Four, Church Tower, radio check."

"Church Tower, Revere Four, out." The response, instantaneous,
came from the cockpit of a low-slung twin-V-8 black speedboat rocking gently on her mooring lines in a boathouse on the Western Shore
of the upper bay.

"Confirm twelve hours." The communicator again ran the circuit.

"Twelve hours confirmed." Others were making the calculations.

At three A.M. the following morning, the operation entered its decisive moment. It was Sweetman's operation, shaped from his decade and more as a frogman, a SEAL in Southeast Asia, and from the years of the second career, counterespionage with the Central Intelligence Agency. His hearing was dead in one ear, blown away in special operations off the Chinese mainland. The wash of the night rescue helo's rotors had fanned him back to consciousness that night deep in the Gulf of Tonkin. The screaming pain; he hadn't dared touch his head. It felt as if half had been destroyed. Then, the needle and sleep so deep on the hospital ship that even the vision of the wounded and dying being raced on the corpsmens' stretchers to the operating rooms had been blanketed in a total void.

Like an athlete no longer in the game, Sweetman missed those diving years. The white hull with its red crosses flashed through his thoughts as he readied for this new mission.

Bridge traffic was light, barely audible from inside the central trailer. Sweetman's face was smeared with black grease, blending into the hood of the wetsuit encasing him. He pulled black pads of protective fiberglass over each elbow, each knee. His hands worked quickly lacing the calf-high black nylon boots, rubber-soled with fiberglass stays reinforcing each ankle. It was hot in the wet suit; he wanted to get outside again.

The communicator was at his post on the catwalk. The other team-members helped him strap on equipment: two waterproof infrared cameras attached by separate lanyards to a zippered kangaroo pouch on his stomach, a blackjack banded and clipped to his left wrist, luminous-dial wristwatch and compass, radio beacon, infrared beacon light and inflatable waist vest.

He extended his arms to receive the nylon chest harness, which buckled into place supporting a dull black metal breastplate with two heavy-gauged slide grooves running in a vee from the base to the upper corners of the plate. An eight-inch knife fitted in a friction sheath at the base of the plate. Beneath the sheath, a snap-pouch held a coiled ten-foot line permanently tethered to the plate.

The first indication of the Soviets' operation had come from a KGB officer recruited by the Agency as a double agent in Colombo, Sri Lanka. He had just finished a five-year assignment with the Soviet Trade Mission in New York. He had become disillusioned in the new, primitive surroundings, the sickening heat, the absence of the good life. He missed the States. In the course of the first year, he found one buddy, his American case officer, and over the nights of drink he became steadily more expansive about Soviet operations in the United States . . . until, in the early hours of a drink-sodden morning: "Pioneer Point, *cher* colleague!" He had giggled, rubbed his face with his hands. "You study us like microbes . . . San Francisco, Dulles, JFK; the airports . . . tight! The seaports, tight! Tight as a *tick!*" He had bent over in merriment, the giggle louder, lost in the dawn of the Indian Ocean. "Yet, *cher* colleague, you give us total laissez-faire at the dacha. Check on it—but only after we endure the misery of this wretched dawn—really, quite scandalous." The two had clinked glasses, laughed together.

The Soviets' forty-five-acre Pioneer Point estate on the Eastern Shore of Maryland was under constant FBI surveillance. Soviet Embassy employees and their families arrived by convoy in cars and vans each weekend. They stayed put behind the linked chain fence, then left the estate in the hands of its "residents" until the following weekend.

The Colombo report had brought Sweetman into the case. A rare specimen since coming ashore with the Agency, he had the Bureau's respect, reinforced by seven out of eight scores in CIA-FBI operations, the expulsion just two months before of five bloc diplomats using UN cover for their espionage. A Czech military attaché's defection had provided the Pioneer Point link. Others in the Agency had conducted the preliminary interviews. His first statement, six hours in length, had included the words Baltimore and Chesapeake Bay several times. Computer analysis had dispassionately cross-referenced the interview with the Pioneer Point surveillance, a copy of the report going to the Pioneer Point team.

Sweetman had spent a week with the attaché, closeted in safe-house debriefing, working outward from the officer's former duties, the primary mission and interests of the Czech Army and Air Force, their targets in Washington, the United States, their modus operandi with the Pentagon, the contractors, their operations throughout the NATO Alliance . . . and against their pact brothers.

Sweetman had not been interested in the responses. By the time the military vein had been fully bled, the attaché had unwound to a point where their conversations went beyond the world of military hardware. Sweetman drew him out, his personal impressions from the years in Washington, the pressures of surveillance by his own embassy, the Soviets, the Americans. The questions turned to his ties with the American community, with the bloc embassies, the scarcity of home leave, the children held hostage in Prague, the eternal shortage of money, even for time off in the States.

"Vacations; where did you and your wife go?"

"Car trip . . . trailer . . . to New Hampshire, Vermont, Maine one year. The Soviet cruise ship the next . . ."

"Cruise ship, really? . . . always wanted to do that myself . . . from where to where?"

"Baltimore, the Caribbean, Jamaica, time ashore for shopping, touring, Grenada, back to Baltimore." The attaché and Sweetman relived the cruise, retraced it to the return trip in American waters. The ship had been scheduled to dock at six A.M. The Czech and his wife had cursed this typical Soviet stupidity. A great to-do had been made of the night of farewell entertainment. There had been heavy drinking, loud music—American guitar, rock-'n-roll style—and there had been the usual rigid Soviet organization, no one permitted on the open decks, everyone in a preassigned ballroom.

The Czech recalled having felt the ship slow at one point, a very definite change in motion. He had tried to step outside, but his way had been barred. He had been told the crew was preparing for the docking, that the decks were not safe.

Subsequent interviews with Chesapeake Bay pilots who had worked the *Omsk* had revealed that the ship was the usual lousy Soviet construction. She had propulsion problems; machinery trouble had repeatedly forced her to cut back speed. The engine room had always managed some sort of repair, but it was a regular occurrence. None of the pilots liked to work her. More times than not the trouble would hit just short of port, upper bay, north of the Bay Bridge.

Then, the complaint of a Chester River resident had made its way from the Centreville police, to the FBI, into Sweetman's reading folder. The resident had been returning from a weekend's sail to Crisfield. In the middle of the night he had come across one of the Pioneer Point cabin cruisers, out in the bay, beyond the mouth of the Chester River, in clear violation of the well-publicized government-to-government understanding on the recreational area permitted to the Soviets.

A tidy operation. Sweetman had slowly massaged his head at the moment of revelation. The challenge was to pin the charge and make it stick, trap them in the act. The KGB was using the *Omsk*, as probably only her skipper and the KGB agents aboard knew, to run their agents from a westward bound transfer at Kingston to the next transfer underway at night from the *Omsk* to Pioneer Point. Once inside the diplomatic shelter of the country retreat, the Soviet agents were able to hitch the next embassy convoy back to Washington, or to fade directly from Pioneer Point into the U.S. countryside. The entire network was just as smooth on the flip side . . . exfiltration, very tidy.

"Time check?"

"Estimate fourteen minutes, thirty seconds. Revere Three has visual contact." The communicator answered Sweetman as the big man reemerged on the catwalk.

"Jesus Christ, hot in there—estimated speed?"

"Revere Two reports ten knots and slowing. Estimate eight knots at contact."

Two double lengths of black line were flaked along the catwalk, running from the far protective shelters to the center where Sweetman stood. Each line was fitted with a metal coupling for the breastplate, and each coupling had been crafted with a motorcycle-grip handbrake, to permit Sweetman to control the payout of the lines.

The calculations had been checked against the shipping passing beneath the bridge during the past two weeks. With no outward bound bay traffic, and none was expected at the hour of contact, each of the ships heading up the bay had, as anticipated, steered directly for the three vertical white lights marking the precise center of the main channel's suspension span.

The catwalk winches feeding Sweetman's lines were set two hundred feet apart. He would make his drop facing south toward the oncoming *Omsk*. He would have fifteen seconds from the time Revere Three reported her bows passing beneath the eastbound span until she would reach him, then five seconds to complete the descent. He would begin his drop at the thirty-second mark, sliding left or right to position himself over her track, brake his fall mast-high until he was clear of the bridge, mast and midships stack, then drop to the port side of the lifeboat deck. If he missed that, to the main deck aft.

"Six minutes. Revere Three confirms target on centerline track. Revere Four standing by."

"What do we hear from *Omsk*?" Sweetman's smile flashed white in his blackened face.

"Revere Two, Revere Three confirm decks clear."

"Yeah? There'll be some bastards down there, sleepy sailor-boy bastards from Odessa—not so sleepy KGB bastards out to give their buddy boys a good-luck swat on the ass."

At the two-minute mark he stood poised on the catwalk, tongue running over his lips in anticipation, eyes on the growing lights of the cruise ship. At thirty seconds, he stepped into space, held just below the span until he steadied, dropped fifty feet braking to the right, then held again, staring down the throat of the *Omsk*.

The eight knots seemed like fifty. He caromed off a lifeboat and fell to the deck ripping at the release bar which sent both lines silently back into the night. He rolled twice. His arm struck; his chin smacked a deck cleat and he spun to a stop.

"Mother of Christ!" He rolled further into the shadow of a lifeboat, pulled back his hood and lay still to listen, gain his bearings.

A galley ventilator was exhaling the warm, thick smells of food and grease. The stack was forward, well forward; he had just made the lifeboat deck. His eyes shifted to the fading necklace of lights marking the Bay Bridge's westbound span. There were two routes to the starboard side, aft around the open deck or midships through the passageway dividing the ship's officers' country. He felt the change in the *Omsk's* motion, a slow, gentle roll as she continued to lose way. He had calculated five minutes from landing to transfer of agents. Deck clear. He was on his feet, held for half a second at the passageway, was through it and flat against the bulkhead on the starboard side.

He pressed his head and hands back hard against the metal, his good ear straining to interpret the metallic scraping of footsteps . . . behind him, on the interior ladder. Sweetman crossed the deck in two leaps and crouched against the rail behind a heap of drums, life jackets, and other unstowed lifeboat supplies. His hands ran over his gear . . . his chin? He licked two fingers; not much blood, no trail. Within seconds a flashlight beam appeared aft, angled forward in a bouncing path preceding the footsteps.

Sleepy sailor bastard. Sweetman stayed low, the whipsteel blackjack in his left hand. Come on buddy boy, come on; don't blow the main show.

At the passageway, the footsteps stopped, and the beam played forward in disinterested fashion. The light vanished; Sweetman tensed, ready to strike the white uniform moving closer to the rail. For Christ's sake! He's taking a leak! Better watch it buddy boy. Get your KGB buddies wet and . . .

The uniform disappeared, the metallic scraping of feet fading into the heart of the ship. Sweetman checked his cameras. The fast click of each shutter and the whir of the motorized film winds told him both were set. He returned them to the pouch, climbed through the rail, shook the tethered line free from the breastplate base. With the line, he lashed himself to the rail, tested, then with the arms free and feet braced against the deck edge, he hung out over the ship at a forty-five-degree angle, surveying the white-and-black wall of the *Omsk*'s starboard hull.

Nothing. But, the ship was barely moving now, no more than two knots. The lights cast by the passenger-deck portholes on the port side were nonexistent on the starboard. The hull aft of the green running light was completely blacked out. One hell of a cruise. He ran his hands through the cameras' wriststraps, waited.

The muffled screech of metal on metal . . . a door slowly opened in the side of the hull, no light, close to the waterline. A thump . . . cargo netting banging against the hull. The embassy's Pioneer Point cabin cruiser appeared suddenly, running in from the east, darkened, in a sweep that would bring her alongside from the stern. A volley of electronic shutter clicks recorded her approach.

The Soviets worked swiftly. No lines were passed. With fenders over the side, the cabin cruiser was held to the *Omsk* by her rudder as they coasted up the Bay. A figure emerged from the boat's cabin, heaved one bag, then another, up into the ship, reached for the cargo netting, and started the short climb.

Look up, you bastard. The clicks continued. Flash some steel teeth, authenticity, buddy boy. Sweetman dangled like a misplaced bowsprit over the transfer. Two, three, five, six bags were dropped to the cabin cruiser and passed below. The first of the new agents started down the netting. His fedora knocked against the netting and disappeared between the hulls. The soft, laughing curse floated up to Sweetman. Not so fast, boys, not so fast. He switched cameras and recorded the second and third agents as they made the transfer.

The darkened hulls parted. The tremor from the increasing turns in the *Omsk*'s shaft vibrated in the railing. Sweetman eased back onto the boat deck, stowed the cameras in the belly pouch, cut the chest tether, and took off at a run. Others would have felt the increase in speed. It would have stirred the curious among the passengers even in the dead of night; security would ease now.

At the stern end of the boat deck, he skirted the companionway, scissor-kicked the railing, and dropped down the crew's access ladder two rungs at a time. Racing aft on the main deck, his feet shot out from under him. He hit hard on his elbows; a shuffleboard puck skidded away. Light, laughter; the door to the main deck lounge had been opened. Up over the fantail rail without breaking stride, he leapt feet-first the thirty feet down into the bay. Beacons triggered, he treaded water awaiting Revere Four.

Sweetman was barely asleep at mid-morning when the telephone call came from the executive assistant to the Director of Central Intelligence. Pierce Bromberger received the call one minute later at Fort Bragg, North Carolina, where he had just arrived to instruct a six-week course in the political dimensions of terrorism.

Bromberger had scheduled the first class for Memorial Day, a national holiday, to capture their attention and dramatize the urgency of the task. Chalk in hand, he interrupted his talk to take the telephone call slip from the army private who had creaked her way across the wooden barracks floor in her stiff, issue shoes.

"Gentlemen. I will have to take this." He waved the yellow slip at them. "You have on the board the first halting steps we have taken as nations to provide a legal framework for combatting terrorism. In Civil Aviation:

"The Tokyo Convention, the Hague Convention"—he touched each chalked line as he spoke—"the Montreal Convention, each aimed at the hijacking dimension.

"In parallel, as the diplomatic community came under siege, the OAS Convention, and the UN Convention on Crimes Against International Protected Persons. This all in your textbook; damned dry stuff, but worth the effort—if only in that it is revealing in terms of international laxity, the traditional hesitancy of independent states to work together no matter how vicious the challenge. Study these different convention texts. You'll find there's not so much meat in them. An understanding of the timidity and ineffectiveness of the international community is a basic prologue to the heart of our work

together over the next six weeks. That's it until tomorrow morning."
He gave the chalk a professional flip onto the blackboard tray, surprising himself, strode out of the barracks with the young soldier in his wake, took the call, and before noon was on a CIA Jetstar.

Pierce Bromberger looked older than his late forties. He brushed his thin, graying hair straight back from his face, accentuating the darting eyes, beaked nose, and gaunt physique. Bromberger had grown up in and around prisons, the second son of a Tennessee state trooper who had risen through the ranks to become chief of state prisons. Prison rumor, gossip, information—intelligence—had been dinner-table talk, beer-and-cigars talk between his father and the stream of officers always flowing through the family's homes, for as long as he could remember. When he headed out on his own, it was preordained that he would get into the business in some form or other.

The formal language of Washington's growing breed of terrorism bureaucrats was a tongue he had only recently acquired. The world of the terrorist, however, was in the marrow of his bones. He had built his career in operations, in the field in Asia, then Europe, Asia, Latin America, then Asia again in a grinding existence which had thrown him against assassins, agents, murderers—the dark creatures the world now lumped as terrorists.

The van that met him on the far taxiway on Andrews Air Force Base was new to Bromberger, dented, faded yellow with a brown script "Trade—Marketplace, Inc." on the side. The route was familiar enough—parkway, across the Anacostia River, then the freeway. But, instead of continuing on across the Potomac to Langley, they swung right at the 7th Street ramp and headed into downtown Washington.

"Hoover Building?"

"No sir"—the young agent driving the van looked to Bromberger like a Cuban, but his voice was straight, flat Ohio—"close enough." The van turned again, north on 11th Street. Bromberger admired the white marble front of the old Evening Star Building, now an armed forces recruiting center. On the east side, a string of rundown two, three, four, and five-storied buildings ran saw-toothed up the street, some with windows boarded or painted over, a flotsam and jetsam of city retailing—liquor, wigs, donuts, girlie shows, ears pierced, uniforms, breakfast and lunch joints, lofts, maternity wear, costume jewelry, and walk-up hotels.

"I'll keep your bag. Second floor; you're expected, sir."

"Thanks for the lift, Ohio." The driver frowned. Bromberger yanked his tan flight bag from the van, glanced at the dilapidated gray-black entryway with its adjoining cellar steps offering Italo-Hungarian cuisine, and crossed the sidewalk. The prominent creases in his thin, lined face deepened as he headed up the stairway. At the eighteenth step, he arrived on an abbreviated landing ending in a gray metal fire door which slid sideways, opening as he approached, revealing a musty, empty corridor ending twenty-five feet beyond at a second fire door.

The first door thudded closed behind him. "Good afternoon, Mr. Bromberger. Please come in." The voice, from a hidden speaker, extended the greeting. The second door slid open.

"Christ, Hanspeter! What the hell are you doing here? What the hell am I doing here?" The two agents bear-hugged.

"Haven't a clue, Pierce. I answered the great man's summons, and I have been cooling my heels with Mr. Fisker, here, I gather awaiting your arrival. How about it, Harold. What are you getting us into in this den of yours, hard porn . . . ?"

Harold Fisker's lips were shut, but working hard, rolling two cough drops around his mouth. A small, flushed chipmunk of a man with tinted orange hair, he ignored Sweetman's question, flicked a switch beneath one of the closed-circuit television monitors at his desk, then pecked briefly at the word processor console.

"Mr. Sweetman, Mr. Bromberger, I have been instructed by the director's office to show you the spaces you have been assigned." He shuffled to the far side of the reception room, which was cluttered with stacks of publications, newsletters, tabloids, market reports, flyers, and cardboard folders with swatches of cloth and rug samples. "The console keyboard activates the wall switch." He gave a little whistle as he pushed on a section of the wall which swung on a center pivot, then led them up a single step into a large inner room.

"Lead seal in the entry, false floor, lowered ceiling, double walls. Not bad, Harold; you've got the makings of a good carpenter . . . comm center, eh . . . not bad."

The little man shot a quick glance at Bromberger in reply, popped another lozenge into his mouth, and proceeded to a large, multi-screen tan console running the entire length of one wall. "Communications and data terminals here. The entire system switches through headquarters. Your location will not be known to the operators or those servicing your requests—Washington area, no more. You should reveal no more. Facsimile machines here . . . this for open transmissions, and this, encrypted. There is a small lounge—"

"Cut the crap, Fisker, for Christ's sake." Sweetman was tired; his words had a sharp edge. Fisker continued on unperturbed.

"Mr. Bromberger, if I may have your attention. Incoming and outgoing traffic will be slugged 'Shattered Flag,' a category five designator chosen and controlled exclusively by the director."

"'Shattered Flag,'" Bromberger intoned, his voice resigned to accepting Fisker's presentation, clearly a pace that had been set personally by the director.

"There is a small apartment, lounge, two beds, mini-kitchen, and a bath through that door. It is not anticipated that your need for these facilities will extend beyond a few weeks. I will be here seven days a week; my quarters are on the next floor. You will find that you have considerable capability here. My instructions are to augment that capability as you may require."

Fisker paused, ran a pencil up and down the back of his neck, satisfied himself that his mental checklist had been covered. He then keyed the console and led the way back through the wall into the front reception area. "I have a bit of pocket litter for each of you, nothing elaborate, no name changes, just the Trade credentials, a few credit cards, and a smattering of correspondence." He flipped two switches beneath the first of the TV monitors; the inner steel door rolled open. "On this side of the street, about two hundred feet from the entrance to your left, you will find a blue-and-white cab showing an 'off duty' card on the sun visor. The driver is waiting for you, knows you by sight. The Director is expecting you in twenty-five minutes.

Sweetman and Bromberger strode behind their escort, moving swiftly from the director's private, key-operated elevator, through his outer rooms, to the sprawling wood-paneled office overlooking the spring green of Virginia.

Two large hands formed a triangle cradling the forehead of a larger gray head bent over photo enlargements spread in a fan shape. "Hanspeter, Pierce, welcome." The director continued his examination without looking up. His hand went to a particular print. He pushed his eyeglasses up on his forehead and took several moments to examine various details of the photograph through a magnifying glass. "A wedding ring by the looks of it. My sympathy to the bride." He spoke slowly. "A very smart piece of work, Hanspeter." He put the photograph down and turned his full attention to the two men.

"We delivered a set of your snapshots to the secretary of state one hour ago. Not bad service, wouldn't you say? He has invited Ambassador Fedoseyev in for a chat this afternoon. He will reveal our evidence. He will review it with the ambassador, and he will throw the book at him! High time!" The voice rose, then relaxed. "I see you have a small trophy on your chin, Hanspeter—a fine job. Congratulations!" The director came around the desk, shook his hand, turned. "Pierce," shook his hand and returned to the black leather chair.

"Thank you, sir. No damage here; good to hear State's moving." There was relief in Sweetman's voice. With the front office call, he was afraid he had somehow blown the *Omsk* operation, steeled himself for the bad news, searched his mind, every step, during the drive to Langley . . . now, the director's approval. If it had gone well, why the hell the summons? He felt totally drained.

"Sit down Hanspeter, Pierce." The agents moved to the long L-shaped couch which served to frame the glass-topped coffee table exhibiting twenty-eight foreign decorations, each contributing to the professional history of Director of Central Intelligence Ernest Lancaster.

"Pierce; you won't have followed, I trust"—he pulled his glasses down to the tip of his nose and gazed over them—"Hanspeter's exploit. Knowledge, planning, initiative, skill, guts, and luck—landed on the Soviets like a great bat last night and sunk his bat's teeth into their prized spy-running game. Invaluable, absolutely invaluable. You will have to make a point of having Hanspeter tell you about his cruise on the *Omsk*, Pierce. I do apologize for having lifted you from your students before you had the chance to savor the charms of North Carolina. Do you know the South?" Lancaster's voice continued without sentiment, but with a familiarity borne of earlier association. "Of course you do. Your grandparents on your father's side were from the hills of eastern Tennessee, were they not?"

"Parents, grandparents, born there myself, sir." Bromberger nodded, a slight smile on his lips, the outward sign of his deep admiration for the director and his performances.

"Rock-ribbed conservative stock in the hills of Tennessee. Good people, good bloodlines—which brings us to the purpose of this reunion, gentlemen . . ." Lancaster held his next words, observed the watchfulness and heightened attention his two prized officers gave to him.

"The lexicographers tell us that today's society has endowed the word 'cell,' humble in composition, reserved for the most part to science, broadly, and the biological, medical, and penological sciences more specifically . . . we have endowed this humble word with greatly increased prominence.

"Our obsession as a people with cancers, the intrusion of malignant cells and the constant, indeed understandable, chatter offers one explanation. The cell as a unit has also metamorphosed. Once the devout monk's apartment, then the corpus of political action . . . now, the malignant structure of terrorism." Lancaster reached behind him, retrieved a news release from a tray, pushed his glasses back up on his forehead and read.

"I have a release of sorts here from an organization by the name of 'Trade,'"—Bromberger and Sweetman continued to wait him out—"advising that you have affiliated. Excellent!" He tossed the release back into the tray. "Pierce"—he looked at Sweetman as he spoke—"has been sharing with a new generation his appreciation of terrorism. Yesterday, while he was doing so, Constance Burdette was cut to shreds in a bloody, premeditated assassination—all the earmarks of an orthodox act of political terrorism—United States ambassador, newly arrived, cut down to demonstrate *our* weakness, cow *their* governments, flaunt their freedom of action . . . the anarchistic push against rational order, authority.

"The Swiss"—he looked from one to the other—"have apprehended no one. As ever, they are jealous and protective of their sovereign rights. Across the river, here, as ever, our colleagues at the State Department have established a new interagency task force. . . ." His smile was one of disgust. "My designee—neither of you, is a member of that task force, if you please.

"The regional security team is at the site with nothing to report beyond two shattered human forms and assorted automotive wreckage. These photos arrived this morning about the same time as yours, Hanspeter." He sailed a manila envelope across the room to Sweetman.

"Not much left . . . plenty of chops, entry into the car metal . . . looks like automatics, AK-47s?" Sweetman and Bromberger shuffled quickly through the prints of the corpses, the riddled limousine, motorcycle, skidmarks, and glass.

"No, not much left"—the director selected a cigar from an embossed leather chest—"and, at the present rate, not much prospect of any more. Have either of you had occasion to reflect on Washington's won-lost record? We are playing for the World Cup. To win is to allow us to continue, however imperfectly, as human beings. To lose is to yield the field to blind violence—and we are losing. That is not what you would tell your students, Pierce. Yet, we are losing.

"Assassins vanish into the night"—his fist opened with long fingers spread apart—"and we continue along, boarding up buildings already bombed, resigned to battle with local authorities, to likely loss of scent—Like the hell we're resigned!"

"Neither of you had occasion to know our late ambassador, did you?" He inclined his head first to Sweetman, then to Bromberger . . . silence. He made a note which he folded and slipped into a vest pocket. "The late ambassador will be arriving in the United States in a very few hours. She is to be interred at Arlington. I have arranged for both of you to be there. The ceremony will give you, first hand, the necessary perspective . . . a fuller appreciation of the importance attached to bringing her killers into the net.

"That ceremony will mark the commencement of Shattered Flag. Mr. Fisker has given you that name, yes? Harold Fisker, one of my carefully guarded treasures. Mr. Fisker has shown you *your* cell. You will find him a provider, an indefatigable cross between servant and genius. He has his idiosyncrasies, but he is solid, my very best. Count on him.

"You both are extensions of me. We want Constance Burdette's killers while the scent is still fresh. You have the tools you need. I will not need to see you until you have reported the completion of Shattered Flag."

The director rose, thrust his hands in his pockets, crossed to the picture window. "One sees a multitude of people from this glassy perch over the years. Between you, there is a brilliant record. You are honest in your work. You take satisfaction from the exercise of your gifts. . . . You trust no one. Good luck."

The minute hand on the chrome wall clock built into the paneling behind the desk jerked forward to XII in the silence of the meeting's end. Lancaster's back was to them, his large hands digging down through a stack of red folders, when Sweetman and Bromberger retraced their steps to his private elevator.

Chapter 6

"Yes, I must bite your ass."

Her bare foot came down hard on his neck. Paul Head howled, flipped backward off the rope ladder into the sea. In a moment, they were both on deck, naked, bodies together, streams of seawater trapped in pools where her breasts pressed into the golden hair of his chest. She yanked the stops from the ketch's loosely furled mainsail, and the heavy white cloth in folds on the cabin top.

"Clever, bloody clever you are." He dropped down beside her, caressed her erect nipples with his tongue. Her hands ran along his body, skirting the tape on the bandaged side, resting for a few seconds in the sodden curls at the base of his neck, then pulled his mouth to hers. They rolled and joined, the sail cloth crackling beneath them.

She moved her head back, lips apart, her eyes on his, as their bodies thrusted. He paused, broke the hard rhythm of sex, suspended above, a grin on his face, saying nothing.

"Leer, will you?" She reached up, lips, arms, legs yanking him back, locking her ankles above him, riding with him as the ripples of pleasure filled them, their bodies straining in climax.

"Oh Christ!" A benediction, not a curse. They were on their sides, still together, the ketch *Matabele* riding easily at anchor, alone in a cove south of Dwejra Point, some twenty-five miles from Valletta.

His lips moved in gentle kisses along her arm, her shoulder, her neck, and pressed against her mouth, a long, slow kiss of passion matched by the renewed thrusting of their bodies. His hands were beneath her hips. They soared in pleasure, then lay side by side beneath the sun.

"How is that wound?" Her eyes followed a sea gull gliding above the cone of shrouds running to the mainmast top.

"Sharp, bloody jolts, severe pain when I screw you. I'll make it." He ran his fingers along her spine. She pushed away, onto her knees. He followed cupping his fingers on her breasts.

"I'll change the dressing. You'd be a lousy lover dead." She grabbed the curled edges of the tape and ripped off the bandage.

"Bloody hell!" He spun away in pain, peering down at his side at the same time.

"Not so bad." The raw, red crease carved by the bullet was clean, healing. "Lie on your side; give it some sun. I will put a new patch on as soon as Filippo is awake." She touched the fuzz of his new beard.

He lay back on the mainsail. ". . . too much of whatever he's shooting . . . twelve bloody hours, sleeps too long. Did I tell you? I killed another American, pitiful bastard . . . cooking in the boot of his rental at the airport. You fucked up on the passports, took them with you."

"You made it. The hell with your American." She slid off the cabin top, stepped down into the cockpit, pulled on a coarse, white sailor's shirt.

"Where'd he make the hit, Naples? That bloody lot had been cached, hadn't it? . . . One of your masterpieces, Les?"

"Two months ago, Angelo's faction with Filippo. I was with them for the planning, the weapons, but it was theirs . . . clean, a victory for the people." She sat on the deck, her eyes on the sea beyond the cove, her back against the cabin. "A night convoy, Navy, routine, moving munitions from their NATO depot to the Italians. Angelo had tracked them for months, never a change—"

"There for the picking, right? Bloody supermarket." He grabbed her cut arm. "Where'd you do this?"

"Geneva." She continued. "They have so many bases, so many commands . . . more than a hundred in Naples. Angelo knew every minute of the convoy's drill. Two trucks, lead jeep, APC bringing up the rear." She turned toward Head. "Fourteen miles from the depot, the road narrows as it curves up into the hills, a sharp turn, opening onto an outlook just beyond.

"Angelo's timing was to the second. The lead jeep was clear of the curve, moving slowly, waiting for the rest. When the lights of the first truck cleared, Angelo hit the armored carrier with the antitank; it was wounded, but still moving. Three seconds . . . they hit the second truck, shot out the tractor tires. The APC had limped closer, and was spraying fire. He gave it another antitank, and then one into the second munitions carrier. The APC was dead. The curve in the road shielded the first trailer from the second, as planned—tremendous explosion. That brought the lead jeep back into the automatic fire.

"In less than a minute, the convoy had been demolished. Angelo's team, two, were on the lead truck while it was still moving, shot the guard, forced the driver into the pulloff where we had the motor caravans. Angelo knew he would be most vulnerable during the cargo transfer. Even with the electric torches, they could not be sure what they were handling. The munitions trailer was packed. Both caravans had been rigged to accept the roller conveyors. The crates were heavy . . . some too heavy . . ."

"Bloody hydrogen bombs . . ."

"They were sweating out every second."

"The traffic—you had rigged barriers?"

"Detours, at either end, after the convoy had entered the hills, and on the far side. There was no need for them; it was the middle of the night. Angelo had the caravans in Salerno before dawn. There, they made the second transfer—not that morning. Filippo will tell you the rest."

"Italian! Report to the bloody quarter deck." Head pounded the cabin top with his fist. "Italian, this is the carabinieri." He fell back laughing, shielding his eyes from the sun.

The snap as the bullet left the Luger; the powder scorch, the clean double holes, half an inch above his nose, in the sail cradling his head. "Good morning, you bloody addict. Fourteen hours in the fetal position hasn't done much for your aim."

Filippo Tonasi came aft from the forward hatch, barechested, barefooted, only the grooved black handle of the pistol showing above his belt. His small hard body had tight clumps of muscle armoring a torso that had absorbed many a beating by prison guards, giving him a deep, vengeful rage against all authority. "You have a big mouth, you Zulu bastard." He kicked the sail close to Head's wounded ribs. "You'll keep us moving even when we have no wind, you bastard; it's good." His laugh was flat. "You always have a reason for everything, Les; even this big-mouth scum." He leaned against the mast, pulled paper, tobacco, and a small leather pouch from his pants. Turning from the light breeze blowing across the deck, he shook out a fine row of the leaf, enriched it with a dusting of white from the pouch, then drew the leather's drawstring tightly closed with his stained broken front teeth. A forelock of black hair fell forward as he licked the paper, gave it a twist, and lit the cigarette. The first two puffs were short, the third long and deep, with the smoke floating slowly from his nostrils. He closed his darkly shadowed brown eyes. He was tired, his jaw stubbled with black beard.

Leslie Renfro was on the foredeck alone, her mind focused on the name, the words, the use to be made of Oats Tooms.

The noonday sun was harsh. The three sat beneath a canvas awning rigged from the boom of the *Matabele*'s mizzenmast. A yawl flying the French flag—sixty footer, Toulon registry—approached under sail, reconnoitered the cove, and departed. Aboard the ketch, diving gear was spread across the cockpit. Filippo, a fresh cigarette locked in the vee of two fingers, had picked up the recounting of the NATO munitions robbery. "There was little danger. Les had done the planning. That's why I am here." He whacked the tiller with the palm of his hand, his teeth bared in a shattered-glass smile. "Little danger, much work. We kept the caravans in a barn near Salerno for ten days, maybe two weeks, gave the carabinieri gestapo the time they needed to tear up houses, torture another hundred innocents, and move along to newer distractions.

"When we were in Switzerland, they moved again, brought the caravans down to the coast one at a time, transferred the cargo"—he gestured with his black chin toward the unseen crates stowed forward in the *Matabele*—"to a fishing trawler of a friend, Naples faction. By then, I had left you again, rejoined Angelo—"

"That was no bloody *trawler* you scuttled last night!"

Tonasi inhaled deeply, flicked the cigarette past Head into the sea and continued. "We transferred to the trawler, headed out to Capri. The cabin cruiser, Paulo"—Tonasi's words were slow, languid with the dope—"met us the following evening. We transferred again that night at sea—not too rough, no trouble.

"I took the cruiser—you're right—she was a classy boat. You know about her? Angelo stole her last year—changed her profile, paint—classy, fast, twin V-8s. Only Angelo's brother was with me now. It was raining heavily that night, the next day. We made the run to the straits, rendezvoused with the Messina faction . . . made the final transfer for storage at Palermo depot.

"I took the cruiser alone now, through the Straits. Off Catania, a patrol looked me over from a distance, lost interest." He rolled another cigarette. "I continued around Cape Passero to the middle of Malta Channel. The *Matabele* was blinking, and I was home to your arms, Zulu, home to Faction Malta."

"That was a fast, capable boat. Bloody nuts to scuttle her. How the hell are we going to operate?" Head slapped at the canvas, his eyes flashing from the Italian to Leslie. "The bloody psychopaths, the oppressors ignore us! We take out one and twenty more butchers take his place; nothing changes! The plundering pigs, the snakes everywhere piss on us fleas, shake some bloody powder, have us hop away and die! Paris, Bonn, Berlin—the Fascist police, the imperialists kill, rob, crush the people—we connect in Geneva. Bloody laugh! Filippo busts his bloody nuts for a handful of firecrackers, and here we rock in this bloody cockleshell sticking patches on bloody rubber suits. When the hell are we going to wake up? We're playing games. There is no revolution—bloody games! Counts for nothing!

"When we joined forces, two years ago, Les,"—he was on his feet, hands on the shrouds, shouting at her over his shoulder—"we were in the struggle. We had . . ." He spun toward them. "Scuttling that boat was a crime! I'll tell you this, Les; you too, Italian. We see the hatred! The people . . . everywhere are humiliated. With each day, they are bloody weaker, the oppressors bloody stronger. But, you can still feel and see the hate. They have guts; they want liberty, to destroy the Facists crushing them. They want *us* to cut down the pigs. They go to bed; they wake up . . . waiting for leadership!

"Are we waging war against the pigs . . . armed revolution? No! We sink the weapons of struggle!

"The Mediterranean sun is too strong for you, brave Zulu Paulo. It's baking your brave warrior's brain. Better pack your head in ice." The sneer spreading across Tonasi's face sent a surge of fury through Head. His body tensed, poised to leap. He turned his back, spat, made his way forward, the challenge unanswered, his breathing still heavy with anger. Leslie's hand was on Tonasi, commanding silence.

● ● ● ● ·

A single, davit-mounted brass kerosene lamp lit the *Matabele*'s main cabin at nightfall. They had slept, swum again, then in mid-afternoon begun their plans in an intense meeting, which ran through the tinned dinner and half the second plastic liter of red wine. The cabin was clouded with the two men's smoke. Head was morose, Tonasi impassive. But, he and Head were agreed: The time was right, with the turmoil on land, to catch the pigs off-balance, while they were manning their stakeouts, prowling their empty alleys; catch them at sea. Take the struggle to the Mediterranean as planned. Start sending their ships down. Spread them thinner. Defeat the pigs; it was what they had planned.

They had followed her orders, the unexpected orders for the Geneva hit against the American. Now, they must return to their original plan— strike from the *Matabele* by night, fade back into Malta. Months had been dedicated to the *Matabele* cover, the chartering, the dives. Why fester in Malta if they were not prepared to strike? The weapons were aboard. The struggle demanded that they proceed.

The *Matabele*'s cabin could have as easily been a mountain cave or a carefully screened hideout in Berlin. Leslie Renfro listened. She was in command. They would follow her orders, just as they had sunk the weapons runner, immediately, on her orders. They were seated on the bench bunks on either aide of the main-cabin table. A chart of Malta's coast and off-shore waters lay before them half covered with the evening meal's plates. She refilled each cup, her thumb wiping a few drops of the coarse Algerian wine from the pouring neck. When the two had finished, she gave them her appraisal of the faction's responsibilities. They absorbed her message, the quiet power of her words. Only once did her voice rise. She snapped her head from one to the other, her teeth clenched, fists balled. "If one Fascist walks free, I am a prisoner. If one pig lives, I am dead. We live for one purpose: the struggle. If we are to win . . . *if* we are worthy of the struggle, *if* we are to wage the war, you must obey—total commitment, total unity. You must use your heads; it counts for everything—*everything!*" She studied their faces; they were with her. They listened as she continued to lay out her plans.

At 2:00 A.M., beneath a sky white with stars, they weighed anchor, motored out of the cove, set sail, and laid an easterly course. Tonasi was at the helm. Renfro and Head worked through the night restowing the crates from Naples, sealing the forecastle, and dressing the cabins to restore the ketch's charter-yacht appearance.

By mid-morning, with the ketch on a broad reach boiling along at hull speed, they were topside again, touching up rust spots, polishing bright work, checking out the diving sled before relashing it to the rail. The sun sharply defined the slender, finely muscled figure of the leader as she surveyed the rigging and sails. "That shadow; there's the beginning of play in the mainmast hounds. We'll have to rig the chair. Filippo, there are four holes in the mainsail, new; they will have to be patched as soon as we're in port."

It was late afternoon when the *Matabele* rounded Dragutt Point and nosed into her mooring in Marsamxett Harbor. The telephone operator was uncooperative. The pay-booth caller was asking her for something that had never been done. Leslie stood her ground, switching from English to the harsh Semitic of the Maltese tongue to drive home her resolve. With great complaint, the operator discovered and acknowledged the existence of the ship-to-shore connection. Within ten minutes of coming ashore, the captain of the *Matabele* was speaking to Dr. Oswald "Oats" Tooms aboard the *Towerpoint Octagon*.

● ● · · ·

The blue-and-gold Towerpoint crest was emblazoned on the twin scuba tanks and heavy duffel Tooms slung aboard the *Matabele*. Heaving himself up from the rubber zodiac with an enormous grunt of accomplishment, he stood on deck, clasped Leslie's hand.

"Princess, I am delighted. This is high honor." He beamed, turning as he held her hand to admire the *Matabele*. "A fine ketch, not Maltese. A fine boat, yes sir."

"I told you Dr. Tooms, there was no need for you to bring diving gear. We are fully equipped."

"I had to pocket that advice, Princess. Didn't want to impose, and when you're barrel-hulled like me, the fit's not always that easy. I appreciated the offer." He tossed his duffel onto the cabin top, yanked open the zipper, and extracted a small box which he opened to reveal a gold-and-silver filigree dolphin. "Respectfully presented, Captain." His heavy fingers, with surprising dexterity, attached the delicate pin to her collar.

"Thank you, Dr. Tooms. How very kind." She gave the pin a touch. "Prepare to get underway. We'll clear the harbor under power."

Tooms watched the two men respond smartly to the order, bringing the zodiac aboard at the same time that their skipper ducked below to start the engine. She reemerged, gestured to Head and Tonasi to cast off the mooring, kicked the gear lever into reverse, pushed the tiller hard over, then reversed the process catching the lever with her foot, snapping it forward, swinging the *Matabele* clear of the adjacent moorings, and steering her into the harbor's main channel. She scanned the scattered clouds, the flags gently waving on the buildings of Valletta off to starboard. "There will be a good breeze as soon as we clear the point, Dr. Tooms. You may take the sail stops off now; stow them in the lazaret. We will be under sail in five minutes."

Valletta faded astern as the *Matabele* again rounded Dragutt Point outbound into the Mediterranean. Tooms, delighted with his new surroundings, alternated his gaze between the slim woman sailor and the ancient fortifications ashore.

"There's a tale to be told about that breakwater."

"What is that, Dr. Tooms?"

He was looking aft, at the band of rock jutting seaward from St. Elmo's Point. "The run Il Duce's frogmen made on the British fleet anchored in the Grand Harbor back in '41 or '42. Speedboats packed with TNT, human torpedoes shipped over from Italy; they left mamma destroyer in the middle of the night, formed up and headed in—gutsy bunch." Tonasi and Head had joined them in the cockpit; the three listened to the contented drawl of the American.

"They wanted to crack Malta, top priority for Il Duce, but they knew they were facing some stiff defenses. They didn't attempt the main entrance—tried to blow a hole through the chains and nets under the small bridge connecting the breakwater and the point. A grand production—just before dawn—terrible mess. Those in the lead boats blew themselves up; the rest were like porpoises in a net, chopped up by shore defenses."

"Dr. Tooms?"

"Oats, please, Princess. I much prefer to go by Oats in distinguished company such as this."

"Right then—Oats, if you . . . will stop using that asinine 'Princess'; my name is Leslie. Meet my mates, Oats—Paul Head and Filippo Tonasi. We've been cruising as a team for several months—"

"Thought you said the other night you were heading off for a week; you're back early?"

"Five days early, Oats. A member of the party took ill shortly after we entered open water. The others lost spirit shortly thereafter. We had to return to port before the first dive. Tell me, Oats, what have you been doing with your time when you haven't been poring over Malta's history. I should imagine Starring has been keeping you quite busy?"

"Yesterday morning, I journeyed west—company car, the Continental"—he gave a coughing chuckle—"joined the citizens of Rabat as a spectator at the donkey races. Dusty, to be sure, but a festive crowd and willing beasts—No idea who won—no program, no daily double."

"Bloody donkey races?"

Leslie cut in quickly. "Horse races, Paul, a course through the streets, donkeys owned by local families."

"Well," Tooms continued, "following the Kentucky Derby, a dandy Rabat hotel, well situated in the hills overlooking the entire island, was able to offer me a much-needed gin and tonic, two in fact—after which I returned to the ship and, to my great pleasure, received your call." He watched the glistening sea foam along the lee rail. The yacht slid past Sliema and St. Julian's Point, gradually drawing further and further from the shoreline.

When they arrived over the submerged ruins of the Roman convoy off the north coast of Gozo, the *Matabele* was sailing easily, enough wind to tow the diving sled through the thirty to forty feet of clear water. From the deck, the wrecks appeared beneath the surface from time to time as faint, dark shadows.

Tooms had stirred, was in black trunks, swim fins, watch, and leg-scabbarded diving knife. Scratching his chest, he surveyed the scene, put his scuba regulator mouthpiece in his teeth, flipped his air tanks over his head onto his back with the heavy straps settling on his shoulders, and clipped the waist strap over his stomach. He cinched the weight belt, fitted the mask over his eyes, wiggling into place against the chrome regulator, then pushed the mask high on his face and spat out the mouthpiece which dangled from its hose against his chest.

"Don't know, Captain," he was wheezing slightly. "I used to be able to rig myself out a lot faster than that. How do I check out? Everything in place? I have a depth gauge in the duffel, don't think that's required this afternoon."

She circled him. His straps were tight. She gave the tank valve a quarter turn clockwise, then hard over counterclockwise; it was open. She slapped one of the tanks. "You are good for at least a month down there. Bring her into the wind, Paul." The *Matabele* headed up, losing way with her sails flapping and the sled bobbing in her wake.

"Remember, you are buoyant. The sled's hull is filled with Styrofoam. You will run on the surface until *you* are ready to dive. Keep the soles of your fins against the bar stirrups; the backward thrust of the water will make that quite natural. Keep your arms against the sides of the sled, your hands on the plane controls. As you bring your hands back, the planes will take you down, at the same time as your body streamlines—"

"Fond hope—"

"—the tow is set to give you a maximum depth of twenty-five to thirty feet. You will find, given the primitive nature of the rig, that you will have very little lateral maneuverability. Lean to one side or the other. We have designed a rudder, controlled by the stirrups, but that has to await the proceeds from a few more charters and a week or two in the machine shop."

He lifted the weights on his hips, let them settle again. "Tell you what, Skipper; I'll have the boys on the *Octagon* fit you out as soon as we can bring the ketch alongside; same-day service, everything imaginable in those hulls."

She continued to brief him without acknowledging the offer. "Once you are aboard the sled, I will watch for your signal. We will make three runs over the site. When we come about each time, you will surface with the loss of tow, but you will be able to dive again in less than a minute. Signal if you are having trouble. You can, of course, always swim to the surface, but that should not be necessary given your experience."

"I'm shooting for at least three gold chalices, figure you'll claim one as the captain's share. What's your cut, Paul?"

Head had not been following the conversation. "Cut? What the hell do you mean, cut?" His eyes narrowed at Tooms; a hand, in reflex, ran down the front of the T-shirt which concealed his damaged side.

"Settled, one-tenth share; at least a sculpted handle for the helmsman. Over we go!" Tooms again brought the mask over his face and, with one hand against the glass, took an exaggerated parade step into the sea, legs spread to keep his head above water. His fins carried him back in a quick flutter kick to the orange sled. Tonasi, in the water waiting for him, forced the stern down. Tooms mounted; the young Italian pulled himself hand over hand to the ketch. Tooms raised an arm, thumb down, ready. The *Matabele* fell off, filling her sails until Tooms, splashing in wake, engaged the planes and disappeared beneath the surface.

Leslie took the helm, checking her course against the Gozo landmarks. "Cut the line. I'll pick him off when he blows, the bloody bastard!"

"Likes to hear himself talk, like you, Zulu."

"Keep your eyes on the tow"—her voice was with them—"learn to love him." She laughed ruefully, "Our new partner." The braided white line stretching down into the sea trembled against the strain of its cargo.

● ● ● ● ●

After three long passes, Tooms was back aboard, towel around his neck, shaking his head with pleasure. Tonasi placed a chilled Hopleaf ale in his wrinkled hand.

"You folks; you're quite a team, much to be admired. I've done diving enough for three men in my day, but this afternoon was something mighty special. That sled, under sail power, the clarity"—he rubbed the towel vigorously through his hair—"and, the sightseeing, first rate. How long was I down?"

"Not quite one hour, deck to deck."

"Not nearly long enough . . . a dandy sensation . . . like a twenty-foot ray surveying his realm."

She encouraged his enthusiasm. "What would you say the Maltese have down there?"

"Captain, several hulls by the looks of them, broad o' beam, what's left beneath the limestone growth . . . broad o' beam, cargo ships, ordinary merchantmen back when Caesar's crowd was in full sway."

"It has been well picked over. Fortunately, the Maltese have now acted to preserve the site as a national trust. It is officially a crime to remove anything or to disturb the site in any way . . . like the rest of the sea, abused by the selfish few with no respect of the past, no regard for the present, except their own pockets, no thought to the future. . . . Well, Oats; do have another ale. The ice chest is on the starboard side."

Tooms collected her words. There was a purity that went beyond the ancient hulls, beyond Malta; a dedication and *purity* in that half-naked young woman that would hang a veritable halo over the bay research project taking form in his mind. "Damned Maltese! Haven't learned screw-off caps. Where the hell's the grog wrench on this able craft?" He followed this bellow with another. "Got it! Sorry, crew."

He half-emerged from the cabin. "A beer, a wine, some medicinal spirits, Captain? A salute is in order."

"Right at home. Very good, Oats. The Algerian would taste very nice. You will find some cups over the chart table."

The *Matabele* was running home, now, coasting along on a following sea, her running lights lit. Tooms handed out the wine, tossed his cigarettes and lighter to Head, and growled happily in the evening air. "To the *Matabele*, her master, and those who serve on her." He drained the ale and reached behind him for the opened replacement on the cabin sill.

Leslie watched the fat scientist relax. He was propped against the cabin, heavy legs straight out on the cockpit bench, with arms alternating in the delivery of smoke and ale. She prompted him again. "The great Thomas Starring seemed quite keen on some research in America the other night, Oats. I suppose that was no more than the show for that night's guests?"

"You caught me daydreaming, if that's possible at this hour, Captain." He lurched higher into a sitting position and pulled on his bottle. "Today's adventure had me thinking about an earlier dive, a dive ashore—and that relates to your question, which I was about to raise myself. Paul, Filippo, what's the deepest you've been off this ketch?"

They both looked to Leslie, silhouetted in the twilight. "Last year, one hundred and twenty-five feet, off Greece wasn't it Paul? Yes. We had to rig a new decompression line—"

"A hundred and twenty-five feet." Tooms scratched a shin. "About five atmospheres, real diving . . . takes skill. I took a team of four down to sixteen hundred feet a few years back, sixteen hundred feet in a chamber built to my specs at Towerpoint—part of Starring's thrust into deep ocean engineering."

He had them listening. "It's a strange world at that depth. You suck in the helium and oxygen. The human body is flexible, tough, but it's mighty easy to screw up. It's rough at that depth, hard to do the easiest tasks. You get the shakes, your stomach goes, head hurts, can't sleep worth a damn. Then you start the decompressing, not minutes—day after day, a week goes by. You think you'll go nuts with the boredom, but you're fighting fear at the same time. You have to make constant checks, keep the nitrogen from boiling over in the blood, turning you into a burnt-out kettle of mush—"

"Ease the main." Leslie uncleated the mizzensheet, allowing the line to slip through her fingers until both sails trimmed to the shift in wind.

"—that, too, was diving. Thinking about that dive, I was thinking about the three of you. You're a good looking bunch, young, smart, able divers—the skipper a card-carrying member of the Oceanic University crowd.

"You asked about Tommie Starring. I've been hopping, deadline of the Fourth of July. You three ever been to the United States?" There was only the gurgling of the *Matabele* and the sea, the glow of cigarettes. "Well—here goes—I want you all to come to the States, to work for me, for Starring, and it'll happen, on my say-so, if you want to do it."

Tonasi toured the cockpit with the plastic liter, sloshing another round of wine into the cups.

"The Chesapeake Bay, Filippo, one of the greatest estuaries . . . the greatest estuary in the world, runs in from the Atlantic up through Virginia and Maryland two hundred miles, three hundred kilometers—"

"And, what does Starring have in mind, Oats?"

"Nothing . . . everything. I haven't laid it out for him, yet, Skipper . . . research with impact . . . good science, good coverage in the media at the same time the big ships are making their runs—"

"What ships?"

"Ships? The big combo-hybrids he's got on the new Mexican run—eighty percent gas tanker, twenty percent float-aboard barges, everything nice all wrapped in one." The chrome lighter gave a metallic click, illuminated Tooms's squinting face. "Tomorrow, one of the company containerships departs the U.K., diverts to Valletta before picking up her regular trans-Atlantic run—my doing. She'll have an underseas habitat aboard, a pretty piece of work we've had in pier-side storage since the mid-seventies, . . . primed and ready to go. She'll be here early in the week; we'll sling her aboard the *Octagon*.

"The bay's shallow, no more than two hundred feet at its deepest, main channel, thirty to forty feet most places. My thought, and bear with me, is that you three—and Oats Tooms—form Starring's bay research team. We'll have it mapped out before we're in U.S. waters—it's why I want *you* now. We'll mate the catamaran's submersibles—

and I'm talking about the work chariots, not the deep machine—we'll be *in situ,* you know *in situ,* Filippo, by the Fourth.

"I see it as a two-season exercise. We'll fan out early across a broad research front, baseline measurements, shellfish beds, pollution—a broad front. The locals will want to help, and we'll fit them in. But, that won't work for day one, got to have the three of you, got to launch at flank speed."

"You want the three of us to ship with you on the catamaran for America this month." Her tone established a benchmark rather than posing a question.

"About ten days from now, Skipper, ten days. One more data bit and I'll have another Hopleaf to keep me quiet. First, Towerpoint will cover storage of this handsome ketch." He slapped the coaming to confirm the point. "Second, you'll find the pay's mighty impressive by any standard. Stick it out and you'll have enough for a second *Matabele*. Third, if you don't like it, you can be on your way in two months, pay in your pocket. Once we're in the bay working and the media lets the public know it, I'm ninety percent home: two months. Fourth, return passage will be first class, courtesy of Towerpoint." His lips squeaked on the spout of the bottle.

"You are proposing a total, if intriguing, uprooting, Oats. We will talk it over, and I will call you in two days."

Tooms was standing, a hand on the cabin steadying him. "Just in time; we're coming up to Marsamxett. You give me that call, Skipper, and"—he chuckled—"if it'll close the deal, I'll throw in a sack of chestnuts for that dandy iron fireplace in the main cabin, be back with my fur trunks for the *Matabele*'s winter cruise."

• • • • • **Chapter 7** • • • • •

Pierce Bromberger cocked his head against the heavy mist blowing through the gardens of the Rodin Museum. The shorter man keeping to the slow, strolling pace beside him was faceless beneath the downturned brim of his waterstained suede hat.

"They didn't argue with dear old John the Baptist, eh, did they? We don't argue with people like you now, do we Pierce. We shoot you." The brim turned toward the taller man, the smiling face still hidden. Their shoes splashed through the puddles forming on the empty paths, paused before the great bronze of *The Thinker* dripping in his contemplation, continued on another measured round.

"The years have treated you kindly, Stuart. Even your hearing has improved—a sign of rank, I suppose. You have your lieutenants to run your parcels for you now?"

"Bombings, eh? No need, Pierce, no need, not for the moment at any rate. There's a war; that's clear, but not the Jubilee Riots. London and Dublin have taken over, are doing our work for us—colossal great mess. The people of Ulster, the working people, have never been more depressed. Even their wildest dreams reveal only despair. Your information is good, Pierce. If nothing else, you have always had good information. There is to be no settlement without Sinn Fein. The tide is leaving the barren flats of the negotiating tables, turning to us again. Young men, eh, and women, coming in marvelous new numbers."

"And, you have left the field for the import-export business in Paris?" There was a trace of amusement in Bromberger's voice. "Stuart Lynch, proprietor, entrepreneur, risen from the ashes of gelignite, shuffling invoices, sampling rare imports from the north shore of Africa—Paris your residence full time, Stuart?"

Lynch poked at a bottle cap with the toe of his shoe, kicked it to one side. "Here and there, Pierce, here and there as the business requires—quite a bit of travel these days. We're not the xenophobes some would make us out to be, eh."

"And, business is good?"

"Adequate."

"The imports have slowed from my side of the Atlantic?"

"A source of no little satisfaction to you, eh, Pierce? The way your government fumbles around, you can't be having a hand in it. We're patient. Needs are being met. Washington will lose interest, but your Irish will not, Pierce. For them, a united Ireland is not a proposition, eh, not a problem. It's a certainty, as fundamental as belief in Jesus Christ. Now, that's my part of the Royal Inquisition over. Why are we out here tromping amidst this lifeless metal and stone?"

"Constance Burdette."

"Your ambassador, eh?"

"Buried yesterday."

The enormous dome of L'Hotel des Invalides appeared before them, then blurred in the mist. "What would Napoleon have thought of such deeds?" Lynch bit at a thumbnail and spat as he spoke. "I don't think he would have approved."

"Paris is a buzzing hive, Stuart. What's in the wind; which group, Stuart?"

"During the '39-to-'45 war, I had an uncle and an aunt over here, my father's brother and wife—volunteers in the Communist end of the French resistance. He spun some fine yarns—excellent training for my career, eh, Pierce—about the political clashes within the movement, the jockeying for the power in the peace that would come. The difference then, the luxury, eh, was their overriding unity against the bright spit-and-polish of Nazi barbarism.

"A single enemy, Pierce, is a marvelous convenience, one we do not enjoy today. The status quo, eh, authority, order, success, profit—all among today's enemies—not very tidy. Then, there's religion . . . Popular liberation armies are in style today, but you know that. Like the old British Empire, eh, the sun never sets on the red armies—the Brigate Rosse, the Japanese Red Army, the Red Army Faction . . . 'The minstrel boy to the war has gone; in the ranks of death you'll find him.' It's not a pretty song, a sour note for your diplomats."

They turned together and retraced their steps in the near-empty garden, their minds silently ranging beyond the measured chess match of the conversation.

"The empire has pulled all the way back to home waters, hasn't it? But, those waters do include the inner Hebrides, the North Channel, and the Irish Sea, don't they, Stuart?" The brim raised again, revealing a round, pink face, yellow teeth, sandy bushy cocked eyebrows. "I read three or four months ago that the soldiers of the empire, on patrol between County Armagh and County Monaghan, nearly felled a plump bird with their fowling pieces, a carrier pigeon northward-bound from the Continent."

"Umph . . . a wise bird knows the terrain, eh, Pierce, alert to the decoys below as well as the guiding stars above. The British gendarmerie is a shocking drain on Whitehall's treasury, not to mention on the resources and forces of your precious North Atlantic sword and shield. And, what do they accomplish, but to galvanize the people and focus the eyes of the world on their crimes and injustices."

"The mayhem seems to have fallen off in London, for the moment, at least; not your trade so much as the activities of the Arabs."

"Agreed; two points. The Yard is good in any match on the home pitch, damned good, eh, the best. Secondly, the characters you are referring to, the Iraqis, the Libyans, the rest are capable enough when it comes to squeezing the trigger on one of their own at point-blank range, but they're not very clever. You're right, nonetheless, quieter there."

"The Palestinians?"

"Umph!"

"Stuart, the Popular Front for the Liberation of Palestine runs an all-continent operation out of Paris. What were they up to last weekend? We've seen traces—in the flight manifests—Frankfurt, Zurich, Vienna. What about Geneva, Stuart?"

"Your late, lamented ambassador, again. Are you certain her driver didn't do the number, then take his own life. Not every sod can stand orders from a woman, eh—the Swiss would be the worst at that."

"Fair enough; you know the nationality of her driver—probably have the car plate numbers. I have no time on this one, Stuart; who's behind it?"

Lynch pointed to a far corner of the gardens, checked his wristwatch and, with two sharp, barking coughs, cleared his throat. "We are both pressed for time, eh. Paris is a beehive . . . the European brothers in arms . . . increasingly farther afield . . . weekly blasts from our Corsican separatist friends . . . even some recent business with the Revolutionary Peoples Army.

"There is good information, Pierce, exceeded only by better rumor. You know I wish to be of help. I am always flattered to see you, Pierce. Still, there's no reason to believe, based on what I hear, the newspapers, the accounts from Geneva, eh, that there was anything unusual about the assassination. It was your ambassador, not the woman, who was murdered, a new presence, a fresh symbol of Yankee imperialism demanding to be struck down, nothing untoward or out of the ordinary.

"But, ear to the track, Pierce; there have been no Geneva rumblings— plenty of to'ing and fro'ing, the Middle East, Italy, the Federal Republic, but Switzerland has not been in the limelight this month, this year. Your Palestinian Popular Front are busy boys, eh, but not Switzerland—and, Pierce, nothing points to Paris, no fresh scents here."

They left the gardens, moving casually toward the museum exit. "Where are you off to now, Pierce, the Elysee?"

Bromberger thought ahead to the afternoon drive to the suburbs, the probe of the GIGN Gendarmerie Intervention Group, the night drive to Bonn, the day ahead with the GSG-9—the methodical quest, so ingrained . . . "You haven't invited me to dinner, Stuart."

"You're welcome, of course. Sheep's head broth and a pint of plain, ever the best for so important a personage from far o'er the sea."

"On to Geneva. You'll know how to reach me?"

"Indeed."

"By the way, I met some acquaintances of yours at INTERPOL earlier today."

"So I was informed."

"They agree with you. No scent here, or so they say. A worthless session; mouths down, palms up. But, there was the saving grace, Stuart. I could sense they wanted me to give you their very best."

Lynch flashed his yellow smile and touched the brim of his hat in salute. They parted at the street. "I'm going to see the heirs of le Grand Charles exercising their mouths at L'Ecole Militaire. Hope the weather's not too bad for the rest of your stay. My best to your dear mother." Lynch hadn't changed; loud, nonsensical small talk for any prying ears.

Bromberger turned and lengthened his stride along the Boulevard des Invalides. As he neared the Seine and the Quai d'Orsay, a worn gray Renault pulled over, door ajar. The car continued to roll. He hopped in. They crossed the Pont de la Concorde.

"Embassy?" the driver asked, not expecting an answer, keeping a close watch on the Place de la Concorde's grinding traffic. He slowed at the American Embassy's gates.

"Keep moving, normal pace—any of our little black-buggied amis?"

The driver glanced at his mirrors. "Yes, black Citroën, three occupants, six or seven cars back."

"Reassuring, isn't it? Do you share the same garage, or just give them a ring every time I am scheduled for a visit?" Bromberger reached under the front seat, pulled out an ancient, wrinkled black raincoat. "Lose them for half a minute."

The Renault spurted ahead through tight traffic. Bromberger draped the coat over the high headrest on the back of his seat, spreading the cloth to its fullest around both sides. "What the hell happened to the head-and-shoulders outline I recommended the last time through? Can't afford cardboard these days? Don't answer. You and the coat keep our friends occupied. If they stick with you, give it about an hour. There—at that grocery half a block ahead. So long!"

The gray sedan turned a corner, shielding the passenger's side from the rear. Bromberger exited, mingled with some shoppers, selected an elegant cauliflower, watched from the corners of his eyes as the solemn faces of the Surete Nationale rolled by. He ran an admiring hand over the white, cerebral lobes, flipped the vegetable back in its bin, retuned to the sidewalk and flagged a cab. He slouched half-sideways checking through the rear window—no tail. There was enough blood being spilled in the city streets of France; the Surete, DST, and GIGN had better change their ways, he thought, no longer any profit in such black-on-black chess moves, when all play should be directed against the red. Stuart hadn't lost his edge. The red side of the board was changing, crowded with some strange new pieces, complicating, even neutralizing orthodox strategies.

The cabdriver stabbed at his brakes, swung out around a slow-moving tourist bus. Bromberger's thoughts skipped back to Sweetman and the ceremony twenty-four hours before.

● ● ● · ·

The three rifle volleys had cracked the heavy stillness of the Arlington air. "The field's clear; we have our dead. Resume fighting." Hanspeter Sweetman's words hissed from the side of his mouth at Bromberger. They stood above the hillside gravesite, watched as the six matched grays —lead pair, swing pair, and wheel pair—had drawn the empty caisson away, watched the intense conversations among the president and those clustered around him, then the clean, silent procedures of the Secret Service, the sweeping departure of the president's motorcade.

"Impressive. Lancaster was right, the first team."

"No riderless charger with inverted boots; I thought that was part of the drill."

"Your career evidently has not included a hitch with the color guard, Hanspeter. No jet missing-man formation either." As the funeral crowd thinned, the two officers returned on foot through the cemetery to the Ft. Myer Chapel parking. "The caparisoned horse, older than Genghis Khan, is reserved for the warrior, not the diplomat, a steed for the long marches and the charges in the hereafter. Then again, it's not everyone who draws the president as a graveside mourner."

"That's the first time I've seen him in the flesh." Sweetman laughed, his eyes on the walk, "First time I've seen a secretary of state for Christ's sake—couldn't get him to take the leap onto the *Omsk* with me. The president seemed hard hit, more than you'd expect, even though a woman had been blown away—relatives?"

"You'll be the reigning expert a day from now. As I understand it, they were shacked up at some point, not front-burner stuff, but a close connection. That's why the president's thumb is on Lancaster's button."

As Sweetman checked his watch, Bromberger instinctively did the same. "Sunday, I'll hook up with you in Geneva. Fisker has it laid on. I won't know whether I'm coming straight through until I have a better feel for the file. What the hell"—he slapped Bromberger on the shoulder—"you should have it busted by then. But, save any violence for me, Pierce. You're the national asset."

Bromberger's unmarked sedan left first, headed west for Dulles to connect with the night flight to Paris. Sweetman's followed, turning east across Memorial Bridge, past the Lincoln Memorial toward downtown 11th Street, moving easily against the mounting flow of the afternoon rush.

As the second of the steel doors locked behind him, he spotted Fisker negotiating the step down from the communications center. "Harold, what the hell have you been up to? Ready to prime my pump? Let's get on with it." Sweetman flung his jacket and tie on the reception room table, sending a stack of magazines sliding to the floor. Fisker thrust a sheet of teletype at him and shuffled past to restore the display and retrieve the clothes.

The director's message was brief:

Shattered Flag
President called from motorcade during return from ceremony. Requested status report, which I will provide him, opening of business tomorrow. Asked my best estimate on time. I told him weeks, not months. This, as you will understand, has been accepted as fact. No reply required.

"Clods of earth still clumping on the coffin lid, for Christ's sake! Makes it all easy, doesn't it, Harold?" Sweetman started to crumple the message. Fisker retrieved it, guided him into the communications center. The walls of the room had been transformed into bays of an art museum, a montage created by Harold Fisker from the newly acquired albums and scrapbooks borrowed from the Burdette and Starring families.

"I would recommend, Mr. Sweetman, that we approach this in two phases: a quick run-through"—a cough drop clicked against his teeth—"to give you a feel for her life. Then we can go back through it again, addressing your questions, your requirements of me."

"What the hell was this all about?" Sweetman was studying a full-color magazine tear sheet. A tweed-suited Constance Burdette, beaming at the reader from her executive suite, was posed with one hand on a floor-to-ceiling map, a patchwork quilt of numbered oil exploration blocks superimposed in the North Sea—TOPIC—THE TOP PICK!

"That was about four years ago, Mr. Sweetman, her days in London." Fisker set to work at 5:00 P.M. They finished at half-past three the following morning. Sweetman began to absorb the family names and relationships, at first; moving from the storybook childhood through the revolt against her family, to the failed first marriage. On the second run-through, Sweetman would break into Fisker's commentary, questioning, confirming, etching this woman Connie into his brain, marking each event that would require investigation. "If she were still alive, she wouldn't like you, Harold. You know too much about her—Okay, both parents deceased, no uncles, aunts—"

"Possibly one left of the older generation, an uncle who would be in his late eighties, on the mother's side, reputed to be the clan loon, a nomad of the South Pacific. Last known address Port Moresby; we should know more tomorrow."

"Enough, Christ; he wasn't the hitman. We've got the widower husband—"

"Robert Burdette. Professor of Literature, City College—"

"Two kids, twins, right, Bruce and Evelyn . . . and two brothers: Thomas Starring, Towerpoint superstar, and kid brother Adrian. One living ex-husband, and . . . a string of ex- and current lovers running from the obscure of Europe—"

"Just London, as far as we have determined—"

"—from London to the White House."

Fisker guided Sweetman back to the point of last interruption. He described Constance Burdette, the girl and young woman, as an exotic blend, exotic in the sense of chemistry, of physical beauty enveloping resilience and resourcefulness. As the family business of STARCO had grown during her childhood, her father had made a point, quite unusual for the time, of treating her as her brothers' equal. Beyond that, there had been nothing really out of the ordinary—horses, ballet, boarding school, two schools in fact, summer trips to the family's home in Nova Scotia, to France, an unexceptional first three years of college, and then the encounter with Victor L. O. Long, her first husband.

Fisker tapped at one of the montage photos with the eraser tip of his pencil, pointed to Connie and Victor at New Westminster, British Colombia, six months after their marriage. The print had appeared in *For Her* magazine's biography just the month before. "Mr. Long was an instructor in literature and an unpublished playwright who was eleven years her senior, on exchange to Radcliffe from the University of Toronto. At the end of his first visit to the Nova Scotia residence, the young woman informed her parents that she was pregnant and that she and Victor were going to marry—a total uproar, parental prohibition, revolt, the flight across Canada, a civil ceremony in Vancouver—"

"No kid?"

"No kid. The *For Her* article didn't dwell on the subject." Fisker traced the flowering and the collapse of the marriage, the passion she lavished on Long, her discovery that he required more than her companionship, three different women within the first few months. She returned to the East Coast of the United States. Her family embraced her, helped her through the divorce, the death of her father, several months of barren depression. She was only twenty-two at that point.

"What do we have on Long?"

Fisker had anticipated him, taking his incoming message log and flipping through the teletype flimsies. "The RCMP has run a check. Long is in Australia, married to an Australian national, five children—"

"She must have tied him to the bed—"

"No criminal record, no travel outside of Australia. And, I have also confirmed there have been no appearances, telephone calls, correspondence since the divorce."

The next years saw a 180-degree shift, with Connie plunging into her brother's emerging Towerpoint empire: Five years as special assistant to President Thomas Starring, several more as assistant executive director for corporate planning, then the jump to vice president. Sweetman clamped shut the thick file. "According to you, Harold, as smooth as silk on the outside, a cactus lady with her colleagues—but, no vendettas or violence?"

"Not at that stage—now, there were half-a-dozen death threats each of the family members had received in their capacities with the corporation, at the time plans for the new coastal research center were announced. Each case has been carefully documented and closed. The protests were of an antiwar, environmental nature. Two people eventually went to jail. The threats stopped. The two are out now; the Bureau is running a check."

"Then, our husband Robert Burdette entered."

"Yes, he had written her, before they had met, on college letterhead, inviting her to address one of his seminars, no obvious explanation. We do know the event rekindled her academic interests, a gap that apparently had begun to disturb her. She removed herself from the day-to-day Towerpoint operations, moved to the board of directors and launched a self-appointed sabbatical year, graduating *cum laude* and absorbing Professor Burdette . . ."

"Then she had to cut Adrian off at the pass."

"Yes, a quick, harsh tangle in which she emerged as senior vice president. He was capable. She was far quicker, by now a master of each of the Towerpoint divisions. More importantly, she now had a grip on Wall Street and the money market—her new degree. When the clash came, Adrian could talk Towerpoint. She could talk Towerpoint, the Big Board, foreign bond issues, commodities, spot metals, market position—and relate them to the family empire."

The two men took a break from their work. The smell of fried meat and coffee filtered through the rooms of the cell, before Fisker again took up the thread of the victim's life. The next ten-to-twelve years had seen planning for major expansion of Towerpoint International, the operations in the North and Irish Seas, the creation of Towerpoint Petroleum International Corporation (TOPIC), headquartered in London with Connie as its first president.

"Elegant town house isn't it?" Fisker had followed Sweetman's eyes to the color photograph of the Burdette's London mansion. As soon as she had unpacked, she cleaned out half the British employees from the TOPIC start-up. The firings produced several weeks of sensational journalism, branded her, really, and made for three of four hard enemies—"

"The Yard come through?"

"Their report is being transmitted tomorrow."

"Give them a hard look; flag anything important."

"That is in train, Mr. Sweetman. She obviously knew what she was doing. TOPIC's profits leapt; operations expanded. Then, in her third year, an off-shore rig was lost, capsized, in the North Sea with loss of life. There was labor trouble in the east of England, a barrage of work actions and protests. Until we have the Yard's report, I won't know whether these translated into specific threats against her. She chose this tempestuous moment to make the first of her public appearances with two new male companions."

"Husband Robert was benched?"

"Not formally, not divorced or even separated, simply encouraged to return to his courses while she ran the London end."

"We have Timothy North, art collector, and the rising congressman, now president."

"The three of them began to make appearances from time to time at concerts, exhibitions, the best restaurants and midnight clubs, with North lavishing attention on both . . ."

Sweetman rubbed his eyes. "Too late for a soap opera, Harold. I know the rest of the file—campaign trail, victory, Geneva, pow! She must have kept a diary?"

"Three volumes have been made available to us by her family; the fourth is in Geneva with her effects."

Sweetman pushed out of his chair and began to pace. "In this performance of yours, Harold, and damned good, too, you haven't mentioned a single goddamned threat. Aside from that coastal research exercise, no political or criminal violence, no attempted sabotage, kidnappings, letter bombs, or property destruction against this woman who's just been blown apart. Is that right? We're sure?"

"No surer than I have indicated."

"It all says U.S. ambassador—international—political assassination. It's too easy, but no one's making political hay. That doesn't track, Fisker. We're not looking at nuts, lunatics—not the way they cut her down. What are we looking at Harold, some sort of new strain?" Without waiting for a reply, Sweetman snatched up another folder. "What about Chairman Tommie and his wife? Yeah, Tina, the actress, right? She's taken a few swipes at Burdette in the press."

"Mr. Starring is en route back to Europe tonight, apparently rejoining his wife on a company ship in Malta."

"I'd better grab them personally. Christ, Fisker, my head keeps saying European hard core, but my guts—keep digging. This London file. She was all over the map. Let me know what the Yard tells us— they'll be holding some of it back. Get a couple of hours sleep. We'll need a firm location on Starring. Meeting him is the first step, Malta or wherever; then I'll hook up with Pierce.

"After he and I work Geneva over, I've got to check out the TOPIC operation. I'll need the London files. Lay the groundwork; fill me in with one of your 'Shattered Flags.' And look"—Sweetman went over to Fisker, engulfed him with a great arm around the shoulders— "tell Lancaster after I go that he can have my bunk down here. He disappeared into the lounge, returned, still laughing, with a can of beer. "Do that, Fisker?"

"Mr. Sweetman, the director has loaned you *his* bed."

·····● **Chapter 8** ●···· ·

A t 2:00 P.M., June 4, Hanspeter Sweetman was admitted to Suite 401 of the Hotel Excelsior by a plainclothes security officer. Tina Starring was standing on the balcony, her back to him, watching the goings and comings of a balmy afternoon on Rome's Vittorio Veneto.

He spotted another woman in one of the bedrooms off the drawing room, in black and white, hotel staff by the looks of her, on the telephone. *"Si, si. E urgentissimo! Si, si cabbiara lo stile, si Excelsior tre e mezzo. Grazie, grazie."* She saw the visitor, hung up, and scooted to the balcony.

"Mr. Sweetman. I do apologize. You're from the embassy? Do sit down." She looked into his eyes, gave him a long, soft smile and led the way to a cluster of sofas. She sat down and tucked one leg beneath her. "It's just across the street, isn't it—the embassy?"

"I'm in from Washington, Mrs. Starring, working on the Burdette case."

"Oh my God, yes." She bent forward to retrieve her cigarettes and holder.

"I want to thank you and Mr. Starring for seeing me, good to catch you while you are in Rome, makes it a lot easier." He took in her beauty as he spoke, the body, the face, the blonde he had only known from the print and television, sitting four feet away, barefooted, in a black, longsleeved cotton shirt and silver slacks.

"*Mr.* Starring? Oh, I'm afraid you'll have to *scusi* Tommie, Mr. Sweetman." She gave him the full beam of her smile, tossed her hair before lighting her cigarette. "We've just flown in, too, from Malta, after a late, very *liquid* evening"—she clicked her tongue, shook her head in disapproval—"and there was a lovely gold-and-white invitation from the Quirinale Palace, propped against those beautiful flowers. Tommie is lunching with the brother of the president of the republic.

"I was indisposed, and will remain so until the hairdresser has exorcised the demons of Malta's sea air. You really do have a better solution, don't you, Mr. Sweetman? Oh, don't think I'm being rude—just fuzzy. I know Tommie will want to see you." She turned slightly, caught the maid's eye. "I'm going to have a very long, cold, revitalizing gin and tonic; will you join me?"

"Sure, gin 'n' tonic's great."

"That's great. You're great. Tommie's secretary, Muriel Sullivan, is also here somewhere in the hotel, Mr. Sweetman. She will make the arrangements for you with Tommie. Now—you wanted to talk to me about Connie?" She halted the glass on its rise from the tray to look across the rim at him, then said, "Salute," before taking her first sip. Her blond hair fell away from her neck as she tilted her head back, eyes closed, feeling the cool drink, searching for the words she would use with this investigator. "She was murdered by terrorists, wasn't she? It's so cruel, just when she had made so brilliant an achievement."

"Mrs. Starring, are you aware of anyone who ever threatened Ambassador Burdette, held a grudge against her, was outspoken against her?"

"Oh, I was all of those from time to time, but don't think of me as a suspect. Connie and I were not friends. She really was . . . quite insensitive, at a very difficult moment in my life, but that's . . . that's that. She did not approve of her elder brother's second marriage. They were even there, as on so many other points. Tommie didn't approve of either of hers." Tina's mouth pointed into a small smile; a layer was falling away. Her words began to flow more comfortably, no longer of rivalry, but of history. "I don't know how much you know about my late sister-in-law, but she was an exceedingly capable, aggressive person, very destructive of other people. She made enemies quite easily."

"Who are you thinking of, Mrs. Starring?"

"Don't misunderstand me. I'm talking about closet foes, not homicidal enemies—men and women she had injured, damaged, swept aside—who suffered their bitterness and their defeats quietly. I could give you a hundred names if you really wanted me to."

"You're saying that you are unaware of any explicit threats?"

"None that ring out. You see, we might run into each other in New York, in London. We were not together that often, Mr. Sweetman; our careers were usually on different sides of the Atlantic. She ridiculed mine, told Tommie that he had married a sex object with a little girl's mind trapped in a worthless, make-believe world. Goodness. We didn't speak for two or three years after that. She broke the ice with a long, intelligent, thoughtful letter tinged with apology. I had my agent reply.

"A few months later, I sent her tickets, a box, to one of my performances, my biggest Broadway opening. *Her* secretary sent an acknowledgement"—Tina laughed softly, resettled herself on the sofa—"saying that the tickets had been given to some deserving younger employees, My, my . . .

"The closest to a threat that I can recall, Mr. Sweetman"—his thumb flipped open the cover of a small notebook he had been holding in his left hand, causing her to hesitate—"was from Arthur Jenssen." She watched him write. "A double 's'—N-S-S-E-N. God; it must have been ten years ago in New York. He had learned that Connie was engineering his removal from the board, one of those situations where he was up for reelection, you know." The circular gesture of her hand left a corkscrew of smoke between them. "He cornered her in an alcove, yelled, told her she'd rue the day, etcetera, etcetera, etcetera."

"Jenssen of the Alabama division?"

"Yes—you have been investigating—told her to stay away. Tommie told me this; I wasn't eavesdropping . . . told her that shipyards were dangerous places. I have never followed the Towerpoint business, Mr. Sweetman. But . . . I was aware at the time, and that meant that Jenssen was aware, of the plans to bring in a new man. It was Connie's idea to cut him off completely, even deny him his consolation prize on the board."

"Where is he now, Mrs. Starring?"

"Oh, I have no idea. Someone told me that he was breeding boxers, dogs." She leaned across, touched his arm. "He's retired, well-off, of course, quite old, not your murderer.

"Really, I am sorry—and, I'm relieved that I can't be more help-ful." Her shoulders hunched in a shudder that rippled through her body. She caught his eyes watching the movement of her breasts. "In a way, Connie was right in her criticism of me . . . living, imperfect people, not money . . . not power, are my life. It hurts me to talk about flaws. There isn't time. I cringe at death, block it out, a can of black paint hurled against a delicate, wondrous canvas." She paused, her lips apart, her eyes questioning him. "You are an admirable man . . . in the service of the United States. Your business is death, some-thing that I can understand but not accept. Do our rules permit me at ask you a question?"

"Damn right, go ahead." He put the empty glass down.

"Are you armed? Do you carry a gun?"

His right leg was crossed above his left. One hand rested on the polished mahogany boot disappearing beneath the trouser leg con-cealing the pistol lodged in its holster. "I carry a gun."

"I won't ask if you have ever killed. Obviously, you can kill, swiftly. The man outside the door is armed. He can kill—the squeeze of a finger, the blink of an eye; a growing stem is cut, life gone. Shouldn't there be fewer guns, a better way to deal with each other as *living*, imperfect beings? Tommie doesn't agree with me . . . but, we are seeing violence run amok, finding it harder and harder to distinguish between civilization and savagery. I have always been so struck, Mr. Sweetman, by the British bobbies—unarmed, unique really, aren't they, willing so bravely to shape their protection of the British people on the principle of civilization, not savagery, life not death?"

"More Brits are armed than you'd like to think, a necessity unless you move to Masada. I don't want to take up too much of your time, Mrs. Starring, just a couple of more points."

"Connie and the president?"

"No." The simple negative. She relaxed. The light shifted and soft-ened in the suite with the back and forth of the questions and answers in the lengthening afternoon. "You mentioned being with your sister-in-law in London. Those were controversial years for her?"

"Dear, dear man, that was Connie at her zenith, her most notori-ous. She was in the news more that *I* was, but, really, I didn't follow it. I have left the lucrative, boring affairs of Towerpoint and Towerpoin-tees in Tommie's very capable hands—so much so, that I presently am studying Arabic—Ar-r-abic!" Her professional voice played with the word; Sweetman's pen had stopped.

The maid emerged to answer a gentle knocking at the door, the security guard, a few whispered words. "Hairdresser, signora."

"Oh . . . lovely. Well, Mr. *Sweet*man, the curtain falls on my bedraggled head. I don't envy you, and I do hope that you are as capable as you look. . . . Helicopters terrify me." Her eyes were wide; she had taken one of his hands. "This morning at Malta's airport I saw two small children standing, gripping their father's hands, enthralled by the sight of a bristly, noisy helicopter preparing to take off—those terrifying blades. We're a resilient bunch, aren't we? The young aren't afraid. If only we could crossbreed courage and curiosity with greater love and humanity."

"I'm afraid you're dealing with oil and water there, Mrs. Starring."

Still keeping a firm grip on his arm, she accompanied him to the door. "That precisely is my hairdresser's problem. Do you know Italy? Your face says 'no'—neither do I, and I want to know. A lady friend is going to show me one day—Ancona, Ravenna, Verona, Vicenza, Venice. You are invited."

"I'll leave a couple of numbers with the front desk for Mr. Starring's secretary. You're a lovely lady, Mrs. Starring, not my place to say so. Thanks for your time today."

"My time? Ha ha. I thank you. You're the one who is doing the important work, and," she released him, "if you can't do it in Italy, in two weeks, we have the return to the States on Tommie's favorite toy, the flagship *Octagon*." She followed him a step into the hall, watched him bypass the elevator and disappear at a silent lope down the hotel stairs.

Like other American wars of the twentieth century, Vietnam and the U.S. military adjustments that followed had produced new bonds among the world's fraternity of warriors, firmest among them within the secret societies of special forces—contingency planning, training—bonds based on formal responsibility and personal respect and admiration. Ze'ev Shostak greeted Sweetman with an expressionless nod and firm handshake, showed him into the worn, windowless interior of his cover air-shipping office tacked onto the side of a freight hangar on one extremity of Rome's Ciampino Airport. Shostak was with Israel's General Staff

Reconnaissance Unit, part of the antiterrorist network his nation continued to build throughout the world, with the dual assignment of moni-
toring Italy and contributing to the security force's responsibility for El Al
flights transiting Ciampino.

A message from Fisker via double-link communications in Jerusa-
lem had alerted the Israeli to Sweetman's coming. Shostak was eight
years Sweetman's senior; from the lines in his face he could as easily
be twice those years. The U.S. experience in war could be studied in
its separate chapters. For Israel, the first chapter of its history as a
nation had begun almost forty years ago. The fighting had continued
and would continue, he knew, long beyond the contributions of his
lifetime. Israel—smashed schools, the broken forms of schoolchildren,
including his own—was the eternal target. He was part of the shield.
Any human being, any ship, aircraft, or vehicle moving to or from
Israel was the target. With his expertise in the terrorist's ways—the
training, methods of attack, the flow of arms, false documents, laundered money, and laundered killers—Shostak was part of the shield.

Together they reviewed the patterns of ingress and egress that terrorists on the attack in Switzerland, or using that nation as a sanc-
tuary, had developed over the years. In clipped, carefully chosen
words, the Israeli provided a neatly catalogued review of terrorist
developments in Italy and the region, dwelling in particular on the
theft of NATO munitions, given its implications for Israeli security.
He tapped a wall-mounted air route map of the Mediterranean with
a one-meter metal ruler.

"Based on what has been pieced together so far, really just moni-
toring what you have underway with the authorities here, I believe
we can anticipate a new base of operations . . . very special mines,
and unless they are just to be discarded, a new base of operations
specializing in their use. We have tracked the shipment to Naples.
They could be enroute to Sicily, Palermo perhaps, could be enroute
to Greece, to Syria, possibly Libya.

"If they have these mines, they want shipping. Cyprus would have
them at our throats, but they know that we know that. By the time you
are out here"—the tip of the ruler was on Crete, jerking along the coast
from Iraklion to Khania—"you are already at a point where the Mediterranean is so broad that you would have to mount a major seaborne
expedition—really, beyond any known group's capabilities—unless you

are content to hunt the Aegean." The ruler continued west. "They might be going here. These little islands, Malta, the historic choke point, but unless Maltese are actually in on the planning, a most unlikely prospect, there is not much cover for an extranational terrorist operation."

● ● ● · · ·

During their brief Rome meeting, Sweetman was to make a deep, extremely favorable impression on the Towerpoint chairman. A week later, Starring recounted the conversation to Oats Tooms on the owners deck of the *Towerpoint Octagon* in the Grand Harbor. The agent had made no promises, but he had shown confidence, the mind of an expert. He had told Starring that people too often magnify the skill and operations of the terrorists, that they are criminals, nothing more, that they leave a trail of clues like every other criminal.

"A powerful man, Oats; he gave the impression he wanted Connie's killers physically in his hands, to wring the life out of the bastards there and then." Starring picked up the deck telephone, rang Sullivan, and dictated a message to the White House, let the president know he thought he had a good man on the job.

Tooms had just returned from his hastily arranged trip to the United States, and reported to Starring that key pieces were falling neatly into place. They would be set for crew, set for gear, vehicles, habitat, and full political support from the Chesapeake Bay research community. "They snapped at it faster than a blue can hit cut bait. Research money is scarcer than hens' teeth. The folks back there are half starved, a mite overwhelmed by your generosity. And, best yet, our mermaid, Leslie Renfro—you remember, the reception a few days back—and her partners, two good young divers, have taken the research crewing offer."

"Confirmed? Superb work, Oats."

"Confirmed." He checked the calendar on his watch. "Today's the eleventh of June. They'll be tying up a few loose ends and should be aboard by the sixteenth or seventeeth. If the Maltese tugboat and yard unions will oblige, we'll already have the habitat swung aboard and set to work."

"When did the *Pacer* arrive?"

"She's in French Creek, over yonder, came in Friday. We've been promised action by the middle of the week."

Starring went to the rail, studied the distant, distinctive, hollow-box fantail of the long, clean-lined trans-oceanic barge carrier *Towerpoint*

Pacer. The canvas-shrouded habitat cylinder was barely visible aboard one of the big ship's barges. "I wonder what the Russian trawlers must have radioed when the *Pacer* went by?" The corners of his eyes wrinkled in amusement. "I hope, my friend, they reported a dangerous new development on their hands, a strategic plot, new missile, new size, new shape, on the move in the Med—Goddam 'em, Oats. I can't help thinking they had a hand in Connie's murder!"

His gray eyes stayed fixed on the *Pacer.* "We're missing a simple bet, Oats. Her barges are too wide for the catamaran's well. We're wasting time, dependent on an overage port, unions who would rather be on the dole than work. We should be free, able to make this transfer with no outside help. We need to build on the barge concept, continue to refine it—some half-width units, pre-position them in multiples, the home ports, and regional transfer hubs."

"It'll be a new chapter, Tommie, but you're the leader"—Tooms waved a heavy hand toward the *Pacer*—"taken the technology and built it into the entire fleet."

"The rest are deaf and blind, Oats. It's a tragedy, the rest of the pack. But, mark my words, Oats, no matter how hard any of them try to fail, the United States is too good! Somewhere, some kid, eight, ten, twelve, still a youngster, is beating along in a dingy, the play of that small craft in his hands, his arms, his entire body—some kid a hell of a lot smarter than either you or me who is going to splice it all together, take up where *we* left off, and send the United States another thousand miles ahead of the pack. Tell me, Oats, who were you dealing with on the bay project?"

"The fates were with me. I touched down at Dulles, made a few calls, twigged to the fact that Senator Darcy Parsons had a day's hearings scheduled for the successor to the Corps of Engineers' Chesapeake Bay model. I chugged over there, Maryland's Eastern Shore, and settled in for an afternoon and evening with the good senator and a cross section of competing power elites."

"Parsons has been helpful, hasn't he?"

"More than helpful. The upper bay would never have been dredged—no coal-port expansion. We wouldn't have had the channel depth for the *Partner* and the *Mayan*. Beyond that, you owe him on the entire LNG project. He's not blind to environment, not by a long sight, but he's pushed hard for development. He's made some enemies, is up for reelection this fall and feeling exposed, the reason for the hearings."

"How can I help?"

"By not changing a thing. Your research project is the ticket he's been looking for. It'll be all you can do to keep him dry and out of the habitat. That bay, for all its one hundred ninety-five miles, is one of the most fragile ecosystems on the entire globe, shallow and vulnerable. And, even though it's been studied to near-exhaustion, the data is never up to snuff when a *new* problem comes along. The bay stays under a magnifying glass twelve months out of the year. The Federal boys and girls are obsessed with the bay. Why? Because they swim there; they boat there; they eat its catch.

Tooms helped himself to an ale from the tray, just delivered. "Sometime back, we had the Kepone scare, down around the James and York rivers. The first, you remember, wiped out the blues, the striped bass and rocks, wiped 'em off the table—carcinogens, raised hell in the gentry's minds about everything else, turtles, oysters, shad, catfish.

"Each year, there's a new scare. Last year, the menhaden, alewives ran into trouble. The spotter planes went up for the purse seiners; the schools weren't there. Then, they showed up, millions and millions dead, stinking up twenty miles of shoreline. The cry went up again. 'The Bay is dying,' and the cry spread: 'Keep Starring and his goddamned ships out of here—too many ships, too much shore runoff, too much, too much.' Well, there had been an oxygen imbalance that had caught the menhaden at the wrong time. The bay was healthy enough, and this year those skippers stand to get rich.

"But, this spring, they're at it again. A research team on the upper bay has discovered, or rediscovered since we've been finding them for the past decade, different traces of chemical compounds, polynuclear aromatics, and the name alone has whipped up a whole new wave of fear—a wave that has come splashing down around the good Senator, steamy politics."

"Environmental, EPA, his opponent the most vocal?"

Tooms growled affirmatively, lit a cigarette. "In the lead, but not alone. Wading into the middle of all of this, I laid it on the line. I told the folks that if they were worried about your new tankers, it was time to dispel some of those worries, that they didn't have to believe me, you'd help to prove it for them, and prove it now. I told them proof costs money, plenty of it, that you were set to underwrite an across-the-board subsurface, surface, atmospheric objective research program led by an international team, with a full and open invitation to each of the marine research institutes to participate over the course of two seasons, and to share in all data.

"Well, Tommie, a lot of fleas started hopping toward this hound's back." Tooms swatted at a fly buzzing around his calves. "I invited their nominations, said we'd be prepared to accommodate them aboard the *Octagon* this August first, and I suggested that we get together the following morning to share some thinking on the best public presentation of their institutes' roles in the project. At that point, Darcy Parsons's smile was only a mite larger than the one you're wearing now."

"You've done well, my friend. Those taxiboats dart around the harbor like water bugs, don't they?" Starring gave a wave to the passengers of the dghajsas passing beneath the *Octagon*'s bow. He brought their conversation to an end, crossed to the door of his suite. "See to it that I have an early meeting with our young team of divers. I do remember the girl—what was her name?

"Leslie Renfro."

"That's right." The door closed. Tooms stretched, rubbed the trans-Atlantic fatigue from his face, took a fresh ale, and headed to his cabin.

● ● ● ● ·

Leslie Renfro placed three telephone calls on June 10, the first to Oats Tooms to confirm that she, Head, and Tonasi would sail with the *Towerpoint Octagon*. The second was to Smith & Kalkara Commercial Ship Chandlers, Ltd. The third was an unlisted telephone number in Naples; her message, without salutation or identification, was brief. "Xavier is twenty-one. Fishing party Saturday night. Xavier is twenty-one." That weekend, the *Matabele* left harbor to keep a 4:00 A.M. rendezvous with the Palermo faction.

On Monday, June 13, the *Matabele* motored to the chandler's wharf to take aboard four twenty-man, self-inflating life rafts, paid for in cash. They were heavy, each packed into a hard, white fiberglass cylinder two meters long, sealed with breakaway banding, the most modern shipboard rescue equipment in Malta. The ketch again left Valletta for the privacy of the Gozo anchorage.

The false bulkhead was dismantled, reopening the forecastle, the crates knocked apart, the boards taken ashore, smashed and burned in several small, separate fires under cover of daylight. The gunmetal-black-and-bronze shapes, still half swathed in protective packing, were winched up by the jib halyard, from the cabin floor, through the forward hatch, each placed in a separate life-raft container. The length and circumference of the cylinders were right, but the fit imperfect. Strips of the rafts and pieces of the crating which had only partially burned were exhumed and retrieved from the beach. When the cylinders were resealed with metal bandings the shapes were packed tightly inside. Additional hours slid by. The three carefully hand-painted the identification—FRAGILE—SCIENTIFIC INSTRUMENTS—RENFRO RESEARCH—on each cylinder and tagged them and a metal sea chest for transfer to the catamaran. When the *Matabele* returned to Marsamxett Harbor two days later, the white cylinders were on deck as before, carefully lashed. They were much heavier now, sixty kilograms each.

● ● ● ⋅ ⋅

Acrid diesel exhaust from the idling engine of the *Towerpoint Octagon*'s workboat hung in the still harbor air as the gear was transferred from the ketch. Diving equipment, clothing, and personal belongings, such as they were, were packed in new, blue nylon duffels, with names already stenciled in gold, a gift from Starring.

Leslie Renfro was below reinspecting the ketch from stem to stern, cuddies, lockers, the bilge, and engine spaces—clean. She blotted the film of sweat on her temples and upper lip. "The yard is expecting one month's storage in advance; you have it?" Tonasi touched his hip pocket, nodded. They moved out into the cockpit, stood close together, their words masked from the workboat crew by the deep gurgle and sputtering of the engine outtake. "There should be no questions. The yard has been told that an Italian diving club is chartering the ketch for the summer. The club should arrive to take her in two weeks; her documents have already been forwarded to the club's officials. Remember that, a diving club, nothing more. I will send this crowd back to pick you up in three hours." She crossed into the workboat, which pulled away and threaded its way back out through the yacht basin to the Grand Harbor.

● ● ● ⋅ ⋅

Tooms led the way along the *Octagon*'s main deck, guiding his discoveries into Starring's suite. They were a fine-looking trio, young, tanned, trim, the men well muscled, each wearing one of the new blue windbreakers with a circular patch on the left breast showing the contours of the Chesapeake Bay in pale blue with the yellow Towerpoint habitat superimposed, the words CHESAPEAKE DIVEQUEST INTERNATIONAL arching across the top, and RESEARCH, KNOWLEDGE, PRODUCTIVITY along the bottom.

"Sit down, my friends; consider this ship your home. Welcome! You are honored guests and partners in what I know will be a thoroughly rewarding adventure." He watched them absorb the surroundings, oiled oak paneling extending from the deck to the rub rail halfway up the bulkheads, met by a robins-egg-blue silk wall covering, richly hung oils and wall sculptures, illuminated by recessed lighting.

"I have been careful to be correct with this ship. She is, after all, a working ship; I'd like to show you." He led the way to a semicircular bannister, its newel a white-robed maiden, face averted, bearing an earthen water urn, the railing curving down to the next deck. He stood aside, inviting them to take the lead. "When I was very young, my father traveled to Europe each summer. The family went with him, always on a *French* ship, at my mother's insistence."

The stairway opened onto an interior, bordered garden, trimmed in pink marble, with a centerpiece bronze dolphin spouting water into a bronze sea scallop shell. "We're on the second deck now; you'll get your bearings. For years, we sailed on the *Ile de France*, a magnificent four-stacker, clumsy exterior. Then we sailed the *Normandie*, a masterpiece of naval architecture. The trans-Atlantic ships were still climbing toward their peak of glory. The *Normandie*, Oats will know this, had medals struck for each of her passengers, commemorating her new record, medals loaded into her holds before she left France on her first run! There was pride then, confidence. She was brilliantly engineered, clean lines—a tennis court between her funnels.

"Now,"—he gestured around him, the oiled teak floors, mirrored walls with cascading crystal wall chandeliers—"we cut away a section of the main deck. This saloon is two-decks high—but, enough. I am departing for the United States later this afternoon. Nothing can be more important to me than your work this summer. Tell me, how have you been doing since your arrival?"

Tooms responded. "A little more than a week from now, Tommie, we'll have the *Octagon* in the States with you. We weigh anchor today right after you shove off, ETA 1600 June twenty-ninth at the

capes. In the meantime, this team's breaking in as smooth as glass."
He reported that the two work chariots, originally a four-man Navy
design, reworked for the North Sea, had been reworked again, cockpits
and external racks modified, instrument panels upgraded as a result of
several good suggestions by his young mermaid and her colleagues.

"The electrical shop is humming, Tommie, coming up with inten-
sified illumination for the compass, depth, speed, and attitude indi-
cators—she even raised a damned good question about the battery
reserves. I don't know how the hell we did what we were able to in
the North Sea sometimes."

"Have London run a check on the logs, Oats." Starring never welcomed such criticism. His eyes hardened, then a new, flashing smile.
"And, what else, my friends?"

Tooms barreled ahead. "The work chariots' after cargo racks have
some freshly welded extensions and stronger antifouling tie-downs to
accommodate the bay experiments. And, a telex is on its way to some
of our bay colleagues calling for some bottom density readings, calculations we'll need to gauge habitat leg penetration. We'll probably end up
modifying the fittings on the way over; bay's soft, mighty soft."

Starring glanced at an antique porcelain clock above the sideboard. A
ship's officer entered, reported that baggage was aboard the helicopter
with departure for Luqa scheduled in fifteen minutes. Starring had barely
exchanged a word with the three, but he exhorted them, admonished
Tooms to be sure that the catamaran had sufficient wet suits, coveralls,
other gear with the expedition's emblem for Parsons and other distinguished visitors. They followed him to the flight deck to see his departure.

"Good evening, Mrs. Starring. Mr. Starring's instructions were for the
ship to sail upon your return."

"Sail away, my dear captain. You have met my coach and tor-
menter, Joan Rorie, haven't you?"

"Yes, ma'am, earlier today and a few passages ago." The captain
saluted the guest, turned to make sure that the right orders had been
given to three crewmen, each with a wooden crate, puffing after the
climb from the launch.

"One, two, three—there were four." Tina was peering over the
railing. "Where's the fourth? Here it comes. You must take very good

care of these purchases, Captain, thrillingly beautiful ceramic tiles, each handpainted by a gorgeously talented Maltese artist. They form a . . . twelve-foot by twelve-foot mural, or is it a mosaic? of the voyage of Odysseus. I am thrilled. It is a surprise for Tommie, for the back garden in New York. They are precious, aren't they Joanie?"

"Lovely, lovely, lovely. Put them someplace far away, Captain, or we will spread them out on your big helicopter deck." Joan Rorie was a pudgy woman wearing tiny, square sunglasses, sandals, with a pup-tent cotton dress bridging the intervening expanse. "*My* purchase." She held out a white crocheted woolen shawl. "Survival gear for New York City's hideous air-conditioning. Survival gear." She looked around her. "Really, Tina, every time I sail on this mad ship, I feel I should have one of those octopus helmets on, and lead boots to do some clomping around . . . breathe through a hose, look as if I belonged!"

"We can arrange that, can't we, Captain? Joanie please do put a helmet on, with the little windows closed during our sessions. It will make you less oppressive; I'll pass in snacks."

The Grand Harbor pilot came aboard, proceeded with the captain to the bridge. The accommodation ladder and ship's launch were secured for sea. The crew of a harbor tug freed the shackle of the massive steel U-bolt securing the *Octagon* to her mooring buoy; the anchor chain was winched aboard. The captain and pilot strode briskly from wing to wing of the bridge. With the pilot's order, a long, reverberating blast from the ship's horn filled the harbor. The decks took on renewed life with the vibration of power from the engine rooms, the first turns of the ship's screws.

Lofty jets of water arched from the fireboat saluting the Towerpoint flagship moving slowly through the Grand Harbor. A friend was departing. The ship's flag dipped, returning the honor.

Geneva, the fireboat's water jets . . . Head turned to Tooms. "Treat you like bloody royalty and you bloody love it. It's obscene; it won't—" He checked his words.

Tooms was soaking in the historic harbor. "Treat *us*, I say again, *us*, young Paul. You're on the Towerpoint payroll now . . . service . . . honor . . . the whole lip-smacking smorgasbord. You're going to enjoy this shindig, isn't he, Leslie?" The scientist snapped two cigarettes from his pack, lit Head's sheltering the lighter's flame from the stiffening breeze.

"I would like to work with you this evening, Oats, to take a harder look at the schedule you have drawn up. I believe it is too light. Much more work will be required during this passage if we are to make the fullest, most productive use of the first days of the submerged operations in the Chesapeake. That is what Starring wants. You will not be able to give it to him with your present planning. I have some specific suggestions for —"

"Done, done, but tomorrow morning. If you listen carefully, a tray of drinks is on the way. There's a certain protocol, not too heavy. If the three of you guppies take a swing by your cabins, you'll find a note from Lady Starring inviting you to a dinner down in the glass palace tonight in honor of her coaching pal, little Joanie, and yourselves. Not as cozy as roasting chestnuts in the *Matabele*'s fire, but cozy—tomorrow, we'll work until we drop."

When Tina Starring emerged for dinner, she removed her high heels to negotiate the curving stairway. Her white cocktail dress was low-cut, a graceful acquisition from the trip to Rome. She slipped back into her shoes. "How indecorous. I apologize, and I must seat you. I am host and hostess tonight, while poor Tommie is nibbling from another lapful of cellophane airplane food—and, here it is." Stewards filled the six tulip-bowled champagne glasses.

The evening's gin caused her to bang the glass. Filippo's dark hand caught it, brushed against her own.

"Now, that was *very* clumsy. Thank you—and, name is—?"

"Tonasi, Filippo Tonasi."

"Thank you, dear Filippo." She rose, champagne in hand. "Oats doesn't count. We found him in the ship when it was built. It's lovely to welcome the rest of you, my dear Joan Rorie, and our team of beautiful, talented divers who are so very important to us. A toast!" She looked across her glass at each of them, settled for a second on the young man beside her. "Welcome, a happy cruise, God's blessings on your endeavors, *Allah-i-haiyikim.*"

"Dear Tina! I am touched." Joan Rorie remained seated, raised her glass in return. "I know you'd be disappointed if I didn't have at least one point to make. Your Arabic is *most* impressive, but I would recommend against bringing champagne into the Bedouin camp—"

"Stick to the elocution, Joanie, but—" Tooms raised his glass, "play up the bubbly. Harems always drink at sea. Here's to Tina's play. Here's to the play in the Chesapeake, and to work until we drop." He tilted toward Leslie. "Bottoms up!" Tooms drained the glass and accepted a refill.

"Salute."

"Salute . . . Filippo."

Rome was the focus of the dinner's conversation, crisscrossing conversation that continued over coffee on the owner's deck. The great catamaran thrust westward through the Mediterranean, steady as a rock in the moderate sea, no rolling from the twin hulls, only a comfortable, barely perceptible hobbyhorse motion.

"And now, my dear Filippo, *you* must come with me." She led him from the deck into her suite. "You are a very special creature." Her lips left his just long enough to praise him. The second kiss was deeper. Her hands ran along the ripples of muscles on his back, beneath his shirt, across his stomach, up along his hard chest.

"Do come." They crossed to the bedroom. She pushed the door closed with a hip, wrapped her arms around him, and pulled him down ever so gently on to the bed.

"Oh . . . wait, just a minute. Some music for my lovely beast . . . a lovely, lovely . . ."—she was searching the shelves of a bookcase on the far side of the cabin—"lovely tape. Here."

Filippo was silent, on the edge of the bed, the pouch in his teeth as he rolled the cigarette. She floated back to him, took a whiff— "Oh . . . very special"—then a puff. She held his head in her hands, brushed back the thick black hair, floated away.

"'The Swan,' Filippo, the *Carnival of the Animals*. Do you know the 'Swan'?" He watched as she danced, her arms out, head back, her dress opening into a circle of white as she turned and turned. "You . . . you are my whirling dervish, Filippo, but I will dance for you." He smoked, expecting her to fall, but she was steady, spinning with the tempo of the music, turning again and again, her blond hair flowing, her outstretched arms above the plane of her skirt. "I dance . . . to mourn the thought of separation from you, to whirl and whirl . . . and whirl . . . in the ecstasy of my desire . . . to be with you." She reached behind her, stepped out of the dress as it fell, her naked body turning in the soft light, wedded to the music. She faltered and he caught her, brought her down to the bed, her white breasts against his chest, her lips roaming his face with kisses.

"Do you know William Blake, dear Fil . . . li . . . po? We are in his 'Lovers Whirlwind.' Save me from that hell. Make love to me, Filippo."

· · · • • **Chapter 9** • • • · ·

"This Worker's Autonomy Movement . . . ?"

"Italian, small stuff, on the left. The Swiss intercepted a sedan five weeks ago, on the border, handguns, political tracts, three men still being held."

Hanspeter Sweetman, Pierce Bromberger, and Major Karl Pitsch of the Grenzschutzgruppe 9—GSG-9—were working from identical sets of documents.

"Not bad, Hanspeter, not bad. You are more of a European hand than I would have imagined." The German counterterrorist took two walnuts from the bowl in the center of the dining room table, cracked them open in one hand, and went to the chalet balcony to toss the shells. Beyond the blue-greens of the evergreen tops, the lush, lighter hues of the spring meadows dropped gracefully to the surface of Lac de la Gruyére five hundred feet below. To the south, through the crystal air, the peaks of the Northern Alps, heavy with late snow, stood high above the treeline.

Pitsch had been assigned by Bonn as Bromberger's liaison. Following the visit to GSG-9 headquarters, the American agent had asked him to continue on to the safehouse tucked on the hillside between Geneva and Bern. They had made the journey in an Opel sedan whose armor and Mercedes engine lay hidden beneath the unpolished rusting exterior. This instrument of counterterrorism was silent in the garage beneath the balcony, beside the battered, deep-blue armored Saab which had brought Sweetman from Rome.

Pitsch stood for a few moments enjoying the heat of the sun on his face and forearms. Acts of violence against Americans, whether in the Federal Republic of Germany or elsewhere in Europe, were his primary GSG-9 responsibility. Seven months before, his unit had infiltrated the largest of the three terrorist cells targeted against U.S. Armed Forces in the Federal Republic, saved two hundred and fifty armored division lives, with the tip and the counterstrike two hours before the bombing.

Pitsch's talents had been forged in the furnace of twentieth-century political violence. He was the expert. His psychological and tactical grasp of hostage survival, from capture to captivity, negotiations with the abductors, and dealing with the traumas of post-release marked a professional skill unknown a generation before. Five feet eight inches, he was physically unexceptional in his white shirt, collar open, sleeves rolled above the elbows, brown wool slacks, and brown shoes. As with the machines of war parked beneath him, this was a deception. Pitsch was a warrior in time of peace, trained for a lethal, more demanding fight than required of any commando at war, trained for the decathlon of terrorism—light and heavy arms, explosives, storming buildings, aircraft, armed and fortified positions. He was adept in land, sea, and air actions; in the use of communications; in the timing and movement of men; in the precise application of force by hand, karate, knife, and fire power.

Through his violent missions, heroism, and successes, Pitsch had emerged as the recognized GSG-9 counterterrorist—no ribbons, no razor-sharp creases in a peacock's uniform. The spit and polish of the counterterrorist doctrine he shaped lay in his ability to translate the classic requirements of military leadership: to understand the enemy, to anticipate his actions, to exploit the terrain, and to lead his men under fire to suppress fanatical pockets of death-wreaking mayhem in a society at peace.

Pitsch had several hours' headstart over Bromberger and Sweetman in the investigation of the Burdette assassination. But, a week and a day after the killing, the three agents were searching together for the first opening in the wall, the first lead.

At the sound of a voice, the German returned in two strides to the cool shadows of the dining room. "Karl, our Mission has struck out! We've got a regional security officer, Howard Weems, excellent reputation—"

"I've met him once, Pierce. It's clear he blew it, before, during and after—not properly prepared, caught by surprise, panicked. It could happen to the best."

"From what he told me, he left the entire, on-scene investigation play to the Swiss, came home with his goddamned pockets inside out, not even a cartridge shell. No witness interviews—Swiss kept edging him away—unbelievable: I told him to take a couple of days, then we'd walk him through it again. The poor bastard is up to his ears in investigators. We must have four different levels of Washington in town, all mouthing one line—RAF!"

"RAF isn't Weems's problem," Sweetman snapped, "more like RAB, real afraid for his own butt. He leaves it to the Swiss, but you listen to some of the detail he spouts and he had to be in the limo with Burdette at the time of the hit. He's not squaring with us, not yet that is—scared for that nice paycheck of his. We'll walk him through it again and uncover that butt of his, bet your mortgages on it, first clean, solid prediction of this game."

Pitsch savored this without comment, then picked up the conversation with a change of gears. "Has his Highness, the minister of justice, granted you an audience?"

"This Friday. Lancaster had to hit him directly. Is he just ignorant, or is he deliberately such a son of a bitch?"

"You know," Pitsch took two more nuts, "it is convenient to blame all bad weather on the bomb and all European bloodshed on the RAF." He extracted a large hunk of walnut flesh. "In the past, the Swiss have had to contend with six hijackings at Cointrin, Geneva, including that particularly bloody twelve hours with the Eagles of the Palestine Revolution. During the same period, Swiss banks have been hit by terrorists, mainly German and Italian, in need of expense monies. The Swiss have been pinched from the north and the south.

"Ten weeks ago, the authorities here moved in on three Bader-Meinhoff, as you are aware, in a Zurich flat—not my responsibility, but our people were cooperating. The bankers receive a steady flow of death threats, abduction attempts, linked to the terrorists' ransom demands, the demands for release of imprisoned killer colleagues— threats stretching from Tokyo to Belfast. In the past two years, there have been four attempts, one successful, against Swiss Army muni-tions depots. The pace has continued to quicken for His Excellency, Minister Grabner. He is overworked, feeling raw, exposed, and—it is all because of these outsiders. His blood pressure dances high in the warning zone; his stomach is shot; and, as you are learning, he is not given to collaboration."

"I don't see a single shred pointing to or from the RAF at this point, Karl. The killing itself was political in style, the weapons, the close-in moving operation. Hell, she hadn't been here long enough to be a target for Swiss crime. The escape was also the work of professionals. But, and here's where I shift gears, no telephone calls, aside from the lunatics, no messages, no contact with TV, radio, the press?"

"In other words, no exploitation, and that's not political."

Bromberger prowled through the loose-leaf notebook before him, scanning the dossiers of terrorists with recent footprints in Swit-zerland, the names of the cells, factions, armies, movements; their avowed purposes, home bases, size, composition, leadership structure, *modus operandi,* record of actions. The file was thick: FRG, France, Iraq, Ireland, U.K., Italy, PLO, Spain, Turkey, Brazil, Chile, Colombia, Argentina, Uruguay. "All these Latinos, the South Americans; there's nothing there, radicals in exile, just like the Corsican National Libera-tion Front, all scheming against the mother country—"

"The same is true for Spain," Sweetman said. "Those poor bastards are dreaming of the easy days of La Pasionaria. 'It is better to die on your feet than your knees' . . ."

Pitsch's head turned with the words. "La Pasionaria, yah, yah. A Madrid!"

"*Dolores a Madrid!*"

"*Dolores, si!*"

"*Si, si, si.* . . the old war cry."

"It's rough there. The Basque Separatists are gunning from one flank; GRAPO's guns are mowing down the Army from the left."

"This summary shows GRAPO in Switzerland this year, Karl." Bromberger held up a smudged onionskin page.

"Money, not politics—robberies to fund the paternal feud. Grab-ner will have the details. They weren't after your ambassador. Tell me, Pierce, these are good dossiers, well constructed; why isn't there a U.S. section; are you that confident?"

"Hell, no. Washington is also working the case as a possible domestic homicide. But, if it were a U.S. political action, we are fairly confident we would have heard from the killers. Down through the years, a lot of bombings by the Puetro Rican independence types, Washington, New York, attacks against our people in Puerto Rico, Even then, publicity has consistently been part of their game."

Pitsch sat back, a finger through the front of his shirt, scratching his hairless chest. "That is grand; an approach you cultivate only in the New World. You must export some of your confidence, Pierce, a private consignment to S-9. We run low from time to time."

"Confidence comes with keeping the specimen under the glass at all times—better links, better cooperation between people who know what the hell they're doing. The computers are OK, but only if you understand what they're feeding you. The more we know, the narrower the field. The surveillance printout is not worth a damn after the bomb has blown."

Pitsch laughed. "Yah—there are limits. By the way, the other day, one of my colleagues alerted me to one of your private U.S. firms—I forget the name—a company specializing in the newly prioritized trade of security for executives, a company apparently making less than discreet inquires about a deal to handle the protection of one of *our* largest houses! A few checks around—we found these same swashbucklers were offering their services not only to Germany but to Israeli Aircraft Industries, with letters to the president, the executive vice president and the corporate vice presidents!" He laughed harder. "And separately were dangling another proposal before the untempted eyes of Aermacchi, yes Italy, to look after its president and managing directors. You will do us all a great favor if you pass the word to these new security commandos that if they ever should land such a contract here they would be in so deep that there is every prospect they would stay there permanently, at least six feet deep in the earth."

Sweetman swatted a hand in the air, batting away the idea. "Takes solid brass, the bastards have no place over here. But Karl, you don't seem too worried. You know, getting back to the U.S., we've got a good track record against all prime suspects. We don't have your problem! The action's over here, and you know it. You! You're seeing some damned good results, ought to be wearing the Iron Cross, or whatever the fatherland awards these days. The sweeps!—the new multinationals, how many did you bag in Bordeaux?"

"Twenty-six, completely off-guard. A formal headquarters, gentle-men, eleven *million* marks in four currencies, passport facility, two crates of grenade throwers, five hundred kilos of ammunition, pis-tols, submachine guns, nine of the latest Italian Anti-Terrorist rifles, snipers with infrared scopes, six Czech rifles—more. Quite a group, RAF, Red Brigade, and two Iraqi strays—the first time that we had coordinated a strike step by step with the British, French, and Italians."

"What weight do you give to those pious assurances of your bud-dies the PIRA, Pierce? How about you, Karl?"

"They're all over Europe, with two principal missions, buying arms and assassinating the British. Switzerland is off their beaten path; and there's still only one focus, the Brits."

"It may be somewhat more complicated, wouldn't you think, Pierce, given their decision to establish liaison with the PLO training operations in Syria?"

"More elaborate, not more complicated. Their objective hasn't changed."

"This circling of the quarry has had its value, if only for its process— moving in from the periphery of the continent—of elimination." Pitsch drew a circle on a yellow, lined pad as he spoke, then, with quick strokes, turning the page with each new mark of the pencil, added a succession of arrows shooting in from the circumference to the center. He circled the circle with a larger circle and slapped the pencil down. "Similarly, there is nothing we are aware of that would implicate, in terms of hard evidence, any of the Middle East madmen." His hands leafed through the file again. "The Shiite Military Army, the Arab Revolutionary Army, the Palestinian Commando, the Eagles, the PLO, even though they are spreading people through Europe faster than a measles rash."

"The Libyans?"

Sweetman pushed his file away. "The Swiss can smell a Libyan on the far side of the Alps."

"Yah, tight surveillance. They have been very successful there in pick-ing up the right wavelengths. The Libyans prefer Italy, anywhere in Italy; they prefer Paris, anywhere over Herr Grabner's hospitality."

"What about a Soviet crossweave; I don't see it."

"The only eyewitness reports that the Swiss have shared refer to banana-shaped magazines on at least some of the killers' weapons."

"Kalashnikov—AK-47s."

"Probably, but not a certainty. If so, that would hardly be a finger toward the Soviets, the AK-47 is a very available weapon. It is manufactured in what, half-a-dozen countries? It is everyone's favorite—cheap, easy to strip, no neat holes, kills more than it wounds."

"Naw, that's a blind alley."

"We don't have governments running against governments here. The stakes are too high with an ambassador; scare the hell out of themselves, risk a goddamned war. The big bear isn't going to do that."

"There's another slant here, the thousand-to-one chance that we're dealing with some free-lancers, killers you wouldn't find in these files." Bromberger rifled through a few pages as he spoke. "My unsavory friend Lynch hit on this the other day, a new dimension of murders for other than political purposes carried out so as to leave the footprint of the terrorist, and confuse the scent."

"Of course, of course it's a possibility," Pitsch replied. "We have records of such murders in France and in England. No, you cannot discount murderers. She had her enemies. You can't discount madmen. You cannot discount the killer seeking thrills—but there is no pattern for such activity in Switzerland, not Geneva."

"The enemies, the enemies' angle needs a hard, fast look, hard and fast," Sweetman said. "We've played it against the computers in Washington. From what I know, the Yard has also. Nothing. How about your megabyte monster in Wiesbaden, Karl? Let's feed it everything we've got and play it off every stray dog and hatchet man this side of the Atlantic." He walked over to the trio of telephones, started the process of a secure call to Fisker. "I'll start the feed from our end now and get the U.K.'s flowing as soon as I reach London."

"No, no need. I agree it's worthwhile. I'll also handle that from here. Leave it to me."

The calls completed, Bromberger resketched the morning's findings. "Even choosing the free-lance option," he said, "the facts are there, and the facts say that there has been no pattern of threats of violence against any other American installation or diplomat during this period?"

"None."

"None last week." Pitsch contemplated the pencil rolling between his thumb and forefinger. "Until her death, I had been enjoying a quiet period—six weeks since Bader-Meinhoff claimed credit for—the destruction of your consul's vehicle in Hamburg, minus, thank

God, the consul. Two, two-and-one-half weeks before that, a US/
NATO munitions convoy was hijacked outside of Naples, loss of
American lives, an extremely damaging theft of munitions. It has
been kept out of the press to a certain extent. The terrorists claimed a
victory, but they didn't release their inventory—75-foot lethal-radius
grenades, a dozen crates of rifles and machine guns, ammunition,
mortars and mortar shells, special unit arms, including your new
swimmer mines—"

"Yeah, the SEAL mines." Sweetman cursed: "we hand it to them on a
platter!"

"The Carabinieri's Gruppo Intervento Speciale has the action,
without results so far. There has been a scrap between your authorities and the Italians."

"The Grabner factor."

"Maybe not completely—some smart work going on behind the
scenes down there." Sweetman recounted the Israeli's investigation,
adding "Ze'ev's wired up to us, wired up through the net Lancaster's
established for this operation. He'll keep us posted."

"Smart people, capable people. We had all better know where
that cargo is destined. That said, Hanspeter, Pierce, if there is a link
between the events in Hamburg and Naples it is yet to be evident; if
there is a link between either and your ambassador's murder it is not
yet evident. Herr Grabner will tell you that it is the Federal Republic, period. He will then walk you once gain around the course and
tell you that if it is not Germany, there is a fifty-to-one shot that it
is the Italians . . . and if it is either. . . ." He paused, looked at the
two Americans. "We've made a good start here, good lines of inquiry
developing, good lines of support in place, and a good future agenda.
There is a door we still cannot see, but we are heading toward it. I am
confident—one door, and behind it lies our solution."

He went to the sideboard, opened a liter of mineral water, and poured
it slowly into three glasses. "It is a rich hunting grounds." He placed the
drinks on a tray which he brought to the table. "We have our RAF; we
have the RZ, a curiously vicious cell of bombers, the Revolutionary Unemployed Cells, RZs; we have Haag-Meyer. We keep them, their satellite
groups, and their disciples under the closest watch.

"Last week before you two arrived, my colleagues made an important
arrest, RAF, in Frankfurt. You probably got wind of it. A landlady had

become suspicious about a carpentry truck with carpenters who did not carpenter. A significant phenomenon, the value of custodians in penetrating the seemingly innocent exterior of these terrorists who, however virulent, must still sleep, eat, and attempt to find security in the faceless numbers of the city. Her suspicions were confirmed when we received word and placed the vehicle under twenty-four-hour surveillance.

"Last week, these woodpeckers chose to travel to a wooded site some three kilometers from the main runway. We observed. They would remain in their vehicle, with lookouts spaced up and down the road. With the sound of a flight, they would emerge with dummy GRAILs, fitted with sights, and they would track the aircraft—excellent training, we would all agree.

"We allowed them to complete this work of theirs. When they were safely home, our commando made its entry in a simultaneous strike through every door and window in their flat . . . no injuries. The carpenters were in possession of one SA-7 surface-to-air missile launcher, in three suitcases, with six rounds and the usual assortment of arms and documents. Rigorous interrogation is continuing. They haven't revealed anything of significance yet; and they may not. The papers in their possession point to a logistics link with the PLF—the missile. But, there was nothing in the direction of Switzerland."

"That's the second GRAIL this year."

"Correct, and as Herr Grabner will confirm with his wagging finger, the first was also seized in the Federal Republic."

Indignation, indigestion, and chronic fatigue deepened Minister Franz Grabner's slow speech. He glowered at Sweetman and Bromberger, dabbed with a handkerchief at the sweat on his forehead, and, with a heave of his shoulders, turned his back on them in his swivel chair. He studied the row of amber pills on the shelf behind his desk, swiveled to face them again.

"You are the experts; all the way across the Atlantic, my, my. Did you know that I have never paid a formal visit to your country?" He dabbed again with the rumpled handkerchief, extending the operation to the moist gray hairline at the back of his neck. "Tell Ernest that I would be agreeable to his invitation, later this year, perhaps. Tell him that." He settled deeper in the chair, a look of contempt on his face, and studied them in silence.

"Now then, my American experts, would you think that the murder of your ambassador is an indigenous crime of the wicked Swiss?
Is that why you have come to Bern to my family apartment to help
me while away an otherwise empty evening?" Grabner had insisted
on the night meeting. He wanted no American investigators calling
at his office, visible to the Swiss press, adding to his burdens.

"If the killers were Swiss, Mr. Minister, we would have already
received your report of their capture. We would not be here." In the
heavy silence, Bromberger waited for a flicker of satisfaction, but Grabner only slouched further, his body a dead volcano sloping down and
outward with a fine sprinkling of dandruff ash on the upper slopes.

"When you convey my response to Ernest Lancaster's invitation, tell
your director of Central Intelligence how wise I found both of you to
be." The Swiss minister continued to hammer home the point that they
had been admitted to his presence only because of the high-level intervention from Washington. His fat fingers reached for a brown cardboard
box, the size of a double deck of playing cards. There was the sound of
metal, empty shell casings. He examined the contents and again closed
the lid. "And, your friend Major Pitsch—the chalet valet"—Grabner's lips
rose slightly then fell in a failed effort at a smile—"does GSG-9 believe
Ambassador Burdette's demise is the product of Swiss treachery?"

"Mister Minister, from the reports we have had, your department
is working hand in glove with the Germans. GSG-9 has placed itself
at your disposal; we are at your disposal." Bromberger had ignored
Grabner's baiting, responding quietly with a trace of caution in his
voice. Sweetman listened impassively, his fingers pressed together,
forefingers against his chin.

"Mister Minister, the fact that the murder took place on Swiss
territory is regrettable. Nothing we have learned points to a Swiss
suspect, which is not surprising. At this point, however, no evidence
points usefully in any direction. There is increasing impatience on
the part of the American public and government. They want the killers brought to justice. Our director has offered you our services, Mr.
Minister. We see this, sir, as a cooperative effort. You are in charge."

"Nothing Swiss—which is fine—'increasing impatience' . . ." Grabner's words came more slowly than ever. He smashed his hand down
on a foot-high stack of folders, left it there with the uppermost paper
twitching beneath his trembling fingers. The handkerchief again

blotted his brow as if to ensure that every square inch of irritation was clearly visible. "If you are at *my* disposal," the words hissed from his thick lips, "where shall we assign you? Airport security, border inspection? What is your preference? . . . at my disposal!

"No evidence, you say!" The hand rose and again pounded the bruised folders. The chimes of a clock somewhere in the apartment struck 9:00 P.M. Grabner looked at his wristwatch, gave a sigh that rippled downward through the spreading flesh before disappearing behind the desk. He swiveled around to his pharmacy, plucked two bottles from the row, and dumped some pills into his palm. He reached for the water pitcher; it had disappeared. "No evidence . . . umph!"

Grabner pushed himself away from the desk, plodded to the kitchen and returned with the pitcher and a bottle of water. "And, what does the Gruppo Intervento's Lieutenant Colonel Bertucci suggest?" The last word was split in half by a rumbling belch. "And, our Israeli Mossad colleagues, who are giving Switzerland such a population crisis keeping an eye on their Arabs; what do they tell you?"

"Bertucci's out fishing like the rest of us, Mr. Minister. The GIS is deep in the Naples munitions heist—"

"The heist, yes; and was there a message there, Mr. Sweetman?"

"None yet."

"No, and what does that suggest? Don't answer me, Mr. Sweetman." Grabner's body recoiled from another belch. "My business, my American colleagues, is people living and dead, and with the former I fancy myself a good judge of when to change tactics, a judge of the moment when patience threatens to wear too thin." He rearranged the pill bottles. "Good medicine, even though it is slightly explosive.

"Gentlemen," he swiveled toward them, "your collaboration is welcome. Tell your Director . . . Ernest Lancaster, that I look forward to much closer liaison with him and with his close associates in the future. There is no room for exclusivity . . . exclusivity? . . . Yes, in this growing madness. But," Grabner continued, more relaxed now, his hands resting on the desk, opening and closing as he spoke, "we must respect the responsibilities of nation, yes, the national responsibilities . . . the national structure, the national sensitivities each of us brings from our different home to countering this madness. Switzerland, you appreciate, is no longer the chocolate house of Heidi and the yodelers."

Sweetman slid down in his chair and squinted at the pharmacy's labels. *The old tub of lard is changing gears, about time.*

"We are no saints, my American colleagues, but our hospitality as a nation has been abused violently. It is unhealthy for the national spirit. It is unacceptable for law and order." His hand went to his mouth. "Do you know the record of operations of the Germans, the Italians, the Palestinians, the entire international cast in Switzerland this year? . . . Last year? It is unacceptable madness! These scum will be made to realize that it is unacceptable, from behind the cold, hard steel and concrete of Swiss prisons!"

Grabner twisted open the top of a small, round tin, rolled his thumb and forefinger in the contents, tucked the ball of snuff between his gum and lip. "You will not know that one hour and one half ago, we arrested three Italians at the border."

"Four police were shot in Milan yesterday . . ."

"Yes, Mr. Bromberger, so they were, and there is every prospect that the evidence will link these three to that crime—"

"What—"

"We should know soon. And, they will know that Switzerland will no longer be a safe haven for their scum, even if my wretched existence must be claimed in the process."

The minister's heavy cheeks wiggled as he maneuvered a second ball of snuff into place. "Now then, what do we know about your murder? Two people, killed deliberately by gunfire, the American ambassador and her Swiss chauffeur. Three people, wearing hoods, were involved in the killing according to the eye witness accounts. As it was night and raining, and given the professional execution of the crime, these accounts have been understandably sparse. There may have been three killers, maybe more—a van of undetermined make and origin, which, to my regret, is so far not recovered.

"There was a Lambretta motorcycle, recovered, crushed beneath the American limousine. We know of at least one pistol, a Makarov 9mm, at least two, maybe three submachine guns . . . Heckler and Koch 53s, AK-47, and a Czech machine gun. The evidence at the site would so indicate."

"HK-53s?"

"Yes, Mr. Sweetman." Grabner rattled the contents of the cardboard box. "The Kalashnikov was an early favorite of ours, too, but shell analysis indicated that more was involved." He pushed the box across the desk to the Americans. "Basically, Soviet and German weapons. We know, my American colleagues, from the blood samples taken from the limousine and the surrounding area, the blood types of two of the killers. Rh Positive, not the dead driver's, was taken from his shattered window, carelessness, apparently, on the part of one of the killers. Type O was taken from the Lambretta. Now, this was your ambassador's type. However, firm evidence points to the fact that she died where she lay in the back seat . . . never left the limousine.

"We have good evidence, given the total absence of the attackers' fingerprints . . . anywhere, that her killers have experience in their business. Does anything I say diverge from what information you gentlemen have gathered?"

"Please go ahead, Mr. Minister."

"Good. Now, as you will appreciate, we keep a number of individuals under continuing watch in our country. Matching their activities with events of May thirtieth produces a negative result . . . which is to say two things. First, we do not believe that any of those 'in residence' either actively carried out the operation or assisted those who did. We would have been aware.

"Secondly, and flowing from the first, this points to the logical probability that the killers entered Switzerland for the specific purpose of committing this crime. If this is the case, it is still possible—possible—that they are within our borders, holed up until the situation cools, possibly preparing another crime. It is more likely, given the habits of such scum, that our killers have already left." Grabner tilted back in the swivel, with some difficulty locked his fingers behind his head, and invited their reaction.

"Today, your people netted the three Italians, but they were heading north. What about last week's outbound border traffic?"

"Nothing"—Grabner's hands were still behind his head as he pushed the seat around in full circle—"nothing . . . and something." The Swiss minister rose and took an armchair closer to his visitors. "A pregnant something, suggesting three possible clues to one of our killers. Number one, that the killer, not surprisingly, is male; number two, that this male is blonde, of fair complexion; and number three, that English is at least one of the languages he speaks."

"One of your eyewitnesses?"

"No, not with the hoods they wore that night—no, another lifeless body. Last week, a security inspection at Cointrin led to a sedan which had aroused the interest of a security dog. The vehicle, a rental, contained a dead body in the trunk, *no* papers, *no* passport, *no* identification, evidently locked away at least for the time the sedan had been at the airport—June second. The dead man's fingerprints did not produce results in Europe. They did in your United States. The sedan produced no fingerprints of value. It had received a professional's attention, a trait of interest given the timing of the airport discovery and the earlier absence of prints at your murder site."

"Who was in the trunk?" The back of Sweetman's neck burned with anger. There had been no word of the airport murder either officially or in the press. Grabner was a polished performer. How the hell had it slipped by that little runt Fisker? Grabner, the bastard, must have sent off the prints for routine check, not bothering to tell Washington that they belonged to a dead man.

"The rental contained Mr. Henry Cranston, a young American in Europe for summer studies. The folder is in that stack; you are welcome to have a look. The sedan also contained the bullets which took Mr. Cranston's life, a little knocked around, but quite certainly fired from a Makarov 9mm.

"Now, to anticipate your next question, my colleagues, we inquired of the airlines as to any bookings made by Herr Cranston. We were quick to learn that on June second, just before, or more likely just after his death, a Mr. Cranston booked a one-way fare to Cairo on Trans-Global Air. We subsequently confirmed that there was no Cranston on that flight . . . and no one by that name on any flight anywhere since June second.

"Slim pickings, as you say, but, pickings, and that"—his hand again shoved against his mouth to stifle a belch—"is where we are tonight."

"The same gun?"

"The same. We don't have it."

Bromberger had been writing as Grabner spoke. "One, maybe more of the Burdette killers at the airport on June second . . . the bullets, clean cars . . . why kill Cranston?"

"He was hardly one of them; read the folder."

"Blundered into their act . . . saw, heard something that threatened to blow the operation?"

"Possibly, Mr. Sweetman, but unlikely, given the pattern of his activities in Geneva, and given that it was not until the third day that his murder took place. No, I would make the assumption that if Herr Cranston, given his personality, had had information relating to your ambassador, he would have reported it at the earliest moment."

"You're suggesting he was killed for his papers?" Sweetman's words came quickly. "Christ, Mr. Minister, every terrorist on the Continent carries six goddamned passports. How the hell does that square?"

"I reserve my instincts for mushroom hunting, Mr. Sweetman." Grabner had groaned upright and plodded toward the front door to show them out. "The single thread would indicate only what I have suggested. But, we will look forward to continuing our collaboration. You have my message of friendship to Ernest Lancaster."

● ● ● ∙ ∙

In the days that followed, the two agents combed through the testimony of each member of the U.S. Mission, from Pinkerslaw down. The late ambassador's maid, still shaken, took them through the residence and arranged interviews with the residence staff. She opened the ambassador's personal correspondence file to them, having first removed a very few letters which she had judged irrelevant to the investigation and not suited for others' eyes. This she had done in violation of the strict instructions sent to the mission from Washington that all was to remain untouched. She would be the judge of that. Mrs. Burdette would have expected no less.

As the testimony mounted, it was fed back across the Atlantic via the Shattered Flag channel. The pieces offered nothing. At the same time, a single word might hold the key. Fisker was the backstop, as good as automated, sifting, cataloguing, energizing the resources of the entire U.S. community, and keeping his own flow of traffic on the return circuit to Geneva.

With Howard Weems, the mission security officer, they drove and redrove the murder route. An entire day was devoted to the death car, to reviewing the driver's standing instructions, the communications gear, the emergency procedures.

Weems, a retired San Francisco policeman, had made diplomatic security his second career. On Friday June 17, Sweetman and Bromberger returned to his office buried, typical of the trade, deep inside the handsome U.S. Mission. The white paint of the walls was broken by three displays: one, a cluster of full-color photographs, the president, the secretary of state and the late ambassador. Another cluster included a vertical row of framed citations and police awards dating back thirty years, newer meritorious citations from the Department of State, a browning front page of the *San Francisco Chronicle* with a head and shoulders photo of Weems, a photo of the lobby of the hotel, and a diagram of the hotel reception area with a dotted line running from the switchboard and vault to two *X*s where the robbers had fallen when Weems had foiled their attempted holdup. This testimony to heroism inscribed to the ages hung beside a glass partition in the office wall, the third, living display.

The senior sergeant of the watch of the mission's Marine detail sat with his back to them at a desk on the other side of the glass, a smaller office lined with alarm panels, communications and closed-circuit TV monitors. The faint unintelligible crackle of two-way communications penetrated the glass.

"Pardon, sir!" A thin, young marine, close-cropped in crisp uniform, stood at attention at the entrance to Weems's office. "Secure conference room secured, sir!"

Weems checked the digital clock suspended from the ceiling. "1604, right." He beckoned the marine forward and took his clipboard to initial the security form.

"Thank you, sir!" The corporal turned smartly and returned to his post.

Weems spoke with assurance to the two new agents from Washington, polite, unawed by their closely held blue-ribbon credentials, confident of his own, and fully satisfied with the way he was standing up to the successive waves of investigation. Their predicted line of initial questions rained down on him. In his responses, he held to the theme he had developed with increasing polish.

"Gentleman, I think I might be most useful to you, given the demands I've already taken of your valuable time, if I were to recap a few, key points. Protection of lives, security, counterterrorism are my business, our business." No visible reaction from either of them; he continued. "Every diplomatic post in which it has been my honor to serve has been awarded a 4.0 rating, 4.0, two continents. That's the way it has to be and that's the way I'll keep it as long as I'm on the job. Every member of this mission's staff has been trained by me, surveillance, travel, precautionary commuting techniques, vehicle sabotage checks, riot defense, explosives defense, protection and destruction of classified documents, use of tear gas and defense against same, emergency communications, evasive driving, evacuation procedures, escape and hostage situations. When they're trained by me, they're trained from *A* to *Z*! No exceptions; they must meet my standards."

"This included Ambassador Burdette?" Bromberger's question sounded matter-of-fact.

"Of course! The ambassador, God rest her soul, had just arrived. You know that. We covered the basic brief on residence security her first day here, and mission security was already on her schedule; Admin can give you that. The ambassador was a quick study." His voice dropped, his eyes on the cluster of awards. "Let me tell you something, gentlemen. We brief. We train. We upgrade security. We anticipate, stay wired in through the station chief, local security forces, message traffic from Washington—threat assessments, part of the business, vital. We develop our own threat list, the best working document when you come right down to it. We do more than the regs call for. But, there's a limit beyond which *no*body can go, Mr. Bromberger, Mr. Sweetman, and that limit is resources, money!"

Still no nods of understanding. "You take today's modern point-target weapon, a submachine gun which can fire thirty high-velocity rounds in two seconds, and you get what you'd expect when it cuts into a partially armored limo. My case is in the files, gentlemen, and I hold the copies. I've been telling Washington to spend the pocket money involved—peanuts, that's all it is when you're protecting the head of the U.S.A. presence. Spend that money to upgrade where it's really needed—provide us with decent, first-generation rolling stock. I've gotten nowhere.

"We have two limos here, neither one worth a damn, one in the shop for new shocks the night the ambassador died. I don't have to tell you; Washington deals in half measures. Forgive me, gentlemen, if I'm stepping on some toes. They take the floor stock, put in just enough armor to ruin the suspension. The windows, laminates, fused to the showroom glass, weak, added on, not constructed as part of an organic defense. It's OK against a peashooter, but tissue paper against the assault that hit her! Washington has got to get through its head that there aren't any high-risk or low-risk posts anymore. They're all vulnerable. Any time an ambassador moves; you need real armor; you need a chase car . . . that's more people and more money!

"You need dedication, gentlemen; you've got it. You need a security program; you've got it. You need security equipment; you're not halfway there. You need the decision by Washington to give higher priority to the threat, to spotting the terrorist before he can strike. The security officer can't do it alone even if he goes twenty-four hours a day, which I've done plenty of times. I thought penetration was the name of the game. Talk about jungles. We need our people on the inside. This whole continent would sell its soul for what either of you've got in your wallet right now. Spend the bucks; develop the agents. We're—"

"Weems!"

"Yes sir, Mr. Sweetman?" Weems broke off, his response the immediate, rote deference that so often stimulated respect in his visitors.

"Howard, you make some good points, but save them for your inspector general. I keep rerunning the communications, the sequence of transmissions, the comm during that last drive. Either I haven't been asking the right questions, or I'm still missing something. What do you think, Pierce?"

"Go through it again, word by word."

"You were in your car, Weems, when the driver was enroute to the hotel with the ambassador?"

"Right, Mr. Sweetman. I had informed the DCM, Mr. Pinkerslaw, that I would be at the mission command post, even though officially it was a holiday, until we were satisfied that the evening was on track. He had gone out to the ambassador's residence. It was after 8:30 P.M., 2030, the time's in the log."

"I'm with you; keep going."

"When the command post received the call from the residence staff that the ambassador had departed, I took about five minutes to close up, then headed home . . . knowing that I could monitor communications from my car."

"The chauffeur had established contact with the command post?"

"Yep, from the residence; you have that statement from the command post watch."

It was a phone call, from the kitchen, not a radio check, right?"

"Right. He had had a quick coffee in the kitchen—"

"In your car, you had the same voice set, the same bands the chauffeur had?"

"Correct."

"But not the backup radio telephone, the one in the limo's rear seat?"

"Well, it's not a backup, Mr. Sweetman. It's a separate circuit dedicated to the ambassador's—"

"You didn't have that equipment, right?"

"That's correct."

"Go ahead."

"The ambassador had been enroute ten minutes. Her location was somewhere on the Avenue de France, by my calculations, when I received the first attempted transmission."

"You have stated this was a click, repeated clicks, no voice?"

"Yes sir; the driver, as we have established, was triggering the mike with a thumb switch, raising the mike and tilting it toward him to speak. Each time he did so, he broke the connection, wiring worn at the base of the mike, no voice. I knew when I heard them that the clicks had to be from his transmissions. No one else is on that band. I radioed the sergeant of the watch; he was getting the same thing. . . ."

"You returned to the mission?"

"I spun around, tore back. I was only a minute or two out when it happened—the first clicks."

"Did you have the sergeant of the watch contact the limousine; you didn't, right?"

"I radioed him to stand by. I was on my way back. I didn't want to run the risk of an unnecessary foul-up. You know, this was an important evening for the ambassador, and—"

"You returned to the mission?"

"To the command post."

Sweetman ran a hand across his bald head. "A call was coming in, the first clear transmission from the limousine, as you entered?"

"Yes sir. I was winded. I could see from the sergeant of the watch's expression that we had a problem. I dove for the second receiver."

"The sergeant has stated he heard the driver's voice, the call sign, the word 'Urgent,' then all hell breaking loose, and it was happening fast."

"Tell us what you heard, Howard."

"Automatic weapons' fire, unmistakable, a collision, tires, more weapons—"

"All this was coming from the ambassador's set?"

"Correct. Either she or the driver had the button down the entire time—"

"You tried to raise the ambassador?"

"Yes sir. I had just given the call sign, when her voice came through—"

"Calling for help."

"Shouting, screaming—someone was killing her."

"Then?"

"Then—another salvo, silence. I tried one more time to raise the limo, dropped it, ordered the watch to keep trying, contacted the Geneva police and took off to find the limo. I was on the scene in eight minutes."

Sweetman walked over to the framed front page of the newspaper, studied the photos, the diagram, the story as he spoke. "You're a professional, Weems. You've got a good memory. What you just told us tracks exactly with what you've said before—right, Pierce?"

"More detail each time."

"Now Howard, you haven't built a career on memory; that would always have been your word against someone else's. You're a professional. You run a taut ship, keep good files, logs; I can see it myself. The sergeant of the watch keeps a communications log—"

"Correct, Mr. Sweetman."

"What sort of log did you keep of that evening, Howard?"

The security officer sat straighter in his chair, both palms on the desk in front of him, his eyes narrowing on Sweetman. "Of course I keep records, Mr. Sweetman—"

"Come on, goddamnit, Weems; cut the bullshit! We've spent a week with you! You're holding back!" Sweetman was half across the desk, shouting. "What is it?"

Weems remained motionless for a full thirty seconds, only the sound of the clock in the room. His hand slid open the center drawer, withdrew a pocket tape recorder, placed it on the desk between them.

"A tape? You taped the goddamned killing? Jesus Christ!"

"I only wish I had taped those communications, gentlemen." He gave the recorder a small shove, dropped his eyes. "Background noise, gunfire, nothing more; it's worthless. I was winded, probably half in shock, holding the tape too far from the telephone. You know . . . I was trying to hear, to raise the ambassador, and to record at the same time. Worthless!" He gave the recorder another shove. It dropped into Sweetman's pocket.

Sweetman departed for Washington the next morning. On Monday afternoon, June 20, Harold Fisker had the first lab analysis of the tape. The words were indistinct. But, unmistakably, there were two women's voices.

·····●Chapter 10●·····

Sea gulls, hundreds, lifted in a gray-white fluttering from their perches on the Victorian roof and clock tower of the pier A Marine firehouse jutting out from the Battery into New York Harbor at the southern tip of Manhattan. Circling and screeching, they swooped low toward the food in the outstretched hand, veering away in fear only at the last second.

"Sullivan, did you know these sea gulls are retired harbor pilots gone to their reward?" Tommie Starring tossed a chunk of bagel into the harbor air, whooped at the steep plunge of two of the birds, the snatch and flight of the victor. "Tell that pushcart vendor we've got some hungry pilots on our hands, Sullivan. We need another one of these things, two more. A splendid, splendid morning; good meeting coming up today. I smell success!"

In the days following his return from Malta, he had been closeted with the Towerpoint inner team preparing for the July stockholders' meeting. His Mediterranean tan gave him a look of extraordinary fitness. His spirits were soaring with the morning birds. He was on the verge of tying the last knots in the multibillion-dollar Sea Star consortium. Oats had reported from the *Towerpoint Octagon* that the ship had cleared Gibraltar, the research team in the traces pulling hard. The president had called the night before to report a promising lead in Connie's case, one that he could not discuss over the phone. He had encouraged Starring to come to Washington; he would personally bring him up to date.

Starring and his secretary started up the west-side waterfront, followed at a discreet distance by another of his blue Continental convertibles. The president's call had led him to make a two-fold decision. First, Muriel Sullivan was instructed to arrange his call at the White House, if possible, for the first weekend in July. Second, she was instructed to reserve the Octagon mansion two blocks west of the White House for his personal use over that entire weekend.

For years, Starring had toyed with the notion of staying at the historic Octagon, President Madison's home following the burning of the White House. Now, he would do it, take the time he needed . . . alone . . . in retreat, within those historic walls to put his hand personally to the stock-holder's speech he would deliver in mid-July. It would be far more than the usual bookkeeping account. He wanted to relate the Towerpoint programs to preceding and future generations, to provide the conceptual underpinnings that would make the corporation's contributions lasting.

"You don't build on sand, Sullivan. Look at this deserted harbor, piers in decay, not even a garbage scow in sight. Just a few years ago, the Hudson River, these buildings, trembled with the powerful horns of maritime commerce. Mile after mile of piers, six hundred miles of waterfront, were teeming with ships and cargo. The old Ellerman Bucknell and United Fruit had piers just ahead on the left. The U.S. Lines, Panama Pacific, Cunard White Star, our STARCO, Grace, Clyde Mallory, dozens and dozens more were up-river. It was a sight—national strength, maritime leadership, employment! Now, mismanagement, poor politics, a vanishing act. Those ships still working have gone across the river, south to the gulf—thirty to forty shipping lines. The mind aches at the loss."

They steered away from a sanitation truck giving the streets their morning washdown. "The Octagon house, what arrangements have you made?"

"I have been assured by the Institute's hostess that nothing is booked other than normal visiting hours for the entire summer. She told me the house may be leased any weekend you wish. She did ask for the courtesy of a week's advance notice, as there is often touch-up repair work going on."

"Book it. What is today, the twenty-fourth?"

"The twenty-fourth."

"Oats and company are due on the twenty-ninth; we'll have the bay arrival ceremonies. Book it for the entire Fourth of July weekend.

Confirm the appointment with the president's staff. Then organize me, organize my papers for the Octagon."

"You alone. No Mrs. Starring, no staff?"

"Absolutely no one; a retreat, Sullivan, a retreat!" He scowled at the question. They crossed West Street, arrived at the southern face of the World Trade Center's twin towers. "Ha-ha! Here's Adrian looking well washed and combed. Mother would be pleased." They entered One World Trade Center, swept upwards seventy, eighty, ninety floors to the corporate headquarters of Towerpoint International. A coterie of executives fell in behind the two brothers. The procession moved through the reception gallery in the direction of the boardroom.

"I won't be two minutes, Adrian. Have everyone take their places." The younger brother relayed the order and caught up with Tommie who had passed the first of two, internal security checkpoints enroute to the corporation's plot center. Watch officers jumped to their feet. Starring strode past them, halting before the thirty-foot by ten-foot electronic chart of the world. Towerpoint ships, yards, offshore platforms, and support facilities glowed in color-coded lights. He addressed the senior watch officer. "You have us running smoothly this morning."

"A fair amount of activity, sir; nothing unusual."

"Where do you make the *Towerpoint Octagon?*"

"South of Santa Maria Island, sir; the Azores, 35 degrees 16 minutes north, 26 degrees 30 minutes west."

"To the south?"

"Yes sir. There's a good-sized storm building to the north. The skipper made the course change fifteen hours ago." A green light flashed with increased intensity on the display screen. An orange dotted line appeared, flicked across the screen to the western Atlantic seaboard. "Her projected track, Mr. Starring; she's still on schedule."

"Landfall the twenty-ninth?"

"Chesapeake Light, 1600 the twenty-ninth."

"The LNG tankers?"

The orange light of the catamaran faded. Two new green lights grew in intensity. "The *Towerpoint Partner* has just arrived in Baltimore; she'll be offloading . . ."

"Not as much ruckus as predicted."

"No sir. She'll berth there until the third. The *Towerpoint Mayan* is in the gulf, enroute Baltimore." Another orange, projected track appeared, marking a long curve from the Mexican coast around the tip of Florida northward into the Atlantic. Starring moved left a few paces, studied the Pacific, then left the plot center, giving the watch a brisk, saluting wave.

The board of directors' portraits lined the entrance to the conference room, one heavy gold frame draped in black. Cumulus clouds reflected in the gleaming mahogany table which paralleled the wall of glass looking down on lower New York Bay, past the Statue of Liberty, Governor's Island, Staten Island, the Verrazano Narrows Bridge to the opening to the Atlantic, a spectacular panorama of the famous harbor.

Starring beckoned his directors to take their chairs. The next two hours were dedicated to an intensive review of the planned report on the Towerpoint Defense Weapons Systems programs: the *Staghound*-Class antisubmarine heavy destroyers, the *Cunning*-Class nuclear attack submarines, the *Neptune* submarine rescue class and the newest, *Valor*-Class nuclear command cruisers. The corporation's production, yard-by-yard, class-by-class, played on the conference room screen. There had been seventeen launchings over the past twelve months, in the black, orders on the rise despite the problems with Washington.

The presentation had good color, schematics, the right mix of statistics aimed at bringing the stockholders aboard, giving them the plankowners' view of each ship's weapons suite, the engineering plants, armor, and sea-keeping built into each fighting hull. Starring ordered another run-through. The slides flashed by quickly. The directors were a study in concentration.

"Tight. A good report on the present, with good flow into the yards' modernization for the future—excellent report. What is your opinion, Mr. Counsel?"

"We've given it a good look, Mr. Chairman. The presentation is solid from the legal viewpoint."

The board's secretary turned a tab divider in his book. The lights came up in the room. "Mr. Chairman, looking to the actual meeting, we anticipate a goodly number of questions from the floor following this presentation, a few plants from known detractors—fed from the left and, of course, from official circles."

"Of course." Starring turned his pen end over end. "Of course there will. I plan to preside during the Q-and-A session. We're going to emerge from that session, my friends, with the stockholders and the media on our side."

He leveled the pen at the secretary. "We will want a complete transcript, unedited, of that session ready for distribution by the second day. For my own use, I will want identification of each questioner. We'll break now for ten minutes, airport next."

Muriel Sullivan met Starring at the door prepared to receive his next volley of instructions. She followed him into his office, past the clusters of furniture, across the enormous rug, to the view of the harbor. He put an eye to the long glass to take a closer look at the Staten Island ferry beginning her swing, to line up with the Manhattan slip. "What's up?"

"When you and Mrs. Starring were in Rome, you met with an agent, a Mr. Sweetman, investigating your sister's death."

Starring looked up momentarily, returned to the glass. "I remember."

"Mr. Sweetman called this morning to ask for your personal intervention—"

"Nothing to report?"

"I tried to draw him out. He was very noncommittal, said it was essential that he have your authority to examine all, he underlined the all, of your sister's London TOPIC files—"

"Nothing on leads?" The long glass swung up-harbor, settled on a tug shepherding a fuel barge.

"He said that the evidence was such that they could not rule out anything, even the possibility of a British connection—"

"What do they have?"

"He wouldn't go any further, Mr. Starring."

"I understand." Starring moved his examination to the far reaches of the harbor, pushed the long glass away. "He's a good man—an Irishman, Sullivan. Of course he has my permission. Damn it; it's going on a month now. Connie's blood still dripping from those bastards. Give London the necessary instructions." He gave an enormous stretch, checked his appearance, and returned to the conference room.

"*This* is Sea Star!" At the sound of Starring's voice, the directors melted away from the eight-foot-square scale model. He bobbed his head as he peered through the Plexiglas dome. "Remove the cover—and keep it off for the stockholders—reflects the light." He studied the detail, the airfield runways, hotel, ports for the surface effect shuttles, recreational craft, and commercial shipping. "Far superior to that damned film. Proceed."

The curtains closed and the Towerpoint symbol appeared on the screen with SEA STAR—SUPERPORT COMPLEX. "Mr. Chairman, this coming fiscal year marks the beginning of Stage Two of the Sea Star complex, as approved by vote of the Towerpoint International stockholders a year ago."

The next slide presented a bird's-eye view of the five-pointed, star-shaped airfield afloat in the open ocean. Two eight-thousand-foot runways angled along the star's edges, one running from the northern point to the southeastern, the other from the western point to the eastern, crosswind runways designed for the new and projected generations of commercial and military aircraft. The control tower topping off the structure of the terminal was spotted in the center of the star. Tree-lined access roads ran to the base of the southwestern point where they merged with the fountains and gardens at the front-entrance drive and side-serviceways of the terraced Sea Star resort hotel.

A semi-submerged breakwater curved from the tip of this point, sheltering the passenger transit and recreational harbor. Another breakwater, sheltering the cargo piers, curved south from the eastern tip, giving the entire ocean complex the appearance of counterclockwise motion. The next slide showed a hazy photograph of twenty jetliners stewing in their jet exhausts, the skyline of New York in the background, awaiting clearance for take-off.

"With the coming of Sea Star, America enters a pioneering new era of transportation, relaxation, safety, efficiency, and commercial progress unique in the world."

"'Relaxation, safety'? . . . Hold those points; build them in later."

"Yes, Mr. Chairman . . . enters a pioneering new era of transportation, efficiency, and commercial progress unique in the world." Successive slides reported on the complex strata of planning being devoted to Sea Star, the consortium organization, the stages One to Four of financing, the time-phased meshing of industrial participation, construction, and final assembly outlays, projected employment in the tens of thousands, projected revenues—the timetable from first letting of contracts through the first landings and takeoffs.

Starring's voice cut into the presentation again. The lights came up and the drapes slid open. He looked sharply from one director to the next. "Sea Star is more than a leap into the next century. It is the essence of Towerpoint, the superior technology, the concept, the sheer volume of construction, and the benefits to the nation. This presentation is uninspired; give it a lift!" He turned to the project manager. "How many semisubmersible columns support Sea Star?"

"Two thousand plus, Mr. Chairman."

"What are the dimensions of each column?"

"Three hundred feet long, sir, thirty-five feet in diameter—"

"The length of a football field, the diameter of a nuclear submarine—more than two thousand. That's the theme you want to build on! The unparalleled manufacturing in graving docks along the eastern seaboard; the talented thousands of men and women; that's the message. The shaping of Sea Star, the fleet of ocean tugs towing each column to the site, the technology—greater than the space shots—tipping each column vertically into place, joining them together on the open ocean, module by module, the physical phenomenon of this stable, semi-submersed city with the decks, the airfield riding above the energy of the waves."He glanced at a police helicopter darting over the tip of Manhattan, "and, Sea Star contributes to the nation's defense. You have a line on that?"

"In the event of national need, the Sea Star port and airfield could make an immediate contribution to America's security."

"Vague—good, as it should be. We know we are looking at a tactical air base, a refueling and replenishment field, a carrier capable of projecting air and sea power. My friends"—Starring stood with one hand on the model, the other on his hip—"it is your task to present this message—experience and brains; no one else can match us—audacity and tenacity. We have vision; we have guts; we succeed."

Muriel Sullivan was at his side. "Mrs. Starring sir, calling from the ship. Shall I tell you will call her back? You should be leaving for your meeting with the secretary-general."

Starring nodded at the whispered message, returned to the conference table. "We're going to have an outstanding meeting this year. The year's record is superb, every division. You should all take great pride. This model leaves for Washington tomorrow for my meeting with the president." All rose as he left the conference room.

The blue Continental slowed, passed the Washington Square Arch, and rolled to a stop in front of Starring's brownstone town house on Washington Square North. An unmarked New York City police car was parked a third of a block away. The three detectives were relaxed, windows open, enjoying the balmy late afternoon. Starring chatted for a moment with the plainclothes UN security guard, a member of the secretary-general's personal detail, at the entrance. He spotted the slender, transparent two-way radio tubing running from the guard's ear beneath his collar. "Is the secretary-general on schedule?"

"Yes sir, still showing arrival 5:30 P.M."

Starring trotted up the steps into the house, showered, dressed in fresh clothes, and was at the door when the black UN limousine arrived. He bounded back down the steps to greet the secretary-general. A cluster of agents formed an immediate protective perimeter around the two men.

"Lars, you do me great honor."

"Quite to the contrary, Tommie, it is always a reinvigorating pleasure for me to see you again."

Starring pointed across the park. "Did you know that FDR used to keep an apartment on the Square, that tall brown building?"

"Truly? No, I didn't know that. Campobello, Hyde Park, Hot Springs; I thought I knew them all."

"He used to arrive as only he knew how to, an open car behind a swift, flying-vee of scarlet motorcycles. They stopped for no one."

The secretary-general shook his head. "I'm afraid open cars are a luxury of the past, at least for some of us. You've just come back from Europe, haven't you? Any developments about those responsible for your poor sister?"

"Those bastards. It's promising, Lars; nothing firm, but I think our people are about to pop it. I should have a better picture in a very few days."

They started into the house. Still another police car had halted traffic a block away. The three New York detectives were at work, stationed on either side of the street, scanning the buildings, watching the movements of the curious who had gathered to observe the event whatever it might be.

"I have just returned from Europe, Lars, Malta, in fact. Tina, by the way, is coming home by sea, making the crossing now. I just got off the phone; she sends you her most affectionate love."

The secretary-general beamed. "Tina, such a lovely lady. You're very generous to share her with the world. I am a devout admirer and an opening-night regular. You know that!" He laughed again.

"She has your tickets; the Fourth of July, if you're going to be in town. Now, come inside my friend. I want to tell you what we're doing with the international Oceanic University program in Malta."

The door closed. Two agents remained outside at the head of the steps. The detectives returned to their car to wait for the departure. The curious thinned. The roadblock was removed, and yellow cabs resumed their flow along the city street.

·····•Chapter 11•···· ·

The light was as soft as the evening rain when Sweetman emerged from the TOPIC skyscraper on the south bank of the Thames. Straggler river boats swept past him speeding up-river, home, on the incoming tide. The raindrops felt refreshing after the stale air of the sealed building. He creased the papers in his hand, tucked them into a breast pocket, and, paralleling the Thames, lengthened his stride toward Battersea Park.

The letter from the president, then congressman; the terrorist threats against the off-shore rigs; the loss of the driver; the hate mail, hiss and cry of the press, strikes threatened and real, raced through his mind after a full day, locked in a vault, submerged in Constance Starring Burdette's most private files. One letter, almost corny, stuck in his mind: "An eye for an eye Burdette. Their murders shall be avenged." Words and letters cut from newsprint and glued to the inside of an air-letter form postmarked Amsterdam. It had been sent to Scotland Yard along with the rest, returned—dead end, inconclusive analysis. The thread of Amsterdam, not limey hate mail, too many players moving through Amsterdam—could be a visceral threat, just for the principle of the thing, no intention of action—maybe not, a thread worth hanging onto.

And there was that other correspondence. He pulled the papers from his pocket, kept them partially folded against the rain, and again read the top letter.

Darling, dearest Connie,

New week, Tuesday, I will be with you again. I ache for the moment, for you, my love.

Reservations at Claridges, as usual. I'll pick you up, Madame President, at your office, if I am still considered presentable. Then, the evening is in your lovely hands.

Connie, my love. Do you realize how important it is that you are already a president? Because, I shall be one very soon, it's in the stars, and you will be my guide even, damn it, if you won't say yes to being my wife. Not yet, not yet—rush not, my love.

Connie, do you think about us, how completely superb our life together would be? It would . . . it will. I will continue to propose over dinner, lunch, breakfast, in the theater, in the middle of the night. I do love you so; I respect you as much as I love you and I admire you as much as I adore.

If you still insist on remaining Burdette, I will love you with every ounce of my life, in London and, mark my words, in the White House. Grover Cleveland did, you know, dearest Connie. But! Do not call me Grover, sounds like the family pooch.

Until Tuesday, I dream of you.

All my love to you,
TGG

Sweetman returned the letter to his pocket, waited at the Vauxhall Bridge road for the light. The sky was clearing. Cars hissed along the wet pavement which shone in the evening's sunset.

He frowned; Bromberger was in Rome. Grabner's catch was probably starting to sing. Italians bumped her off. Action's down there—No! He corrected himself, made the turn inland from the river to circumnavigate the Battersea Power Station. It wasn't true. They were still cold as ice. Where in hell did anyone get off signing a letter like that TGG for Christ's sake. But she had kept him on her string, never played his game.

Sweetman sifted through the disconnected evidence. Grabner's blonde male . . . airport . . . Geneva, the name of the American, ticket to Cairo . . . the voice . . . that incompetent bastard Weems . . . second voice, Christ . . . woman, talking English or American, anyone but a goddamned Mongolian could say five words in English! Fisker, the little prick, had worked the tape inside out with his lab-speak boys . . . the ambassador's name . . . the even tone, no emotion . . . the death shots, then her hand had released its grip on the phone . . .

A man and woman, husband and wife by the looks of them, were on the cinder running track as Sweetman entered the park. A jog, a shower, a couple of gins, roll in bed with honey, not bad. They passed him, chatting as they ran. Connie Burdette had been alright in bed. North, her Brit lover, had his share of space in the TOPIC vault, fawning letters, cards with the gifts, gallery opening announcements, all in the files.

The vault's contents went far beyond her personal life. From Scotland Yard, the reports in response to every threat were comprehensive, professional. The Yard had assumed full responsibility, a single, plainclothes twenty-four-hour-a-day detail had been assigned without publicity because of the national uproar she had created. But the Yard's reports dealt with nuts and hotheads. Only one person had ever been detained.

Connie Burdette had thrived on battle with the British, and on fighting the Labor government and its offshore energy regulations. She had burst out once in an interview, "Socialism is a sickness. It will be the death of you!" END IS NEAR: ERUPTION FROM MT. BURDETTE had led that evening's headlines. During the years in London, she had seen eye-to-eye with the government on only one issue, terrorism and the threat to the rigs. The vault's papers revealed a close and continuing liaison with the Yard, the Royal Navy, and the commanding officer of the Special Boat Squadron commandos.

The Navy monitored the TOPIC rigs as part of its North Sea patrols. There were not enough ships, and they could not protect against the underwater threat. On her orders, subsurface inspections were conducted daily. This, too, had been kept from the press, as had all rig security measures.

Each member of each crew had to pass a background investigation. The rigs were not left in isolation, ever. Each carried communications and backup systems. The security teams inspected all incoming supplies. Access from the sea ladders and helicopter decks was sealed, to be opened and manned by security only when a supply ship or flight was scheduled. Even if saboteurs were to make their way aboard, the rigs were as terroristproof as possible—automatic shutoff systems, dispersal and redundancy of vital gear to minimize the damage from both explosion and fire. Fifteen rigs; big operation; smart lady.

Sweetman crossed the Albert Bridge into Chelsea. Smart lady, but not smart enough to win against seventy-foot waves. Who the hell is? He purchased a bouquet of yellow roses and peach iris from the flower stall on the corner of Royal Hospital Road. The Chinese-red door was ajar when he reached the small, white-brick row house on Radnor Walk.

"Sherri, where the hell are you?" Sherri Easton was on the telephone, pointed at the receiver, gave him a wave from the kitchen door, and continued her conversation. He tossed the white paper cone of flowers on the sofa, engulfed her in his arms, gripping her round bottom, working upward across her hips, along her back to her shoulders, then down again. She wiggled beneath the massage, turned in feigned annoyance as the long fingers continued their travels to her breasts. Divorced, a friend and lover of Hanspeter's from an earlier life, Sherri was arguing with her night city editor.

"Yes, yes, yes, yes, yes! The flat was demolished, furniture and paintings smashed . . ." She listened. "Yes, struggle, torn hair, blood everywhere!" She rolled her eyes at Hanspeter, moved the phone away as he pretended to take it. Her voice grew angrier. "Look, lovie; I don't know what's bothering you tonight. The story *is* the way I wrote it, and it is a goddamned exclusive unless you bugger it up!" He was talking again; she broke in. "I was at the side entrance, alone, away from the pack when the coroner came out, was climbing into his car. We know each other; do you hear me? . . . bruises on the neck; the stab wounds probably came after she was dead . . . alright?" She held the receiver away, then close, "Good, good boy, lovie; don't bugger it up." She hung up with a sigh.

"Sounds like a profitable day."

"Oh, Hanspeter, that man is suffering from senile dementia. Our resident Balkan duchess managed to have herself splattered about her Regents Park flat this afternoon. The fool at the night desk is in a trance, paralyzed by the finest story he's had in weeks, all but accused me of fanaticizing. We haven't heard the last of him, either— and you?" She put her arms around his neck, rose on her tiptoes, and they kissed a long kiss blending the distant past with the night ahead.

"And me?" He picked her up, strolled around the living room hugging her. "I've been wasting money—a very neat puzzle. We're dealing with a tight cell, hard to penetrate, modern weapons, good operation; a neat puzzle, but I'm pocketing some pieces, kiddo."

"Shall we go out to eat?"

"Aren't you afraid your buddy boy is going to call you back?"

"Oh, you're the optimistic chap." She put the flowers in an empty wine carafe, filled it from the kitchen tap, and returned the bouquet to the living room.

"If you've got a pail, I could get some beer and sandwiches."

"That's an idea, Hanspeter, a picnic at the foot of our bed!" She smiled a loving smile, snatched her purse from the front hall stand, and trotted up to the second floor. Sweetman followed the outline of the panties beneath the tight cotton-knit dress. "No," she called down the stairs. "Night desk is under control. It's a gorgeous evening. We're going for a walk."

It was after midnight. Sweetman's head was propped against a pillow, his pale, muscular shoulders illuminated by moonlight. Sherri raised herself on an elbow in her darkened bedroom to take a sip from the beer he was nursing. She stretched out beside him again. The dinner had been good. They had come home and made love.

"I've been followed from the moment I cleared customs at Heathrow."

"Rather foolish, isn't it, for anyone here to follow you?"

"Part of the business. They want to know why we're here. We didn't broadcast my arrival. TOPIC must have tipped them off."

"We've been followed tonight?"

"Right to the doorstep."

"Not inside—semi-public sex?" She laughed, ran her hands up his hairy thighs, fondled him. "And, why didn't you shake them, Hanspeter? What were you, a commando, a frogman, no—a SEAL." She gave him a squeeze. He pulled her tight against him. "I remember the night you taught me the proper way to hold a fighting knife, long, long ago when you were protecting me." She had one arm out of the covers. "Handle reversed, blade pointing back up the arm, purse as a shield in the left hand, the opening—slash, thrust—didn't you, you dangerous SEAL. Why didn't you swim across the Thames submerged tonight, leave them baffled ashore on the South Bank?"

"No need to, not until this morning."

Sherri brought a cup of coffee to Sweetman at daybreak while he shaved. She left the house first, walking along Kings Road to Sloane Square where she hailed a taxi for her office. Sweetman emerged an hour later, turned up Sydney Street, and slipped into the waiting black American sedan just before Fulham Road. A gray British Rover confirmed its interest in the American party. The two cars pushed through the beginning of the morning's rush toward Grosvenor Square. Sweetman's car disappeared into the embassy's basement garage. At almost the same instant, a black van emerged from the interior garage ramp. The Rover was at the curb, two of its occupants on foot surveilling the main and consular entrances.

● ● ● · ·

Sherri's red Triumph sped through the outskirts of London heading northeast toward Yarmouth. " —And, Mr. SEAL, you guarantee we're not being followed?"

He glanced over his shoulder. "Impossible, not a chance with you as wheelman. The black balaclavas wouldn't stand a chance, let alone the Yard."

"Are you working with our Special Air?"

"Indirectly." He stroked her shoulder as she drove. "Did you have to take the day off for this?"

"Almost, said I had to have some work done on the car, back by noon, that sort of thing. Did you see the story?"

"Was it okay? Lovie come through?"

"He did, strangely enough, front page, in fact. I do have to be back by two. I have a meeting with another inspector, Hanspeter, a good friend—"

"We're all good friends."

She yanked the Triumph toward the side of the road in mock anger, sped ahead. "—a good friend who has promised—oops, here we are"—her car bounced through ruts in the gravel outside the car rental agency—"who has promised to fill me in on the autopsy. The car is in my name. Will you be back tonight?"

He shook his head. "At least a couple of days. Send the bill for any damages to my great uncle George, Main Post Office, Anchorage, Alaska."

"Air mail?"

"Surface mail's fast."

They kissed. He emerged from the office with the keys, climbed into a green Jaguar coupe. The two cars headed off in opposite directions.

An unreasonable chill blowing off the North Sea had the gold-and-crimson sign of the Lord Nelson swinging from its hinges when Sweetman pushed his way through the double doors of the waterfront pub on the evening of June 29. The loss of the oil rig *Topic Universe* had pointed him to Great Yarmouth. The London files had been far more detailed than the information scratched together by Fisker. It had been rough, and Connie Burdette had been in the bull's-eye, loss of the rig, loss of the diver, several injuries, work stoppage, then the unsolved death of the rig crew chief.

"Over here!" A cane jabbed into the smoky haze. Sweetman spotted it over the capped heads and made his way through the jabbering crowd to a booth in the far corner. "You told me you'd be tall and bald, and that you are. Sit down." The old union leader, crippled with arthritis, used both damaged hands to lift the pint to his lips. "Throat still works, God be praised. You want to talk about the wreck of the *Topic Universe*? A bloody, sorrowful business." He set the mug down, his weathered face looking hard at Sweetman through watery eyes. "A villainy, death brought on by greed!" His voice, a shout, was lost in the din of the pub.

"Harry? . . . "

"That's right, Harry."

"What can you tell me about those two deaths, the diver and the rig chief?"

"Two? . . . In good time, Sweetman. Here!" He poked a hole in the smoke again. "Two pints—two!" He caught the barmaid's eyes. "Now, these are very unhappy times, Sweetman. For all the talk of progress, the working bloke gets shoved further and further to the rear. And"—his head trembled as he framed his thoughts—"this is not something that has come on us overnight! Nor is it unique to that one rig!"

He batted at the empty mug. "Go to the west; ask the miners. Take a *look* at the idle cranes, the empty building ways on the Clyde. Ask the factory sods in Glasgow and Clydebank. They'll tell you, Sweetman, tragic unemployment, in the double digits."

"Come down the coast a wee bit. Stick that fine nose of yours into Hull. This nation, you know"—he paused to hoist the fresh pint to his face for a long, slow pull—"this nation is no more than a lump of coal surrounded by fish! The Hull fishing fleet was the finest. But, stick your nose in there today and you will see a tragedy, a dying city, closed factories, rusted, idle ships, empty of catches, an entire fishing industry vanishing—mismanagement and the curse of government!"

"Drink up, Sweetman . . . and, who suffers? You know before I tell you . . . I like your look . . . and it's the likes of you and me. The blokes who work the foredecks, the nets, the flaming engine rooms —the blokes who work the wharves, the waterfront, the freezer works. God help us. The wives, the aged grandparents, the wee boys and girls, the worker and his family suffer.

"And then, you continue south to Yarmouth"—he cleared his throat, spat on the wood floor— "the great boom city of North Sea energy— oil and gas flowing like liquid gold—rubbish! Another tragedy, not a boom, Sweetman, another pustule of worker exploitation.

"Hear these blokes?" He glared into the mass of bodies. "The bloody laughter of despair, half of them unemployed, on the dole, unable to look their families in the eye." He drank again, clanked his pint with the American. "Now the crime of the *Topic Universe*. What brings you from the States to the Lord Nelson these years later—still settling insurance claims, lawsuits, is that your business?"

"On May thirtieth, the former president of TOPIC, Constance Burdette, was murdered."

"Aye. The news flowed like quicksilver through this wretched port."

"Harry, I don't know what if anything the loss of that rig had to do with her death. I am an investigator—"

"So you said."

"I need you to tell me, Harry." Sweetman pushed his mug forward for another clank. "I need to know as much as possible." The empty pint in his upraised arm brought two more.

"There were no tears, Sweetman. God rest her soul, there were no tears. She was a greedy bitch, a foreigner—unlike yourself, concerned only with profit." He rubbed the wrinkled brow beneath his shaggy yellow-white hair. "Profit to the exclusion of all else— including human life!

"She has gone to her grave, Sweetman, with the blood of Yarmouth on her hands—and the hatred of those of us still living within us." He thumped his heart with a gnarled paw.

"This is where you can help me, Harry."

"What do you want to know about the *Topic Universe*?"

"You tell me."

"Right." Harry Jones steered the mug to his mouth. "The *Universe* was a four-legger, a jack-up rig about thirty-eight miles out." Sweetman knew the off-shore business. He let Jones talk. "The jack-ups, the semisubmersibles, the drill ships, the fixed platforms each have their uses. The jack-up, you see, gives you the benefit of feet on the ground, so to speak, stability when she's on site with her legs planted in the seafloor. And, she lets you raise the legs and float her away to a new site when the first job is done. Simple enough, and very nice, if you know what you're doing."

"The jack-up has her drawbacks, too. Those long legs, some three hundred to four hundred feet you know, can lead you into a tremendous thicket of troubles. Each of the legs bears a tremendous weight, which pushes them into the muck, down into the seafloor. When it comes time to pack up and move, if you've sunk too deep you must fight a terrible suction—fight with the risk of one or more of those spidery legs crumpling!

"Mind you, Sweetman, no rig's invulnerable. The semis have their perils, too. But the jack-up, she's in a delicate stage on the up and on the down. The companies have their experts, the marine geogra—no, ge*o*logy blokes, the engineers paid so handsomely for their calculations. Down the hatch, Sweetman . . . calculations to keep the rigs drilling with great profit, as advertised to the investor.

"Well, Sweetman, they covered it up; the late Mrs. TOPIC and her lieutenants. A bit here, a bit there. The *Topic Universe* was cutting corners, shaving the safety edges to keep the front office happy, hap-py—two syllables, Sweetman, four letters, C-A-S-H.

"The *Universe* was thirty-eight miles out, being jacked . . . down, at the end of a job when one of the legs held, wouldn't budge. Then came the next mistake. The crew was ordered to place too great a strain. A storm was coming now, you see—too great a strain, and the leg began to bend. So they stopped, and there she sat.

"It was as if you were taking your leave of a lady, Sweetman, and were obliged to stand motionless in the bedroom with your pants half up and half down . . ."

"What direction was the jacking, Harry?"

"The jacking, aye!" Jones roared his laughter, "Half up and half down, with the husband's keys jangling in the door; the wrong position to be in. Do you know of our storms, Sweetman?"

"The worst in the world, howling winds, shallow seas, tall waves, long fetch—"

"That's it; and that's what was closing on the *Universe*, There was a great deal of consulting going on between the rig and London. The chief, you see, was reporting the storm and the recommendations of the crew that the *Universe* be cleared, men off, until the blow passed. But, the chief was a lizard, trying to play both sides and come out smelling of roses. He was agreeing, you see, with the late Mrs. Burdette when she took the phone at the other end and gave the order to stay with the rig.

"Now, the biggest concern about *Universe*, save being blown flat over, was the swirling currents churning in the storm. The concern was they would scour away the seafloor from around the sick leg, the one with the bend. This meant divers, and the chief diver, chap named Renfro, God rest his soul . . ." Harry Jones gave a moment of silence, his watery eyes blinking past Sweetman, one paw nudging the mug handle back and forth on the pub table. "Retired Navy diver, the best in TOPIC's employ, prepared to go down."

"He was the chief diver, you see. He knew it was too dangerous, but he knew his duty, absent orders to the contrary. . . . But . . . he ordered the rest of his crew to remain topside. He'd do it alone, you see. Down he went, one frail soul, into that bloody, roiling murk of a sea to pack—picture it, Sweetman, to pack great sacks of aggregate around the footing of the bent leg, to save it from the sea."

"Long odds, Harry."

"No odds at all. They sent him to the diver's grave. They had him rigged like one of them Punch and Judy mari, mari—bloody puppets, with one safety line running to the surface and another to be clipped to the cage delivering the aggregate. In twenty minutes, the winds were tearing. The support ship standing off the rig was reading thirty-five, forty, forty-five, fifty-foot waves, and rising . . . some would say seventy before it was over. Then the *Universe* buckled, not enough to collapse, but a sickening lurch which sent the rig crew off in their rescue gondolas. Not the diver's mates, mind you, but the rest of the crew. They bobbed around like so many apples until the support ship could maneuver to retrieve them.

"And, Renfro. That lurch tipped the loaded cage, binding the poor bloke in his own lines, and there he dangled, Sweetman, absolutely cut in half, held together only by the rubber suit he wore. And, that's how his mates would find him! We'll have another."

They drank. Sweetman allowed the old man to catch his breath, then moved him on again. "The rig went down, didn't she, Harry?"

"She did, turned turtle, capsized two days later. Cocked over as she was, the strain had been too much for her. The loss of the *Universe* was a scandal! Renfro's loss was a crime! But"—he worked the mug to his lips again—"there were to be no formal charges. The inquiry, orchestrated by the late Mrs. Burdette, was unable despite its deepest searching of the evidence to find fault. *Force majeure*, Sweetman, that's what they found."

"On the words flowed from their mouths, through their typewriters, into the presses, and onto the tele. And, a deep and lasting bitterness settled on Yarmouth." His eyes narrowed into a challenging squint. "You don't have to take my word for it, you know. The man you'd want to be talking to would be old Collie, Colonel Colin Tully, Royal Marines, knows more about the sordid mess by far, worked with the Navy, in charge of off-shore security." A paw waved in the direction of the North Sea. "Old Collie, back in Scotland now with the Forty-fifth Commando, a friend of Renfro's, mourned his passing."

"Harry, let's have another. You're looking half dry." They drank, and Harry Jones recounted the turmoil that followed Renfro's death. "Tell me about the rig chief, Harry."

"The rig chief? A short tale—mashed by a car one black and icy night; hit and run you'd call it . . . perhaps an accident, perhaps no. Few mourners; no witnesses came forward. But, by God, that was not the last of the dying. The diver's lovely wife, Mary Renfro, was destroyed by her loss. She gassed herself the morning after the inquiry findings were published, and, Sweetman, their child . . . a pretty girl, simply disappeared!"

While Harry Jones and Sweetman were shutting down the Lord Nelson, the *Towerpoint Octagon* was slowing to ten knots, coasting along toward her Virginia landfall. Only the twin wakes of the big ship's hulls indicated motion on the flat, glassy sea.

Leslie Renfro, Head, and Tonasi were sprawled on the starboard foredeck, taking a short break from the heavy, self-imposed transAtlantic training schedule, absorbing the glib gab of the ship's bosun.

His hands were working line and marlinspike. He gave an occasional turn to the glossy wood handle of the ship's boat hook he was dressing with coach whipping, a braid of flat sennit, to be finished at either end with Turk's head ropework. Oats Tooms appeared at the owner's deck railing with Tina and her coach, growled down an oblique greeting to his Maltese colleagues. "Better put that shutterbox to use, Tina, document the blood, sweat, and tears the team is putting into Chesapeake Divequest International: Filippo, research; Head, knowledge; and Princess Leslie, productivity, pardon the expression . . . three lizards baking in the sun."

Tina trained her camera along the foredeck, bringing the viewfinder to rest on Tonasi. A turn of the telephoto lens brought up the rugged young face sharply. The brown eyes opened, as close to her as in the stateroom. The shutter clicked, clicked again. The eyes closed . . .

"Oh, ho! Over here, Tina, better camerabait still." Tooms was pointing to the north, his arm following a speck paralleling the ship, level with the horizon. "Got 'im; good lady. That's going to look just fine when Tommie throws it up on the screen. That bird, here, he's circling back—take a few more—that's the greater shearwater, one of the true oceangoing birds, distinguished by his black burglar's mask. See it? They breed on Tristan de Cunha, eight thousand miles south of here, circle the North Atlantic for the better part of a year, then fly south to breed again. He's a rare sight this time of year, usually further north by now —and a fine specimen."

"It must be terribly boring. He just looks lost zooming around out there."

"Joanie, I don't think you'd be too good at it, not even with feathers." He hugged her ample waist. "That shearwater has more navigation systems than this entire ship. Celestial—the sun, the moon, the stars—and we're only beginning to understand."

"Does he have a glove compartment for his little charts?"

"Used to, Joanie, but that's been overtaken. He carries all he needs in that onboard computer just aft of the beak. Now! See yon speck, off to the east, beyond the bows? Yon speck approaching is the Honorable Thomas Madison Starring, roll of drums."

● ● ● · ·

The helicopter settled on the flight deck. Starring and Darcy Parsons emerged, their heads low beneath the cut and wash of the blades. Two steps behind them, immigration and customs officers jumped to the deck; the Towerpoint front office had done its job well. The formalities of port entry would be met without the rigors of formal inspection.

The helicopter refueled and departed. The Chesapeake Light Tower was abeam. The black hull of the pilot's boat rolled along in the bow wave of the starboard hull; the pilot transferred to the catamaran.

In an hour, a helicopter returned, bigger than the *Octagon*'s own, carrying TV remote crews—two reporters, two cameramen, two sound technicians—the twins of the electronic media with their Towerpoint escort. They set up quickly, the reporters—one man, one woman—selecting the angles for their crews.

A *Reliance*-Class Coast Guard cutter led the welcoming flotilla, a Newport News fireboat, chartered press boat, and a growing gaggle of power and sail spectator boats. One of the launches came alongside; more staff and guests transferred to the flagship. Amid the growing chatter, watches were checked. The press conference was scheduled for 4:00 P.M.; the remote crews and their videofilm would be ashore again in time for the evening network news. The senior member of the Towerpoint media team cupped his hands to his mouth, set the ground rules and identified the participants for the "on the record" press conference. Starring, Senator Parsons, Tooms, the members of the expedition, and the directors of the participating Chesapeake Bay marine research institutes were announced. The TV remotes were told to be back on the helicopter deck immediately after the conference ended. All others were invited to the owner's deck for a buffet and cocktails.

The press was led down a ladder, forward. Klieg lights were playing on the port side of the ship, and on the yellow, cylindrical habitat and its glow-white-and-orange supporting legs, suspended from the bridge crane and lowered in the center well to a point of maximum display, with its top even with the main deck.

Across the center well, on the port side of the ship, Starring and his supporting cast, each in an expedition windbreaker, were arranged in a semicircle at the center well railing. One of the two midnight-blue-and-gold work chariots gleamed in its cradle behind them. The *Towerpoint Octagon* was lying still in the water, the captain keeping her on a northerly heading with an occasional touch of the main screws and bow thrusters to hold the afternoon light at the back of the cameras.

"Ladies and gentlemen . . . I trust we have the acoustics right"—Starring was at the microphone, one hand on the shoulder of Senator Parsons—"we are delighted you have found time to join Senator Darcy Parsons and Towerpoint International this afternoon as we prepare to embark on one of the most exciting scientific expeditions ever launched in the bay region, or indeed, on this side of the Atlantic."

"The findings from this research will translate directly into benefits for the people of Virginia, Maryland, and Delaware—and the entire Chesapeake system and the headwaters of the great rivers which feed that system"—he followed the pencils scratching across the notepads—"the Rappahanock, York, James, Potomac and Susquehanna." Starring broke his introduction to point to a class of forty-foot racing sloops, hulls well over in the freshening breeze, good background footage for the cameras.

"You have press kits, I believe." Starring turned to Tooms who nodded, used to fielding his boss's questions whether he was certain of the answer or not. "Tomorrow, this ship will be at the dive site, which we have already surveyed. The habitat before you will be lowered into place, and the first team—I should emphasize, international team of marine scientists and technicians—will be in the water aboard their work chariots. This first phase of research, most fittingly, will be launched on Independence Day."

Starring's smile broadened as he looked across the center well to the media corps. "It is now my pleasure to introduce those with me. I look forward to showing the members of the press around the ship following some important remarks by Senator Parsons and Dr. Tooms and, of course, following your questions."

Parsons and Tooms were brief; the questioning began.

"Mr. Starring, Jerry Harrison, *Evening Herald*."

"Yes Jerry?"

"This Sunday, July third, the LNG tanker *Towerpoint Partner* is scheduled to depart Baltimore—"

"Yes."

"It has been suggested, that Sunday, given the triple-wage scale and"—Starring winked at Senator Parsons, ran his hand along the microphone shaft—"given the fact that it's a holiday, make it an unusual time for sailing. My questions are: First, are you attempting to avoid more public protest by sneaking out over the weekend? Second, isn't this diving expedition—laudable as the goals described by

Dr. Tooms may be—really a cover for the ecological damage to the bay caused by your new ships and shore facility?"

"Very fine, my friend." Starring paused; he had their attention. "On the timing of the *Towerpoint Partner*'s departure, that has been set to mesh with the launching of the Chesapeake Divequest International expedition. The *Partner*'s pioneering run, her delivery to our new bay LNG facility, and the arrival of the ship you are now aboard, the *Towerpoint Octagon* with her embarked expedition, mark two significant new pages in this nation's seafaring history. These ships will salute each other in the best maritime tradition as the *Partner* stands down the bay and the *Octagon* delivers her scientific team to the bay floor over the Fourth of July holiday. The timing, Jerry, my friends, marks a page in history."

"Now, tuning to the goals of the expedition: As my colleagues from the leading research institutes on the bay will confirm, we have consulted closely. One cannot invest too much in the marine research that gives us the data, the baselines, the knowledge we require if we are to understand the marine environment from the creek marshes and coastal wetlands to the deepest ocean toughs . . . if we and future generations are to enjoy this bay's bounty"—his hand chopped the air—"and to take fullest advantage of all that our splendid natural resources hold out to us . . ."

Another voice from across the well: "Mr. Starring, you haven't answered the question. What about the damage your ships . . .?"

"In just a few minutes, you will all be enjoying the most succulent seafood in the word, freshly steamed, chilled blue crab claws from this bay. Towerpoint has followed the development of the bay over many years, studied each new commercial enterprise, fed it into the Towerpoint data base to understand its impact on the bay —nuclear power, the first LNG projects, the challenging, inspiring march out of decay that we have witnessed with the redevelopment of Craney Island, Portsmouth, Hampton Roads, the Patapsco River, and Baltimore. We have analyzed the associated dredging and improvements to aids to navigation required to bring new ships to those ports.

"The Towerpoint ships bringing the sorely needed, clean, natural gas energy from the Yucatan to the mid-Atlantic United States are the best engineered, the finest, pollution-free ships in the world!

Towerpoint would not be here, Mr. Harrison, ladies and gentlemen, if it meant damage to the region!"

● ● • • ·

"Didn't lay a glove on you, Tommie; masterful!"

"Oats, too many people are afraid of their own shadows. We ought to do more of these. People like someone who will take an honest question and give an honest answer." Starring and his chief scientist emerged from the owner's suite and proceeded to the reception.

● ● • • ·

In Yarmouth, it was 3:00 A.M. the following morning. The night desk clerk had had to ring Sweetman's room six times before the bedside telephone had cut through the deep blanket of Lord Nelson lager.

"Telephone call for you, from the States, a Mr. Fisker; shall I put him through?"

"Good, yeah, Fisker?" He waited, clicks on the line, sounded as if the connection was falling through. Lancaster wanted him back in Washington, no time to make the trip to Arbroath, Scotland. He had called Fisker on the open trans-Atlantic commercial line as soon as he and Harry Jones had parted company, told him that business was good, new orders coming in for Trade, prospect for more in Scotland. The Trade Washington office should put a call through to jarhead Tully, should find his address in the forty-fifth group of the customer printout, tell him Trade wished to be of service. "Fisker? Yeah, what have you got?"

"Mr. Tully is delighted to learn of your interest, sir, and is looking forward to hearing from you. He wanted you to know that their new address is double two, not thirty-seven, that he would be pleased to receive you any time after eight-thirty-five, but that he will be catching a flight at four-eighteen. Otherwise, give him a ring again in two days; he'll be in from nine-fifteen to five-twenty."

"Thanks, Fisker; stay sober." Sweetman hung up, copied the chain of numbers down a second time, this time more neatly, and extracted the telephone number Fisker had neatly laced in them. Sweetman checked out at dawn and had the green Jaguar coupe halfway back to London before he pulled off the road and searched out a pay phone.

Fisker had done his advance work well. The Royal Marine colonel knew who was calling and why. His account of the TOPIC rig disaster meshed with all the other pieces Sweetman had assembled—a different slant, more authoritative and less sudsy than that of Harry Jones, and as Harry had predicted, there was more to be learned about the tragedy of the diver's family.

"I was told last night, out in Yarmouth, that Mrs. Renfro killed herself?"

"That is correct, unfortunately."

"And, I was told that there was only one kid, a girl, and that she's disappeared?"

"No, I think I can help you there. Again, unfortunately, your information is not quite right. There was one surviving member of the family, Leslie. But, she is not a girl, very much a grown woman. I am not so sure that she has disappeared, but, given my affection for John and his wife, it does trouble me to think what may have become of her."

"How do you mean, Colonel?"

"Even before her parents' deaths, she had fallen in with new acquaintances—a summer vacation, touring the Continent, France, Holland, Germany. I recall her father being quite worried about her new, radical ideas—"

"Anyone in particular?"

"No, there I have no idea."

"You say France, Holland, Germany" —Sweetman subconsciously touched the copies of the letters still folded in his breast pocket— "were any of these new friends in Amsterdam? Do you think she's in Amsterdam?"

"I am sure she had been through Amsterdam, Mr. Sweetman. Holland is not that large a country is it? I cannot say for certain where Leslie Renfro is today; not a case of her disappearing. Quite possibly, she is on the Continent. In fact, I heard some time ago from a mutual acquaintance of the Renfros that she had been taken in by John's brother and his wife in Malta."

The tip of Shostak's metal rule reemerged in Sweetman's mind. He returned to the coupe and encoded a message that would pass from London to Fisker for Pierce.

• • • • • **Chapter 12** • • • • •

"I'll be damned if I know what the hell blew those cameras!"

"Don't worry about them. The replacements will be here next week. We will keep meticulous logs; there is really no need for the television monitors, you know."

Tooms cuffed one of the dead overhead monitors, "You're right, Princess. Damned near see us from the surface as it is." He ducked beneath the CO_2 scrubbers, flipped open the catches on the face of the charcoal air filter and, satisfied with his inspection, snapped the face back into place. His forearm swiped at the sweat trickling down his face. It was hot and humid in the metal cylinder despite the cold air being blown through the access trunk from the mother ship. He glanced at his partner, Leslie Renfro, running through the habitat's main electrical board checklist. Cool as a cucumber; how the hell does she do it? Aboard the catamaran she had the reputation of a perfectionist. In Malta, during the crossing, she had driven Tooms and the rest on every phase of the expedition.

On the curving bulkhead over the worktables of the habitat's laboratory space, she had mounted the charts of the expedition site, the salinity tables, the sediment tables showing the clayey-silt overlaying the fine-grained sand of the bay floor, phytoplankton tables, bar charts summarizing the sources and trends of pollution over the past decade, and depth, tides, and current charts. Her large-scaled chart of the site's oyster bar, with a clear plastic overlay of the research grid lines to be run during the first days' underwater work, was taped to the worktable.

With Tooms, she had modified the layout of the habitat, with the storage space previously reserved for scores of oxygen and helium bottles during deeper saturation dives turned over to the equipment of the bay dive: cases of sample bottles, instruments shipped in from the local institutions, a five-drawer file cabinet, tubular steel spools holding thousands of feet of braided buoyant nylon line to be carried underwater, paid out from the work chariots' cargo decks during the Phase One construction of the grids, and the large white cylindrical canisters marked RENFRO RESEARCH.

This gear was stowed at the end of the habitat furthest from the access trunk. Closer to the trunk, on the right side of the chamber, the laboratory was neatly placed, together with the banks of meters, panel lights, and switches for atmospheric control and treatment, electrical power, illumination, and communications with the surface support ship.

Crew quarters lined the left side of the cylinder, curtained, double-decked bunks, clothes lockers, a compact galley, curtained shower and toilet, and a large open-faced locker for wet suit storage. On the bulkhead beside the heavy rubber diving gear, tables spelled out the number of divers' decompression stops required from bottom to surface, a safety measure she had taken even though the expedition would be limited to average depths of forty feet or less, with no danger of nitrogen buildup.

Six thick, conical, acrylic plastic viewports dotted the habitat's steel pressure hull. The steel grid dock for the work chariots was hinged into place on the exterior of the habitat's base and lashed against the hull for lowering into the bay. When the habitat was below the catamaran, with its footings solidly on the bay floor, the docking deck would be opened at a right angle to the access trunk, permitting efficient transfer of divers and gear between the habitat and the submersibles.

"This freeze-dried food reads right fine in the press kits—"

"Starring feels his press conference was a success?"

"Flawless. We're sitting pretty, Princess—on location, big splash already on the nets, the glossy weeklies still to come, a month's breathing space. As I was saying, I don't know about you, but I'm having steak and trimmings catered from topside." Tooms surveyed the interior of the freezer, closed the brushed-chrome door. He gave the entire interior another slow look. "She's in good shape, ready to go." He stopped at the bulkhead dividing the bunks from the main working spaces. Full-profile line drawings of the *Towerpoint Partner* and *Towerpoint Mayan* were mounted above the navigator's charts of the northern and southern halves of the bay. She had covered every phase, recorded the tankers' schedules, plotted their projected tracks in the bay's main channel, the site and timing of the ceremonial links with the big ships, which Starring attached so much importance to . . . what detail had she missed? . . . What detail? Goddammit, not like her to have those cameras out, and what the hell purpose does some of that detail serve?

They troubled him from time to time, these Maltese dolphins. Mixed in with their good work were the hours they remained closeted in her cabin. His cynicism—his envy—had tried to write it off to another generation's morals, group sex. But not day after day. Jesus . . . a hard trio to fathom . . . her bolts of crusading language, some sort of hybrid Carrie Nation/Joan of Arc . . . goddamned expressions on Tonasi and Head, looked like they both belonged behind bars half the time . . . hard to fathom. They were getting the job done; he suppressed the fleeting dark thoughts.

"Leslie"—Tooms plopped down on one of the stools at the lab table—"what you have going for you is your modest ability to do everything! You've got this show under control; it's a smash hit. Starring's pleased. I owe you one hell of a lot. Goddammit it's hot . . . stun a Finn in this sauna." He snatched up a towel, blotted his head and neck. "The thing of it is, you're a throbber, a real throbber. There's no rest in you, and . . . " His eyes caught the cameras again, the questions returned. "Christ!" He lumbered to his feet, wrestling with the need not to question, not to insult. "You know, I watch those hands of yours; things come alive in them. I swear you could turn lead to gold."

She received his floundering words with a cool smile of attentive silence. It had taken years, the discipline of the huntress and the hunted. She had learned that discipline, how to lock her emotions away, to pursue her quarry. She had steered Head and Tonasi to the new target. Together, they had allowed Tooms and Starring to create their roles. Now, they were positioned. She listened, and when Tooms had finished his ramble of affection, she smiled. "The habitat *is* set, Oats. We should be back on deck; it's much fresher there . . .

high time to sink this can, that is what you call it?" She slipped down through the access trunk, back onto the deck of the catamaran.

● ● ● ● ●

The swallow-tailed white and blue, signal Alfa/Alpha flag, 'I have a diver down, keep well clear' was at the *Towerpoint Octagon*'s yard when the habitat began its bubbling descent into the translucent green-brown of the bay. The cables of the ship's crane paid out until the cylinder's legs settled on the bottom, stirring a cloud of sediment which spread to the surface and carried away on the current.

Four divers in scuba gear—Head, Tonasi, and two members of the ship's crew—went below in inspect. The legs were squarely on the bottom with the access trunk well clear. Head's voice came up on the radio from inside the cylinder, reporting the status. If topside agreed, they would set the work chariots' docking platform.

Tooms gave the go-ahead. In twenty minutes, they were back on the surface and lifted aboard. Tooms scratched out a quick message reporting the first success to Starring, who had already departed for New York with Tina and her coach, having left strict instructions with the chief scientist for detailed status reports on every evolution prior to his return on the evening of July 2.

In the early afternoon, they were on deck again. "Well, my mermaid and two boys on a dolphin, we're ready to roll, July first, on target, damned proud of you." The ship's crew secured the crane slings to the first of the work chariots. Still on deck, Renfro and Tonasi prepared to climb into one submersible, Tooms and Head into the other. The results of weeks of intensive preparation crystallized in the crisp responses to the pre-dive checklist.

"Emergency ballast secure?"

"Secure."

"Main propulsion clear?"

"Propulsion clear."

"Rudder clear?"

"Rudder clear."

"Diving planes clear?"

"Planes clear

"Structural damage?" Their hands and eyes ran along the sixteen-foot hulls, including the bottoms.

"Clean."

"Marker buoys secure?"

"Secure."

"Salvage lift padeye?"

"Padeye clear."

"Cargo deck, clamps, clear?

"Clear."

The checklist moved to the interior of the open fore-and-aft, two-seater cockpits. In each submersible, the pilot faced forward, the crew aft. A manipulator arm was fitted to the rounded bullet nose of each craft. From the bows, the smooth hulls ran to the cockpits, rising on the upper surfaces in streamlined, hydrodynamic contouring, providing for the instrument panel housing.

The two compartments of each cockpit were divided by a narrow bulkhead, wide enough to house reserve oxygen supply, contoured to receive the back-mounted twin scuba tanks of the divers. By facing aft, the crew had ready access to the cargo deck. A green light, button-activated, on the panel of each compartment provided the visual, intracrew communications, with the numbered sequences of flashes indicating forward, stop, submerge, and surface.

"Batteries?" Tooms boomed out the checklist item. The gauges flicked positive for each of the eight, silver-zinc batteries packed in oil in their compartments at the base of the hulls. "Batteries check."

The calling of the list and the responses continued: instrument panel illumination, sonar, gyrocompass navigation display, depth gauge, emergency ballast release, diving planes controls, rudder control, throttle, reserve air supply, external light forward, and light aft.

"Manipulator?" The two chariot skippers reached forward, flicked the activator switches. Both of the three-jointed metal claws mounted on the bows went through their exercises. A push forward on the control, and the hydraulic command sent the claw in an outward reach with smooth extension of the finely machined metal wrist, elbow, and shoulder. A retraction of the control, and the arm folded back against the submersible. A turn to the left, and the metal wrist rotated to the left. A thumb pressed on the "pickle" in the center of the control knob, and the claw opened, thumb released, the claw closed. "Manipulator check."

"Hopleaf?" Tooms stomach was shaking with laughter beneath the wetsuit. They checked one another's diving gear; they were ready for the water. The slings were secured to the second work chariot. The crane operator tested the double load, raised the submersibles a foot above the deck . . . rigging sound, raised them higher, then up over the railing into the center well. The blue-and-gold hulls grew smaller, seemingly more fragile, as they dropped through the shadows between the hulls. The operator again jockeyed his controls, testing their buoyancy on the surface. They rode well and were rafted either side of the catamaran's work boat.

"A nice breeze, surface is calm; your expedition is underway, Dr. Tooms." She and Tonasi stepped easily into the creases of the two slings the crane had returned from the well and rode down to the surface. The slings returned for the other team.

"Taking on ballast, going to operational buoyancy."

The trim tanks filled with bay water until the submersible rode with only the panel fairing, the tip of the rudder, and the divers' heads and shoulders above the surface.

"Propulsion."

"Propulsion." The work chariots' propellers responded instantly to the command of the electric motors. They eased forward, clear of the work boat. A Towerpoint photographer worked both still and motion picture cameras recording the official start.

"This ain't the Mediterranean. Turbid's an understatement, more like minestrone soup. Use your heads. Stick to the game plan; get used to traveling surfaced"—Tooms bellowed his instructions—"then we'll take 'em down and run them through their paces." They slid out into the bay.

Constant shoreline erosion and influx of river sediment combined with the rich marine plant and animal life to create the murk which limited visibility beneath the surface. The low yield of ambient light, the apparent contradiction with the bay's bountiful yields, were central to Phase One of the expedition. Visibility targets would be arrayed above the nylon grids to be suspended just above the bay floor. The submarine photography would be taken systematically, then shipped to the institutes to be processed and catalogued by date, time, location, and reading. In parallel, during Phase One, the divers would collect subsurface water samples, and measure the dissolved oxygen, salinity, and temperature . . . the ingredients of the minestrone.

The water swirled past Leslie's shoulders; the submersible felt easy in her hands. She cut away from Head and Tooms, scanning the navigational displays arrayed across the instrument panel. She was running northwest, paralleling the Western Shore, with the luminous, magnified bubble face of the magnetic compass swinging between 330 degrees and 335 degrees. The miniaturized gyrocompass was a showpiece product of Towerpoint ocean engineering, shipped out to Malta during the fitting out for the expedition. The submersible's heading appeared in the form of a grid display on the center of the panel, with high-intensity yellow-green light beaming the readout across two feet of water to the eyes of the pilot.

To the right of the gyrocompass, a second rectangular display, in high-intensity orange for contrast, gave the submersible's location in relation to the network of sonar buoys, which had been anchored at the trapezoidal corners of the expedition's site as soon as the *Towerpoint Octagon* had steadied on her anchors.

The hard sole of her neoprene boot pressed down on the starboard rudder control. The grid displays flashed the new headings; the compass swung through 355 to 0 to 15 degrees. The motor fed more power, with increased throttle. The pressure and gurgle of the surface water increased. The work chariot was now at four knots, maximum speed. She throttled back, then gave the submersible maximum speed again. The displays held steady. She was satisfied; it was sound.

At the end of the first hour, the two work chariots lay still in the water on either side of the work boat, five hundred yards from the catamaran. Following a conference, the teams were underway again, the first to the north, the second to the south to minimize collision risk.

Tonasi gave his mask a reflex adjustment with the "submerge" signal of the communications light. They were a third of a mile from the main channel in forty feet of water. The light of the subsurface faded rapidly as the submersible dove to twenty-five feet. She held at that depth, steering a course from south to west. The cool pressure of the bay forced past them, the rhythmic inhale/exhale of their regulators, the flickering readouts of the instruments, and the nudging play of the foot and hand controls shaping the submarine world in which they were traveling.

She surfaced, running at three knots, the blue and white catamaran a small dark triangle to the north. Tonasi pushed out of his seat and turned against the flow of the water. He pressed his mouth close to the side of her head. "She's good! She's good!"

The pilot gave a vigorous nod, swung the work chariot toward the main channel, still running on the surface. Another dark form was on the horizon. Tonasi saw it at the same time she did. She altered course, jerked her thumb down, hit "submerge," and the chariot dove. She leveled at fifteen feet, the bright green-and-orange displays playing before her as they pushed through the dark-green wall of water. They ran for five minute before she surfaced again.

The loaded black-and-ocher hull of the ladened, oncoming ore carrier lay ahead, off to the right. She altered course, went down to fifteen feet and leveled. The run continued in the blindness. Her pulse thumped against the wetsuit. She bit on the mouthpiece, held her breath steady, eyes locked on the displays, suppressing the urge to surface.

The first faint throbbings of the big ships propeller and machinery cut through the rush of the water. The noise built quickly, steadily, as the submersible pressed ahead. Her left foot punched the rudder control. The compass spun from 30 back to 355 degrees. The water darkened. The thrashing of the propeller crashed in their heads as the first turbulence of the passing hull enveloped the chariot. They rolled sideways, down into the darkness, leveling at forty feet with another fifty feet still beneath them in the main channel. She brought the chariot around to 270 degrees, eased back on the joystick bringing the chariot on a gliding ascent to the surface. The ship's green-and-black stack spewed a trailing black smoke which half obscured the stern.

"Japanese." He was again at her shoulder. She spat out her regulator, pushed her mask back on her forehead. The submersible was running surfaced for the catamaran. "Handles better than I had expected, Filippo, sensitive—"

"I was up, on my feet, both hands on the cargo deck from the first sound of the screws . . ."

She twisted against her back tanks to look at him. "And?"

"Okay, okay. Locked my legs against the curve of the cockpit; I can work." He gave her shoulders a squeeze. "Here the bastards come." The catamaran crew had spotted them; the work boat was closing rapidly.

"One or two more dives—plenty of battery!" She had to shout over the boat's diesel exhaust. "We have time?" She checked her watch, shaded her eyes against the sun.

"Plenty of time. We lost you for a while, there. Glad to hear no problems. Dr. Tooms and the second sub made one dive, had to haul her out of the water again. Steering wasn't answering the way it should."

"They alright?"

"Yep, nothing too serious."

"Thank you for keeping an eye on us; we're off again." The boat skipper gave her a thumbs up, backed, and swung in a return loop for *Octagon*.

In the murk of the bay, the external lights of the submersibles had one purpose, to assist in the mating and decoupling with the dock. The chariot took the descent slowly, touched forward first, settled on both of the semicircular cradles. Tonasi was in the water working his way forward, around the hull, clamping the four mooring hooks. With the lights extinguished, the darkness was almost total. They felt their way across the grating toward the glow of the trunk, emerged in the dry, bright interior of the habitat.

Leslie hung up the intercom, threw a blanket across her shoulders, slumped onto a bunk and stared at the deck, exhausted by the run. "They should keep up there for a few minutes. Tooms was babbling away more than unusual."

"Paulo did well." Tonasi yanked off his hood, combed his hair with his fingers, and rubbed his eyes and whiskered face. "Take time to repair that pin, fucked up until tomorrow, next day maybe? We've got time, don't we, Les?"

"We have to move. Tooms is excited, unpredictable. His last words were that he would stay above, but, I don't trust him—"

"He's a pig, full of pig shit!" Tonasi was at the far end of the habitat. "A pig! How much longer?"

"Two days. We strike on the third."

He rolled one of the white cylinders to the center of the deck space. "Two fucking days. He'll be the first!" They were on their knees, warriors with impassive expressions. "Up on the bunk, have to turn her over, panel's on the other side." Tonasi braced one leg against a steel upright. They eased the fifty-kilo antiship mine onto its back. He studied the streamlined form, sucking in air, approving through his broken teeth.

The mine was new, designed for the U.S. Navy's SEAL teams. Its bloodlines ran back for more than four decades to the early days of the Second World War . . . to the limpets strapped to the waist of a swimmer, clamped to the bilge keels of the enemy's ships. The limpets had left no trace. Their victims had sunk or been scuttled no matter how good the submarine nets or the deck watches.

Tonasi removed the access panel, set it on the deck. His mind lingered over his suppressed hatred of Tooms. The screwdriver spun in his fingers. He released the timing mechanism from "lock-storage." Malta, the *Matabele* should be in Capri by now. "*Matabele* in Capri?" His eyes flicked to hers with the question. "Take this." She held the timer, keeping her fingers away from the numbered wheels.

"Angelo said two to three weeks."

"He will do it faster. She's in Capri."

"You are right Filippo. They should have her there."

She passed the plate back, watched as his scarred brown fingers set it in place, tightened the screws, turned to the second, propeller-activated timer. He removed packing from the tapered end of the mine. A circular shroud housing a small, bronze, three-bladed propeller was freed by his action. He turned the propeller slowly with one finger, studied a second set of dials. "Not hard to build . . . see, the shaft, gland seal, direct drive of the timer from the push of the water." He set to work on the second, delayed-timing mechanism: this one elapsed knots rather than hours. "Minex Bravo, Les, this explosive." He patted the shape. "Makes TNT look like sneezing powder, go through a tanker like a bullet."

Her mind went to the night kill in Geneva. She had seen his eyes beneath the mask . . . intensity, not emotion. The bullets were of no significance to him when he had closed for the kill. His young life was soaked in the acrid smoke of high explosive. For him, each murder was justified by the act itself, each shedding of blood, a retribution for a great, dimly defined evil.

Tonasi finished with the dual activators. "Thirty-two hours, right, Les?"

"Strike plus thirty-two. We want the first to blow in the open ocean, after the strike on the second. They detonate together."

"She'll blow."

"You can handle the mines?"

"She'll blow. You get me there. These were designed to be delivered by swimmer vehicles—not heavy when you're in the water. These grips, I keep the fat end facing me. The mine rides on the pallet, magnets down, insulated by the wood . . . for how long? Ten minutes? Fifteen minutes? When we submerge, I hit the activators." His hand skipped from one to the other. "When the tanker takes us and we start to close, I cast off the last tie-down, wait . . . until we have the hull. When I hit 'surface,' the mine will be on the hull. She'll blow."

•••• Chapter 13 ••••

The *Towerpoint Partner* slid under the twin spans of the Chesa-peake Bay Bridge at 10:00 A.M. on July 3, four bells clanging in the wheelhouse, precisely on schedule for the down-bay rendezvous. She and her sister ship, the *Towerpoint Mayan*, had been designed and built for the Chesapeake-Campeche run, the ultramodern, hybrid creations of Starring's naval architects.

The streamlined bow of the nine-hundred-ninety-foot ship pushed cleanly through the bay with only the thinnest of curling white bow waves peeling off to port and starboard. To hold to schedule, she was loafing along at twelve knots, half her normal operating speed, only token demand on the fifty-thousand-shaft-horsepower gas turbine power plant driving her single, twenty-four-foot, five-bladed bronze-alloy propeller. At the foot of her bow, beneath the water's surface, the hull extended forward in a protruding bulbous nose shaped to mold the flow of oncoming water encountering the enormous hull.

Above the waterline, the tanker and her sister looked like no other ships in the world. Their paint was the Towerpoint scheme, midnight-blue with block-gold lettering on hull and stacks, white superstructure. From the forward lookout mast, the main deck stretched back eight hun-dred feet, its surface curving upward from sides to centerline to sculpt the housing for the six cylindrical holds which carried the liquefied natural gas. This long white housing was topped by port and starboard catwalks and bordered by deck cranes and machinery for the loading and offloading of her cargo.

The *Partner*'s slim superstructure and twin smokestacks rose behind the cargo housing, with the hull, seen from either side, continuing aft main-deck high for another one hundred twenty before chopping off in a clean perpendicular cut at the stern. Viewed from her churning wake, the tanker's stern revealed a raised barge-lift elevator recessed between the sides of her hull. A snub-nosed pusher tug was secured athwartship on the elevator. Barges loaded with machinery and supplies for the Campeche gas field and port-support facility rode forward of the tug. The *Partner* and the *Mayan* helped to produce the gas they hauled.

The *Partner*'s second home port had been carved from the Campeche Banks, where the west coast of the Yucatan Peninsula curves north from the State of Tabasco, along the Gulf of Campeche, before opening out onto the Gulf of Mexico. Inland from the banks, their lagoons and sand dunes, the peninsula bakes hot and dry. For centuries, only the Mayan pyramids at Uxmal and Chichen Itza had risen above the swamps and porous soil as the only heritage and visible reminder of a greater life. For generation after generation, the peons had scratched the poorest of existence from that land, harvesting the tough-fibered leaves for the manufacture of sisal rope, twine, and sacking.

In the 1970s, new pyramids of structural steel had sprung from the land and coastal waters of Mexico. To the north, in a belt running from Monterrey to Reynosa, lay the first major discoveries of gas. To the south, in Chiapas, Tabasco, and the Gulf of Campeche, production crews had driven the drilling bits of their towering rigs into the earth to tap the expanding oil and gas reserves.

Towerpoint International had stayed on the fringes. The exploration and production had continued, and the economics continued to turn, until Tommie Starring struck the deal he wanted, then presided in person at the laying of the *Partner* and *Mayan* keels. From the outset, the entire operation had been designed as self-sufficient.

The Campeche gas flowed from the off-shore wells to the liquefaction plant on the Yucatan coast, where it was transformed by refrigeration into liquid at minus 270 degrees and pumped through insulated pipes into the ships' insulated cylindrical tanks.

The *Partner* was steaming in ballast now, her first cargo already pumped ashore to expand more than five hundred times into gas again, and her tanks purged with inert nitrogen to reduce the risk of explosion. She moved without a tremor through the bay. The ship's master cocked an eye at the blue sky, and handed the message board back to his second officer. "We have a good day. Have the deck crew rig the bunting from the starboard catwalk. We'll want nothing adrift this afternoon. This young lady will be on camera. Make sure there's a good, full belly to each bunting loop. You've read the instructions on flags?"

"Yes sir—the national colors, Mexican flag, house flag—and the swallow-tailed 'mission accomplished' pennant from the forward mast."

The pilot stood beside them, smiling a sympathetic smile as he listened to the exchange. He had been briefed on the pass-in-review before boarding.

The *Partner* continued south past the long line of empty ore carriers riding high at anchor. Her great blue hull glistened with reflected sunlight from the surface of the bay. Figures appeared along the ships' railings to watch her pass. The master took the clipboard from its rack beside his chair, began to draft:

FOR TOWERPOINT OCTAGON, HONORABLE THOMAS STARRING, CHAIRMAN OF THE BOARD, TOWERPOINT INTERNATIONAL.

1. TOWERPOINT PARTNER, ENROUTE GULF OF CAMPECHE, FIRST CARGO DELIVERED ON SCHEDULE, SALUTES TOWERPOINT OCTAGON ON COMMENCEMENT CHESAPEAKE . . .

He hesitated, searched for the page with the title, continued:

DIVERQUEST INTERNATIONAL EXPEDITION.

2. HONORED TO BE MEMBER, TOWERPOINT INTERNATIONAL TEAM. VERY RESPECTFULLY, J.A. WILHELMSTEAD, MASTER.

The *Partner*'s radio officer received the master's instructions to transmit the message on first sighting of the Towerpoint flagship.

● ● · · ·

At the dawning of July 3, Starring thought back to the *Partner*'s keel laying when he awoke aboard the *Octagon* . . . the shaping of the new venture, the bands, the bunting, the one-hundred-ton keel sections being lowered into the graving docks. He had kept the pressure on, ignoring the squeaks of the timid. The LNG operation was now a fact, a new, black profit bar of projected revenue in the stockholders' report.

Martin Tambling had died the day before, heart attack on the street, a tough competitor, the news a shock. Starring's heart was steady. He could feel it as he tossed the sheet and blanket aside and sat for a moment on the edge of the bed. He didn't like Tambling's death, the reminder of mortality. So much to be done, so much— needs brains, guts, stamina. Tina worried about his health, the steady strain. She'll be dead long before me. He turned on his bed light, flipped through the advance copy of her new Playbill. It had been with his papers when he returned from New York the night before. Good photo; she was working hard, would have a success . . . the cover, a splash of paint, made no sense.

While he shaved and dressed, his mind was already twenty-four hours ahead, rehearsing his meeting with the president. With the development of Sea Star, he was reaching a generation into the future, in platforms, hulls, technology, the entire engine of ocean enterprise. He bathed his eyes with cool water, toweled his face and neck. He had to chart the route to the next higher peak from the summit on which he alone now stood. This he would share with the president and seek his guidance.

The owner's deck was shining with the earlier rain when he took his first deep breath of air rich with moisture and the sea-smells of the bay. Puffs of fast-moving gray clouds, the tail of the storm, were blowing to the east. As they thinned, wave tops shimmered silver in the emerging sunlight. From the far side of the bay, the faint engine coughings of boats still beneath the storm carried across to the catamaran. He took his binoculars from the bulkhead case. Commercial crab potters, three of them, were working separately in the quiet of the holiday Sunday, one waterman to each of the long, low white wooden hulls.

Their boats were stacked with wire crab pots, a yard to a side in size, already baited with menhaden, each pot rigged with a coil of line and a marker float for retrieval later in the day. Only the engines' *pock pock* reached his ears. The pots went silently over the side, leaving a lengthening line of white dots bobbing on the surface.

On the foredecks, the crew was readying the catamaran for the day's ceremonies. The string of signal flags was run up the dressing line to the masthead. Starring followed the ascent of the uppermost flag. There was blue sky above the mast, fair weather. It would be Towerpoint International's day.

● ● ● · ·

Filippo Tonasi prayed in the darkness of his cabin in the predawn of July 3. The words, their utterance, the ceremony had stayed with him from childhood. Neither religion nor fear brought the prayers. The words were spoken to honor the importance of the day. He rose from his knees, rolled a doped cigarette, and stuck it behind an ear, to smoke on deck before they dived. He rolled a second and leaned back on his bunk, sucking each drag of smoke deep into his lungs.

Paul Head was in the facing bunk, asleep, chest down, head to one side, one eye partly opened with only the white showing, the hand beside his face clenching, relaxing. He was at the railroad station in Geneva, on the platform, attempting to board his train. People, Swiss, were crushing against him, shaking their heads at his clothes: the coat, tie, and black wetsuit pants. The conductor was speaking French loudly at him, waving his hands in his face, barring his access to the steps of the waiting train. The faces on the train were African, silent, watching, pressed against every window.

Head had his ticket, his passport outstretched. The conductor hit them away. Steam hissed from the cars' undercarriages, exciting the crowd, driving him back. His voice—he was shouting. His father had pushed through the crowd and was glowering at him . . .

Tonasi sucked in smoke, watched the fluttering eyelid, the hand —"Paulo! Zulu!" He gave the blond head a shove. The lids opened, the eyeball rolled into place. Head jammed his face into the mattress, then pushed up from the bunk, struggling to awake.

"What were you up to, Zulu—at the castle, trouble with the queen?"

Head was sitting up, his face blankly absorbing the cabin. He stuck out a thumb and forefinger. Tonasi passed him the cigarette. He hunched forward, the smoke circling around his eyes, the coal glowing from his lips. "Fuck you."

Leslie Renfro was ready when they knocked. She had slept until four o'clock, then arisen to prepare. She had rubbed lanolin deeply into her face, arms, legs, and body to fend against the hours of submergence. As her hands worked the heavy oil into her flesh, the fleeting happiness, death, horror, awakening, and revenge of her lifetime drove her subconsciously. Her mind again rehearsed each minute of the coming day.

The three walked along the floodlit open decks to the galley. Theirs were familiar faces. The crew went about its business. They drew coffee from the urn and drank in silence.

"Big day today?" A cook slid a plate of glazed brown rolls before them with his greeting.

"Fucking right, mate," Head answered across the lip of his mug. She waited while they smoked. When she rose, the two men followed. They shed their shoes and coveralls, returned them to their cabins. Most of the *Octagon* was still asleep, the bridge watch unaware. One by one, they climbed the center well ladder. Only the rubber fenders of the surface support float squeezing and complaining against the hull plating broke the still of the hour.

Above them, through the crane, Venus was at its brightest. They dove, each with a hand on the toggled intervals of the marker guideline, down to the faint circular glow of the habitat's access trunk.

"Stale!"

"Smells like bloody Italy." Head ran a hand across the atmosphere exchange panel, purged the canned atmosphere with fresh air from the surface. Tonasi stood naked in the center of the deck. She had already shed her suit, accepting their eyes, then pulled on thermal long underwear. The sweet smell of talcum mixed with the fresh flow of air. They lubricated the inner lining of their wetsuit bottoms with the powder, pulled them on.

"Another day with your fat friend, eh Paulo?"

"Shut up!" Her command brought silence. She covered the length of the cylinder, checked the mikes to make sure they were in their hooks, that they would not be overhead. The second hand on the bulkhead chronometer ticked past 5:30. She spun on both of them, eyes flashing, voice controlled. "Break out the weapons. Check them, pack them in the transfer container. We will want to take them up with us to the ship when we return."

Head and Tonasi wrestled with the fourth heavy cylinder, cracked its seals, laid out their arsenal on two of the bunks. They stripped and reassembled each piece, matching weapons with ammunition. With combat nearing, Head, without a word, took the first pistol, stuffed it into his nylon bag at the foot of the bunk. Bloody nuts to keep all the guns together. While they worked, she took them through the mission.

"Tooms is the one we have to watch out for. His routine has not varied when Starring has been aboard. He will sleep until six-thirty; be sent for at seven-thirty to hold Starring's hand, embroider on the lies they feed upon. He will find a note from me on his desk, which he will search for and find after Starring asks about our plans.

"This will happen at nine. He will call down. I will tell him that we are heading out, working off the Western Shore, laying the first lines of the grid. He will be worried, because of Starring, but he is obsessed with that grid and the productivity experiment, so he will be pleased—"

"One more day for pleasure!" Tonasi slapped home the twenty-round magazine, fitted the silencer to the machine pistol. "One more . . ."

"Tooms's pleasure will be brief—the concern that we may not be back in time for today's obscenity. I will tell him that we will be there. When we are not, there will be a second call. He won't be able to come down at that point, to leave Starring before their ships pass. You will take that call, Paul. You will tell him you are supporting us, that we are on a second run. We have had luck. We should have an entire grid completed today—and, he will know that this will be far more important to Starring's interests than our presence on deck.

"If he presses you, tell him that you and he should resubmerge the second submersible for a test run as soon as he is free. He may or may not decide that is what he wants to do. If I am wrong, Paul, if he decides to make an appearance, he will probably call down, first. Whatever he does, stick with your story. We are on the first grid."

They made coffee and rested. It would be light now on the surface. At 8:55, the call came from Tooms to Renfro. Starring had him in the traces topside, perplexed about their decision to make the grid run. See them in two to three hours . . .

"He's out of the way. The tanker is enroute, on schedule."

"He does good work for a pig." Tonasi clamped his arms around her, hugged her hard, and kissed the back of her neck. "You are a hungry hunter. You want that ship. I will get her for you. Breathe, Les, breathe. Relax. I will get her for you!" He let her go. The tension was broken. Together they traced the route on the chart of the main channel.

"They are planning to pass as close as possible. They navigate at all times at load depth, thirty-eight feet, even though the ship is in ballast. Allowing for shipping in the opposite direction, the tanker will be exactly here"—she made a mark on the chart, moved the calipers to the chart scale—"when abreast of the catamaran, closest point of contact—we will be here—the shoreline, from here to here." She placed the calipers beside the chart. "I *know*—we will sink this ship. You have to do everything required to achieve this victory. You have lived among these criminals. You have endured them to make this possible. By tomorrow night, your *victories* will be known to the world. Three swift cuts of the guillotine will have ridded the world of a criminal! You will lift the hearts of all in the struggle, and you will strike *terror* in the oppressors. What we do today and tomorrow is more than anything before. Our victory, the justice, will be remembered long after we are dead."

"Paul, Filippo. The ship today is only the first blow. We have thirty-six more hours. Keep your heads. Do not reveal today's action in any way. My body will scream to cry out victory, but we cannot. Victory today! Victory tomorrow! Anything less will betray all who hunger for this blow. We cannot fail." She took their hands in an act of communion.

● ● ● · ·

There was one hour, now. Tonasi and Renfro zipped the jackets of their wetsuits, pulled on the hoods, gloves, and buoyancy compensator vests. Head inspected them. They moved the cargo to the deck of the work chariot. Their bodies slithered back and forth from the habitat. At noon, the work chariot rose from its cradle in the darkness of the bay, hovered, then proceeded in a slow circular run, climbing, descending. Head's masked face and clenched fist were illuminated as the chariot passed the habitat and then disappeared instantly, its lights doused.

From his after station, Tonasi kept watch on the cargo, which was riding well. The deep-green canvas sea anchor and surface buoy were lashed to the reel of nylon line. The tail of the line ran forward from a slot on the outer rim of the wheel, along the chariot's hull, through the padeye on the forward deck, to a metal ring in the grip of the claw. The mine rode top up, its shrouded propeller jutting into the cockpit, the powerful magnets insulated from the chariot's cargo grating by the lashed wooden cradle.

Instinctively, Tonasi worked his jaws to compensate for the changing pressure. The water above was a dark gray-green. They were running closer to the surface. He ran a gloved hand across the smooth curve of the mine's shroud, checked his position in the cockpit, the surfaces against which he would lock his legs. He felt no tension.

Only the physical sensations of the submerged run kept his interest before the attack. He allowed his body to bend with the water's steady pressure. His face moved close to the black skin of the mine, the raised white arrows of the settings. The chariot banked to starboard. The water was lighter. Renfro had made the turn east and was climbing on the final run into the main channel.

Renfro's occasional glance at the panel told her what she already knew; they were running smoothly, on course, on schedule. Her watch read twelve minutes into the mission when the bubble compass steadied on 90 degrees. The speed held at four knots. In five minutes she would slow to one knot, recheck her bearings. Life aboard the *Matabele* was finished. They would have to abandon Malta; that had already been decided. As the future fed through her mind, she nudged the joystick, increasing the upward glide of the submersible. The next day they would be ashore, would separate. They had money. Tooms and Starring had seen to that. She throttled back, hit "surface," her thoughts still on their routes out of the country, cover stories, the separate arrivals in northern Europe, the rendezvous in Copenhagen. There they would decide, separate again—permanently?

They were running in pale green. She did not welcome the return of light. The blindness of the submerged run was also its invisibility. Silence enveloped the chariot in its slowing glide. The fathometer reported the increasing depth beneath them . . . eighty, eighty-two, eighty-four, eighty-eight feet. She could see the underside of the surface. It would not be rough, but there would be enough wave action, she could see it, to help conceal them.

Her body tensed with the first sound of the distant thudding. Early! she thought. Immediately, she rejected the notion, adjusted the chariot's trim. As they continued to rise, she forced her head back against the resistance of the tanks, gauging the surface. She did not want the upper blade of the rudder or the curve of the reel and sea anchor exposed. The chariot was steady, hovering. She pulled her legs up and stood on the seat. The wave action was greater than expected. Tonasi was also standing. She gestured upward, climbed into the submersible's compartmented divider. Held firmly by the legs, she studied their location. The thudding—crab boats off to the east—no interference. The red gong buoy marking the far side of the channel was rocking slowly, some five hundred yards to the northeast. She turned; the profile of the *Octagon* was precisely where she wanted it, 180 degrees reverse bearing from the buoy. She turned again . . .

Tonasi felt her dive through his hands. She yanked him down into the cockpit. She had missed spotting the sailboat beating to windward from the southeast. It had been blocked by the rubber sidewall of her mask. When she did see it, the sloop was on them, no more than one hundred yards away, knifing diagonally up the bay. She waited. Forty-five seconds flicked by on her watch; then she stood again.

The yacht had already faded to a small patch of white. There was a merchantman barely visible to the south. They would have at least fifteen minutes. She took the controls, brought them closer to the surface, but she would not risk being spotted by binoculars from the catamaran. She knew their habits; the chariot's hull would stay completely submerged. She thumped Tonasi's tanks; they dodged waves as they spoke.

"The mine?"

"Ready . . . one hour?"

"Less. One ship closing from the south. We should deploy the anchor."

He nodded yes.

"I will run to the north to stretch the line to its fullest. The freighter will have passed. When the line is out, signal."

Both masks and regulators slid back into place. She swung the chariot onto the new course, taking it down to fifteen-foot running depth. The nylon line was attached to the rigid, circular opening of the canvas sea anchor. The anchor, eight feet in diameter, was weighted from the bottom, buoyed at the top to hang suspended at eight-to-ten feet beneath the surface, with only its white flotation buoy on the surface. It was away. Tonasi kept the canvas close to the hull until he was satisfied that the cone had filled and was towing unfouled. With the brake released, the metal reel on the cargo deck began to turn, paying out the line in response to the forward motion. He counted the yellow, one-hundred-foot interval markers emerging slowly. She knew the timing. He felt the chariot slow just before the tenth marker, one thousand feet of line, appeared. They surfaced. The red gong buoy was abeam. The freighter they had anticipated was passing. Another ship was southbound, heading toward them.

"Her?"

"No, container ship. We are well clear. I will run forward. Pay out the last of the line; jettison the reel. We will wait. I want to see her before we cross the channel." They waited, heads above water, masks off, the bright chrome regulators on their chests beneath the surface to avoid betraying glints of sunlight. The vibrations of three passing ships throbbed through the chariot, the waves from the wakes washing over their heads. They waited. Then, they spotted her.

"One-forty-five? The bastards are early?"

"No. She will slow. The planning has called for three knots from the start. I checked that with Tooms and the lot on the bridge."

"Slow and sexy for the great man—good, good for us, Les. She's high in the water, a goddamned wall of bottom paint—okay"

"She's alright. The nose is still beneath the surface. It will catch us."

Tonasi scanned the horizon; a few distant sails, no other ships. "She's dead!"

"Activate switches; prepare to release tie-downs. Take manual control when you feel us begin to tow." They were at their stations. The turns increased on the submersible's propeller. She held it on the northerly course to keep the line taut to the trailing sea anchor.

At 1:50 P.M., the chariot submerged with rudder hard over and swung to an easterly course across the channel.

● ● ● · ·

The message from the *Partner* to the *Octagon* clattered from the catamaran's teleprinter. The communications officer clipped it neatly into a folder and took it to the captain for delivery to Starring, who immediately dictated a glowing response.

"My God, Oats, what a sight; what a stirring sight!" The details of the giant LNG tanker were emerging. She loomed larger and larger in making her slow, stately approach. "Where's your team, the divers? Have them join us. That bunting makes a show against the white. We're having this filmed, aren't we?"

"Three cameras, two motion grinding away, one still, Tommie. Higher duty has called our Maltese porpoises. They went below at the crack of dawn to lay the first research grid—spoke to Leslie a couple hours ago. She promised they'd be up, but they haven't made it yet." Tooms fished in his shirt pocket for a cigarette, preparing for the blast.

"Bad planning, damn it, Oats. I'm damned well not pleased, wanted that shot of the expedition members with the *Partner* in the background—

who the hell can I rely on? Damn it Oats!" He slapped his hands together, turned his attention to the blue hull continuing to build. "Make sure that we get it tomorrow when the *Mayan* makes her pass up the bay—No, damn it, I won't be here. I'll be in Washington, and—I'm going to take that young Renfro with me. Have her see me as soon as they surface."

● ● ● ● ·

Standing on the wing of the *Partner*'s bridge, the pilot took his eyes off the catamaran to glance at the tiny crab pot float off to starboard, cocked at a strange angle . . . looks like it's moving with us . . . tricks of the eye. They were abreast of the *Octagon*, and the tanker's great, bass horn shook the bay in sounding her salute to the Towerpoint flagship. When the salute ended, the baritone of the *Octagon* rolled across in response. The swallow-tailed pennant snaked gracefully from the forward mast. The *Partner*'s master was elated; Starring's message was in his hand.

● ● ● ● ·

The work chariot faced south, hovering six feet beneath the surface, the braided line disappearing to the west through the grip of the manipulator's claw. The slow beat of the *Partner*'s propeller increased in volume, letting them track her approach. Tonasi glared through his mask, ordering his eyes to see the ship they could not see. Forward, Leslie Renfro was concentrating on the instrument panel. She had to maintain depth, to anticipate the split-second maneuvers required when the submersible and ship were joined.

The thump of the blades was so close, so loud, she thought the propel . . . they surged forward! The *Towerpoint Partner*'s bow nose had slipped under the line stretched across the channel at the same time the tanker had thundered its salute. The bow had the line in its teeth, drawing it taut in a vee, bringing the chariot and the sea anchor aft, and in toward the port and starboard sides of the enormous hull.

Pulled by the line in its claw, the submersible fought against its controls, began an arcing slide, then leveled and steadied under its pilot's command. The compass was swinging wildly under the influence of the tanker's hull. The propeller beat was fierce. The tow continued to draw them inward, now in that darker water of the ship's shadow. The chariot pulled hard against the line, yawing, attempting to roll. Strain was tearing at her legs. She bit hard as a sharp jolt of pain shot from arm to arm across her chest. She snapped her head to the side, straining to see through the water . . . the ship had to be there! Nothing! . . . Green blindness, pain! The chariot bucked, fought to roll. She leaned hard against the stick in the turbulence of the tons of water being forced along the sides of the great hull. Then it was there! In the swirling chaos, a wall of orange-red rushed toward them.

The starboard bow plane . . . she knew she had to guard it. She fought for more port rudder, swung the submersible in stern first. Now, now, now! Her mind blocked out the violence engulfing them, screamed out to Tonasi, *Now!* She heard the thud. *Green!* He had hit the surface signal. The mine was on the tanker.

Tonasi had seen the approaching hull first. He was standing, legs braced, half turned, unaware of the weight of the mine he held against his chest. Maybe not? Maybe not? His worry drummed in cadence with the propeller. He had not expected such violence. As the chariot bucked and veered toward the hull, there seemed only one possibility. They would smash. The chariot rolled again—his left elbow! The sea was a tempest. The pain struck so severely he thought his arm had gone, but he still held the mine. With a sharp twist, he reached across the hammering, battering divide, shoved the black shape from his chest, His hands stayed with the mine after impact. He pulled; the magnets held.

At the flash of his signal, she thrust herself half onto the bow, feet locked behind her. With two slices of her knife, the line slipped through the padeye, through the claw, and was gone. She banked the chariot into a long, circling dive away from the leviathan they had just condemned to death.

They surfaced, exhausted, struggling for breath, watching the high, open stern draw rapidly away. Tonasi kissed her hooded head, patted her shoulders. The left sleeve of his wetsuit had torn away at the shoulder. Blood was flowing freely from the gash. His voice was slow, deep. "I'll live. The big one won't. She didn't like having her belly tickled." He took a strap from the cargo rack, wrapped it tightly around his upper arm.

The chariot began its return run, working to the north and west in a methodical zigzag course until they spotted the surface buoy. Tonasi stowed the line beneath him in the aft compartment. The sea anchor came back aboard. They altered course for the *Octagon*, dove, and returned the chariot to its habitat cradle.

• • • • • Chapter 14 • • • • • •

A chalky film of limestone dust settled on Pierce Bromberger's shoes during his walk up the path of crushed white rock winding from the road to the walled residence. The nameplate carried CAPTAIN WILLIAM ROGER RENFRO, DSC, ROYAL NAVY RETIRED in two lines of engraved brass. He rang the dolphin clapper of the bell mounted beside the gate in North Bluff, St. Georges, Malta.

This intrusion on the silence of the Sunday afternoon brought the high answering bark of a dog. Bromberger had Sweetman's message with him. The quest for the Burdette killers had just entered its second month and, finally, the first cracks were beginning to appear. Grabner had been true to his word. His men were excellent. A week before, the Swiss had taken an interest in the activities of a hotel caterer in the resort town of Lugano. He had several vans, one parked at night inside a small garage, others on the street outside his flat. His specialty was Italian delicacies for the Swiss hotel trade. The vans were well known at the border for their regular runs to the markets of Milan, fifty miles to the south. The pattern had begun to vary in June, more runs, different hours. This had not made an impression on the border police until Grabner's special units had reinforced the posts with the sharper eyes, minds, and the newest computers of counterterrorism.

The vans were placed under surveillance but not challenged; their runs to Lugano, Milan, Zurich, Lenx, and Geneva were plotted.

While the number of runs had increased, the number of hotel deliveries had stayed the same. In Geneva, a van had gone twice to the same city garage for gasoline, disappeared down an inner ramp, then reemerged for the return drive to Lugano.

Grabner personally had authorized night entry of the garage. Swiss security then discovered another van under canvas, snap-on license plates, and with hidden storage compartments, including a cargo hold beneath removable floor decking.

The GIS in Rome was given this information. The authorities in Milan observed one of the vans being unloaded from a closed truck on the outskirts of the city. Within less than an hour, the van which had driven from Lugano to Milan was aboard the truck, and its replacement was heading back toward the Swiss border.

This exercise had led the GIS to Naples, Palermo, and a stunning raid forty-eight hours before on the Messina faction. Half the stolen NATO munitions had been recovered, two terrorists killed, and three others captured in the harbor aboard a stolen powerboat. Official silence was maintained. A harsh interrogation had begun.

Bromberger rang the bell again . . . more barking and, this time, a voice. An elderly woman in a white-collared black dress was watching him from the second floor of a neighboring house. Someone, still out of view, was coming. He reread Sweetman's message:

SHATTERED FLAG—FOR BROMBERGER
Pierce—UK investigation has produced lead requiring immediate follow-up. Burdette years loaded with controversy. Findings here have narrowed-in on death of Burdette company diver—name Renfro—R-E-N-F-R-O, killed in TOPIC offshore rig disaster. Wife—name Mary—M-A-R-Y—took life. Rig foreman subsequent victim hit and run. Surviving member Renfro family, daughter Leslie—L-E-S-L-I-E—apxm. 25 years old, left UK following parents' deaths. Subject has history of contacts in Amsterdam, Paris, Berlin. Reliable source indicates subject radical. Source further indicates subject may be residing in Malta with Ret. Navy Capt. William Roger Renfro—W-I-L-L-I-A-M R-O-G-E-R—brother of deceased diver, address North Bluff, St. Georges, Malta.

Based on Rome investigation, reviewed with you and Pitsch, Malta possibly more than coincidence. Essential you interrogate subject soonest. Would handle myself. However, Lancaster has called me on quarterdeck, returning Washington this P.M. Regards, H.S.

"I'll be right back there; be quiet!" The voice called first to Bromberger then to the dog.

"Mr. Bromberger?"

"Pierce Bromberger. Good afternoon, Captain."

"I do apologize for having kept you out here in this sun, and for the misconduct of Mr. Ajax." The elderly man took a gentle swipe at the black-and-white springer spaniel sniffing at the visitor's trousers. Captain Renfro extended his hand; it was cold, with heavy blue veins crisscrossing the bones along the frail white arm.

"Do follow me. We will have our talk on the veranda. I kept you waiting, you know"—he laughed softly, his eyes on the path ahead—"because I couldn't find a slipper. Imagine! Do you know Malta?"

"My first visit."

"Quite a lovely place. My home now. My wife is buried here. The gardens never looked this way while she lived . . . a shambles isn't it?"

He paused, surveyed the half-empty flower beds, the grass in need of a cut. "This is a juniper tree. Do you know juniper?" He broke off a bit of the evergreen and gave it to the American. "Gin! That's what juniper does so well."

He continued toward the house. "This is a lemon, still bearing, and"— he swung his cane toward the next trunk—"a palm; you will know that one from the States." He stopped again, bent slowly to pick up a fallen tan frond. "The one creature who causes us to keep our heads high is lovely lady wisteria." He halted at the edge of the path, his hands planted on the cane, the hollows of his thin face folding into a deep smile. "My wife and I planted lady wisteria when we retired here in St. Georges. My wife fancied lavenders and lilacs—clothes, flowers, jewelry, scent— Lovely, isn't she?" The lush flowers of the great vine twisted and looped across the entire front of the house looking out over the Mediterranean.

"Do have a seat, Mr. Bromberger." Captain Renfro took the chair beside that of his visitor, studied the face. "I shan't offer refreshments; I do not feel up to that. I do apologize, but we will have our talk. Ajax, Ajax!" The dog left Bromberger, lay down beside his master on the cool tiles of the porch.

"Captain Renfro, please do not go to any trouble. If this is inconvenient—"

"No, no. We will have our talk. As I told you this morning on the telephone, you are fortunate to find me here—to find me at all." He nodded and smiled toward his guest, heads and hands trembling. "As I told you, I have just come from the hospital—pneumonia. I dare say, a few of the staff lost a pound or two—that is, a dollar or two—on me. But the fates would seem to have decreed another summer at St. Georges, my last command, sir—HMS *Vegegarden*, greens of course, and tomatoes. They love it here." Captain Renfro drew himself straighter in the lounge chair. "Now, then, Mr. Bromberger, you have asked to talk to me about my niece, Leslie."

"Yes."

"And, if I sounded reluctant this morning to make our appointment it is"—the voice stopped, eyes fluttered closed, his head resting against the creaking caned back of the chair—"because there is so precious little I may tell you about dear Leslie."

"I had been advised, Captain Renfro, that your niece might be living with you. Apparently, she is not. Do you have an address . . . ?"

"Really, Leslie does not have an address here, not in the usual sense. I am not certain, indeed, Mr. Bromberger, if she is in Malta. She most certainly did not visit me while I was in hospital, lest it was while I was unconscious or asleep." He slowly brought himself forward again, struck by the implication of his last remark. "She's a lovely girl, sir, but she has caused me sadness, a sense of frustration, you know, at being unable to do more for her. You say you're a detective?"

"I am conducting an investigation for the U.S. Government, Captain Renfro. Our embassy will vouch for me."

A bony hand raised from the cane to dismiss the words. "That is of no interest to me, sir. You are then aware of my niece Leslie's tragedy?"

"The loss of her parents?"

"Quite so—far more than a loss of parents, you know. It was the harsh, quite violent end to the life in which she had flourished as a child. Her father was my younger brother. We are both Royal Navy . . . although he earned his ration far more honestly, more sweat, bravery, contribution to the Crown than I would dare to claim.

"Leslie's father was a decorated diver in our Navy. He taught her to swim . . . in these waters. At the high point in my career, I was Chief of Staff, Flag Officer Malta, for more years than one might normally expect to serve in that post. My brother, his wife, and daughter would take their annual holiday with us each summer. We did not live in this house then, a bigger house, quite elegant official quarters."

Captain Renfro reflected for a moment, then continued. "My wife and I had no children. My brother's visits were special times for us, and we competed in the fuss we made over Leslie—she was a gorgeous child. When a ship of the fleet was in the Grand Harbor, her uncle would take her aboard. Of course, she was the pet as soon as she set foot on deck. Malta had a cherished place in her childhood, and in our lives. Her father, as your inquiry will have told you, retired, still a young man, and began his second life as a commercial diver. This was at the time when Great Britain had made her vast energy discoveries, very important, and he was very enthusiastic about his new career. They moved to Yarmouth, and that is where he was to die, on the job, in the collapse of the *Topic Universe* oil rig. You have this history?"

"The niece, your niece Leslie, came here when, Captain Renfro?"

"My brother and his wife were deeply in love, sir. Love, I have always believed, is strengthened when there is risk, physical danger present in the marriage. His death caused her to take her life, and Leslie, God bless her, arrived here unannounced within six weeks' time.

"Mind you, Mr. Bromberger, my wife and I had journeyed to Yarmouth for both funerals, such an incredibly grim time. We had urged her to come stay with us, and we were so completely relieved when she arrived. We were ecstatic to have her with us.

"Leslie was in torment, Mr. Bromberger. She refused totally to accept the tragedy. I remember . . . so distinctly, she had chosen to keep her mother's ring. There was no will. Apparently, it was something they had agreed on while the mother lived. Leslie chose to wear her mother's ring as a remembrance. She would brandish it at my wife, at me, when she cried out against her loss . . . when we tried with such inadequacy to console her.

"She was a grown woman by then, of course. I should be clearer with my words. Her mother had left no will. Leslie had a small sum by way of inheritance from her father, what little my brother and his wife had set aside—not much, you will appreciate, from the Navy. She stayed with us for three or four months and then took a flat in Valletta."

"Do you have that address, Captain?"

"Please, please. I shall tell you what little I know. Her address then is not her address now. I will guide your inquiry to the extent I can, sir, and it is for this reason—unless you prefer to end our talk—that I am relating this to you!" The old man's face stiffened with indignation. He awaited his visitor's reply.

"Beg your pardon, Captain Renfro. I didn't mean to rush you." Bromberger resisted the urge to check his watch: the captain's pace was maddening. "It's helpful, very helpful to have this information. Please go ahead."

"Well . . . never mind. We saw far less of Leslie after she left our home. What we did see offered troubling suggestions of what I would describe as a change in personality. She had become a much more reserved young lady, a cooler person . . . fair enough, I suppose, given that she was now an adult on her own. But knowing her as we did, the reserve was disturbing in that I saw it more as a suppression of her rage, the bitterness she seemed unable to put behind her, almost as if it smoldered within her and could burst at any moment into flame."

Captain Renfro rocked his body in the chair, one hand on the cane, the other jutting out, cutting up and down with its crooked fingers as he catalogued the changes, clearly upset by the memory. "By then, she had begun to travel on the Continent a good amount of the time, doing what we knew not, but traveling and jotting off a very occasional post card to us here at North Bluff.

"Then, Mr. Bromberger, she returned, just before my wife died. Yes, Mr. Ajax, just before she died." He let a hand fall, stroked one of the spaniel's long, silky ears. "Leslie had dinner with is. She was quite shocked to see my wife, her aunt, so close to the end—much as she would be to see me now, I dare say—and she was solicitous.

"This was genuine on her part. She loved my wife and was to grieve her passing. Leslie also asked over that dinner if I would loan her a relatively small sum of money, about fifteen hundred pounds, to supplement her own savings. She wished to make an investment.

"I have told you Leslie was a good swimmer. She was extremely capable in every way on the water. My brother had raised that side of her as a son. She had now set her mind on the purchase of a yacht. She told us that she planned to start her own business here in the Maltese Islands, a charter trade, you know—tricky financially, an off-and-on, risky sort of enterprise. Never mind. I loaned her the money. I was pleased to do so, and she promised to take us for a sail around the islands, which she never did—my wife's death, you understand." Captain Renfro leaned further to the side, gave the dog's head and neck a long scratch.

"These are exquisite waters in which to sail. Apparently, she had spotted a market for her chartering . . . you must excuse me, Mr. Bromberger." He hoisted himself slowly out of the chair. "You wouldn't feel it, I am sure, but the afternoon has brought a breeze that is chilling through me. I am going to fetch my sweater, and serve us some tea. I have an electric element. It won't take a minute."

He disappeared into the house, followed by the spaniel. Bromberger had known better than to ask for details of the yacht, its location. This would come when the captain saw fit to deliver . . . Christ, the weekend had slipped away. Nothing! He silently cursed Sweetman. There was a clatter of cups, followed by the old man's call.

"Thank you. Thank you very much, indeed." Captain Renfro sighed, laughed at himself as they took their seats again. "The Navy impressed upon me, from the first schoolboy days at Dartmouth, the importance of discovery, of being able to identify, and being willing to accept and digest new information. I have now discovered that one cannot carry a tray and, at the same time, walk with a cane. One needs either a third arm or a third leg. There are no biscuits in the house; I do apologize."

"Perhaps I could help, Captain—any stores open around here?"

"No, no, Mr. Bromberger. I have a servant, a very faithful girl, who will be here in the morning. Mr. Ajax will have his nose in her basket. We will be fine; very thoughtful of you." He slipped the tea.

"To continue, Leslie purchased a yacht, in Italy; I have never learned the port or the builder. She brought it to Malta, and, as I was saying, apparently she managed to make a success of it. Within a short time, less than a year, she had repaid the loan, even though I had urged her to keep the money as a gift."

"Captain Renfro, did her charter operation have a name, an address, the yacht . . . ?"

"Yes, I will surprise you here, sir. I have the answers to your questions. The address was in her name, of course, in care of the post office, Valletta. I know that because I told her I must have the information. She was still receiving a few bits of mail here—"

"Do you have any?"

"No, and I told her I had to send it on to her. Now, the name of the charter was rather formal, Renfro Research. She had an oceanographic aspect to her cruises, Renfro Research, Main Post Office, Valletta." He carefully raised the cup to his lips, satisfied that the information had prompted the American to begin taking some notes.

The captain's fatigue was increasingly evident. Bromberger framed his next questions hoping they would allow him to close the interview. "Captain Renfro, was your niece running this charter trade single-handedly? Did she have employees?"

"You must tell me why you are making this inquiry, Mr. Bromberger. You told me when you telephoned that you had no reason to believe Leslie is not well. I trust she is well?"

"Sir, I said I was hoping to meet your niece, that I was hoping she could help us with some information. I didn't want to take much of your or her time, but I did want to talk to her—"

"Well, that was a mouthful of words, wasn't it?" He turned from the American, gazed at the sea. "I must rest, Mr. Bromberger. I do hope you will excuse me." He eased himself to his feet. "Allow me to show you to the gate."

"It would be helpful if I could telephone a taxi."

"Yes, yes. I keep a card with the numbers. The telephone is in the front hall."

● ● ● ● ●

The cab ordered, they walked slowly from the house. "You asked about Leslie's crew?"

"Yes Captain; did she have people working for her?"

"I didn't approve, you know. She took me for a drive one day, down to the yacht basin to have a look. She was a young lady, unmarried, living afloat—with two men!" The captain stopped on the path and turned to his visitor to share this information.

"Did you know them? Were they friends of your niece?"

"Know them? Hardly. And I didn't wish to, Mr. Bromberger. But Leslie would have none of my counsel. We were on the quay admiring the yacht, a ketch, very able in appearance, when they came upon us the one time I met them." He stopped again. Took Bromberger's arm in the grip of his hand. "They were scruffy! . . . ."

"What nationality, Captain? English-speaking, can you describe them?"

"One was, after a fashion—a dirty man, unshaven, scruffy blond beard."

"The other?"

"Lord knows, a Maltese by the looks of him. She would have none of my counsel. Here we are, Mr. Bromberger. I will say goodbye and wish you well in your inquiry. If the yacht is still in Malta, you should find her in the main basin."

Bromberger took the cold hand. "You've been a help, Captain. Thanks for your time. Get well. Looks like you are going to have some gardening to do."

Yes, indeed. Thank you."

The American visitor turned as he stepped through the gate. "What was the name of the ketch, your niece's yacht?"

"Dear me, yes. I should have told you that. *Matabele.*" He spelled it; his visitor jotted it down. "A most peculiar name for the yacht, you know. The *Matabele* were called the vanishing people, Zulu in origin, whose sole business was war."

Captain Renfro followed his visitor's descent to the road, gave the gate latch a testing jiggle. "Now, Mr. Ajax. It's going on your suppertime." The spaniel stayed at the old man's side, the stub of a tail wagging in response to the words. They made their way back to the house, pausing for a moment at the front to contemplate the wisteria.

· · · · ●Chapter 15● · · · ·

eslie Renfro sat motionless, repulsed by Starring's touch. He stood behind her in the catamaran's ornate dining room, hands on her shoulders, announcing that she would accompany him to the White House on the Fourth of July. She listened, incredulous that she had not known of his plans. Their strategy had called for him to be on the catamaran until July 5. During the crossing from Malta, his schedule had shown the fifth.

Her eyes shot to Tooms. He had said the fifth. His face was locked in a drunken smile. She felt the secretary, Sullivan, observing her from the far end of the table. She met her eyes, forced her to break off the encounter with a dab at her plate.

It was late evening. Starring had held them, insisting on a celebration to mark the majestic appearance of the *Towerpoint Partner*, the mirror ceremony for her sistership *Mayan* on the Fourth, the launching of the expedition. She was exhausted. She looked around her. Head's face was waxy with fatigue. Her mind ached. She argued briefly against the plan, but Starring would have none of it—this would be the most important Fourth of July ever.

"George the Third would still have given it a pretty low rating, maybe one out of ten." Tooms gurgled to himself, enjoying his joke, held his glass up for the stewards.

"You need some sleep, Oats; we all do." Starring was at the stairway. "Sullivan, what time do we depart?"

"Noon, tomorrow, sir. Your meeting is at two P.M."

"Excellent. Give Miss Renfro the details. She will be with you at the hotel. A splendid day, my friends. You have done us proud."

● ● ● · ·

At 3:00 A.M., Tonasi's voice was a low, doped snarl, dismissing her doubts. "The next one's loaded with gas. She's loaded; we'll boil the fish! You hit that son of a bitch. You kill him; you're the important one, Les. Kill him; watch yourself—Paulo . . . ?" He tugged on the blond beard, shrugged off Head's punch to his injured arm. "Paulo will be like a mother to me, Les. We'll be in Copenhagen. You take care of yourself. You're the good hunter, the leader—Copenhagen— we'll be there." He left them, walked slowly to his cabin, lobbed the packet she had given him on his bunk, and collapsed asleep.

Head was certain they were making a mistake, and he continued to argue. "The hell with the bloody tanker. Starring, this bloody ship; they're our targets. We should take them now. Rig the mines; blow them before dawn. We'll be out of the States together, before the pigs know we're still alive!"

She held firm. She would take care of Starring. The second tanker was essential to the peoples' victory. Head would be in command. The death of the ship was his responsibility. "The criminals will never recover. Make it work, Paul; in three days, Copenhagen." Their hands parted; her cabin door closed.

The mining of the first tanker . . . hours, days, weeks ago? . . . only hours . . . impossible. She was awake, tense . . . 3:30 A.M. . . . force yourself to sleep, but not yet.

The thought that Head would take her place in the second attack tore against her instincts of combat. The mission would be out of her hands. They had just spent two hours in preparation, reliving the first attack. She saw the great red hull, again, rushing toward her. The draft? He knows she will be deeper. He must be deeper, run at least twelve feet. They would talk after he had slept. She damned herself for her carelessness.

When they attack, I will be with the U.S. president. Her head snapped involuntarily at the thought. She would be stalking Starring, in Washington, in the White House. It was staggering. She would kill them both! Could she? There would be secret police, their agents. She grappled with the new unknowns, crossed her cabin to recheck the door lock, picked up the Beretta pistol, removed the thirteen-round magazine from its plastic wrapping, placed the pieces on the bunk.

The Skorpion machine pistol was big beside the Beretta, a foot long with the butt folded double over the barrel, more than two feet with the silencer fitted and the butt extended. She would need two twenty-round magazines for the Skorpion—fifty-three rounds in all. She could not take more. She rolled the pistol and its clip first in a plastic sheet, then in the tight roll of a blouse. She set the insulated bundle aside, checked her two passports, the currencies, her cover documents, and placed them in the bottom of the expedition's nylon shoulder bag. She would wear the expedition's coveralls and windbreaker in the morning—that would please Starring. She packed the leather gloves, the hood, more clothing, then the rolled blouse. The four pieces of the Skorpion were next; she tied the rolled shirt with a belt, placed it in the bag. Her eyes were burning in the artificial light. She stuffed cosmetics in the pockets of her raincoat, folded it, and stuffed it over the rest and zipped the bag. Everything else in the cabin, she would leave as always, nothing unusual to arouse the curiosity of the stewards.

She lay on her side, her eyes closed in the darkness, and listened to the cabin air vent and the faint clanking of night maintenance far off in one of the hulls. She forced her body to breathe slowly, steadily, slowly—to lie still. She forced her mind to a different time and she slept.

● ● ● · ·

"Eleven-thirty; we have a few more minutes." Starring, in his suite with Tooms, was flipping through the morning news file prepared for him by the ship's communications officer. "Had a telegram from Adrian earlier this morning, Oats—good coverage of the *Partner* on the networks last night, and in today's press. A grand sight, wasn't she?"

"A knockout!" Tooms leaned forward, balancing his coffee, to reach for the clipping held out to him by Starring.

"A nice piece on Tina's opening this afternoon, apparently a first, this Fourth of July matinee. She's unhappy with me for not being there. I'll make it up to her; she's unhappy when I'm there. Give her a call this morning, Oats. She'd like a good word, some reassurance."

Starring was on his feet, shot the French cuffs off his white shirt, slipped into the dark-blue pin-striped suit jacket held out for him by the steward, adjusted the silk tie, giving it a critical look in the mirror—blue, fine red dots, went well with the suit. "Give her a ring, Oats."

"As soon as you are airborne, Tommie. She'll be okay. Joanie's happy with her."

"Another piece there you ought to read, an attempted hijack of spent fuel rods from a Colombian reactor. What good are spent rods?"

Tooms picked up the reading folder, searched for the page, skimmed the article, let his glasses drop to their familiar perch on his chest. "Plutonium, by-product of the reactor's fission. You start off with U-238 in the fuel rods, fission, power from the reactor; in the process, the U-238 transforms into plutonium 239; that's what you need to build a bomb."

"Not that easy is it?"

"Hell, no!" The reading folder skid as it hit the table. "Those banditos are lucky they were caught, stuff's tricky to handle. They would probably have glowed for a day or two after they started playing with it, then gone to a higher calling in the sky."

"It's getting a hell of a lot worse, isn't, Oats?" Starring cast an approving eye at the clear sky, only the faintest haze, as they walked aft to the flight deck. "The proliferation of sabotage, terrorism, destruction." Their feet clanked up the metal ladder.

"Do a message to Adrian, in my name. My guts tell me we've been leading a charmed life—these stories are appearing every day. Have our best people pull together a complete statement of our security procedures. Bring in a good contractor. I want the report to take a hard look at the threat, the new weapons and tactics, the growing pattern, if there is one, around the world. I want a candid, emphasize that, candid appraisal of deficiencies and a hard list of recommendations. . . . Ah ha, the ladies are already aboard. I'll give your regards to the White House, Oats."

Starring slipped out of the jacket, climbed into the co-pilot's seat of the bubble-topped helicopter. Renfro and the secretary were squeezed together in the rear of the small craft. He greeted them, passed his jacket back to Sullivan, took the headphones from the instrument panel, and leaned out to Tooms again. "Make sure we have good coverage of *Mayan* today, important part of the historical record!" Tooms nodded vigorously. Starring slapped him on the shoulder. The flight deck crew closed the bubble door, made sure the chief scientist was clear, extended his arm in a vertical, circling "start engine" motion.

● ● ● ● ●

"You're a darling, Oats. You're always a darling. Everything is fine. How are you and that funny boat of yours?"

Tooms had returned to the owner's deck to place the call. He sat with his feet propped on the railing, the first ale of the day cooling his left hand, soothing the damage of the night before. "You left too soon, Tina. I'm in charge today, another parade, a dive with two of my Maltese dolphins this afternoon, a hot shower, an hour of whiskey sours, and an evening of fireworks *a la Towerpoint Octagon*."

"The Ritz."

"The Ritz."

You can dance with Sullivan and little Miss Whatshername, Tommie's pet fish, can't you? Muriel probably has a secret—she tangoes! Give her a double, Oats darling, after your shower."

"After, to be sure."

"Bring out the best in her. There, that was small and mean enough. I'm girding for my matinee."

"No dancing aboard ship tonight, m'lady. They've both flown the coop, off to Washington."

Her voice hardened. "I thought this was to be Tommie's famous *retreat*, solitude, an ancestral enrichment? They're not going to be with him?"

"Poor choice of words on my part, Tina, apologies. He'll be solituding tonight. Sullivan and Renfro will be manning the hotel suite. He's taking Leslie—"

"Yes, dear Leslie?"

"Tommie will be taking her along this afternoon as a live exhibit for the president."

"Lucky, lucky, lucky."

"You must be about ready to head up to the theater?"

"Yes, darling, one of Tommie's lovely blue mobiles is out front waiting, and tyrant Joanie is stomping around downstairs yelling for me. I'm off as soon as I tear myself away from you."

"Tina, I've never seen the boss so charged up, excited about his rendezvous with the Leader of the Free World. He loves you—"

"*Yes*, of course he does—"

"—told me he was going to make up everything to you"—Tooms took a long pull from his bottle—"probably buy you Martinique or the Bahamas."

"Not Bermuda? Good."

"He knows your tastes. Don't let me keep you, Tina; break a leg. Got to get going myself—got the tanker photo pageant, messages to write, young Paul Head and Filippo—"

"Those wonderful eyes . . ." She was silent for a moment. "Have I ever told you Oats, I find all three of them slightly unsettling. Make them behave. I love you for calling."

Unsettling . . . they'll behave. Tooms mulled the words, gently rocking the receiver in its cradle. Behind his bubbly façade, the entire Divequest escapade had become seriously troubling to him. The dolphis were into some sort of double game that he still could not fathom. He was in the homestretch now and knew he had to stick with them. But he would have them out of Towerpoint forever, paid off and back on their Mediterranean rock, at the first chance.

What the hell was it that had started him churning just a couple of days before? "Timer," that was it, timer. Head and Tonasi had been taking a smoke, backs to him, leaning against a rail when he had come across them and heard that goddamned word, and had seen them clam up as soon as they had spotted him. What the hell were they talking about timers for. Those two little bastards; he was going to hawk their every step.

Tooms checked the *Mayan*'s schedule with the watch, then proceeded to the communicator's shack, mentally outlining the contents of Starring's security directive to Adrian enroute. The boss was right, an important message; it would have to be transmitted in code. That was good, force him to keep it brief. He checked the designators and heading with the communications officer, took half-a-dozen message forms, and dragged a chair over to the spare typewriter. He made a hash of the first form, balled it up, and continued to type.

● ● ● · ·

"I can't read the bloody pressure, Italian. Check my tanks."

"Three thousand pounds."

"Both?"

"Both. You're set, Zulu."

"We're going to bugger this if we're not out of here now!"

They dropped through the habitat's trunk into the bay. Head set himself in the forward cockpit. The glowing faces on the work chariot's instrument panel came alive. Tonasi cast them off, swung into his seat, and stabbed at the "forward" signal. They rose with the first testing thrust of propulsion, then pushed ahead with full turns of power. The bubbling exhaust of his breath trailed aft. The chariot drove at maximum speed toward the center of the bay.

When they surfaced, they were on the edge of the main channel, with less than an hour until the attack. The sky had taken on a yellowish cast, the haze of early summer heat. The surface was flat; nothing was near them. Sails off either shore hung near-motionless in the water. In the distance, a triangle of holiday flags pinpointed the *Octagon*.

Tonasi was out of his seat, talking to Head as he had to Leslie the day before. "Keep us low, Paulo. You're good; you're good now. Just our heads, no sea today, easy to spot us. You ready?"

"Do it in my sleep. After this one, we'll put the next on the bloody catamaran—port or starboard hull?"

"Inboard, starboard, split her in two."

"They'll blow tonight!"

"Ten o'clock—all three of the bastards. This fucking tanker will be the bomb—*arhhrumph!*"

"What are your settings?"

"Eight hours—*arhhrumph!*—need an asbestos suit within five miles."

"We'll be bloody further than five miles; on our way, Italian."

"On our way. We should pay out the anchor, to the south, just enough turns to keep the line taut. I'll watch for you."

They slipped beneath the surface. Tonasi counted the markers emerging from the reel—"Ten!"—they were still under way. He hit "surface." The submersible slowed, rose. He worked the last of the line free from the reel, brought the tail forward—all clear. It held. He had rigged it himself. He released the empty reel, followed its plunge to the bottom. His left arm was bad, his gash reacting to the renewed immersion. They broke the surface. The pain was terrible. He reached for his knife to slice off the new sleeve, bake the arm in the warm air. The knife stayed in its sheath. Both hands went to the mine instead, ran along the curve of the shroud. They waited.

First the compass, then the throb through the water, a ship, a big ship—the swinging dial, the vibration of energy; where was it? Mask-high in the water, Head craned his neck to spot the approaching hull. He was going nuts; there was nothing! He cursed into his mouthpiece, kicked at the chariot's controls—bring it up some more. He spat out the regulator, shouted over his shoulder, "Where is the bastard? Where, bloody hell?"

Tonasi had spotted it. They were too high on the surface. "We're okay, Zulu. Down, down, down again. We're okay."

The thin vertical line had appeared from the north, no more than a stake in the center of the channel. His eyes had found the white of the bow wave next, then the curve of the hull. "Submarine, Paulo, running on the surface." As the distance closed, the angle opened, revealing the sleek black sail of the conning tower, the top of the tear-drop hull, a streamlined shape broken only by the raised missile housing, then white wake and trailing behind, as if detached, the black trapezoidal blade of the rudder.

The sound racing through the water was different from that of any merchant hull, power tightly packaged, finely machined to a deadly precision. The heads and shoulders of the men atop the sail were silhouetted against the afternoon sky. The black beast of war slid quickly to the south, her ensign snapping in the sixteen-knot breeze generated by the forward thrust of nuclear propulsion.

They followed her, braced as the wake slammed into them, carrying the full size and strength of the seven-thousand-ton ballistic missile submarine. Head brought the chariot back on course. The horizon was clear. The "submerge" light had them diving to fifteen feet, swinging slowly to port at two knots, little more than pivoting against the pull of the sea anchor. The compass measured the maneuver in its quarter turn from 180 to 90 degrees.

They surfaced. It was time. Adrenaline was pumping through Tonasi, the excitement of the kill. "Good work, Zulu, good as yesterday." His hands worked the mine's mechanisms—cocked and running, all but one restraining strap gone.

Head had not heard Tonasi's words. A fat, black bug was on the southern horizon—not the sub, fat, wide as the channel —"Bloody bitch is here!"

Tonasi's eyes were to the north. He squinted hard at the still indistinguishable shape—and the shock ran through him. He and Head were back to back. "Two ships!" Head's shout, the single word "Dive," and they were angling beneath the glassy green of the surface.

● ● ● ● ⸱

The pilot aboard the *Towerpoint Mayan* had already established the course and speed of the approaching hull, a Greek cruise ship under charter out of Baltimore on one of the off-season holiday excursions to Florida, St. Thomas, and return. He rubbed the fine stubble on his chin, took his decision.

His instruction from Towerpoint had been to slow to three knots. This would have him pass the cruise ship port-to-port when abeam of the flagship *Octagon*. Under these circumstances, the Greek would obscure the view. He could not slow the ladened *Mayan* beneath three knots and wait for the Greek to pass. He would not risk a thousand feet of loaded LNG tanker near dead in the water with no maneuvering room.

He crossed the bridge, conferred briefly with the *Mayan*'s master, who immediately nodded his concurrence, and stepped into the wheelhouse to radio the *Octagon*. The *Mayan* would give the Greek another forty feet of channel and maintain twelve knots, beating the cruise ship to the point of ceremonial salute abeam the flagship, providing a clear field for Towerpoint's photographers.

White waves curled from the bows, hissed back along the deep-blue hull before rolling free on either side, fanning outward in a spreading vee. The bridge watch sung out the ranges and bearings. Two minutes, then four minutes passed. The pilot's lips flexed in approval. His calculations had been correct. The Greek was still a quarter-mile up-bay when he crossed to the port wing of the bridge beneath the rolling thunder of the *Mayan*'s salute.

● ● ● ● ⸱

Head fought back against the panicking jolt, hauled with all his strength on the forward planes control as the tanker seized the snare line at twelve knots and dragged the chariot forward, sideways, down into darker water. As his body wrestled with the machine, his eyes, blurring with the violence of the encounter, caught the instruments. The line tore free from the bow claw. The pull on the chariot was now from the forward deck padeye, slewing the slender craft sideways out of control, rolling the cockpit toward the hull. Head battled furiously against the almost useless controls, his mind raging at the tanker's counterattack.

In the aft compartment, Tonasi had locked his body against the inside walls of the chariot's hull, straining to right the craft, to escape from the unbelievable force which held them. In the struggle, he bit through the rubber in his mouth; the regulator was gone, trailing from his back tanks in the gray-green hell. The speed, the first hard, diving roll had snapped the mine from his hands, and it had vanished in an instant, now a part of the bay. A minute later, he was dead, smashed against the *Mayan*'s hull, skull and neck destroyed, body plucked from the chariot and sucked aft into the cut of the bronze propeller. Head blindly cut at the tow.

The great bass horn had brought the passengers of the cruise ship to the port rails, and when the sounds had silenced and the two ships passed, they pointed with pleasure at the enormous blue-and-white hull of the *Towerpoint Mayan*, so patriotic and handsome in her holiday bunting, forging past them on her voyage up the bay.

·····•Chapter 16•····

As the deep-blue convertible, its silver grill gleaming, approached the concrete barrier the uniformed Secret Service agent had swung open half of the heavy steel gates, welded to resemble ornamental iron, guarding the Southwest Gate of the White House. He checked the names against his list and shifted his attention to the chauffeur.

"Straight ahead; follow the blacktop across the South Lawn; left turn will bring you back up and across to the diplomatic entrance." The agent waved them ahead as soon as the second half of the massive gate was clear of the drive.

Despite the mounting haze and humid heat, the White House grounds were vivid in their beauty. The historic trees planted by two centuries of presidents were in full foliage. A deep carpet of red geraniums ringed the sparkling jets of the South Lawn fountain. As the convertible crossed the grounds, the South Portico appeared, then disappeared behind one of two knolls of elegant lawn, landscaping added by Thomas Jefferson.

First General Sherman, glowering astride his bronze mount, then the columns of the Treasury Building showed through the trees beyond the fenced grounds. The chauffeur made the turn toward the president's residence.

"Good afternoon. Please do come in where it is cool." A butler in tuxedo opened the rear door.

"It would be best, Sullivan, if you stayed in the car, I don't want to overimpose." Starring gave the order in a clipped voice, turned smiling to the butler who had gone to the other side of the car.

"Please, sir; please, madame, follow me." The butler extended an arm toward the red carpet running beneath the canopy's shade to the diplomatic entrance.

"Good afternoon, ma'am. May I please have a look in your bag?" The lean, young face beneath the sculpted black hair had delivered the words so quickly—Who? Leslie Renfro's mind raced to recover. He was five steps from her, enormous shoulders beneath the dapper suit, strong hands, one already extended—extended to receive her weapons, the money, false papers. Who had done this? This was their method, these secret agents! They know; they have Paul and Filippo. They have discovered! How? Who? Something had gone wrong on the catamaran; when? No rush of police; no guns in sight. But, there were others. She had seen them. Now, they have sprung their trap, silently, swiftly. They will destroy . . .

Not a flicker broke the calm of her face when the agent had made his request, emerging from the shadow of the doorway. "Thank you for reminding me." She looked down at her bag with amusement. "I didn't mean to bring this with me. I meant to leave it in the car. Thank you." Her voice was light; her eyes and smile projected thanks.

She was on her way back down the drive to the convertible parked beneath the trees before anyone could offer assistance. She fought the fear that clutched at her, the ice in her stomach and palms, the pounding in her chest. She turned the corner of the low hedge swinging the bag casually from one hand to the other. In the heart of the night she had selected the place and the moment of Starring's death. She felt the July sun on her neck, dropped the zippered bag over the passenger's door onto the floor of the front seat. The chauffeur was leaning against the car, Sullivan seated on the grass; the presidential park was so silent. 1:45 P.M. They would be on the attack in the bay. Justice depended now on her alone. The fingers of her left hand ran along the top of the hedge; she turned again under the canopy.

The agent followed her with an admiring eye—a swimmer, an athlete of some kind by the looks of her in that outfit, a good-looker, for sure, one of the better parts of the post.

"Thank you, again. I really was not planning to move in."

He returned the smile. "No problem. They're inside." He folded his arms across his chest, shifted on his feet, thankful for the break in the tedium. He raised a hand to one ear, adjusting the clear plastic ear-phone—command post confirming Marine One lift-off; the president was in the air. The agent removed a speck of lint from the sleeve of his sharply tailored tan suit, resettled his arms, and continued the watch.

An oval rug, dark and light blues with gold, added to the museum-silence of the mansion. She stood for a moment at the inner door of the softly lit lobby. Starring and a woman were at the far end of the room.

"Here we are, Leslie; this is the president's hostess. . . ." She didn't hear the name; they crossed the room to greet her. The woman was attractive, late thirties, brunette, pretty cheeks and mouth, a blue-and-white print dress with matching jacket, and two fine strands of pearls.

"I've told Mr. Starring. We are so pleased to have you with us. The president is on his way down by helicopter from Camp David. I understand you've just arrived by helicopter." The hostess gave a long smile of greeting, her eyes examining the young woman's Dive-quest outfit with practiced interest. "We have your exhibits in the Map Room just next door. I know the president is so looking forward to seeing you and learning about your work. Would you like a glass of iced tea, iced coffee, a refreshment?"

"No thank you. I would like to sit down."

"Of course." The hostess led the way to a row of straight-backed yellow silk chairs and love seats lining the oval room and took a seat beside her. Starring studied the exhibits. Minutes ticked by. She popped up in response to his voice.

"The Oval Office, the president's office, isn't just above us, is it?"

"No. This is one of three oval rooms, one on top of the other here in the residence. The Oval Office is a relatively new addition dating back to President Theodore Roosevelt's time. It is in the West Wing of the White House . . . your architectural instincts are very good."

Starring admired the finely detailed wallpaper lining the entire room. "Hudson River, the Palisades?"

"Yes."

"And this?" He approached the portrait over the mantle, studied the gaunt, craggy face, the tousled white hair.

"Andrew Jackson?"

"Yes. An excellent portrait, in my opinion, by Ralph Earl. If you would like to see the arrival of the helicopter, we should move back out to the drive." She led the way, Leslie almost at her side, measuring her steps to avoid the hand she knew Starring would attempt to place on her.

The twin-turbined helicopter had turned from over the Potomac and made its first appearance out of the south, to the right of the Washington Monument. The approach down across the Mall, Ellipse, and the South Grounds was swift and precise. The pilot brought the big machine, nose slightly high, to a near-hover and eased toward the landing site on the lawn. No more than one hundred feet from the entrance, he held the helicopter in a hover and swung the tail, revealing the craft's port side, dark-green lower body, American flag painted on the white topside, the presidential seal on the door just aft of the cockpit. The roaring downwash of wind and engine exhaust blasted across the lawn, generating a loud clatter among the heavy olive-green leaves of the ancient magnolia trees bordering the mansion.

The pilot braked the main rotor and cut the engines. Leslie took the count; six more agents had deployed on the lawn, uniformed agents everywhere in the distance. The gleaming, waxed front door of the helicopter dropped open, forming a set of gold carpeted stairs bordered with chrome stanchions and cable railing. The marine crew chief trotted down the steps and snapped to attention.

The president, tanned, in tennis sweater and shorts, ducked slightly as he cleared the doorway. He touched his forehead with two fingers in casual return salute, nodding his appreciation to the marine sergeant.

"Tommie!" He recognized the white head of hair. They met at the edge of the grass. The president took his hand and arm with both hands. "How very, very good to see you—Tommie Starring on the Fourth of July, makes it all official. Hello Jennie. Hello—"

"Mr. President, may I introduce Miss Leslie Renfro, the very important young star in our expedition in the Chesapeake."

"Yes, yes, of course. I am delighted to meet you, Miss Renfro." He took her hand. She could only stare back at this powerful, handsome presence she had so reviled. She heard the words "Thank you," her voice. He had moved on toward the mansion, Starring close at his side, gents and aides fanning out in front of them. Once inside, he excused himself for a few minutes, then returned.

"This is the Map Room, Tommie, no longer used as such. The name harkens back to FDR's days. You may know the story. When Winston Churchill visited Roosevelt at the outset of World War II, the British were already heavily engaged in battle. The prime minister brought along a case of war charts, which he pored over during his stay. FDR was impressed, emulated the practice."

"You've taken it a long way since then, haven't you, Mr. President, your Situation Room, and—"

"Quite a ways, Tommie, but not as far as I would like." The president moved toward the Towerpoint display. "The more instantaneous the communications, the more complete the global reach, the more glaring are the gaps in the information required for any well-reasoned decision. We tend to swamp ourselves with the current information, to the neglect of thought and analysis. It is a constant battle for me."

He held out his hand to the young woman, inviting her to join him. "I've always liked the Map Room, a convenient place to have a visitor drop by for a talk without the glare and pressures of publicity" —he laughed—"not that I'm trying to keep you two under wraps. Now, tell me Miss Renfro, what am I seeing here?"

She spoke quietly, mechanically, guiding the president through the exhibit she herself was seeing for the first time. The three-dimensional scale model included the *Towerpoint Octagon* on the surface, the habitat and two work chariots on the bay floor, multicolored lines running from the habitat out across the bay floor and up into the blue-green plastic plane depicting the water, each of the lines keyed to a legend summarizing the principal Divequest experiments.

"Your work is a great credit to you, so important, international research. I know we'll benefit. Tommie has a reputation as a good boss. I hope that's still the case." He turned to Starring. "Tell me, Darcy is interested in this, isn't he?"

"He is, indeed, Mr. President, and he has been a great help to me. In fact, he was on that ship for our press conference last week." Starring touched the catamaran.

"And this"—the president had moved on to the next display—"this is your Sea Star?"

"It is, sir."

"What an incredible achievement. I don't know as much as I should. It's almost a mile across, isn't it?"

"Closer to a mile and one half, Mr. President.

"Incredible!"

"It tends to test my patience at times—still blueprints and bankers, Mr. President, but we're almost ready to begin construction." The two men made their way around the eight-foot model, with Starring firing off highlights of the oceanic air and seaport.

"Tommie, if we had another ten like you, this country would surge ahead to stay, like Citation. Your drive and accomplishments are staggering. Keep it up. . . . 'With firmness in the right, as God gives us the right, let us strive on to finish the work we are in. . . .' Lincoln's words, his Second Inaugural.

"This has been fascinating. Thank you both so very much for having taken the time from your holiday to give me this personal appreciation of all you are doing. I understand that you will not be able to stay on for this evening's party and fireworks. I'm told we're expecting more than half a million down there tonight. I've invited the Cabinet and their families." The president pressed a buzzer tucked beneath the edge of a sideboard. An aide appeared and received instructions to retrieve the briefcase from the president's flight.

"Please do have a seat. Before you go . . ." The president held his words while he opened the case and withdrew one of a dozen slender folders. ". . . I mentioned to you, Tommie, the other evening, that I thought there had been important developments in Connie's case."

The moment Leslie heard the name, the dark, wet streets of Geneva came flooding back. Her eyes darted down, looking for the fine pink scars on her forearm covered by the sleeve. She watched the president draw his chair closer to Starring's, his voice lower, grave.

"I asked Ernie Lancaster, my DCI, to pull these notes together for you. His report arrived at Camp David last night. I wanted you to have a look yourself, without my attempting to interpret." The president handed Starring the double sheet, waited in silence, elbows on his knees, hands clasped together while the brother of his slain lover read. The text ran only one-quarter of the second page. Starring returned the file, blinked, still absorbing the information.

"Ernie's a cautious man, Tommie. We're not there yet"—the president measured a narrow gap with thumb and forefinger—"but he's certain it's only a matter of days—"

"A woman? He says there was a woman—and two or three of them, either British or American? That's a surprise, an entirely different direction, isn't it, Mr. President?"

Her breath stopped. The president hesitated, struck by her intense stare. "Mr. Starring's sister, Ambassador Burdette, Miss Renfro—a brutal murder."

Her eyes engaged his, the easy smile she had offered earlier to the agent returned to her lips. "May I?" she asked, glancing at the folder.

The president bent forward as she spoke, raised the briefcase lip, and tossed the file inside. It carried a high classification, marked for his eyes only. He had already stretched one of his strictest rules having shown it at all. He covered his action by returning to Starring's question. "No, you're right, Tommie. Ernie still expects the main break to come from Italy. I'll continue to keep you posted. God rest her soul. My God, how I do miss her—dearest Connie—I had such hopes."

They both rose with the president. The Continental was at the end of the canopy, a cab drawn up behind. Starring stopped inside the entrance. "Mr. President, I blasted the networks, sent telegrams to all three a couple of weeks ago, over the unfair play they're giving your programs."

The president laughed a full laugh, clenched his fist, and tapped him on the shoulder. "We can't let those boys get us down. We're sitting pretty for the midterm elections, Tommie. They're bored, trying to stir things up a bit, make better news. But, thank you! Keep after them. Now then, you're heading just down the street, aren't you?"

"I am. You were just lamenting the lack of time these days for thought, analysis. I'm prescribing my own remedy, an evening to myself at the Octagon mansion. I've left strict instructions, no calls, no interruptions. I am to be left alone, sir. How it does rankle a staff—our annual stockholders meeting is coming up, and I'm going to see if I can't go beyond the usual boilerplate, try to place Towerpoint International in perspective, give fresh meaning to our philosophy, our principles, our future direction."

"Oh, I envy you your night with James and Dolley. They were a good pair, Tommie—Madison a good president in a difficult time. His problems were enormous. With firmness in the right, Tommie. Keep up the spectacular work. You and Towerpoint are the heart-wood of America."

The president and his protective envelope of agents had already returned inside when the convertible and battered black-and-orange cab began to roll slowly down the White House drive. The cab, with the two women, turned north on Seventeenth Street. The Continental continued straight ahead for another block before rounding the corner and parking in the back courtyard of the Octagon mansion. The deep-red-brown bricks of the Federal period structure formed a unique architectural achievement, rounding in a curve above the steep front steps and pillared entrance, continuing from this frontal bow along straight sides in a set of faces to shape the octagonal shell housing an elegant, intricate collection of circular, triangular, and rectangular rooms in three main stories. It was 4:00 P.M. The gates closed behind the convertible.

● ● ● ● ·

The excitement of Starring's meeting with the president was far from Tooms's mind in mid-afternoon as he rode the sling of the overhead crane down to the surface and plunged into the water on his dive to the habitat. Those bastards! Those bastards! He pulled hard against the guideline, working his way deeper, repeating the curse again and again. He was furious. He had called each of their cabins, no answer. He had checked with the ship's watch only to learn they were already below. His anger continued to build. The guideline markers bumped through his fingers.

He could make out the glow of the access trunk, the dark outline of the habitat. With no breathing gear on, his lungs were already hurting. He kicked hard, came level with the submersible platform. The chariot . . . one still topside, the other gone . . . where the hell were they? He twisted his heavy body into the diver's final approach to the trunk, painfully banging a knee. Inside, he struggled to his feet, bracing for the confrontation.

The habitat, full of strewn gear, was at the same time eerie in its emptiness. He blotted at the water streaming into his eyes, flung the towel in frustration at one of the dead cameras. Damn it to hell!

His mind raced. . . . Bring the second chariot down, get out there and herd them back. His air tanks clanked against the hull as he snatched them from their rack. He cursed the jumble of equipment, wrestled halfway into his scuba gear before he decided against the plan.

Running across the other submersible out there in that soup would be sheer chance. If he missed . . . he had to take control. They'd be back, damn it to hell. He'd wait them out. He made his way to the far end of the deck where one of the Renfro research cylinders lay open. What the hell? He kicked the side. Packing shifted, strips of rubber fabric that had compressed into a stream-lined cushion tapering back to a smooth semicircular hollow with a mate in the facing side. His breath still came heavily. The bay water on his brow had turned to sweat. He gave his face another wipe, knelt down, rubbed a forefinger along the erased metal plate on the interior of the cylinder. A double game . . . what kind of game? He had seen or read every piece of oceanographic gear ever built, give or take a few, even the unsuccessful prototypes. This jury-rigged casing didn't ring a bell, looked more like military gear from the impression it had left in the packing. A bomb? . . . military gear . . . driving that damned chariot around out in the bay . . . planting some sort of gear on the bay floor. The bastards were saboteurs; they were going to sabotage the habitat or the Octagon . . . but that didn't square . . . they were already aboard, didn't need a submersible to do the job.

His finger again stroked one of the smooth packing hollows . . . Use the submersible as an escape vehicle, maybe . . . nuts; it's nuts. They wouldn't be making a run from something with Leslie due back the following evening. The shape intrigued him. He knew what it was, but his mind was holding back the answer . . . some sort of circular base . . . circular, for what? . . . The form worked in his mind's eye slowly, then sharply took focus as a shroud.

"Bridge, this is Tooms." He had dashed the length of the habitat and had the intercom mike at his lips. "Give me a position on the *Towerpoint Mayan*."

"*Mayan* is up-bay, sir; passed abeam maybe five minutes ago moving at ten to twelve knots, right on schedule"

"She's okay?"

"Pretty as a picture, Mr. Tooms. Right on schedule enroute to Baltimore."

It didn't register on Tooms that the tanker's speed was ten knots faster than the planning had called for. She was already up-bay, safe; at that speed no submersible could touch her. What the hell were they up to?

"Bridge, I'll be below in habitat. Relay any incomings from Mr. Starring. Tell the comm shack that I'll want to be patched through to the boss as soon as we show him we're finished with this afternoon's schedule. Keep a weather eye out for one of the chariots, and give me a shout if you see it, or any unusual small craft activity around the ship or the dive site." He thumbed a triple sign-off click.

With a great grunt, Tooms heaved the tanks off his back, propped them on the deck and, grim-jawed, again surveyed the habitat. The failure of the TV monitors had taken on new meaning. Gotta be something in here to show their hand. Gotta go through the place inch by inch! He yanked open the drawers of the lab's file cabinet . . . manuals, research reports relating to the Divequest program. He turned to the crew's quarters, swept gear off the locker shelves, ripped open the zippered pockets of the coveralls . . . nothing: cigarettes, a roll of tape, ballpoint pens. He had started toward the bunks when he again spotted the white cylinders at the end of the habitat, not the two open halves on the desk, but the two others. He rubbed at a string of sweat, glanced at the seals, lumbered to the workbench, pawed through the tool drawer, then returned with a compact metal-frame hacksaw and a pair of needle-nosed pliers. He turned both cylinders to get the right angle. One was heavy as lead; the other was light. Its two halves sprung open . . . empty . . . as he set it on the desk again . . . empty, identical packing. He swung around to the third white can. The saw's rasp filled the habitat chamber.

Paul Head had very nearly died in the disastrous attack on the *Mayan*. He had slammed hard against the tanker's hull, cut free in the chariot, then spun away, his entire right side numb, hauling back on the controls with what little strength remained, fighting desperately for deliverance. The submersible was severely damaged. The Italian was gone!

From the cockpit, awash on the surface, Head struggled to orient himself. He knew he had broken a shoulder, maybe more. He did not try to stand for fear that he might lose his balance, pass out, and drown. He told himself he would hear Tonasi. He forced himself to search, twisting in the cockpit beyond the limits his body would bear, and screamed in a voice torn with rage and pain: "Italian! Italian! . . ." Nothing . . . "Tona-a-a-s-i! Goddamn you, bloody Italian!" The sight of the *Mayan*'s massive stern, already half a mile away, told him Tonasi was dead. He sensed his own quick, shallow breath. He had to move; the submersible might go down. The starboard plane had snapped and was floating alongside, held only by a cable. The port plane still answered to the stick. He applied power; the chariot responded, moving in a slow circle. He could not see the stern . . . bloody bent rudder! With the controls hard, he found he could force the chariot on a near-straight course. There was nothing to be gained from searching for Tonasi; the hell with him. He steered for the Octagon's triangle of flags, possessed by the pounding in his brain, the need to rig the last mine, blow the bloody catamaran, and, he knew, himself with it.

● ● ● · · ·

With the thud on the hull, Tooms dropped his pliers on the one restraint still to be broken, turned on one knee, and glared at Head, obviously injured, clawing his way up through the habitat's trunk and gasping for breath on the deck. He stood over him, arms at his side, fists clenched. "Well, well, well, the cat's away and the two mice do play! Missed the point of my last speech, you little bastard. Where the hell's Tonasi? First, he damned near rips off his arm, and now you're a basket case! You dumb little bastards! Where's Tonasi? What the are you up to, you little bastards?—all over now!"

Tooms turned away, spun back, enraged by the silence. Head couldn't speak. He kept shaking his head, his eyes on the American. He hunched himself onto an elbow, then onto his knees. The bunk he had to reach was several feet away. He crawled, his tanks banging the back of his neck, his right arm wedged against his crippled side. Ignoring Tooms's ranting, he maneuvered his left side to the expedition bag at the foot of the bunk. With a gasp, his back to Tooms, he found the pistol.

"You're the bloody little bastard!" Head cursed the fat, goateed face. "Over there!" He waved the gun from Tooms to the lab table. "Both hands on the table, Tooms, spread your bloody legs!" Tooms obeyed. Head lurched behind him, jammed the pistol barrel against the base of his skull. "You're dead, you pig!"

"Goddamnit, Pau—" The pistol slapped hard across Tooms's mouth. He could taste the blood.

"You're a dead pig. Your pig's face, it doesn't understand. Keep your fat, bloody mouth shut! . . . Pig! You will understand." He banged the pistol against the back of Tooms's head, pushed him toward the research cylinder. "Open it! It would be a waste if you died bloody ignorant!"

Tooms's hands were wet with sweat and the blood of his face. He popped the remaining band knowing what he would find. The halves of the cylinder were a snug fit. He had to hit the joint twice with the heel of his palm before it parted to reveal the professionally machined dull black and bronze of the encased explosive. "Mine! You—" The pistol cracked him again, hard against the back of his skull. He fell against a bulkhead, tried desperately to clear his mind—to stay alive.

"You're bloody right, for the first time in your criminal pig's existence, Dr. Oswald Pig Tooms. Not one mine! Three bloody mines, pig!" Tooms recoiled as Head measured him with the gun. "The tankers are dead; Starring's dead; you're dead!"

It was too enormous; too sinister. Head couldn't be lying. Tooms slowly made his way to a bunk, unsure of his life second by second. "You're nuts, Paul." The chief scientist's face, blotched by the blows it had taken, peered at the pistol. He pushed himself into a sitting position. "A hophead—"

"Your last rites, pig; the pig's final bloody statement."

"Hophead. I know you're on heroin, Christ!" The words broke with a deep, tearing cough. "Don't you think I've known it since we shipped. Everywhere you go, you and Tonasi smell like half of Singapore. Get out of here . . . up, over the side! I don't give a damn where. I'll say I never heard of you!"

"Enough, pig!"

Tooms heard the click, saw the pistol level at his chest. Head's eyes, tight with pain, had narrowed still further. "You're going to blow some things up now, are you, young Paul? Listen. This cylinder wasn't built for your Wild West show. Start popping off with that and you won't get near your pet mine! . . . Right through to the Chesa-peake, sonny boy, and we'll go together."

Head had staggered closer, was almost on top of him. "No more, pig. This bullet's going straight down through your pig's body, no holes in the bloody habi—"

Tooms slammed his heel into the outside of Head's knee. The snap of the bones and cartilage carried through their violent grunts and the crack of the pistol. Tooms didn't feel the bullet rip through his thigh. As Head fell toward him, Tooms's left arm came down hard on the inside of his elbow. His right hand fought and grappled for the gun. The second shot entered beneath Head's chin and exited at the back of his skull. Head's blood splattered onto his own. Tooms pushed the corpse away and stumbled to his feet before collapsing unconscious on the deck beneath the intercom.

At 5:00 P.M., July 4, twelve noon in Washington, Paul Manikata, co-owner of the largest yacht slipways in Valletta's Marsamxett Harbor, crossed the bridge onto Manoel Island enroute to his office. He was intercepted at the door, told of the American in the market for a yacht who was waiting for him.

They shook hands; Manikata introduced himself. "I don't know if you know Malta. I've just been down the coast a bit, Birzebbuga, on Pretty Bay, part of greater Marsaxlokk Bay . . . no, I can see that you don't. One of my better customers has not yet mastered his new auxiliary diesel. Rather late now, closing time really. How may I help you?"

Pierce Bromberger held out a calling card, name only, which was accepted and given an approving examination. "I'm glad I caught up with you. My flight leaves tomorrow morning."

"We do not have quite as many Americans as we used to. Here, sit over here, a bit more comfortable." Bromberger moved to the tat-tered leather armchair facing the desk.

"We're in the business of siting our new branch office, Mr. Mani-kata. Malta, Monaco, Venice are all in the running." Bromberger could see the wheels of calculation beginning to turn behind the tilted, smil-ing face. The search for the *Matabele* had not taken long. He had begun early that morning, strolling along the stern-to-quai yacht berths of Msida Creek, then Lazzaretto Creek and Manoel Island. It was on the island that his casual inquiries had produced the needed response. "Yes, on the far side, big ketch, anchored off the slipways. Manikata is the one to see." He had continued his stroll past Fort Manoel and the yacht club around to the slipways where he spotted the hull.

"Wherever we decide to put down our new roots, Mr. Manikata, I won't be content to stay ashore. Yachting is second only to women in life, and I like what I see here: good lines, and, important to me, real character. I've checked around and been told that you have the best stable in town, in the country for that matter. Is that so?"

"We have some very fine boats. Indeed, I am expecting a shipment of new Victor offshore thirty-two-foot sloops any day now."

"You're talking glass?"

"Yes, indeed. Fiberglass hulls, teak decks—"

"Not for me, Mr. Manikata. Keep your glass. If you can make a few more minutes for me, I'd like to take a look at two or three of your yachts."

"It's late, but, yes, of course." The yard owner hitched his chair toward the side of the desk, pulled open a long, green metal file-box drawer, poked through a row of cards, extracting five. The American's card had been genuinely engraved. He could feel it in his fingers . . . a visit most unexpected, most welcome. Manikata led the way through the rear door of the office into the now-deserted boat yard. He shouldered a wooden ladder and headed for a venerable, deep-keeled sloop high out of the water in a boat cradle. Bromberger climbed aboard, made his way through the boat, asking questions about her history, removing a deckboard in the cabin to jab at the bottom planking with his penknife. "She's a beauty. You say you are the owner?"

"Bought her three months ago, none better for off-shore cruising."

They inspected two more before Bromberger pointed to the ketch in the harbor. "There's one more I would like to see, well rigged, good hull, looks like she has a generous interior—good for entertaining."

"The *Matabele*?" The yard owner turned from the American to put the ladder away. He needed a minute to think. That boat was supposed to have been called for. He already had had to shift the mooring. The owner, that girl, probably wouldn't mind the prospect of a premium price, with a proper commission for him. He walked out onto one of the small finger piers with the American. "That ketch is not mine to sell, Mr. Bromberger."

"Is the owner aboard?"

"No, no one. She's locked up, in storage so to speak."

"Sounds promising. They might be willing to let her go. Mind if I take a look?"

The thought of the commission loomed again. "Yes, of course you may have a look around. You understand, I really must close down the office. I'll get you the key to the cabin hatch. Take the dingy over there."

The elusive person of Leslie Renfro grew more elusive still—departed England, gone from her uncle's residence in Malta, and now, by the looks of it, gone from the *Matabele*. Bromberger worked his way through the ketch's cabins, yanking open the empty lockers, the chests, the bunk-bed drawers, running his fingers along the hidden recesses of the interior. His mind went back to Switzerland, to the fragments of the case they had in hand—to the questioning under way in Italy—to the futility of this trip to Malta. What were they extracting in Rome? Damnit, that's where he should be.

His hand stopped behind a bunk, pulled out an empty drawstring cloth sack, tobacco, Italian marking. The old captain said the boat had come from Italy. He tucked the bit of cloth back. In the cabin shadows of the approaching evening, he took the penlight from his jacket, pointed it here and there into the dark corners. The chart drawer and table were empty. He poked through the galley, aware that Manikata would soon grow impatient. The pieces of the case . . . Sweetman had seventh, eighth and ninth senses . . . now, in Malta, still nothing . . . what was missing? One of the killers was a woman. He was looking for a woman, Sweetman's lost diver's daughter. What were the odds; about four billion to one?

He flipped two brass bolts, removed the cabin stairs, and pointed his light back into the dark engine compartment . . . nothing extra, the dark gray enamel of the engine wiped clean as it should be. This daughter . . . she, they—the old captain had said there were three of them—knew what they were doing. The ketch was well-maintained. Three of them . . . Grabner and his blond Englishman . . . the GIS . . . the Prima Linea . . . blond scruffy member of the *Matabele*'s crew? For Christ's sake . . . they were in Malta, how the hell many miles away from Geneva? . . . Aboard the ketch when Burdette died. Where the hell were they now? They didn't fit. If he had found her, talked to her, he would be on his way back to Rome!

Bromberger replaced the cabin stairs, stuck his head out of the hatch, and called across the boat basin.

"She's great, really great, be back over in a second."

He ran his light along the electrical box on the bulkhead over the toilet, raised the toilet lid. A coating of grayish mold covered the small circle of water at the base of the bowl. They had been off the ketch for sometime. He walked the length of the cabin, stopped at the open grate of the cast-iron fireplace, bits of black wood charcoal amidst the ashes. Someone keeping warm, hardly necessary this time of year, not in this part of the world.

He bent down, played his light against the back of the fire chamber. His eyes, at first, had tricked him. It wasn't a panel in the metal. It was a thin piece of wood stuffed up into the back, charred black on the side facing into the cabin, but not consumed before the fire had died . . . squared-off at one end, nail hole, broken at the other end; pine crating, the same the world over. He rolled the wood in his hands. Nothing . . . he caught the variations in the black. In searing the surface, the flames had burnt some lettering or numbering.

He twisted the wood until the penlight offered the best distinction between the blacks . . . stenciling . . . probably a company name or consignment code . . . consignment code. What he saw was immediately familiar to him, yet the reason escaped him. There were two partial lines, in fact, both half deleted, both broken by the narrow breadth of the board. The numbers, groups of two and three: above them, the perpendicular and V of a letter, two inward diagonals and what appeared to be a crossbar, another V, then a break and a repeat perpendicular and V, this time another perpendicular curving out to the right at the tip, then the broken end of the board.

N. It's an N. He continued to work through the puzzle. NAV . . . NAV . . . NAI . . . NAV . . . NAP . . . "NAV NAP!" He shouted in the cabin, "Sweet Jesus God!" He thrust the wood into his jacket pocket, too long. He wiped his hands on the nearest bunk cushion, unbuttoned two buttons and slipped the wood beneath his shirt, locked the *Matabele*'s hatch, and pulled the few oars' lengths back to the yard.

"You find the ketch to your liking, Mr. Bromberger?"

"Very much. Where can I find the owner, Leslie Renfro, Mr. Manikata?"

The Maltese yard owner was amused by the American's impatience, so typical. "I'll put you in touch, sir, but it cannot be . . . how did you know her name? Of course, some identification in the cabin. It cannot be done overnight. I will have to confirm that the ketch is in fact still for sale. I have a professional obligation to check with the owner, as you will appreciate—and she and her crew are in America, your United States, Mr. Bromberger." He chortled over the coincidence. "Yes, they left Malta at least a fortnight ago with your famous American industrialist aboard that splendid ship I had the honoring of visiting—"

Bromberger was already on the run out of the yard before Manikata had uttered "the *Towerpoint Octagon.*" He had to alert Sweetman—new players on the pitch!

The stifling boredom of Lancaster's Eleventh Street retreat offered no redeeming charms. 8:30 P.M., July 4. Goddamned Lancaster, goddamned evening shot. Hanspeter Sweetman lay sprawled, stripped to his shorts, on one of the beds in the lounge of the Fisker Hilton. Sherri Easton and her cozy pad in Chelsea floated by him. What a lovely number; who's in the rack with her tonight? . . . More power to her . . .

"A message, 'Shattered Flag,' coming across from Mr. Bromberger, Mr. Sweetman." Harold Fisker's small orange head had appeared in the doorway.

"Fisker, you'd make a lousy lay, know that?" The orange head had already disappeared. Sweetman shouted after him. "The hell with Pierce. Any word from the son of a bitch Lancaster?" He had busted his butt for the director, pulled together an update on the Burdette case as soon as he had arrived from London. And, Lancaster had told him to stand by, keep himself available . . . and, he was standing by. Sweetman pulled on a pair of pants, left the belt hanging loose, the fly open, and moved into the communications center.

"Buddy Pierce wasn't too happy with me, Harold. What's he got?"

"Second section coming off." Fisker stripped the emerging message from the machine, gave the original to Sweetman. The director's line lit. The little man jumped to take the call. "Mr. Sweetman,

Langley's patching through a call from Mr. Bromberger—for you—he's on!"

"Pierce, Hanspeter. Yeah . . . what's churning?"

"Have you received my message?"

"It's coming across right now, important? What the hell time is it over there?"

"Midnight, after midnight—damned important, couldn't risk a transmission foul-up. The woman, the diver's daughter you had me running a line on, apparently is with the ambassador's brother, Burdette's brother Thomas Starring—"

"For Christ's sake! . . . "

"With him right now, do you hear me?"

"Yeah, yeah, keep going."

"There are two men with her, don't know much, one apparently blond, English-speaking . . ."

"Christ, Grabner's boy?"

"Could be . . ." The voice faded on the overseas circuit, came back in. . . .

"Pierce, Pierce, you dropped on me. I missed your last—English-speaking, and . . . ?

"Right, one blond, English, the other, possible Maltese, Italian; can't confirm. The three of them were living aboard a yacht in Malta. I just went through the boat—message spells it out, Hanspeter."

"You're coming in strong. Go ahead."

"Piece of packing crate in cabin . . . I checked with Rome before message to you . . . serial numbers are part of that NATO Navy Naples munitions heist the GIS just scored on in Italy—Navy swimmer mines—confirmed that—"

"*Those* mines, for Christ's sake?"

"You got it. There was nothing else—boat clean. Now listen. The woman, the daughter Renfro—"

"Go ahead, I'm reading while you talk."

"She and the two males are reported to have shipped two weeks ago from Malta, bound for the United States on the Towerpoint flagship, with Starring, Burdette's brother, aboard."

"Right."

"Ship's name, *Towerpoint Octagon*. That's it—you celebrating with Fisker?"

"Yeah, eight-forty-five on the Fourth; Harold and I are going strong. Pierce . . . I feel a jolt, think you may have sprung the lid . . ."

"Only a crack, but it's a goddamned crack running straight in one direction. Find out where that ship is, what the hell they're up to . . . for all I know, she may have said that's for the ride, and is on her way to Toledo . . ."

"Like hell Toledo; I'm signing off."

"I'll be working the Rome end through the night."

Sweetman's powerful arm slammed the phone down. "One clean chip off the falcon, Fisker; we've spotted the jewels. Get Coast Guard Ops on the line, run a line on that ship"—his finger ran along the message—"the *Towerpoint Octagon*. Tell 'em I want to patch through to Starring."

Fisker slipped a cough drop into his mouth, took his seat at the console, worked swiftly, placed his hand over his receiver. "They have me holding. Coast Guard's checking with the Towerpoint Corporations Ops Center in New York. I should mention, Mr. Sweetman, Coast Guard Ops records these calls—"

"We're all big boys, Harold."

Fisker was on the line again. "Yes, do, very important. . . . The ship apparently is nearby, at anchor somewhere in the Chesapeake Bay. Coast Guard is patching us through to her now. . . . Hello, Special Agent Sweetman, Washington, calling Mr. Thomas Starring. Hello?" Fisker repeated his words. "I have someone in ship's communications, Mr. Sweetman; Mr. Starring is not aboard."

Sweetman grabbed a second phone. "This is Sweetman. We're dealing with an emergency. I want to speak to the ship's captain, now!" A voice started at the other end of the patch . . .

"I don't give a damn, even if he's shaving his goddamned legs," Sweetman burst back, "tell him to get his butt to this phone now, you simple son of a bitch. Coast Guard put this call through, didn't they? Tell him if he doesn't believe we both got a problem, he will when he's fired! . . . "

"Let me know when he's on the line, Fisker." Sweetman slammed his receiver down, went through Bromberger's message line by line.

"On!"

"Captain, sorry to trouble you. Two questions. Where can I reach your boss? Yeah, Starring, absolutely vital. . . . Fisker, you got that? Go ahead, Captain . . . okay, okay, I read you. That number's the hotel.

Second . . . What?" Sweetman clamped his hand over the phone, still listening. "Get this down, Harold; you're recording, make sure . . ." He was listening intently to the *Octagon*'s captain. "No response? . . . I get you . . . just discovered them, one dead, one wounded. Can you put him on? . . . Still below, too weak to move, barely conscious. I read you. Okay! . . . Captain, you've got a woman, Renfro, yeah, two men . . . She left with Starring! . . . One dead, one missing! . . . Christ! Captain, I'm ordering a cutter out to your ship. You have? Okay. . . . These people have ordnance. When the other shows, hang on to him. I'll leave it to you. We have some questions for him. Okay? Keep him under guard. The Coast Guard will be there to lend you a hand."

Fisker was speaking to him as he ended the call, took the receiver from his ear. "Mr. Starring's secretary, a Mrs. Sullivan—"

"Right."

"Line three."

"Mrs. Sullivan, Muriel, hello? Hello, Hanspeter Sweetman. You cleared me into TOPIC London, yeah. I need to talk to your boss, Starring, immediately; literally life and death . . . where?" Sweetman slammed his hand against the wall. "Christ; you've got to be kidding. What's that address?" Fisker was on an extension, taking down her response. "You've got Renfro with you, right? . . . She's not there? Okay! I hear you. I hear you. He doesn't want interruptions. He may have some. I'll be in touch."

Fisker ran after him into the lounge. Sweetman's shirt was already half buttoned; he was kicking around for the rest of his clothes. "Harold! One, get back to Coast Guard Ops. Get the cutter out there. Two, need both pieces; where the hell are they? Ankle and shoul—you got 'em . . . God bless your little orange head. Three, wheels outside?"

"Twenty-four hours a day."

"Four, this has the makings of a miserable goddamned mess"— Sweetman inspected the pistols, strapped the first to his leg, grunted as he pulled the boot on—"so get on the horn to Lancaster, direct, no flunkies. Tell him what's going on, okay? . . . Up to speed!"

"He will have received Mr. Bromberger's message at the same time that we did."

Sweetman thought of his earlier references to the director in his exchanges of traffic with Bromberger, shot Fisker a rueful glance.

"I'll give him a complete report as soon as you're on your way, Mr. Sweetman."

As he buckled on the shoulder holster, sweat was already seeping through his shirt. He yanked out the ASP pistol . . . loaded. The 9mm cartridges angled forward, upward, visible through the slotted sides of the seven-round magazine and the clear plastic grips of the pistol.

Fisker was back at the console with the Coast Guard, on the line when Sweetman raced through the communications center. "Your driver's standing by!" The words chased the big man through the opening in the wall. Fisker's hands flipped the switches activating the outer doors.

The cab pulled through a squealing U-turn, ran two red lights on Eleventh Street, near-empty southbound.

"What have we got?"

"Only ten blocks"—the instructions had already been passed over radio by Fisker—"but tonight . . . going to be tough!"

Sweetman's eyes were with the Agency driver's, trained on the police barricade ahead. The avenue was blocked at Fourteenth Street. He strained to recall the details of the girl, Renfro, the scraps he had assembled in Yarmouth. People, thousands of them, were coming into view on the far side of the police line. His ID was already thrust out the window. "Put the light on the roof, damn it," he snapped at the driver as the cab nosed to a stop.

"Special agent!" He drilled the words at the officers who gave instant respect to the badge. "Going through; pull 'em aside!"

"Can let you through, but it won't do you any good. It's solid a block ahead, wall-to-wall people. You couldn't get through if you tried to ram a path!"

The driver already had the cab in reverse, pulling back to make a run north around the crowd. The officers at the barrier shouted after them, "Don't know where you're headed . . . entire area's roped off, as far north as H Street!"

"Stop this son of a bitch!" Sweetman was out of the cab. He spun toward the driver. "New York and Eighteenth, northeast corner, right?"

"Straight ahead, follow the curve of the fence past the White House!"

"Goddamnit!" Sweetman vaulted the barrier, raced westward into the thickening mob flowing through the twilight to the national fireworks.

·····•Chapter 17•····

In the twilight, the first starshells soared to their apogee above the Washington Monument and burst into red, white, and blue chrysanthemums, which dissolved into shimmering silver globes. Fifty mortar salutes tore the air. The Fourth of July crowd stopped in its tracks to watch and roar a whistling, shouting approval. Sweetman had covered only half a block, was forcing his way now at no more than a walk. With first explosions of the celebration.

Leslie Renfro pressed against the shadow of the high brick wall bordering the rear gardens of the Octagon mansion. The fireworks flashed down through the antique glass of the windows, played through the facets of the drawing room's Waterford chandelier, flickering pastels of reflected light around Tommie Starring.

As a young man, Starring had felt embarrassment with his first reading of the history of his distinguished ancestor. The British had held America in such contempt, had prevailed with such arrogance in the depths of the 1812 struggle, flaunted Madison's government, which had stumbled from one error to the next.

Starring had pored over the maps, shocked at the ease of the two-pronged British advance, to the east overland through Benedict, Upper Marlboro, and Bladensburg, to the west, by water up the

Potomac. The humiliations had piled so high, the burning of the White House, the self-destruction of Fort Washington—and, responsibility had lain, ultimately, with his forebear.

Madison's good qualities, his judgement, his coolness, in fact, in the midst of great crisis, his skill as a political thinker and his statesmanship had gradually moved to center stage in Starring's mind through the years. Tonight, Starring walked alone from room to room in the mansion. His euphoria magnified the elegance of the restored interior, drove him, as he knew it would, to reflect on the history of the young nation, and of Madison—looking for the words to translate that spirit, the ultimate success of that struggle into the contributions to history that he was now making.

Starring had eaten lightly from the food Sullivan had had catered. The shape, the theme of the message he was striving for, was starting to emerge. Heartwood—heartwood, exactly. The president's optimism, his perspective, waving off the critics . . . the Lincoln quote played in his thoughts. He pulled the stopper from the middle crystal decanter on the sideboard, poured half a glass of sherry. Resuming his stroll, he caught his reflection in one of the gilded swan mirrors on either side of the mantle at the east end of the room. The reality threatened his inspiration. He departed the drawing room for the coolness of the circular, marble-tiled front hall. A sip of sherry rested on his tongue. His eyes followed the curve of the wooden doors.

The architectural details were extraordinary, the rectangles branching from the circle in which he was standing, the drawing room to his right, the dining room adorned with the china and the pastels of the first owner, the hidden doorway, half open, leading to the narrow, zigzagging upward triangle of the servants' stairway, and, in front of him, the grand sweep of the main, oval stairway.

The rear double doors of the Octagon were open to the night. The silhouette of his armed chauffeur, the one concession he had granted his staff, was rocked back in a chair enjoying the endless succession of color bursts and the echo of the rocket shell explosions bouncing from the curved glass façade of the modern architectural headquarters towering behind the Octagon.

Starring stepped forward into the well and gazed upward through the half-light radiating from the second floor to the glint of the single chandelier suspended in the darkness. He traced the elegant, white spindled bannister from the post at his side to the top of the third-floor landing.

Having replenished his sherry, Starring started up the stairs, count-
ing them in his mind . . . fourteen to the first landing, another eleven,
the end of the carpeting, the hard wood of the second floor. What
burdens Madison bore up these stairs, night after night . . . incredible to
contemplate . . . Towerpoint today, as big as all of Madison's America!

The hallway flickered in the stuttering red reflections of a skyborne
snaking dragon. He crossed into the Treaty of Ghent Room, the mansion's circular study directly over the front hall. A fresh, snapping stac-
cato of showering golds and greens commanded the sky, bounced
through the glass of half-shuttered windows and played again off the
polished surface of the fish-eye mirror above the white mantle.

Starring drew back the wooden chair, took a seat at the circular
wooden table, ringed with pull drawers, in the very center of the room.
It was here, in the elegance of this chamber, so refined with its central
chandelier, white ceiling, white ornamental cornice, green wall hang-
ings, and golden drapes that James Madison had signed the Treaty of
Ghent ending that war. Here, Madison and Monroe, comforted only by
the victory at New Orleans, had weighed the balanced words crafted by
the U.S. and British delegations in Ghent, carried across the Atlantic to
New York, then overland to Washington, to this room, a treaty no better than the war, but a treaty that had brought that war to an end at last.

Starring slid his hands across the smooth surface of the table,
took up the text of Madison's second inaugural address from the
stack of papers assembled for the evening, and reread the principles and the course that Madison had set for his young nation once
again at peace. ". . . to foster a spirit of independence . . . to respect
the rights and authorities reserved to the States and to the people
. . ." Towerpoint, the heartwood of America. He sipped from the
sherry and began to write.

● ● ● · ·

The two women had not spoken during the short ride from the
White House to the hotel. In the lobby, Leslie Renfro had slipped
into the first shop, until Sullivan was on her way upstairs. With the
secretary out of the way, she crossed to another of the many lobby
boutiques and purchased a pair of sunglasses and a fashionable straw
hat, which she immediately put on. At the front desk, she obtained a
street map, which she took with her into the elevator.

In the Towerpoint suite, one of the three bedroom doors border-ing the sitting room was already closed. Two dozen long-stemmed roses gave fragrance to the surroundings. The fourth side of the suite opened into an alcove with a dining table spread with trays of wine, cheeses, and a pyramidal bouquet of fresh fruits. The third bedroom, separated from Sullivan's by the larger middle room, bore her name, Renfro. Behind the closed door, she charted her route, left the hotel to time it, then returned to await the evening.

At 9:00 P.M. she departed again. In sixty minutes, the pride of his empire would be destroyed. He would be dead, and terror would strike millions. This trilogy of ordained fate drummed with the steps taking her with the flow of the last of the fireworks' throng down Connecticut Avenue, through Farragut Square, beneath the bronze of the victorious admiral.

The crowd was being filtered between white wooden barricades erected by the police to block auto traffic. Instinctively, she turned a block before she had planned, the alarm of the agents in the after-noon still ringing in her head. Separated now from the crowd, she glanced at the street signs, crossed, heading south on Eighteenth. Beyond Pennsylvania Avenue, the street was deserted. A police patrol car rounded the corner, headed toward her. Her eyes straight ahead, she kept her pace; the patrol rolled by.

With the downhill slope of the final blocks, she slowed. Noise . . . a group of young people, drunk, crossed behind her. The dark gray stone of the tall building on her left gave way to a closed, heavy iron gate marking the beginning of the Octagon's grounds. On the far side of this gate, a high brick wall ran with only one opening, a smaller, closed wooden door, to the mansion.

The shine of the limousine caught her eyes as she dashed across the ivy border for the cover of the wall beneath the first chrysanthemum aerial display. Kneeling, she eased the machine pistol from her bag, fit-ted the silencer, clicked the loaded magazine home, and shifted the fir-ing lever from safe to single shot. With the Skorpion half hidden by her shoulder bag, she eased back, studied the wall. The driveway gate was too heavy, too exposed, too distant. She returned to the wooden door. The *thut* of a silenced bullet bursting the light, interior padlock, was lost in the machine-gun snapping of half a dozen silver-and-crimson aerial bombshells. She slid through the door, easing it closed behind her.

With the next skyburst, she saw the shrub-bordered path to the Octagon's rear door.

"Hey! Who goes?" The chauffeur jumped to his feet, toppling the chair off the brick steps.

"Jake, Jake"—her voice was friendly, soft, reassuring—"it's Leslie, Leslie Renfro; no cause for alarm."

"Miss Renfro, what the hell are you doing here? Strict rules tonight, no visitors." His hand had left his weapon. He knew her voice. He saw her young face at the same moment the elongated barrel leveled against his chest. A second *thut*, little more than the rush of an African blowgun, then a third, and she stepped across his body into the rear hall. The bag eased from her shoulder; she stood silently, waiting for her eyes to adjust to the interior light. The Octagon was without a sound . . . no . . . easing forward into the stairwell she heard a book being closed, the rustle of paper. He was on the second floor.

Her left hand ran before her up the banister railing, guiding her up the steps, to the level and turn of the landing, and the rise of the second flight. She stood in the doorway of the room where he worked for nearly a minute before he turned, sensing her presence.

"Miss, Miss Ren—Leslie?" His mind was centuries in the past, his pen on the future, at the moment he focused on the woman who had penetrated his solitude. The light of the chandelier fell across her face, the shadow of her neck, the flesh at the opening of her white blouse. His physical attraction for her had been intense from the first evening they had met aboard his ship in Malta. She had frozen his most subtle advances. His good judgment had prevailed, but his attraction remained strong.

"Leslie, you're looking lovely this evening, my young friend. What are you doing here? Where on earth did you find that gun?" His eyes had traveled from the vee of her blouse, to the skirt he had never known her to wear before, to the incredible weapon she cradled in her bare arms. He rose, offering to take it from her. His face suddenly lined with concern. "Has there been some trouble, at the hotel . . . on the street? You're alright?"

"Sit down, Thomas Starring." It was 9:30 P.M. The fireworks splashed with mounting intensity against the glass of the Treaty of Ghent Room. Her voice was deep in its dark, ordering tone, her words so unexpected that he retook his chair before realizing he had accepted her command.

"In half an hour, Thomas Starring, your *Towerpoint Mayan* will be blown apart with a force that will shatter the entire Chesapeake Bay. In half an hour, a mine will destroy your *Towerpoint Partner*. A third mine will blow your catamaran. You must know that now, Thomas Starring. In half an hour, you will be dead."

He looked at the muzzle of the gun aimed at him, raised his eyes to study hers, his hands planted on the arms of the chair. She's drunk . . . some sort of breakdown . . . too much pressure today, the visit, the rushed pace of early dives . . . too young for all of that. Good God, always the unexpected!

"Leslie, put that gun down, over here on this table." He half rose again. "Jake!" His voice carried out into the rest of the mansion. "Jake will take that for you. We'll get Sullivan down here to help. Everything will—"

A single bullet ripped through the priceless rug beneath his feet. "Sit down, Thomas Starring. When you are dead, we will publish our report to the world. We will tell the people of your crimes and of your punishment. The world will rejoice at your death and the destruction of your empire. You are the ultimate criminal, Thomas Starring. Your sister paid for her crimes. You will now pay for yours —after you have written your confession."

Starring's face was set, the gray eyes flashing, his thoughts surging in anger now at this interloper who threatened him. "Jake!" He could not understand the lack of response, until the ugly automatic weapon waving him back to his seat gave him the answer. He reached slowly across the desk for the brass letter opener. A fresh kaleidoscope of colors sparkled through the mottled glass.

"Push it away, on the floor!" The machine pistol trained on his hand.

"See here, Miss Renfro"—his voice was at its sternest, the boom he sent across the board room—"I have absolutely no idea what has brought on this sickness, these hallucinations. You need help. I want to get you that help. Frankly"—his lips were apart, teeth set—"frankly I am annoyed. I want you to leave immediately! You have inexcusably intruded. Please go!"

"Take a fresh sheet of paper, Thomas Starring. We have twenty minutes." His hand drew back from the blunt knife. She swept it away. "Write!"

"Yes." He was subdued, placed a sheet in front of him, studied her more with his mind than his eyes. "Miss Renfro, you mentioned my sister—"

"She was in a white suit that night, Thomas Starring. The bullets from this gun entered her brain, her nose, her jaw, her throat, and the cavity where there was no heart. Does that confirm your top secret reports of her capital punishment? Justice was not served. She did not confess before she died."

Renfro, or someone close to her, had killed Connie! Goddamnit! He did not sense fear, rather a challenge to be met. He burned. He had been taken. She was not the innocent . . . she . . . Christ, hard to know, hard to fit it all together . . . but that gun. He had been briefed, Don't resist. The expert on hostage survival reappeared in his mind, the Trade Center briefings. . . . "What would you like me to write?"

"Confession, all capital letters, at the top of the page." She moved one step closer, to monitor.

"Confession? . . . Yes." He penned the word in large letters, "Yes?"

"I, Thomas Madison Starring, confess the crimes for which I am about to die . . ."

Don't resist . . . the briefings, the words of the expert . . . where the hell is that damned chauffeur . . . dead? "You know my middle name?"

"Do not talk, Thomas Starring. Read what you have written."

He read the line.

She resumed. ". . . to murder, to imperialist repression . . . and to the most vile criminal acts against the innocent people of the world. . . ."

The words, utter insanity; her voice, so calm. He continued to write.

"I confess to plundering the innocent. I"—she followed as the pen scratched the line—". . . confess to the plunder and wanton destruction of the earth and seas. . . ."

He placed the pen on the table, looked through the upper panes at the man-made thunder and lightning bursting in the sky, contemplated his leap at her, time to end this.

"Sixteen minutes, Thomas Starring." Her voice was harder. "I confess to these horrendous crimes."

Starring wrote, laid the pen down again with a look of total contempt.

"I confess"—now her words rose, emotion surging in her throat,—"to the vicious murder of Commander John Lloyd Renfro, and to the vicious murder of his wife, Mary Jessica Renfro—"

"Goddamnit!" He leapt from the chair. "That's totally false crap!" His face trembled with emotion; he had shocked himself with his words. The bullet passed through the leather arch of his right shoe, through the foot into the floor. He fell sideways, horror stricken at the red oozing through the leather and the lace, even before the pain.

"Sit down, Thomas Starring. We have thirteen minutes." She placed the silencer against his face. The stench of cordite burned in his nose. "Take off your belt . . . now!"

He obeyed.

"Strap it high above the knee, as high as you can . . . tight!" She repeated her parents' names.

Starring's face was white. He bled, but he still could not write those impossible lies. "Miss Renfro." The room was spinning . . . My God, I'm passing out . . . He pushed himself straighter. "Miss Renfro, I have murdered no one!" He steadied himself, probed her face for understanding. "Put that weapon away. You have wounded me. You . . . you couldn't have killed Connie. We both need help. I . . . Jake!" Still silence. "I treasure you, Leslie"—his voice caught with emotion—"and all that you have done for me, for Towerpoint. . . . ."

"Write!" The pistol leveled at his head. He carefully recorded the words dictated to him for a third time.

"These names, who . . . ?"

"You are the murderer of my father and my mother!" She had control again. The condemnation was cold and hard.

"My young friend—"

"No more. Write! There are ten minutes."

"Renfro, Renfro . . . your father? He was the one who lost his life in the storm . . . your mother?"

"Murdered by you. You would not know, would you? Nom the gas of the oven, the destroyed soul, a spark of God ground beneath your obscene heel. Write!"

Starring stared at his shattered foot. The bleeding had stopped; pain was jolting through his leg. He had expected more blood. He twisted in agony. The pain surged upward through his hips, his spine, thrashed in his head. He forced his eyes to hers again. "I . . . I didn't murder your parents, Leslie, you poor child. I mourned your father. We established a fund." His face was chalk beneath the crystal.

"Drink your glass!"

Again, he obeyed, draining the sherry.

"Do not move!" She read what he had written, returned it to the table. "The final sentence: I am guilty of these crimes, accept death as my just punishment, and call on the innocent people of the world to rise against their oppressors." His hand was still, his face twisted in pain and revulsion.

Thut, another bullet sliced through the embossed leather of the Treaty of Ghent table, splintering the side in its exit.

"You don't know what you're saying. You're sick, a sick animal! You are part of the cancer that is devouring the civilization mankind has carefully shepherded through two millennia—"

"No, Thomas Starring. You almost deserve pity. You are the cancer, the virulence that destroys. What chance has the individual against your power? What chance has this earth you march across with your billions, plotting its desolation, shaping its ruin as a sterile monument to your greed?—fascist, imperialist pig that you are, Thomas Starring. Write!"

He wrote, head propped against his left hand, fingers locked in the elegant white hair. Across the table, the text of his stockholders' address lay scattered, scarcely begun. She again examined his work. "Sign and date it. We have eight minutes."

● ● ● ∙ ∙

Two policemen, one plainclothes, the other uniformed, had spotted Sweetman, moved in on him as he struggled through the crowd packed on the sidewalk, the street, seated and leaning against the White House fence. He had all the earmarks, "Up against the fence; spread 'em!"

The crowd in the immediate area forced itself back, attention split between the rockets and the new, electric excitement of the arrest. Sweetman, streaming with sweat, knew he had to be quick: two, three seconds from the first shouts before their frisking hands hit his weapons. "Lieutenant!"

Who the hell knew the rank of a plainclothes cop?

"Lieutneant, left rear pocket—ID Check it now!"

The searching hands produced the leather badge cover. They blurted apology. Sweetman destroyed them with his glare, pocketed the badge, and was gone, swallowed by the crowd. He broke across the street, through the expanse of green honoring the First Division, a wake of curses and complaints as he hurdled the picnickers and the lovers in the grass.

The mob was still thick on Seventeenth Street. He waded across, turning right, north, along the front of the Corcoran Museum. If she's there, she's armed . . . if he's not dead already! Christ, there may be two . . . a lookout?

He rounded New York Avenue. Fireworks illuminated the brick mansion at the end of the block, and then faded into blackness. He dashed to the far side of the empty avenue, broke stride to catch his breath, to study the random pattern of dim lights on the first and second floors. Alive . . . Lancaster's going to want them all alive!

His pistol was out of its shoulder holster. He pressed against the brick wall, crept toward the front steps, froze until the next silver burst shimmered down into the night. No one! He strained to spot any sign of life . . . no one. Up the stone steps in four bounds . . . Locked! He listened, still silence. Sweetman vaulted the stair railing, dropped to the grass, and moved north along the Eighteenth Street wall until he came to the open courtyard door. The thumb of his left hand found the destroyed padlock.

● ● ● ● ·

"Give me the confession. You must move, now!"

The effect of the sherry had gone. Starring's stomach was twisted in nausea, his body laboring under the surges of pain. "I've done what you have asked." He was terrified by the tremble of his hand. He brought it to his brow to wipe the sweat away. "For whatever purpose, you have the words you have dictated. Please, I urgently need a doctor. I am bleeding to death, Miss Renfro."

"On your feet." She moved behind him, placed the silencer snout of the Skorpion at the back of his head. "On your feet. No more talk!"

"I can't—God . . . I . . ."

She fired twice at the fish-eye mirror. The glass sprayed through the room. He heaved himself up, crashed to the floor in pain.

"Get up! The next one will be into your other foot. Think of John Lloyd Renfro. Think of Mary Jessica Renfro. Their noble deaths will give you strength." She backed up two steps. "Out into the hall, up the stairs!"

Starring's mouth fell open in horror. He had told himself that he must play along, play for time, for the unknown, for life. Jake, someone had to deliver him from this insanity. *But . . . the stairs . . .* "My foot, I can't put weight—"

"We have five minutes, Thomas Starring. Your foot will then no longer be a problem. Crawl!"

● ● ● ● ·

Sweetman's heel squashed down on the lifeless muscle of the chauffeur's arm. He saw the blood, a shiny pool of black. He pulled his second pistol from its holster, held his breath . . . voices, too faint to understand, still no move to intercept him. Okay, alone. She's probably alone . . . where? He crossed the threshold. Not down here . . . a laboring sound, a woman's voice. *"Upstairs!* Three minutes. Ten stairs more!"

There was another deep groan, dragging, thumping. Sweetman darted to the far side of the stairwell. He could see them now. The fireworks' reds and greens had bounced from the glass of the architect's headquarters, flashed through the rear windows of the Octagon, illuminating the two figures, one low on the stairs, the other erect.

"Move, you pig! To die on these stairs is to die a pig's death. Die with the glory and respect you so desperately crave. Faster! Your ships will go down with honor." Her words fell like hail. He struggled higher. "Do you want to die moaning at my feet?"

No shot from here . . . Renfro, got to be her, and, she's got me if I try to make it up the stairs. Sweetman eased back out into the hallway, searching the ground floor . . . cupboard, plates, goddamned dining room. He returned to the hall. Door . . . closet? . . . He explored the space with the heel of his hand, taking care not to bang the weapon . . . not a closet. His hand had found the base of a railing . . . stairs! He pulled the door closed behind him, lit a match. A narrow, triangular stairway cut upward at sharp angles through the gloom to the upper floors. His thumbs checked his weapons, both safeties off. He started up, one shoulder sliding along the outer wall to guide and steady him in the darkness.

The stairway door was open again at the second floor. He kept climbing. Their voices began to return. He continued, easing up step by step. His muscles locked! A shaft of red and gold; it was gone, light from the reflections in the sky, long enough only to reveal the crack of the opening at the third floor landing.

"One minute, Starring! On your feet! On your feet!"

He hauled himself up by the railing. "I cannot . . . reason with you . . . I am not guilty . . . of any crime. . . . You, you are guilty! You and the slime who tear down, tear down, never build. Love is not founded on"—he shuddered, clung to the bannister—"your hate and destruction. You shame and disgrace your mother and . . ."

"Your time has come, Thomas Starring. Jump!" The gun barrel swung over the railing. "You have the same vision into the future that those you murdered must have known. Your ships are exploding now, torn and sinking, more deaths of more innocents, and the blood is on your hands. Enter the vision. Jump!"

He was fully erect, turning away from her toward the void of the well when his face contorted, a puzzled expression, and he crashed down against the banister on the third floor landing.

"Drop it, Renfro, goddamnit!" Sweetman burst onto the landing, snapping off two warning shots, the 9mm ASP trained on her. She spun, flipping the Skorpion to automatic with the first flash of his pistol. A spitting line of bullets tore along the wall, closing to stop his charge. Her foot turned in Starring's stomach. The Skorpion flew from her hands; she plunged back first over the railing. The machine pistol rattled to a stop at the base of the second floor stairs.

Sweetman pressed four fingers against Starring's neck. The heart was pumping. He had fainted, saved his own life. From the third floor of the Octagon, the agent could see by the twist of the form on the marble below that Leslie Renfro was dead.

At first light, the helicopter came in low toward the *Towerpoint Octagon,* rippling the water around one of the two Coast Guard patrol boats lying off the catamaran. In the night, the *Towerpoint Partner* had been lost at sea. A second explosion, with no loss, had churned the waters of the bay. The *Mayan*, well up-bay, had been halted. A Navy SEAL team was conducting an urgent inspection of the enormous hull. Sweetman was met on the flight deck by the *Octagon's* captain, cleared through the Coast Guard checkpoint, and escorted to the main deck center well.

Head's body was the first to emerge from the habitat. Shrouded in a rubber bag and lashed to a wire basket stretcher, it was taken to the ship's reefer to await shipment ashore. The rich July orange of the sun's upper curve had broken the horizon by the time the ship's doctor had Oats Tooms ready for the trip to the surface. Details of the terror had been kept from him. Still fully conscious, he was buoyed by the knowledge that Starring had survived. The questions that dogged him would soon be replaced by the impact of the attack's shocking magnitude.

With scuba gear on, he was lowered through the trunk, strapped to the same wire stretcher, and lifted to the main deck. The face mask and tanks were eased from him. Flat on his back awaiting transfer to the medevac flight, his eyes traveled first to the white and blue flag with its swallow tails snapping from the ship's yard, then to the powerful bald agent peering down at him, to the dull black of the wristwatch identifying him as a member of the underseas fraternity.

He squinted at Sweetman, "Got some patching to do on . . . be back . . . tell the skipper not to strike the diver's flag."

• • • • • About the Author • • • • •

A. DENIS CLIFT is a former naval officer, editor of the *Proceedings* magazine, and president emeritus of the National Intelligence University. He served in eleven administrations, including tours as National Security Council senior staff member for Soviet Union and Eastern and Western Europe, national security adviser to the vice president, and chief of staff, Defense Intelligence Agency. His books include *With Presidents to the Summit*.

The **Naval Institute Press** is the book-publishing arm of the U.S. Naval Institute, a private, nonprofit, membership society for sea service professionals and others who share an interest in naval and maritime affairs. Established in 1873 at the U.S. Naval Academy in Annapolis, Maryland, where its offices remain today, the Naval Institute has members worldwide.

Members of the Naval Institute support the education programs of the society and receive the influential monthly magazine *Proceedings* or the colorful bimonthly magazine *Naval History* and discounts on fine nautical prints and on ship and aircraft photos. They also have access to the transcripts of the Institute's Oral History Program and get discounted admission to any of the Institute-sponsored seminars offered around the country.

The Naval Institute's book-publishing program, begun in 1898 with basic guides to naval practices, has broadened its scope to include books of more general interest. Now the Naval Institute Press publishes about seventy titles each year, ranging from how-to books on boating and navigation to battle histories, biographies, ship and aircraft guides, and novels. Institute members receive significant discounts on the Press's more than eight hundred books in print.

Full-time students are eligible for special half-price membership rates. Life memberships are also available.

For a free catalog describing Naval Institute Press books currently available, and for further information about joining the U.S. Naval Institute, please write to:

Member Services
U.S. Naval Institute
291 Wood Road
Annapolis, MD 21402-5034
Telephone: (800) 233-8764
Fax: (410) 571-1703
Web address: www.usni.org